Critical Acclaim for Maureen Duffy

Maureen Duffy

was born in Worthing, Sussex, in 1933. Educated at the Trowbridge High School for Girls, Wiltshire, and the Sarah Bonnell High School for Girls, she took her degree in English at King's College, London, in 1956. She was a school teacher for five years, and in 1962 she published her first novel, *That's How It Was*, winning immediate acclaim. Since then she has published twelve novels: *The Single Eye* (1964), *The Microcosm* (1966), *The Paradox Players* (1967), *Wounds* (1969), *Love Child* (1971), *I Want to Go to Moscow* (1973), *Capital* (1975), *Housespy* (1978), *Gor Saga* (1982, dramatised by the BBC as *First Born*, 1988), *Scarborough Fear* (1982, as D.M. Cayer), *Londoners* (1983) and *Change* (1987).

She has had six plays performed and has published four volumes of verse. Her *Collected Poems 49-84* appeared in 1985. Maureen Duffy has also written a critical study of the supernatural in folklore and literature: *The Erotic World of Faery* (1972), a biography of Aphra Behn, *The Passionate Shepherdess* (1977), a social history, *Inherit the Earth* (1980) and an animal rights handbook, *Men and Beasts* (1984).

With Brigid Brophy she made and exhibited 3-D Constructions, Prop Art, in 1969. She received the City of London Festival Playwright's Prize in 1962, was co-founder of the Writers' Action Group, joint Chair of the Writers' Guild of Great Britain 1977-78 and its President 1985-88.

Maureen Duffy lives in London.

MAUREEN DUFFY

THE
MICROCOSM

PENGUIN BOOKS—VIRAGO PRESS

PENGUIN BOOKS
Published by the Penguin Group
Viking Penguin, a division of Penguin Books USA Inc.,
375 Hudson Street, New York, New York 10014, U.S.A.
Penguin Books Ltd, 27 Wrights Lane,
London W8 5TZ, England
Penguin Books Australia Ltd, Ringwood,
Victoria, Australia
Penguin Books Canada Ltd, 2801 John Street,
Markham, Ontario, Canada L3R 1B4
Penguin Books (N.Z.) Ltd, 182–190 Wairau Road,
Auckland 10, New Zealand

Penguin Books Ltd, Registered Offices:
Harmondsworth, Middlesex, England

First published in Great Britain by Hutchinson & Co. Ltd. 1966
First published in the United States of America by Simon and Schuster 1966
This edition published in Great Britain by Virago Press Limited 1989
Published in Penguin Books 1990

1   3   5   7   9   10   8   6   4   2

Copyright © Maureen Duffy, 1966, 1989
All rights reserved

LIBRARY OF CONGRESS CATALOGING IN PUBLICATION DATA
Duffy, Maureen.
The microcosm/Maureen Duffy.
p.   cm.—(Virago modern classics)
Originally published: Great Britain: Hutchinson, 1966.
I. Title.   II. Series.
PR6054.U4M5   1990
823'.914—dc20   90–40357
ISBN 0 14 016.215 1

Printed in the United States of America

for J.G.

'World is crazier and more of it than we think,
Incorrigibly plural. I peel and portion
A tangerine and spit the pips and feel
The drunkenness of things being various.'

Louis MacNeice
SNOW AND ROSES

AND I think by now you must be earth, earth or slime. 'Your water is a sore decayer of your whoreson dead body,' and we're three parts water, slime, mucus, snot, excretion, all the things tabooed for us as children with their foretaste of corruption, death. Gone under grass yet not stirring this Spring morning as bulb and tuber poke through the top soil with blunt leaf fingers, resurrecting; the dancing legs rigid in bone, muscles liquid, taut tendons dissolving, only the hair still bright-tipped, grown long and thick, darker at the roots.

Sometimes I think we're all dead down here, shadows, a house of shades, echoes of the world above where girls are blown about the streets like flowers on long stalks and young men strut by on turkeycock legs thrusting against the March winds, all a little more dead by your real dying since you've come to haunt this place, your laughter jazz-noted, harsh, the dusty floor recoiling under the thudding feet, a glimpse of remembered features in a face in profile, the shock of a turning head. We wait for you to come down the stairs every evening, lifting a hand, a grin; shedding a coat, a scarf; the possibility always there.

'Would you like to see poor, dear Carol before she's screwed down?' As if he had said, 'Bury her forever, compose memory under the waxed features, pad it down in white satin.' But no one went to see.

It rained of course. Did you know? Snivel and rain on the mourners' faces, the words chattered through clenched teeth; a charade but I was atoning for all the other funerals I'd left un-attended, the mockeries I'd refused to suffer. And something else too.

'Working on the coroner's court you sees all sorts. Turn all colours, they do, when they've topped theirselves. Gas is pink. You wouldn't think that would you? And leave 'em long enough they'll go green.'

'Do you believe in ghosts, Matt? Do you believe when someone's died suddenly, violently, they come back? I'm scared, going back to that flat alone. Scared I'll see her. I wouldn't want to see her like that. Have you ever seen a cat when it's been run over? It was like that. There was a nurse—she said she was a nurse—with a ring on her little finger; I think she was one of us. I don't know where she came from, just appeared from nowhere. She stayed with me all the time and I just held onto her hands. But I've got to go back. Sandy said she'd come with me, but I said no. I want to be by myself. But I'm scared.'

At first you'll see her everywhere, turn and see her standing there. But don't be afraid. If the dead do walk it's in their best clothes, upright and smiling though they lie in the gutter in blood, the neck snapped like a flower stalk.

'And there's no bitterness now. Even though I found out what I did afterwards, reading those letters when I went through her things. I don't hate anymore, not anyone. I'm glad, glad she had the chance of happiness. You know what I mean, Matt.'

Betrayal itself is a death and a kind of murder, and all deaths are one's own. I sit here in the corner, a watcher, a party to murder in my own betrayal.

'Are you happy Matt? Will it last?'

Faces look down from the brown walls.

'I'm going to do the whole place up. Take down all the pictures, scrap those of people who don't come down here any more. Been there fifteen years, some of them.'

'It was nicer in those days: afternoon tea and a piano. D'you remember, Billy? He was a marvellous pianist my dear. He could really play. Not all this stomp, stomp you get today. Then when we went again it was full of youngsters in Teddy-boy suits, and a screaming juke-box. Billy was in the forces and I was on hush-hush work for the admiralty. You looked marvellous in uniform B. We hardly ever go there now.'

'Such a waste! All those kids about seventeen; some of them very attractive too. I look around and think what a waste.'

Why don't the scars show? Faces can be too young. Am I getting old? Who'll love me when I'm old? Don't listen to the mirrors, reflecting eyes set in the painted walls, glimpse of a half-face, flicker of twisting limbs. The mirrors multiply death.

It's early yet. Cy behind the bar, lean knife form in clinical white coat, light glinting on grey hair harsh as a scouring pad, polishes glasses detached, the ash falling in the washing-up water. First-comer feeds the squatting juke-box through its slit, pursed lips, the coins dropping into the metal paunch, hiccuping through the steel intestines to belch thick chords into the unmoving air. The floor lies empty, flat on its back under the muted lights. Three shapes huddle in separate corners, dragging deep with every pull, hands turning glasses slowly, eyes not seeing water seep through liquor like green smoke or smooth alcohol climb the steep tumbler walls; drowned.

Is it different? No, not different; yet not the same. What do you see through my eyes? The features are different but the masks are the same. Who's that in the slim-boy jeans, kicking the fire into flame with a black boot. I don't remember. Look closely. She loved you too.

'You're lucky Matt. You're different from the rest of us. You're true.'

'Am I so different?'

You recognise the voices? Did I say that? Look again. They're coming.

Come down the stairs slowly, adjusting your mask; a nod at the bottom for madame. Push through into the cloakroom and unwind the wrappings that hid you in the world outside. Turn to the mirror.

'Who are you in my eyes?'

'I am the captain with pipe and blazer.'

'I am the rake. I'll stab you to the heart with my pointed shoes and cut your pretty throat on the blades of my sleek trousers.'

'I am the boy next door.'

'I'm beautiful. Say I'm beautiful.'

'I loved my mother. Mother?'

'I love myself.'

It's Jill isn't it? She's changed. Perhaps.

7

'You're early. I didn't expect you so early. All alone?'

'Rae's not well; been in bed all day. I'm off the hook this evening.'

'You missed a good night last night. Have a drink.'

I watch her cross the floor to the bar, sauntering bravely, invisible in a careless cloak. You still love her. Of course. I know what you mean. Yes, I thought you'd understand. And Rae? That's different. Yes, I see that too.

They're coming faster now, individual ones and twos clotting into groups, too many to push past the desk at once, tumbling down the stairs like a waterfall; banging of car doors, the stuttered diesel tick-over of taxis, dying whine of a scooter. March winds playing a crazy game whirled them up from bed-sitters and flatlets all over the city, hurried them through the dark streets and sucked them in at the door, down the stairway funnel into the gut of the earth.

'Are you a member? Are you dead?'

They press in through the cloakroom door, helmeted, hooded, fly-fronts hidden under duffle-coats, too many now for the mirror to question, eager for music, comfort of close humanity, the quick release of a hand cupping a glass.

'Shall we do this one?' The record is spinning a web of remembered sounds that unites present and past, binding the room and all its separate elements in a mesh of memory. We move out onto the floor. I take her loosely in my arms and we begin to turn gently with a hesitant swaying step like a fading carousel, the other couples rising and falling around us. 'Not much talent here tonight.'

'There's your beatnik over by the bar.'

Over my shoulder I see a child's lost face above black sweater and tights through the haze. 'She drinks too much.' Once, at a party, I kissed her. She was barefoot and we danced an improvised Apache step together while the room drew back to watch. I saw her smiling to herself as she tried to follow the patterns my feet traced on the floorboards. Afterwards, in the kitchen, I kissed her, reaching deep down in her mouth for the live, soft tongue. The next time I saw her in the house of shades she was drunk and crying. We danced together, this time a formal step hemmed in by others.

'What's the matter?' She shook her head, dark eyes overspilling tears. I held her closer, the full warmth of her puppy flesh drawn to me, her breasts firm against my body. 'Why's she crying?'

8

'She's lonely.'

'She's a nice kid.'

'That's what they all say. You ought to do something about it.'

'I'm a married man.'

'Oh shit that!'

The violence of her friend's reply shocked me. Now I looked for her guiltily every time, wondering if I should ask her to dance, if she'd found anyone to ease the ache, shifting my vague intuition of responsibility onto some mythical lover.

Beside us a couple are already lost, eyes closed, his mouth against her neck, arms binding each other tight and who can say whether it's the prelude to a one-night stand, a brief affair or a years-old marriage. I no longer judge. Her hands are round his neck, fingers tangle in his hair, hips move against each other. For this interlude two undistinguished people appear beautiful in tragic masks.

You've changed too. Are you still there? When you remember me.

Yes, I've changed. We're older, all of us. Matthew, the boy with the book, the word, glad tidings, good spell, where's he now? Become like everyone else, part of the darkness, a shade.

Do you remember the last time we joked together, two butch boys strolling in the sun by the summer-slack river? I promised you a stick of Blackpool rock. Did you know then that you too would suddenly grow older?

I knew. And then you went out and died and left me to carry on down into the dark alone.

Mine was a different dark, thicker, earth filling the eyes.

I'm sorry, for a moment I forgot.

It was lonely at first, lying in the rain beside the railway lines, hearing the trains fly by, after the flowers faded among the straight dead. Once or twice I made my way here but they were all strange faces, no one I knew to talk to.

And now we're all here.

No, not all. There are still some to come. But they're coming. Wait and see.

The wind is blowing stronger through the hidden places of the city, gathering them in, filling their veins with its restlessness, intimation of Spring, the urge to dance, break hearts with a look, flex stiff muscles in the attitudes of youth, in Notting Hill Gate among the chocolate faces and fashionable writers, beside the creek at Barking, among the bright brick boxes of Suburbiton.

'There's Judy.'

'I'm not speaking to her.'

Brilliant, sad, surrounded by a whirl of satellites who are drawn closer or spin pale, disconsolate moons away on the fringe of light as her eyes flash negative or positive, she passes to the bar. They revolve anxiously, hovering to see who will be summoned for their sun's warmth this chill evening while the rest are left to reflect in each other's eyes or slip away into the shadows by the wall. Her mask is immaculate, meticulously built up touch by touch before the mirror; the whole day dedicated to dressing the window, the dummy on which this flawless jewel, no longer flesh and hair but enamel and paste, will be mounted. The hands betray, coarse and red-skinned like a chicken's wattles.

'You're opting out?'

'What's the use? She's a fool. I told her so. The years are slipping, I said. The autumn of our lives.'

'You must have been drunk to come up with anything as trite as that.'

'I was. But it shook her.'

'Why waste your time? She'll still be coming down here in another ten years, a bit more anxious, with a new bunch of adolescents clustering round her like a thirties movie queen. The rest will either have had her or passed her over. Where's the point?'

'It's alright for you.'

'She gets her kicks out of scenes not sex. Life's too short for that kind of masochism.'

'But then we're not all obsessed by sex like you. There are other things.'

'What's gone wrong with you today?'

'Me? Think I'll go and dance with that little blonde over there, the one I picked up on Thursday.'

'You do that.' She pushes through the packed bodies, twitching and posturing on the floor. I stand watching, eyes glazing, wondering why I'm here.

'Where's Rae, then?'

'Hullo, gorgeous!'

'Hullo, sexy; not wearing your leather pants tonight. I love a feel of them leather pants.'

'She's terrible Jonnie. I don't know how you manage her.'

'I don't mate. She wears me out.'

'When you going to tell me the name of your tailor?'

'Like it?'

I finger the smooth dark suiting. 'Nice tie too.'

'Bought me that for Christmas, didn't you, darling? We went over her mum's last week and she give me these socks and all. She's lovely, her mum.'

'I hate my dad. I never speak to him now since I left home. I go when I know he won't be there. He knows I go sometimes and give me mum a few bob, but he never asks after me and that's how I want it.'

'Does your mum know about you?'

'I dunno. Sometimes I think she does but she don't say. Sometimes I think she still don't know about things like that. I know when the kids called me a les at school and I come running home to ask her what it meant she never knew. She said it was just another sort of nickname and not to take any notice. Funny, ent it, cos my brother's the same.'

'Does he know?'

'Yeah, I think so, cos I asked him once if he had any old cravats for Jonnie and when he come down from looking in his drawer he said no he hadn't but here's a couple of ties. I felt meself go a bit red but I never said nothing and we've never mentioned it since.'

'How do you know he is then?'

'Oh he's always liked boys. I remember one he was going with when he was in the army. This boy was so feminine you'd have thought he was a girl if you just looked quick. Georgie was ever so upset when he left him; just sat about the house when he came home on leave.'

'Does he live at home now?'

'No, none of us does except my little brother, he's thirteen. My dad don't hit him like he did the rest of us and he don't hit mum so much neither. He's an angel, my little brother. Does all the shopping and two paper rounds and gives all the money to mum. I think more of him than of anyone else in the world except Jonnie and mum. Even dad can't fault him, that's why he can't hit him.'

'Can I borrow your wife for a dance, Jonnie?'

'Take her mate and the best of luck.'

Sadie shimmies and shimmers in watered silk, the iridescent folds flowing round her, all womanflesh, young girl showering red sparklets of liquid fire as she dances.

'And I said to him, "No, I'm not like that," because I didn't want to believe it. I was ashamed. "I'll prove it," I said. "Come on." But I was shaking like a leaf even before we got to his room and he turned round and looked at me and then he said, "It wouldn't be any good." I reckon that's the worst thing a man can do to you, put it inside. It's cruel.'

'Sometimes when we get to bed she turns to me and she's all keen, you know. But I'm tired. I been at work all day and I want to sleep.'

As I dance with Sadie I feel the thoughts throbbing between them like singing telegraph poles on a summer's day as you lie in the warm, prickly grass beside a dusty road; a memory from childhood.

'See that black butch? She can't half dance.'

'Could you fancy her?'

'No, not really. They're different from us somehow. Some girls like them though. I think they're smashing dancers.'

Africa glistens and stamps by the juke-box in cowboy boots and check sweatshirt, by slavey out of Haarlem, heavy muscled, flake white eyes highlighting the oiled dark skin.

'How can you be more subject; black woman in a white man's world?'

The slim nervous boy from Ceylon flutters his Demarara hands, his eyes two moist Greek olives under thick lashes. A temple dancer from Siam, poised head flowering from a gold lamé calyx, sandals of gold wire, silvery finger- and toenails, sways cat-eyed against a deep blue sari bordered with silver.

'They say she's butch, that Indian.'

'You wouldn't think they'd be like it too.'

'Oh, the Indians have been at it longer than most. All those harems. They had to pass the time somehow while waiting for a turn with the old man.'

'I wouldn't fancy that. Don't you go getting any ideas, Jonnie. One's enough for you.'

'You're enough for anyone. Come and have a dance.'

You've forgotten me again. No, not really. My wife's just come in. Who's she with? Are you jealous? Why not? I'm dead. Sometimes I don't recognise you, Carl. Maybe because I was more alive than most I resent it more. Resent?

It's an intrusion, a distortion of the natural order. Don't believe the people who say it's a necessary part of it. They're alive. Sometimes I seem to forget myself. Then you say my name and I remember. Was she upset? You know things weren't going right between us?

'We don't even fight anymore now, Matt. We're just sort of indifferent.'

Did I say that? Yes, I remember. Even so, the strings remain.

She was shocked at first, then there was too much to do: the inquest, the police, your family.

'My dad never cared tuppence for me. We've had some terrible rows.'

He looked stunned, broken. A big man in an assured suit who suddenly found his hands would tremble if they didn't hold on to each other as the parson's hurried words dribbled through his skull in the bleak cemetery chapel with the noise of women crying a monotonous backing.

And then? Then they descended like settling vultures in their mourning plumage, shuffling their obscene wings, thrusting their beaks into every corner of the corpse that had been your life and carrying off everything that could be sold or split between them until she was left with the bare bones of furniture, half paid up, a bundle of letters, mostly to another woman, and a promise to come again and pick over your clothes.

My clothes? They said there weren't enough, that you must have had more.

'And that was the last thing I could do for her, see that they never found out. So I made a pile of her drag clothes, photographs, papers and Sandy took them away. And you know what hurt me most Matt? I wasn't allowed to identify her. They sent for one of the family. And it brought it all home to me just how outside we are. I knew her body better than my own.'

Poor Chris. I told you to make a will. And the bike? A write-off. Like me. They sold it for two quid scrap. I was fond of that old bike even though she let me down. Dance with her.

'How's it going then darling?'

'Not too bad Matt. How are things with you?'

'Fine. It's good to see you looking happier.'

'Thanks. Not everyone thinks like that. Some people won't speak to me.'

'What are you supposed to do: sit home and knit for the rest of your life? Carl wouldn't have wanted you to. She wasn't like that. You be happy if you can.'

What did she say? I told her I was glad to see her looking better and that you would have wanted her to be happy. I hope I was right. You were careful to use the past tense. Maybe it's made an introvert of me.

'My God if they let anymore in here we'll be squeezed out through the chimney. Makes you feel like Alice or a tube of tooth-paste.'

And this too is wonderland, the world turned back to front through a glass darkly. The tourists stand about, backs to the wall in defence, amazed, amused at the underwater life trapped in this hazy aquarium whose thin, transparent walls might break under a probing finger, letting these strange forms of life swim free among the plump goldfish in the garden pond.

'How many do you reckon?'

'A couple of hundred when I can see for smoke, and all well away. I saw you dancing with Chris.'

'Where were you?'

'Over there with Eve. She's breaking her heart because Judy's dancing with that South African butch.'

'I always told her what she really wanted was someone to master her.'

'Thanks very much. I thought you were supposed to be my friend.'

'It was before your time. You'd better keep an eye on Eve. She's a strange kid. She might blow her top.' I lean wearily against the mantelpiece, eyes smarting with the bitter smoke and the jagged reflections from fragments of broken mirror.

'Cheery, cheery. The little feller looks miserable.'

'Got a headache. Thinking too much.'

'Have a Scotch; do you good. I'll buy you one.' Money. This place must be a gold-mine. Underground. In the hall of the mountainous king. Midas.

'All I touch. They told me I was a fool to buy it but I knew what I was doing. I've made it the most popular of its kind in London. Keep it select that's the way to do it.'

'Those men, what are they doing down here? They shouldn't be allowed in. They only come to gape; tourists, perverts. Roll up and see the queers dance.'

'Rod,' she cried, 'I've been a fool! What I wanted all the time was a man. Take me Rod, here now. I can't wait.'

'Attractive couple over there. The redhead looks like a model. What do they get out of it? What do they do? Wouldn't mind a crack meself.'

'No, it's not true. I'm not like that. Why did I come?'

'And the first time I went down there I went home and was sick. I was ill for a couple of days but I had to go back again and again until I was there every night, couldn't keep away.'

'Where else is there?'

'We hardly ever go now. There's always someone ready to step in and break it up if they think you're happy.'

'And I said to Jack, "What a waste."'

'Judy's seen something nasty in the woodshed again. I told her, some of my best friends are men.'

'Where's Eve?'

Here's blood in the kitchen,
Here's blood in the hall;
Here's blood in the parlour
Where my lady did fall.

'The silly bitch has cut her wrists in the lavatory. Sometimes I think we're not worth saving.'

Blood in the water making pink clouds; water in pernod green clouds.

'Leave me alone. I wish I were dead.'

'You've made a bloody poor job of it. What did you use?'

'That razor blade. Watch it; she's passing out. Shove her head between her knees. It's fright more than anything. Who's got a clean handkerchief?'

'Don't let Charlie know. He'll turf us all out.'

'It's not very deep but rather crooked. Must have been blunt. Hard work sawing away with that thing.'

'Should we tell Judy?'

'No, no. I don't want her to know. Just leave me alone.'

'Maybe she ought to know, hard-faced bitch, what she does to people.'

'It's not her fault. It's that Franz. She wants everyone, collecting scalps. She's leading her on.'

'Oh, yes, fine: dying soldier defends general who sent him out to be shot to pieces. Come off it. This isn't the games field.'

'I think she ought to go home.'

'Get me a taxi.'

'I'll go with her.'

'Jill?'

'I'm staying. There's a party at Larry's. Should be fun. She'll be alright with Sue. Perhaps you'll learn in time. These things happen. We've all been through it.'

Sounds harsh doesn't she? If she does it's my fault. I taught her. 'If you prick us do we not bleed?' Black, bitter blood from a dead heart.

'I wasn't hard on her Matt. I didn't lead her on.' Judy turns rhinestone eyes up to me, melting now in a liquid sea whose tears are pearls, each one a perfect droplet, cultured. Released by this orgasm of despair, torn from her in Eve's blood, she floats now in a luxury of recrimination and repentance, soothing as a lover's kiss and whispered tenderness before she sleeps. I turn away not answering. There is nothing to be said, and you learn, soon or late but you learn, that in this life forgiveness is the cardinal virtue blazoned on every heart in red wounds.

Sue puts Eve in a taxi to take her home to soft words and a hot drink, the comfort of other arms to cry herself to sleep in, and Judy resumes her evening, drifts across the dance floor, a little sad, rocked on her lover's shoulder, gentle now with all, appeased, almost drowsy.

'And the funny thing is she says she was in love with her mother, really believes it.'

'When if you look into it it's quite clear she was dominated by her and resented it, and has been taking it out on other women ever since.'

'The mothers are responsible for a lot.'

> And what will you give to your own mother dear?
> The curse from hell mother you shall have
> Sic counsel you gave to me O.

O mothers, matres, nestling your hungry infant close. Do you know your little cannibal longs to sink its bony gums in your marbled flesh, torment the rubbery nipple with phantom teeth and pound impotent fists into the soft milky breast where it hangs dependent? Or thrust it off on the anonymous bottle; it will wail abandoned, seeking the lost warmth of your body. Keep it from the rough children of the street, cosset it against the urban savage swearing cops and robbers between the semi-detached and it will grow sickly and clinging, wrapt in a closed world of soft images. Send it to play in the yelling, scuffling lanes of common childhood and watch it tomboy, torn-trousered, rough-voiced, aggressive through life. Such a dear little girl.

O patres, driving the long-distance lorries or away about war or business, you will come home stranger to find it has replaced you, man-about-the-house. Beat, humiliate it; it will reject you. Mice men bowing before your hen-peck, pecking wives it will despise you.

The patterns form in the foetus, at the breast and play, about the house, in teacher's eyes, the eyes of the world, worn in grooves, each one adding a little until the final voice is heard. 'I am what I have become and I will be what I will be.'

'Seems to me you can't win. You try and do your best for them but there's no saying it is the best. Often you just don't know where you went wrong. Her father won't have her in the house since he found out. I don't understand it meself. Been better if she'd been born a boy.'

'And she said to me: "Honey are you butch or femme or just a little old inbetween? Because I want to know who does what." So I said, "Try me and find out."

'I reckon I could go with a man if I tried, but a woman's better.'

17

> 'Girls, girls, girls,
> Were made to love.'

sings the juke-box and the room answers in chorus, stamping out the rhythm of assent on the patient, dusty floor.

I feel so strange. If non-flesh could tremble I would say I was trembling now. Why suddenly? I thought I was beyond all that, beyond feeling cold or heat or the shiver of rain. There is nothing the flesh feels. What moves me?

> *Amor, che al cor gentil ratto s'apprende,*

Meaning what? Words of an old poem. There's more too. Tell me.

> *. . . Nessun maggior dolore,*
> *che ricordarsi del tempo felice*
> *nella miseria . . .*

What use is that to me? No use, of course, only the human condition, mine as well as yours. It's Vicky who moves you. Vicky, is she here? Coming down the steps now, pauses a moment to look about. Why? Why is she stopping? I haven't seen her for months, not since the funeral. She hasn't been down? No. She's looking for old faces; for a welcome I think. Shall I go over to her? A waist so small one arm would do to circle it. Do what you like. Leave me alone.

'Vicky!'

'Hallo Matt.' And I take her in my arms and hold her strongly feeling some of the conviction and love flow out of me.

Others come crowding too, some simply pleased to see her again for herself, some glad to see her bear out their words that she wouldn't be able to keep away. Jealous as amazons at a rite profaned, a priestess fled from the vestal temple, once a girl guide always a girl guide, Euridice escaped from the house of shades up into the light, the outcast crossing the tracks; confirmed in their way of life by her return, the campus spreads its welcome mat and the doors close behind her. I watch her dancing, held close in affection and the stifling folds of Judy's arms. She slips back into place as if she had never been away.

'Oh it's good to be back. I've missed this place.'

'It didn't work out, then?'

'What did you hear?'

'Through the grape-vine, Judy. There was an artist, wasn't there?'

'Yes.'

'All finished?'

'Not quite. But soon, very soon. We're going through the death-throes now.'

I pull a face. 'Tell me.'

'I thought last year, after the accident: "Well, that's over, perhaps I should give the other a try again. Cut all ties." So I did. He understood. He was a bit that way himself.'

'What went wrong?'

'It just didn't work, on the physical level I mean, and that's very important to me. If that doesn't work for me then the whole relationship falls down.'

'Yes, I'm like that too.'

'With a man it's over so quickly. There's nothing to it.'

'Perhaps you just got the wrong man. Try a Frenchman next time. They're supposed to be rather good, though I have heard that once you've had a woman as a lover, a good one I mean, the other's less satisfying. Men don't like to think so, of course. Shall we see what the next one is?'

'Okay.' The music begins and we move away on it. She is slight as a grass stalk in the wind, nothing in my arms. We dance a little apart, bodies not touching, as people do who know their flesh takes fire quickly and who respect each other too much to play with it.

'You know I admired you tremendously for not coming down all these months.'

'I couldn't have, Matt. I just couldn't.'

'Even so I admire you. I'd like to think that a woman would do as much for me.'

'You see my hand Matt. Look at the heart-line there. You see, it's double.' I stare down at her palm, a little moist and flushed, double-tracked from left to right by a deep furrow. 'That's a sign of those who when they love, love deeply, obsessively. In India women with a heart-line like that throw themselves voluntarily on their husband's funeral pyre.'

I think of my own puckered, islanded sign, dipping low towards the head, and say nothing. I remember the strained, taut quality of her grief, the sudden rush of words and the long, held silences.

'Carl was like you Matt. She couldn't have been anything else but butch. Some people can be either but not you two and that was one of the things that attracted me. I can admire another woman's body but I couldn't go with one who was feminine, not in that way.'

You've been a long time. Have I? What did she say? She's attracted by you, I can tell. Only for what she sees of you in me. I'm just a substitute. That's how a lot of things begin. Still, how can I complain? I didn't take the chance when I had it, didn't do the right thing, the honest thing. If I'd come back ... What's the use. I'm no use to her anymore. She must go on, make a life for herself. But there's always that tie, that involvement with a woman you've loved, a body you've known. You're not dancing much with Jill this evening. She's busy.

The evening is going stale on me. More and more I wonder why I'm here as if it's a penance I have to work off rather than a free choice of my own, made on the spur of the moment in alienation and self-pity, yet still a free choice. Perhaps I should phone, the comfort of her voice, pebbles dropped in clear water, or just pack up and go, but I hang on, back to the fire, shifting from foot to foot, eyes wandering absently, cross and double-cross the room, nailing a gesture there an expression here by force of habit. 'Mary, I don't think you're quite with us this morning.' Had to give it up. Don't know how Steve keeps going with all that temptation but then she's not like me.

'We're not all like you obsessed with sex.' The words still sting even though I understand them, know the pain behind them. Wave at Steve through the dense air. She smiles guardedly back.

'A wily one there. You'd find it difficult to pin her down.'

'Me?'

'Not just you, anyone.'

Two people look at each other across a room. 'Perhaps?'

'I don't think so. Not tonight.' Their eyes question and drop again. Time runs down. Hands join against the dark. A lover's arm becomes a shield against loneliness; the empty flat and chill sheets without the warmth of another body breathing beside you. Lie

20

and listen for the soft come and go, comforting as a whisper in the shadowy room. Most who are going to have found partners now. The rest stand about watching in attitudes of real or assumed indifference, catching morsels of talk from the passing dancers.

'Rick and Betty have broken up.'

'Eddie's having a baby.'

'Two butches dancing together. Mike must be on the turn.'

'She's only got six months to live, that one in green.'

'Get you. You're just jealous.'

'Sandy's barred.'

'I'm going to a kibbutz next summer to get the chip off my shoulder.'

'And she's got four children.'

'Tony was beaten up by a gang of teds going home last week.'

What's the news? 'Who loses and who wins; who's in, who's out.' Is it the feminine strand makes us so hungry for these greasy scraps, these gobbets? The boys are as bad, worse, bitchier. Think of all those city gents gossiping down their halves of bitter and calling it a business lunch. Whose business? Our trouble is we cram it all into one or two nights. All the week wearing a false face. Come in. Close the doors behind you. Distil this rarefied atmosphere where we can breathe freely apart from the rest of the world like an ashram in the high Himalayas, or a lost tribe of aborigines buried deep in the heart of the social jungle with its own language and customs, unknown except to occasional travellers through on safari, traders who bring us thin cloth and glass ornaments in return for our silver and gold, slavers from the city who hire our cheap labour for their factories and other cut-rate jobs, scientists in search of strange fauna who will put our brains in pickle, missionaries to educate us and police to see we cause no trouble. We stare at them dull-eyed.

Every so long under the moontime we chatter all together like monkey village in the branches, run like river in the raintime up and down, shake thin fists at stickwall we build keep out wild animal come tear our bodies, wild men come fire our thatches. Keep us in more. Then soldier boys come with smoke bomb, fireflash, guns chatter like monkey village, go hideaway in jungle all same colour as leaves. Soldier boys go away come walk back.

Our young people sharp as knives go walk away to the cities where all talk round, make much of. Come walk back to the village wearing strange clothes colour straw and mud dull after raintime. Talk fast and high like monkey village. Not stay long. Laugh at young girls in purple shiny from the traders, young men in thin cloth like soldier boy, low voice like pig grunt, dancing on the night of no work, tom-tom, tom-tom.

Say: 'We not belong along of you no more. Belong the city now. There we tall people. You villagers small peoples. We not speak for you. We speak all ourselves,' swagger in their straw clothes. Not come walk back.

But one full day come the lightime we stand up all together and go walk away too out of the stickwall and not sorry leave our thatches all fall down. Come to the city and man and woman, friends altogether, speak out loud along the tall houses and our young people sharp as knives put hands each on brother's shoulder, say, 'This too our people.'

Then we too live free among the tall houses, working our living, dancing the night of no work along the tall city peoples, unafraid, never go back to the stickwall. Like it says in the story of the old-time before the jungle grows up thick and we build the stickwall. Peoples come and go walk away from the village to the city all along the same, short and tall, and no soldier boys come with smoke bomb, fireflash only to monkey village in the branches. Then wide path come and go, all happily ever after, amen, laughing and dancing, one full day come the lightime.

It is quite clear that the people of this region are completely untrustworthy, feckless and apathetic. Their countenances express sullenness and suspicion and are devoid of any of that cheerful acceptance of the lot which nature or their own perversity has invested them with, which is customary among backward peoples. They respond but poorly to any attempt to teach them new skills or more civilised accomplishments and are not amenable to the very necessary forms of discipline which the authorities are forced to use from time to time. On our arrival at a particular village we found the inhabitants had all fled into the jungle and were attempting to hide themselves amongst the foliage where however they were easily discerned by a careful observer. One, a little braver than the rest, was encouraged to come forward and answer our questions and to lead us into the village. He said that the tribe did not engage in hunting but foraged for berries and grew a kind of wild oat from which they brewed a very potent form of native beer. Gradually they were persuaded to come out of hiding and to resume their occupations so that I was able to observe them in their natural habitat and make the following notes and drawings.

The females among them are particularly shy, largely I believe because some of them are enticed away periodically by traders and the more enterprising people from the towns, either to serve as concubines or as workers. They are divided into families but a rapid system of divorce and remarriage pertains among them and very few associations last more than a few years. There is a great deal of promiscuity, and, indeed, morality as we know it hardly seems to exist at this level. Naturally disease is rife amongst them and much of their time is spent in smoking, gossiping or drinking the native beer. They only show real interest and animation when the village gathers for tribal dancing. Then they dress themselves in coarse, bright finery, laughing and chattering like children and will often keep up their merriment all night.

They show little interest in religion, although many of them when questioned professed to believe in a God of sorts, and the missionaries make very little headway amongst them since they are either too indolent or lack perseverance to change their way of life. Hence the practice has arisen of carrying away the more promising children to the city where although they remain villagers at heart they may be persuaded to learn more civilised and rewarding habits.

It is clear that they do not lack innate intelligence but rather suffer from gross character defects which make them unable to follow a more normal way of life. What is not clear however is whether these are inborn or the result of environment.

I can only conclude that the government do right in keeping them segregated since, if such habits were allowed to contaminate the rest of the nation, all industry would be at a standstill and free licence allowed to instincts which, in all of us, are best kept under severe check.

It is particularly interesting to note that their language has no form of the verb to be nor any way of expressing past or future time. The philosophical concept of existence or being is quite beyond their grasp. Everything simply happens in an eternal present.

'You going to this party then?'

'No, don't think so.' Jill pulls a face. 'For God's sake I'm tired. I want to get home sometime,'

'Alright then. Means I can't go either; couldn't get back. It's alright for you. You've got your sex life all on tap. Thought you were supposed to be my friend.'

And I know I'll give in again although 1 know too she's half seas under, jealous, unreasonable, unreasoning, spiteful as a spoilt and thwarted child, and just as she knows too in the recesses of herself behind this aggressive façade and will tell me, half pleading, next time we meet. And I wonder again if this is all I've done for any of us, and if it's worth the pain I cause Rae, and Jill, and myself, this desperate clinging to what is right, what has final meaning, has been and still can be something that glows like a sombre pearl in this world of shades, hidden under thick waves, sand, the mirk of the sea-bed, in the fleshly belly of a bi-valve; a love cleansed by the waters, washed and washed again in salt waves, scoured and polished by the harsh sand, bedded soft in living tissue.

'They've turned the box off.'

'Right on the dot as ever. Charlie likes to keep a respectable house.'

'Where is this bloody party? I'm not chasing off to Clerkenwell or the fringes of Essex at this time of night.'

'Not far, just round the corner. Honest. Ah you're a good mate and I love you. Say, remember that time we went to the wrong party, all normals in cocktail dresses and dark suits? I'll never forget that woman's face when twenty of us marched in and all the girls were boys and all the boys were girls.'

'Night-night, Vicky.'

'Night-night, Steve.'

'Night-night, Judy.'

'Night-night, Jon.'

' "Good night sweet ladies,
Sweet ladies, good night." '

Outside the last wave washes over the pavement. We stand about in groups, unwilling to finish the evening, chatting, seeing Steve tucked into her glossy little biscuit tin on wheels, reassuring

Judy. Two policemen stand easy, watching curiously from a safe distance. Further down on the opposite side a young man is sitting in a window-box outside a window full of bright sound and passing silhouettes, a telephone in his hand inviting someone to the party inside.

A tall, fat man in a long camel-hair coat crosses the road towards us, his hair glistening dully in a flat skullcap, his face sallow, heavy blue jowled under the lamp. He stops and stands for a moment staring at us. We look back, wondering if he is lost and wants to ask the way. He walks on and then suddenly turning spits deliberately in our direction with a harsh rasping sound. Then he walks on again. The two policemen have disappeared.

'Filthy old sod.'

'Foreigner.'

The blob of spit glistens malevolently like an eye in the gutter. I feel my stomach turn and look away.

'See you Saturday then Matt.'

'See you.' We climb into our own car as Steve takes off with a pigmy roar and a wave.

'Nasty bit of work.' I feel her fear begin to settle as she bangs the car door to.

'The sort who'd've clobbered you if you'd said anything.' We cruise round an elegantly porticoed square under trees still not brave enough to trust their leaves to the baring winds.

'This is it.'

'A hairdresser's?'

'That's right.'

Tiny flaws appeared on the windscreen. 'God, it's snowing now. Better not leave it too late or we might not get away at all.'

'Don't want to be here in the morning when Lady Tom Noddy comes for her weekly blue.'

Inside we have wandered onto the set of an Antonioni film, hawking aristocratic degeneracy and fashionable despair to an aspiring bourgeoisie. The neon lighting is down to half, greenish glow. Figures huddle grotesquely under space-helmet hair-dryers or try self-consciously to defeat the full-length mirrors that inlay the walls. Someone has half filled a washbasin with scampi and potato salad; drinks are served from the display counter, glasses are in short supply. I work my way steadily through the scampi, swigging from a gassy bottle of light, the drink that inflates but does not inebriate. Jill has latched onto one of the entente cordiale who are always in motion between the clubs of London and Paris. A girl in gold boots, satin trousers and clinging gold sweater like a bare-back rider performs a mock ballet in the middle of the floor calling to a young man and a middle-aged butch with lank face and spare figure to come and dance with her. A youthful Oscar Wilde drooping over his umbrella, pale fudge face caramel above a silk cravat, royal blue, inclines to an animated little figure waving its arms in front of him. I'm reminded of late decadent cartoons, Beardsley and Beerbohm.

Carl, are you here? No answer. How soon can we go? Maybe I'm getting too old for this sort of thing. Used to wonder how I'd react to seeing two of the boys dancing together, caught close like those two there, but it doesn't seem to make any difference. Looks just as natural as two girls or man and woman. What's the flash point then? Why don't I get anything out of dancing with them unless it's a real camping bitch, or with Jonnie or Rick. It's not just the conventions we make for ourselves in imitation of the world outside surely? There's no, what's the word, frisson. Unless you're dancing a young man's dance. Then it's like the dancing of primitive peoples, initiation, war dance, a chance for the young bull braves to show off their virility. Who is the prettier boy and wears the braver dagger? Throw your head back and stamp, seemingly caught by the rhythm of the dance but in fact by the rhythm of the blood beating in time to the feet. Maidens look at me, lithe and strong in the firelight. Tomorrow perhaps I go out to the place where ghost face will touch me with cold fingers. How I will rock you in your beds. Open your thighs and let me in. I am the strong sun, the hot wind. Melt under my touch. 'They were allowed to sit in council and boast of the sexual prowess of their wives but not to go on the warpath.' I am hairless as the apache, except for the legs, of course. All those old photographs of the greatest of the plains warriors and they look like old women decked in holiday finery except for the set, lined faces. Spartans combing their hair before the battle, red-coats in neatly powdered wigs: mistress death we come to woo you. Time to go.

By now she's had enough. I tap her on the shoulder. 'I'm off. Coming?'

'Nothing here to stay for.' The 's' slurs a little. The road is quieter now. The wind has dried the scattering of snow. My head quite clear. No longer the terrible urge homewards like a compass needle swinging always north.

> 'Desire, desire I have too dearly bought.'

and too,

> 'I have been faithful to thee, Cynara! in my fashion.'

Only a quiet, persistent longing to be home.

'Who was that piece of French crumpet, or should I say croissant, you were dancing with?' But she is asleep, her head fallen against the cold glass.

Amtyas drew the cloak closer about the sleeping boy. It was cold in the mountains and who knew what the next dawn would bring. It was good that he should sleep while the dew fell and the birds stirred drowsily in their eyrie above the pass. 'We too should be eagles,' the man thought, 'But for the most part we are only kin to the vulture and rend each other's flesh.' He had brought the boy into the pass of death and now he must watch beside him, perhaps watch him die when the sun rose because the boy's arm was still weak, the young muscles showing promise yet not knotted in the resilient whipcord that can swing the heavy short sword all day until the evening shadows stride down tall from the mountain and even the enemy must rest.

I brake suddenly, switch off the engine, leave the lights, must leave the lights on, throw open the car door and run back down the road a few yards to the junction we've just passed. Already a knot of people is thickening on the corner.

'Has anyone rung for an ambulance?' Blank faces give back the answer. I run on again down the hill towards a block of flats where people are appearing on their balconies like boxes at the opera. 'Have you got a phone?' I turn my face up to them, shouting, doubting the strength of my voice to make itself heard. 'Will you ring for the ambulance?' A man disappears inside. I turn and run back up the hill.

The two boys are lying on the pavement, one propped stupefied against the running board of the car whose nose is butted aggressively against the lamp-post; the other twitching and moaning, drawing his knees up to his chin and shooting them out again.

'It's alright, mate. You'll be alright.' They tell him impotently, holding onto his hands to try and keep him still.

'Turn him over.' They roll him over onto his face. Someone runs up carrying a little tin box with a red cross painted on it, but there is no blood to wipe away, no occasion for bandages and dressings or improvising splints, only the contorted limbs in their leather casing twitching on the dry pavement. His face and hair are hidden by the heavy black armour of the helmet. The bike lies on its side in the gutter; its body broken, ribs bent; the glossy hide scratched and bruised.

I think of Jill waking suddenly in the deserted car, perhaps wandering out onto the road, or the car itself being struck as it waits at the roadside in spite of its warning lights. There is nothing more I can do. I turn back towards the car.

She is still asleep, her head pillowed on the window. I start the engine and pull quietly away.

'And fire that's the worst of all; charred like a tree-trunk they are, like the bark of a tree. You've never seen that have you?'

Red lights ahead, lining my side of the road, pinpricks, spots of bright blood, eyes of werewolf and vampire, ease into third, nothing in sight the full length ahead, pull across into the other lane. Always digging holes: gas mains, water mains, electric cables; veins of the city under the tarmac skin. Halfway now. What's that chap up to? He's shifting it. Have to put his anchors on. The bloody fool, he's coming straight on. Surely he can see. He'll go right through us. Pull over into the mud. Just squeeze by. Two wheels down the ditch. Hold her steady. Missed the barrier. We'll make it.

'Bloody woman driver!'

Gently does it. Always shakes you up. Like falling off a bike. Get back on straight away and ride or you'll never get on again. His fault. Thought because it was his right of way. But I was halfway through before he'd even started. What else could I have done? Knew he'd made a mistake so shouted at me. Was his mistake, wasn't it? 'He's just as dead as if he'd been wrong.' But then you can't win. Only try to stick to the rules. Whose rules? What do you mean? I mean what I say. Tired. Nothing makes sense.

Petrol, must get some petrol. There's that all-night garage before the roundabout. The modern coaching inn. Don't see any pretty little chambermaid running out with a stirrup cup, only George the dumb hostler.

'One of special please.'

'Thank you, sir. Good night.'

Eyes must be bad or maybe it's this neon lighting. It's when they correct themselves, make a joke of it. That old girl in the post office. Close as I am to you. Called me sir all the time. And guv'nor once. That night when we broke down on the bypass. Guv'nor; the accolade. What more do you want? Wake Jill in a minute Hope she can get herself to bed. Tired. Don't want to drag all the way up those stairs. Not tonight.

'See you then, mate.'

'See you.'

'Cheery, cheery.'

I watch her go up the steps and open the door, turn and grin before I let the brake off, the clutch out for the last lap. I see her climbing the stairs, taking off her boots and slacks and crawling into bed half dressed. She'll be asleep before I turn the next corner.

And now he too climbs to his love in her darkened room, not knowing whether tigers crouch on the landing or doves preen drowsily in the attic cote.

She had fallen asleep with the little lamp still alight on the table beside the bed to keep away the bogles of childhood. He turned the wick up and saw the feminine array of cigarettes and chocolate laid to hand and a sudden tenderness passed through him which was indistinguishable from pain. He undressed quietly, dropping his shirt and trousers over the chairback, then stood for a moment looking down at this woman whom he neither knew nor understood but who was part of his blood. His thought encircled but failed to grasp her. At the very moment that it reached out to hold her he found she had slipped away and he was left with only a sense of loss and an image of her beckoning him on from the farthest region of his mind.

Should he wake her or creep into bed without disturbing her?

She lay there childlike flushed with sleep, the dark hair shadowing her face, relaxed. As if his gaze were a light touch she stirred and opened her eyes, and he sat quickly on the edge of the bed, pulled the clothes back a little from her shoulders and buried his face in the soft flesh of her neck, breathing in the flavour of her skin like a rich flower, his lips moving against her throat. He felt her arms go round him.

'Missed you.'

'Missed you.'

'What time is it?'

'About three o'clock.'

'Cigarette.'

He took one from the packet, lit it and gave it to her. She would never let him put it between her lips but reached out and took it from his fingers, and to him this was somehow symbolic of their whole relationship. She allowed him so far and no further. The last recess of herself was never given up. And she would have said that this was how it should be, that there should be an element of mystery in a relationship like theirs. She would be eternally courted; give herself, yet no conquest was absolute; she was always to be taken again.

'Just because you've been hurt once.' But he knew his words made no difference.

In a way of course she was right. She intrigued and held him. But at the same time he was teased and tormented, made insecure, thwarted in his struggle to subdue and bind her, to reach in and seize her at the core of her self and feel the full satisfaction of unqualified possession. 'My pride of course; that's what's really hurt.' She could reduce him to a small boy again, unsure of himself. 'It is alright? Do you love me?' And then she would make a man of him by her surrender and her claim upon his protection and support.

'Everyone asked after you.'

'Tell me.'

He described the evening, stage by stage, watching her as she smoked, feeling his desire tighten as his eyes traced the fine shoulders, the beginning of the downward curve of the breast.

'Jill fell asleep in the car coming home. She'd had quite a drop. Got a bit touchy. Judy was playing about as usual.'

'You always make excuses for her.'

'And for you too. I said you weren't well.'

'I'll just go away. Then you won't have to.'

'I'm the one who should go away.'

'I've got nothing. Nothing of my own.'

He turned his head away, his sense of inadequacy drowning him. He was nothing, could do nothing for her because she would not let him. His love by itself was not enough for her. She wanted all of him as he wanted all of her, but neither was free to give it anymore. There were too many separate years behind them. He heard a bird murmuring sleepily outside and it increased his sense of isolation, his despair that the human condition resolved itself to two people wandering apart in the darkness when they needed only to reach out their hands to each other.

'I only want to be happy like other people are. I see them just being together and I envy them. I shouldn't have to envy them.'

He wanted to say to her: 'And if I never saw her again, never went places she and I used to go together, do you really think it would make any difference? Don't you understand we're not like other people? We can't do things like that. It isn't all cut and dried. If we did that there would come a time when we too would go wrong, when we'd despise ourselves and each other for being small and mean. We must be bigger than that if we have anything worth having at all.' But all he said was 'I love you. Why can't you trust me. It will be alright.'

'I love you too.' She was crying now.

'Don't cry darling. I can't bear your crying.'

'You'll get cold sitting out there. Come to bed.'

He crawled under the bedclothes and lay staring up at the ceiling. The silence grew between them like a tangible thing. He knew he would be the first to break it. It had always been so, with Rae, with Jill, and back as far as he could remember, because his was the greater need, the greater fear of the irrevocable loss. He turned towards her, stretched out an arm and drew her round unwillingly to face him. Holding her against his chest, he kissed her hair and tried to soothe her.

'Hush now. Here, have my hankie. It's not very clean. It'll be alright.'

Gradually as he held her her crying stopped and they lay there quietly in each other's arms. 'Like lost children,' he thought with a wry twist of his mouth in the dark. 'The Babes in the Wood.' The bird twittered again beyond the window. 'And why should she trust me when she's seen me betray, destroy once already.'

'We'll both go away for a little while. A few days by the sea. Have a look at how the Spring's been getting on without us. Would you like that?'

She nodded her head, the tears coming more slowly. 'I'm sorry. I don't think I'm very well.'

'It's alright darling. I do understand really. It's just sometimes I don't know what to do. It's always better when we've talked about it.'

He lay awake for a little while after she had fallen asleep, listening for the bird, conscious of her body curled beside him. His arm fell asleep before he did. He raised her gently and moved it from under her and she murmured and drew closer to him again. He felt his stomach tighten but turned on his back, following a meandering thread of thought that led down into sleep. 'Covered them with leaves. Better than earth. Keep off the rain. Did you know it rained? Raining on the railway tracks Carl, there's that bird again.'

'MISS STEPHENS, Miss Stephens!'

As soon as you get inside the door. Lord behold us and if they only knew.

'Miss Stephens, can I have the key of the blue games cupboard please?'

'Miss Stephens can you umpire our match against 2b at dinnertime?'

'Miss Stephens, I can see no provision for 4a's swimming period on their timetable at all.'

'Steve, the head wants to see us during first period. It's about that kid who slipped and hit her head last week, Sandra Filchard.'

And the protests rise and break against the tongue. It's not my problem, my fault. Wasn't there. Not guilty. Not mine, no.

'As head of the department, Miss Stephens, you are, of course, responsible. You should have seen.' Not there. No, not there.

'Miss Stephens, 3c have pinched all the courts.'

'When can we start tennis, Miss Stephens?'

'*I love Miss Stephens.*'

'But I shan't love you for very long, Rosemary, if you scrawl all over the board before any member of staff has a chance to use it. And anyway my name is spelt with a 'v' not a 'ph' as you should know by now. After three years in this school one might expect you to at least know how to spell the names of members of the staff. You can write them all out for me in alphabetical order, in your best handwriting, with their forms and subjects, just to refresh your memory. Bring me the list in the morning. Who's board monitor for this week? Mavis, clean the board please, and put up the date and your first period. Latin? Well it had better be in Latin then, hadn't it. We don't want Miss Evans to think we're absolutely ignorant in this form. The rest of you stop the chatter and get out your hymn books. Have you found yours yet Sylvia? Then share with Connie.'

'Shall I bring you the list this evening, Miss Stephens, if I've finished it?'

'No thank you, Rosemary. I don't want Miss Rushton after me because you've been doing it under your desk during history. Tomorrow will be quite soon enough. I think I can bear to wait til then.'

That child has all the makings of a masochist already. When she's a bit older she'll be crying out for someone to whip her. Unless it's all a deep laid plot, an excuse to hang around after school and walk me to the station. Must have seen I haven't got the car today. Matt's right. It's nothing but a biscuit tin. God knows what the bloody hell's wrong with it now. 'There's the bell, girls. Is all the dinner money in? Who's absent? Right, all talking stop now. Line up for prayers. Quickly now or we'll be last in again. Come along Rosemary. You'll survive.'

'Miss Stephens, why do we have to go in to prayers if we don't believe in God?'

'To hear the notices.'

'Why couldn't we just go in at the end, then?'

'Rosemary.'

'Yes Miss Stephens.'

'Have 3b gone yet Thelma? Follow on then. Quickly girls before 3c get in first. And remember, I shall personally break the neck of any girl Miss Evans catches talking.'

'Supposing she doesn't catch us, Miss Stephens?'

'Rosemary.'

Bang goes my free period for today. Mary was a fool. Should have reported it whether the kid thought she was alright or not. Always thinks they're malingering. Sandra isn't that kind of child. Ought to know that by now. Still, she never takes the trouble to find out. They're all the same to her. Too tough by half. Can't stand hard bright women. Not a soft spot in her, except when she's with a man. Goes all soggy. Take me I'm yours. The woman's place and all the pap the women's mags hand out. Just for the prestige, the social status. I've got a man. Pity the poor fool she hooks.

The kids don't like her either. Takes all the fun out of it. Just another lesson, another period, to be got through before out and freedom, tellytime, boytime, dancing, playing records, gossip; just another period.

Doesn't understand that either. How much they suffer. Won't let them off; even that poor little bitch Julie. Tortures of the damned. Has her out on the pitch in all weathers.

'Miss Stephens, I've got my period. I can't go in today.'

'Miss Stephens, Elizabeth's not well; she's gone to the sick-room.'

'Miss Stevens, can I have an aspirin?'

'Need I do P.E.. I've got a headache.'

'Miss Stevens, Julie fainted in prayers.'

All that blood and pain, and fear so the human race can go on. Boys get off lightly; wet dreams and itchy fingers. Fear or resentment in the girls, I suppose, constricting the muscles; cramp. Yet they've most of them got boy friends, look forward to getting married, having children. Normal, whatever that may mean.

Not like me. See now, of course, what it was, not wanting any of those things. Trapped by your own body. All you'd always wanted to do shoved back into a corner, made dream stuff in a moment. Trapped in a role that's alien to you. Condemned for life in the bars of your own flesh.

But these kids? Maybe they feel they should; a sort of traditional

34

female initiation rite. Forerunner of childbirth. Or perhaps it's just to get attention, feeling insecure at being pushed forward into life. No, not me. I'm still a child. Mother! We're all mother substitutes. Poor white faces. Maybe it's just chemistry.

The Samuels looks rather splendid this morning; Chinese style, high mandarin collar, green and silver brocade. It's a beautiful face, like Bertrand Russell the bone structure and that wild white hair or what's-her-name in *Jane Eyre*, Miss Temple. Repose or is it conscious control? Wonder if she is? Sublimates, I expect. Handsome, intelligent. Mrs. Masters is potty about her even though she's got a husband and two children. Wonder if she realises. And husband Jack, what does he think? They went on holiday together last summer on an archaeological dig. One of those great emotional relationships with queer overtones. Everyone terribly highminded and intense; not daring to admit the truth. Be shocked if you told them. Couldn't face it. End of beautiful friendship. Magnificent throat, Elsie Masters. Pre-Raphaelite, muscular and smooth. Tendency to goitre, I suppose, but rather fine, all the same. 'Thy neck is like an ivory tower.' Not my type, though.

Hymn no. 281. As long as it isn't one of the 'Praise Him, praise Hymns'. Go on for ever. Must remember not to look at Rosemary Ellis if there's anything about love in it or she'll think I'm interested. Difficult though; always stands on the end of the line where I only have to lift my head to catch her eye. Glad I'm not attracted to the kids. Too many problems. Have to get out if you were like Matt. But then, most of us are looking for our mothers so kids wouldn't interest us. Matt's different. Congenital type? Could be. 'Lead us Heavenly Father, lead us,' Seems harmless enough.

'World's tempestuous sea.' A lot of people see it like that. What does Matt call it? The House of Shades. The lonely ones. Afraid people will find out, outcasts; guilt too of course. Funny idea that of the scapegoat. Is that what we are for society?

> 'Thou didst tread this earth before us,
> Thou didst feel its keenest woe.'

Often wonder if he was. Must have been something or wouldn't have been complete. Not man. Scapegoat. 'And the disciple whom Jesus loved lay in his bosom.' 'Follow me,' and they left their wives and families. 'Lovest thou me?' Bisexual, of course; Mary Magdalene as well. Fundamental principle of life and all that. Where would all the charm and vitality have come from otherwise; the power flowing out, healing, drawing the people, resurrecting. Not asexual; too cold.

> 'Love with every passion blending,
> Pleasure that can never cloy.'

Very nice too. Mustn't look at Rosemary. Not at all a bad prospect. What we're all looking for, I suppose. Only here and now. Not pie in the sky. The perfect relationship; the one that doesn't come unstuck after a few months. Too many casualities, too much first aid, patching up wounds, soothing sore places, teaching the injured to trust again; twisted broken lives.

> 'Thus provided, pardoned, guided,
> Nothing can our peace destroy.'

And there it all is in the proverbial nutshell. Provided. Provided what or with whom? 'The Lord will provide,' they used to say but what do we do in the meantime. Sit with hands folded in patient resignation amen or fix yourself on an occasional one night stand. And then supposing nothing comes along or when it does you're too jaded, hooked on easy sex, drifting dazed between shots and reality passes you by on the other side? So you're back where you started with work and play: the rich full life, badminton and tennis, home to mother every other weekend, the club on Saturdays with not too much to drink, the occasional dance, the spectator uninvolved. Play it cool. Maybe I'll end up like the Samuels, aloof, controlled and very much run after, cock of some little hen roost of a girls' secondary grammar, too old for tennis but with plenty of rewarding interests, courses in child psychology and walking holidays with a friend in the Tyrol.

What'll she have to say to me this morning and whose side am I supposed to be on, anyway? Must listen to the lesson or shan't be able to ask the kids about it and one of them's sure to catch me out. Rosemary I expect. Wearing sometimes having someone so closely attached. Doesn't miss a move.

'Nothing is so beautiful as Spring.'

The old girl certainly knows how to pick them. How much sinks in and how much is right above their heads? They'll never have a chance like this again most of them, the old liberal-humanist tradition in education, and yet so few of them can accept it, turned against it from the start by materialist propaganda. All that raw human stuff subjected to the daily stamping and dyeing of telly, newsrags til they come out true to mould; commercialism pandering to them for their spending power, records, clothes, make-up, giving the baby candy til its little stomach won't take anything else and it lolls its slack, pudgy body on the doorstep, blown out like a sheep tick, too lazy to run out and play while the nice kind old gentleman makes off with its piggy bank.

'Innocent mind and Mayday in girl and boy.'

Hard sometimes to see the kids in that light with their sharp knowingness, clouded too soon these modern times. I bet there aren't more than two intact maidenhoods in the whole of 5b and 5c put together. Wendy Rawlings there with the great dark circles smudged under those wary eyes, tart-tight skirt and her blouse fit to bust. The marks of Saturday night to Sunday morning still not scrubbed off that white child's face and what looks like a bruise on her throat. Sharp teeth the current boy friend must have. Still, we're lucky on the whole, not many actual pregnancies and most of them manage to leave before it's too obvious.

Harder to tell with the other sort. Statistically, four per cent out of a school of eight hundred, that's about thirty ought to be queer, which makes, divide by five years, fives into thirty, six a year, one and a bit in every class. But then it wouldn't show for certain till they'd left. Too much social pressure from the others to follow the normal pattern and you can't tell with the younger forms anyway because they're full of crushes, part of ordinary growing up. Interesting to speculate though. Reckon I could pick out one or two in the fifths and sixths. That'll be the day when I walk down the stairs at the club and come face to face with one of the old girls. Not that it'd matter I suppose. We'd both be in the same boat. No sense in either of us rocking it. Maybe I'd even be able to help. Ease her through the difficult stages so many seem to go through when they think they're the only ones in the world and wish they'd never been born at all. What was it that kid said to me once?

Something about feeling that everyone was pointing her out in the street and whispering about her. Eyes everywhere. Thou God seest me.

Innocent enough they look now, heads bowed. One or two sets of eyes open here and there. Rosemary's of course. Two little devils in 2b nudging each other. A moment's peace before Millie strikes up her rousing march and we all shuffle out to battle.

'Shall we go straight in and get it over and done with? There might even be a fragment of my lone free period left over after.'

'Okay. I don't know why you have to be dragged into it though.'

'Oh you know the old girl always believes in making it a matter for the whole department rather than something personal. Makes for solidarity. United we fall.'

'I feel such a fool though when there's someone else there. I'd much rather she just tore me off a strip and that was that.'

'So would we all.'

The door's open just slightly as always so that no one passes by without feeling that they're observed unless a conference of great weight is taking place inside when the whole school goes on tiptoe. Knock gently with one knuckle and wait for a voice.

'Come in.' Soft spoken, carefully pitched. 'Ah Miss Stephens and Miss Barter.'

'You wanted to see us Miss Samuels?' Like one of the kids.

'Yes. Would you mind coming in and closing the door. I'm sorry to take up your time like this but it is rather important.'

Outside a sudden squall throws the trees about. Inside a thin sunlight gives the room an appearance of calm and repose. She has beautiful hands and knows it. As she turns the heavy down on her upper lip catches the light. What was it Matt was saying about having to shave every day?

'I wanted to see you about Sandra Filchard. She's told me her version but as I pointed out to her there are two sides to every story.'

Careful. Never know where you are with the old girl, whose side she's going to be on. Covering her tracks all the time. Fear of the parents, the authorities. Impartial. Scared like the rest of us.

'I don't know what she told you Miss Samuels so I don't really know what you're asking me.'

Oh Mary, Mary so contrary, for God's sake don't bluster. Looks guilty. Play it cool.

'Just tell me what happened.'

'We were doing group work. I was with the group by the horse. There was only about five minutes to go before we put the apparatus away. Sandra came and asked me if she could sit out because she didn't feel well.'

'And what did you say?'

'I said because there was so little time left it wouldn't hurt her to carry on till I blew the whistle.'

'You said: "Since you've left it so late you can carry on. You should have thought of it a little earlier".'

'More or less.'

'Did you know she'd had a fall?'

'Not then, no. The silly child didn't come and tell me when it happened.'

You think you're saved. No, no. I didn't know. But there'll be an answer.

'Are the children not in the habit of reporting such things straight away?'

'Well, as a rule one of the others would have told me.'

The form busybody. 'Please Miss, 'lizbeth's broke her leg.'

'But 4b and I don't get on too well.'

'Oh?'

Time to step in, stick out your neck St. Steven, ready for the stones.

'I don't think they've ever settled down to the change in staff. I'd had them ever since they've been in the school and you know how difficult children are over someone new.'

'I take them for civics. I find them quite bright and co-operative. They have some interesting ideas once you get them to really talk to you. So you didn't realise there'd been an accident?'

'Not until their netball period when she wasn't there.'

'Did you notice that she wasn't there?'

'Well you see she's the form netball captain so of course it was rather obvious.'

'Yes, she's always been rather interested in games, I believe. So you asked why she was away?'

39

'Oh they told me quickly enough.'

'Jane told you I suppose. They're friends, aren't they? What exactly did she say?'

'That she'd landed awkwardly and the catcher hadn't got a proper hold on her and she'd fallen back and hit her head.'

'Who was the catcher?'

'Wendy Cope.'

'I expect she was gossiping to someone and not doing her job.'

'She's always been a bit of a scatterbrain.'

'Did you enter it in the book when you heard about it?'

'I thought it was too late.'

'Oh no. Had you done that with an explanatory note on why the entry was late you would have still been covered. As it is the doctor says she has mild concussion and I hadn't any official record to refer to to find out how far we were responsible. I hope her mother doesn't think of negligence. She's an only child and mothers sometimes get rather upset over their one chick. You will remember in future. Every tiny mishap must go down. I'm sorry it's taken so long. This is the time you usually have for a departmental meeting isn't it Miss Stevens?'

'It is the only time we have off together to talk things over.'

'I noticed the Blue Games Cupboard was very untidy this morning as I came along the corridor. Perhaps you could get some of the children to help you tidy it in the dinner hour.'

And she will pass by on the other side, accidentally of course, just to see if it's being done.

'That's all we can do then, Miss Barter. Hope that the parents don't want to make a fuss. Miss Stevens if you could spare me a minute or two more.'

As if one had any choice. My turn, No, no. Not there. Judith, that's who she reminds me of. That strange bloodless woman in the Old Testament, using her beauty to chop a man's head off. Holy chastity. Getting the poor bugger impotent with drink and then chop. And that song she sings at the end; all full of herself. Pride, that's all it is. Wait patiently with a polite smile fixed in position, hung on your ears like a pair of glasses.

'Miss Barter's relationships with her forms worry me a little. Of course as you say, children do sometimes take some time to adjust to someone new, particularly when they've been used to a lighter hand on the rein, but I do feel perhaps she's inclined to take some of the pleasure out of what is, after all, meant to be enjoyed. The children obviously enjoy your lessons very much. Sometimes I wonder if this is at the expense of real hard work. They must realise that to obtain any standard there must be some effort in their play. The children like you very much. You are what I would call a personality teacher. This isn't really a bad thing in many ways but it does mean I think that you are tempted to take life a little easy. You know you can get along on your own popularity and this makes you stress the intrinsic worth of the subject itself a little less than it should be. Think about what I've said and if you have any thoughts on the subject, any comments, do feel free to come and talk them over with me. You won't forget the cupboard will you? Perhaps you'd like me to say something in assembly to the whole school about keeping the games stock tidy?'

'I'll write you out a notice to give out if you would. I shan't be able to be on the spot myself this dinner hour. I've promised to umpire a match for the second year. But I'm sure there are plenty of willing helpers who'd like to tidy a cupboard for me. I'll think about what you said.'

'Yes do. Could you send Mrs. Rolfe in to me on your way out?'

'Miss Samuels would like to see you, Mrs. Rolfe.'

The perfect bloody secretary leaps to her feet in a flash. Twitters in with the morning's post. Hens, all hens round one old cock. Steady, hold steady. Just time for a quick one before the bell. How many butches pee standing up? Now wash your hands please.

Look in the mirror. Hair could do with a comb. The wind. Kids'll be all over the place like animals. Funny how the weather affects them. Why does she hate me? Hands still shaking a bit. Mouth acid. Fear and anger. Does she know? Guesses perhaps or instinctive. Clash of two masculine personalities. Maybe she's frightened too. Likes to be popular. Afraid because I'm younger and the kids like me. Putting me in my place. The non-academic. A personality teacher among all these fine graduates. Bitch. Butch. I could have loved you. Not like that, no. But I could have loved you, modelled myself. Where's the use? Sterile. You would never have had me as a friend. You only want satellites. Like Judy in a way.

Pity though, a waste. You'll always be lonely, apart from the rest of life. Never admit that you're like everyone else. 'Thinkest thou . . . no more cakes and ale?' No more beer and fags and a warm woman in a bed. Let that be a lesson to me. Keep trying, never give up. Rosemary can tidy the cupboard. Maybe it's time I left. Tried for a comprehensive. Been here nearly four years. Too long, O lord, too long. Not enough seniority for a comprehensive. Sec.mod. for experience and then a training college. Nice little niche and plenty of talent to choose from. Matt's idea of paradise. What the hell can I do with 1e? Bloody woman's put every thought out of my head.

Stand in the doorway and wait for them to notice and hush creeps through the gym or blow the whistle and smart to attention? God they're kicking up a racket this morning. Always notice it when I've been in with the old girl. Sets my teeth on edge somehow. Aware of all the shortcomings, noise, lack of respect. Snappish with the kids when it's not their fault. I'm the one who's different. Expect her to appear at any moment. Sit in judgement at the back. Silent. Then get up and walk out. Silent. And you wait for the bomb to drop. 'Could you spare a moment Miss Stevens? Would you mind closing the door?' And the kids at their worst, self-conscious. Stumbling and not understanding. Cause one of my little ones to stumble. Must stop this din. Whistle.

'Well 1e, that shouldn't have been necessary should it? Stand still Jean when I blow the whistle, absolutely still. You should know that by now. Yes Valerie, go quickly. Haven't those verrucas cleared up yet Hazel? It's time you were back to bare feet. Right now, when I blow the whistle again I want you to line up in your team corners without a sound. Blues you're taking a long time to sort yourselves out. Who's the vice captain then if Monica's away? Reds that's a very poor line. Point each to greens and yellows. Now running on the spot to warm us all up. Get those knees as high as possible. Good that's much better. Right two from each team get a form and I want you to choose your own exercise. Point to reds for a very nice line. Think of all the exciting things you can do with a form and I want to see as many of them as possible. Good Margaret, that's just the sort of thing I mean.'

Funny little things they are at this stage. Tadpoles or skinny fledglings barely human. Same basic structure as any other little animal. Four jointed limbs, a body and a head. Asexual. No real difference between little boys and little girls. One or two of them just beginning to show signs of a bosom, no more than a fat boy. Still smooth skinned though; almost seem transparent in some lights as if you could see the skeleton through like fish. Small fry. Big eyes in thin faces. Don't wash enough the lower streams. Get a terrific fug up in their classrooms. Hits you when you go in. Valerie's neck's grey. Something funny about her home background. Must look up her card. Dirt between the toes, back of the ankles. Glad I made Nella captain of reds. Why are the West Indians so good at games? Move so much better, better physique. Generations of malnutrition, long hours in factories and shops stunted us. Weeds most of us, grown crooked out of the sun and air, dry barren lives. Funny how she smells different. Different diet: spices. Eat better than we do. Sliced white puff bread, sweety cardboard veg from the deep-freeze, milk bled veal and broiled chicken fluff. Whistle.

'Good. There were some really interesting things there. Now two from each team fetch a mat and put it about three feet from the end of the form and see what you can do with that. Point for the first team to have started. Greens, point to the greens. Come along blues you're all behind this morning.'

Not much to look at myself really. Wiry, that's the word for it. Always was. Poor mother. 'When is she going to get some flesh on her bones, Mrs. Stevens, fill out a bit?' When is she going to begin to look like a woman, something a man can handle, something you can marry off? Flat chest, almost a stoop. Not even the typical games mistress, all brawn and muscle. Run to fat in their forties, traditional heavy butch. Not my style. What was it Jill said? 'Decadent Roman.' Hair helps too and being dark. Short for world conquerors the Romans, like Hitler and Napoleon and Sexy Nelson. Makes dancing a bit difficult sometimes. Head on her shoulder. Dance well together. Wonder if she would? And then what? A few weeks of honeymoon spoon and goodbye cry. Nothing not even friends. Not worth it. Stick to what you've got. Don't spoil the ship for a ha'porth of tart.

'That's very nice Yvonne. You can have a point for that. There

43

blues Yvonne's saved your reputation for you. Four people from each team to put mats and forms away. Team captains get out your apparatus. Reds on the box, blues on the horse, greens the ropes. Yes Mary?'

'Please Miss Stevens they had the ropes last time.'

'Did you Gwen?'

'Yes Miss Stevens.'

'Right, yellows the ropes and greens the bars then. Everyone move on to the next place when I blow the whistle. Just the top two sections of the box as usual reds. I know you can manage the whole thing Elaine, but we're not all trained acrobats. Come along Gwen. Time you had the ropes down by now.'

Too fat that child. Making her captain doesn't seem to have made her any less lethargic. Begin to think it's glands or is she just overfed? Can't tell these days. What can you do when the parents don't know how to feed them? Still, look at Elsie, a snippet of humanity. Wonder if any of them will. Just a dot. Yet how many cells in that little body and every one differentiated? What's the sex of an amoeba? Or hasn't it got a sex? Seems somehow feminine because it reproduces itself. And worms completely bisexual, I suppose, swapping sex like they do, both exactly the same and yet both giving the other something. Like us, only we're sterile; no end product. Little Elsie'll probably end up mother to a great brood of six little dots, six round demanding mouths to suck the life out of her thin body. Whistle.

'Move on everybody.'

Now they're curious about it all. Just asking questions. What was it that kid put about in last year's 1e, that she was pregnant. To get attention. Lived with her grandmother. Fancy thinking that one up at eleven. Had to send her to the child-guidance people for treatment. Seems alright now. Viscous love: worms. Too young even for crushes. That doesn't start till the second year with puberty. How do they make contact? Uttering low cries of delight they squirmed across the rutty mud. Let's go and make love in dead Earnest. How could anyone fancy a child? Often they only play with them. No response. Maybe because they weren't allowed to play with themselves. Girls don't seem to do that so much. At least not in public, in competition like boys. 'Please Miss he's showing his thing.' Who's got the biggest. Something tangible, a symbol of yourself, the little man. Girls have to substitute with dolls.

'Mavis your hand isn't in the right place. You can't give proper support unless you've got it right under her arm. Stop everyone and look a minute. Mavis, stand as if you've just come over the horse. Now who can tell me what's wrong? Nella? My hands aren't in the right position. What might happen if I didn't have my hands in the right position? Yes. She might fall back and hit her head or she might fall forward and twist an ankle or even break her arm. You must remember that girls. If you're a catcher you've got a most important job to do. The safety of the people who are jumping depends on you. Right it's time to put the apparatus away. Anyone who isn't needed go and change and I don't want to hear a lot of noise when I come into the cloakroom.'

Scurry away like little mice; high piping voices. Too short these periods before break to get much done. Hope the tea's poured out. Ten minutes isn't long enough for it to get cool let alone if it isn't even ready when you get there. That's the bell. Must get those kids out of the cloakroom.

'Come along now. Who's going to be last? Those who are ready can go. Wait for her outside Nella then she might be a bit quicker. Whose plimsolls are these? Take them for her Marageret and tell her I want them brought to me tomorrow properly marked with name and form before she leaves them somewhere else and they end up in lost property. Outside now everyone or we shan't have any break left.'

Push open the door. Dearly beloved we are gathered here to partake of the tea of lubrication. Poor dad. The dregs of a religious upbringing. Whither shall I go and where shall I sit me down? Not that table, no. The Knight is there stinking with an acid chemical rankness that leaves an almost visible trail through the air as she goes. Little dogs roll over on their backs paralytic, cats run spitting for the nearest alley. Try the windowsill. Chat up the little French piece. Mademoiselle from Armentiers *parlez vous*?

'Pardon?'

'Sorry. I was thinking aloud.'

'You speak French?'

'*Un peu. Un petit peu.* But your English is better than my French and it is good for you to practise.'

'Oh yes. It is good because at home I am having a flat with two other French girls and we are speaking together all the time in French. Also I don't know many English people.'

'We aren't easy to know. Not always very friendly.'

'You are a little *réservé*.'

'Reserved.'

'Does Miss Holroyd look after you?'

'Oh yes. She is very kind.'

'What do you do in the evenings?'

'Oh I study and sometimes we go altogether to the cinema.'

'London is rather different from Paris.'

'You have been to Paris?'

'Twice.'

'Do you like?'

'Oh yes. Very much.'

'What do you like?'

'The cheap wine. In Paris you can always get a drink. You can wear what you like and go where you like and no one stares at you. Everyone is accepted as an individual. I like the night life.'

'You have seen?'

'A little, in Pigalle and Montmartre.' Tread softly. 'What have you seen in London?'

'I have been to the Houses of Parliament and to the British Museum. That is all. It is difficult when you do not have anyone to go with.'

'What about the friends you share with?'

'They are not interested to go to these places only to drink coffee with other French people in the coffee bar.'

'Have you been to Oxford?'

'No.'

'Would you like to?'

'Oh yes. It would be very beautiful I think.'

'I have a car, only a small one, but we could go one Saturday or Sunday if you would like to.'

'But I don't want to be a trouble.'

'No trouble. I haven't been for years. I should enjoy showing it to you if you'd like to go. It can't be this weekend I'm afraid because I'm going to my mother's but next weekend is alright for me if it is for you. Shall we say Sunday?'

'Oh yes. Sunday is very good for me.'

'There's the bell. I'll see you at lunchtime.'

'Oh yes.'

Oh yes, yes and there's a thing, a pretty little thing. The fool hath said in his heart there is no ding a dong ding. No possibility of my ever again. No more fatuous, infatuated thud-thud of a heart gone suddenly crazy. Oh no, no. And 'Oh yes,' she says. 'Sunday is very good for me;' the flower of her face turned up towards my sun.

'Can we have a practice, please, Miss Stevens?'

'Practise?'

'For the match at dinner-time against 2b. We've picked the teams.'

'You're presenting me with a *fait accompli* if you know what that means.'

'It means something accomplished doesn't it? You know when you do something and tell someone afterwards so that they have to accept it.'

'That's it. Have you got two umpires? Anyone got another whistle. Good. Get started then.'

Gives me a chance to think. The 'A' forms are so much easier. Don't begin with a chip on their shoulders or struggling against work that's too difficult for them. All wrong really. Just doing things on the cheap. Any other way you'd have to have more teachers and equipment and who's going to pay for them? No one wants to pay for education now. Still see it as a social service instead of a fundamental need. A profession for women: child-minders. That's why it's so badly paid. Wonder how much the Samuels gets. A couple of thou. if she's lucky for a school this size, and scientists and doctors run away to the colonies every week because they're only getting twice that. Yet this is where it all begins. They never get another chance to learn.

I was lucky there. At least dad saw we were educated. Funny we should both turn out like this. Must give Tommy a ring. Find out how the latest is getting on. Just as well he died when he did. Wouldn't have been so easy to keep in the dark as mother. She doesn't want to know anyway. Wonder if he was; a bit at least.

47

Tripping round in his little lace cotta with all those handsome young servers. Would make you think it ran in the family. They're having trouble with that ball in this wind. Looks as though we might be in for some rain too.

'Come on. You'll have to do better than this to beat 2b.'

What was I like at this age, getting on for thirteen? Some of them started their periods already. Younger these days; better fed. The pattern was there already, ground in, every line etched deep if I'd only known. Dad asking me if I felt I was ready to consider being confirmed. Sun falling through the study window like the Samuels' room this morning. 'I'm sorry but I don't think I believe enough.' Meaning how could I believe in a father figure, all-seeing, all-wise, just and powerful when you were none of these things? When I'd seen you cry and humble yourself to little men on the P.C.C. and fat fools like the bishop. Your grace my lord to speak a space, compose my face and keep my place. A-a-amen. And the carpets shrank down the stairs, worn through with our feet dragging up to bed until there were bare boards above the first floor and the whole house rambled and sagged at the seams like a down-and-out doused with Red Biddy, the wine of anti-communion. But your cope was of the best and your hands soft and delicately joined over the cup of our bitterness, mine and Tommy's. Dilapidations.

Only the garden was good for growing in, running and climbing and a world of fantasy in the shrubbery; clinging to the top of the tree in a wind like this, asail topmast high; hunting between the dusty acrid laurels knowing if I bit one leaf I'd die; hiding in the undergrowth while mother called and commanded to choir practice. Tommy missed out on a lot of that, packed off to boarding school. Making a man of him they called it. And now we're neither of us anything. What was that old pop song? 'I'm just an in-between.' Maybe we're in love with each other. Two halves of the same apple. Happens between twins sometimes. I took his strength and he took my softness like the worms making love.

Strange today, can't get into it. Mind keeps running off down different tracks. This wind doesn't help; threat of rain and then the sun coming through in jagged patches. Tired perhaps. The long hard haul of the Spring term. Uphill all the way, yes all the way.

Some Spring through Jan. and Feb. Easter soon. The last heaviness of Good Friday and then the resurrection of the year with the yellow splashes of daffodils on the altar and the church bowered for the young god, 'Happy Easter darlings' from mother, and dad's egg hunt through the house. How long is it to go now? Another three weeks. Reckon I'll just about make it.

'How's the score, Linda?'

'Six-four Miss Stevens.'

'Did you change ends at half time?'

'Yes, we were two minutes late, though.'

'Well we won't tell them; it might cause an argument.' Funny self-contained child; completely reliable and they know it too. Three times form-captain and not a bit unpopular because it doesn't affect her and they know she looks after them and keeps them out of trouble. Supposed to be pretty bright too. Don't see enough of that in this subject. Perhaps I should have done something else. Pig-headedness just because he wanted me to carry on with history and I saw it as another form of weakness, lost in the mists, romantic retreat to the past. Mother would have preferred it too. 'And what's your pretty daughter?' 'A games hag; lean, stringy and muscular.' No more pretty dresses, the frills and frillies I wanted myself; the dancing till dawn in the arms of a Valentino who doesn't love the Virgin Mary and the chief server better.

'Miss Stevens, do you think it'll rain?'

'I shouldn't be surprised. It looks rather like it.'

'What shall we do about the match then?'

'You'll have to put up a notice on the boards cancelling it or rather postponing it. Will you do that?' Pray for rain. It'll give me a long dinner hour to spend with my little French frou-frou. Must find out her name. Wonder how old she is. About twenty-two I should think. Wonder how much she knows. Still the French are different about things like that. Oh mademoiselle you'll go to hell if you like me too well. Seducing the innocent that's what you're contemplating Stevens. People like you should be locked up before you contaminate society. I am society. You're sick. So is society.

'Another five minutes and then it'll be time. I'm going round to the other court to blow the whistle there. Make sure they stop on time won't you? Here come the first spots. We'll just about get the game finished before it pours. A pity about the match. You'll have to arrange another day with 2b.'

The devil still does a good job of looking after his own I see. Leaves me with my own form though and we can't use the gym because Mary's got that with 4b. Hall's out. Millie uses it all day today. Have to find a free room to have them in. Think ours has a wireless period for the sixth.

'Hurry through the cloakroom won't you 2a? Linda, I leave them to your tender charge. I would be disappointed to hear any-thing'd gone wrong.' Must get to 3a before they go rushing off to the gym.

'Ah here you are. Have you got your satchels with you? Right make a quiet line outside the hall. Thelma go and find an empty room. Now I want absolute quiet here. Don't draw attention to yourselves while I go and get some work to do too. Mavis that isn't a very good beginning.'

Give me a chance to go over next term's timetable and sort through some record cards. Deal with any form business too that's come up. Keep them on their toes. 'Have you found somewhere Thelma? Right lead on then. No fussing over where you're going to sit. It really doesn't matter for one prep. period. Life will go on Elizabeth if you don't sit next to Mary for what must be quite forty minutes. Yes Joan? No inkwell. Then move to this front desk. Jacqueline come to the front too. I see you've got yourself nicely tucked in the back row for a gossip with Carole as soon as I look the other way. No I know you wouldn't dream of it but come to the front all the same. Is there any girl who feels she hasn't enough to do because if so I can provide her with an essay on either the value of physical education or on games through the ages. No offers. Then I expect you all to settle down and get on with it. I have plenty of work to do and I take it that you have too.'

Some hideous smells coming up from the kitchen, specially designed to put you off your dinner before you even sit down to it. Maybe I can get next to the little French piece. 'And what do you think of English cooking? Oh you mustn't judge by this. Let me take you . . .' Walk into my parlour said the spider to the fly. Funny how we always think of spiders as feminine and yet the horror, what do they call it, arachniphobia, is somehow associated with fear of penetration. The spider penetrating its prey and immobilising it with a shot so that it has live meat to feed off equates with pregnancy fears. Bound hand and foot in a situation you can't escape. No, no, not me. Caught by a trick of the body, betrayed again just like you were when you first stood in front of all those closed doors marked *men only*. 'But why dad, why can't I be a priest?' 'The priesthood is only for men. Women have another vocation.' 'But I don't feel any call to that. I want the real thing. What good would it be if I couldn't administer the sacraments or say mass? There isn't any point in it otherwise. I don't want to go around washing old ladies. I'm not cut out for that. Oh I know what you're going to say: that it's not a true vocation, just pride. If I was really called I'd accept anything that offered itself, not want the exhibitionist glories of preaching and advising people on their spiritual and moral problems, god for the week. But would you? Did you? I'm no different from you.' Poor dad. And now he's justified of course. Quite fallen away; never set foot inside. Tommy too only I don't think he even gives it a thought. As Jill says you can't go back and that would be trying to cling to the roots, refusing to grow up away towards the insecurity of an independent life. Get a great hankering though sometimes, kid myself, specially when Easter comes round; I will go unto the altar of God, my feet shall stand in thy way O-o-oh Jerusalem.

Look at them all bent over their work; adults already by this stage, thinking and feeling like adults. Puberty seems to be a definite dividing line between the child and the adult. They're never the same again. Nearly Juliet's age, moving into the real world out of childhood fantasy and dreaming of lovers. Funny how some kids never have crushes but just go straight on to boys while others like Rosemary go through years of agony. Some have both at once of course and some of us never come out. The faces of love. Too simple to put it all down to arrested development. Time to do the rounds.

How I hated it as a kid, someone standing behind me looking over my shoulder. Most of them seem to be doing maths. Had a lot of trouble with the Knight. Saying they were noisy and un-disciplined. She wanted them herself that's why. Always tries to pinch an a form; likes having earnest moral chats with them. Auntie

Knight's corner. Trouble is they're older than she is already, more experienced too most of them. She hasn't even lived vicariously. Never reads a book except *How God Loves* or *The Calculus*. Must be well into her thirties but with that strange unmarked face like a rather doughy fourteen-year-old, white skin and too fair hair, no eyebrows almost like a mongol. Yet she's got a degree so there must be an intelligence there somewhere. Kids don't get on with her. Instinctive reaction to anything abnormal, incomplete like animals. They'd say I was that of course. The children don't sense it though or the old girl couldn't accuse me of being so popular. 'I can always tell them, spot them straightaway.'

'And what precisely are you doing Rosemary?'

'Reading, Miss Stevens.'

'Is that your English homework?'

'No Miss Stevens.'

'Then you're reading for pleasure? And what is this splendid piece of pornography in its brown paper disguise. I see. And where did this come from?'

'The library.'

'The public library? Does your mother know you've got this?'

'Oh yes. She got it for me.'

'And how many other people are on the short list to borrow it before it goes back? No volunteers? All of you I expect. I hope your mother's got plenty put by to pay the fines while the whole of 3a plough their way through putting their fingers under every word. However since as far as I know it isn't on the English syllabus or in the school library I don't want to see it in school again or I shall confiscate it. If you're all eager to read it I suggest you get your mothers as well trained as Mrs. Ellis. Now put it away and get out something else to do.'

'Have you read it Miss Stevens?'

'Yes.'

'Did you like it?'

'Yes. I think it's very well written.'

'Then why can't we read it in school?'

'Because there are some parents who don't see it in this way and I have no intention of losing my job because you want to satisfy your curiosity.'

'But do you think we ought to read it?'

'When you're ready for it.'

'I thought it was boring.'

'There we are. Sylvia thought it was boring because she read it too soon. You might suggest to Mrs. Parry that you have a debate on censorship in English sometime and you can let me know what conclusions you come to. Now get on with your work all of you. I want you to stop in about ten minutes and we'll have the rest of the period to discuss form business.'

That was a tricky one but I think that was the right thing to do. One of the other staff might have come across one of them reading it and not understood and then there would have been hell to pay. Imagine the Knight's face! Filthy books. My soul is as pure as the driven calculus. One and one must never be allowed to make three. And he added unto them; increase and multiply. No, no. Divide and subtract. Sex is the lowest common factor. Keep my hands free from picking and stealing and my mind from all sin. Find the square root of our being. Reduce all vulgar fractions; resolve our equations to simple terms. In the name of the holy trigonometry, Cos, Sin and Tan. Q.E.D.

'Right, will you put your books away now please. Connie, has anything happened that I ought to know about? Has the form been reported or, much less likely, commended?'

'No Miss Stevens.'

'The formroom looks rather bare. Are there any suggestions for brightening it up? Yes Jacequeline? Some flowers would be a good idea but they might be rather expensive. Who's going to pay for them if no one has any in the garden she can bring?'

'If we all paid a penny a week we could buy some.'

'Yes Thelma. That's a good idea. I'll put twopence as I'm earning. Shall we vote on that? Those in favour of a penny a week from everyone for the flower fund. Anyone against? No. Who will volunteer to collect the money? Not a very pleasant job I'm afraid. Carole. Thankyou. Will you add that to the list of monitors please Connie? Anymore suggestions? Some of your pictures. Yes, that's a good idea. A wall display. News items and cuttings. Suggestions for ideal holidays, and postcards when you come back. Who's neat and good at art to take charge of this? Joan. Yes, that's a good choice.

Anyone want to suggest someone else? No. Then Joan we expect to see some results as soon as possible. There's the bell now girls. Get out of the formroom as soon as possible and along to the hall or the library. Which dinner are you? One. Then it might have stopped raining before you come out. Oh by the way, I need two volunteers; wait Rosemary you don't know what it is yet, two people to tidy the Blue Games Cupboard. Thankyou. I'll be along to see how you're getting on before the bell goes. You know where all the things should be. It's just a matter of putting them back in their places, checking the list and letting me know if there's anything missing. That'll be a great help. I expect Miss Samuels will also be along to see how you're doing so don't let her find you playing football in the corridor will you? And no singsongs either please girls.'

Thank God I'm not on dinner duty today with them all in their formrooms. Let's hope it's stopped before this afternoon. Don't fancy trotting to the baths in this, and then there's the fifth and sixth for hockey last thing. Still it turned on very conveniently maybe it'll turn off again.

Millie's first in as usual; got the table laid and her elbow going before anyone else gets through the door. Goes round lifting all the covers to see which plate's got the most on. Maybe I'll be like that when I get to her age. Must be due to retire next year and this is her only meal of the day apart from a cup of tea while she feeds the pussies.

'Hallo Mary. Recovered yet?'

'Still a bit weak about the knees. What did she want you for?'

'Oh something about the timetable for next term.'

'Not long now.'

'Reckon we could all do with a break.'

'Personally I never find the term long enough.'

'No Mrs. Masters but then you've got a long syllabus to get through.' Avoid that table; the old girl'll sit there. That one'll do. Only our loving couple talking about art and making eyes at each other. Romeo and Juliet the kids call them, the sixth anyway. Wonder how far they go. Rather sweet once you get over the slightly grotesque aspect of it, neither of them being oil paintings. What was that story about Miss Evans going to the English stockroom one day and catching them with their arms round each other and little Cornall sobbing on the Witch's bony chest? Funny how no one ever suspects me. Because I'm still young enough to get away with it I suppose unless Knowing about Peter makes a difference.

'Is anyone sitting here Miss Witchard?'

'No. I'll just move my bag.'

'Thanks.'

'I don't see any sign of March going out like a lamb this year do you Miss Stevens?'

'I don't indeed. In fact looking out of these windows the view is distinctly Turneresque.' Watch her twitter with pleasure now and the Witch get all angular with jealousy. Don't worry mate, I don't want her. All I'm waiting for is little Mam'selle to come tripping through the door.

'You are a dark horse Miss Stevens. I didn't know you liked Turner.'

'Ah, we're not completely without culture in the games department. I believe Mary has rather a nice line in traditional etchings the favoured are invited to view.'

'You should know by now Frances that Miss Stevens is never serious.'

I suppose they put it down to a broken heart or else think I'm hard boiled like Mary, and pity poor Peter and think what a rotten time I must have given him. True up to a point I suppose. Wonder how he's getting on. Must be making quite a pile by now. Weeks pass and I never think of him. It's as if those two years had never existed. Then suddenly I remember all the misery of it for us both.

'You are looking sad. Is it perhaps the English weather?'

'Hallo. So busy thinking dismal thoughts I missed your entrance. That place is empty, sit there.'

'I must go anyway, you can have this one.'

'But you've hardly finished. Aren't you going to stay for coffee Caroline?'

'Have to go and open the library I'm afraid.'

'Isn't Miss Bates doing that?'

'Away. I'll just get them going.'

'I'll bring your coffee up to you.'

'Needn't trouble.'

'There's something I want to get out of the library for this afternoon myself so I'd have to come. I'll be along in a few minutes.'

'Miss Bates away again then?'

'Yes. It's too bad you know. She's just a passenger. Caroline's working far too hard. She's always taking extra classes and she has to take two 'O' level forms as well as the Upper Sixth. She just daren't risk giving her any of them and then her being away for weeks. It isn't fair on the children. They don't stand a chance if they're not taught consistently.'

'What is it this time?'

'Some form of nervous rash I believe. It would serve her right if Caroline cracked up and she had the double work for a change.'

'It's a good job Mrs. Parry seems pretty tough.'

'But she can't take the senior work. She hasn't got the experience. I'll just pour out the coffee and take one up to her. Would you like yours now Miss Stevens?'

'Yes please if you're doing it. And don't you think, Miss Cornall, that it's time you called me Steve like everyone else?'

'Oh. Oh yes, if you think so. Would you like some coffee too Mam'selle?'

'Thank you. That is very kind.'

'The dinner seems particularly repulsive today.'

'You think so?'

'Don't you?'

'I am hungry so I do not notice.'

'There's an admission for a French woman.'

'Should I also call you Steve?'

'Of course. Miss Stevens is too formal.'

'My name is Janine.'

'Janine. How-do-you-do Janine?'

'I am very well thank you.'

'Two cups of coffee. Someone's going to be unlucky; we haven't much left. I'll just pop up to the library with this while it's hot.'

'Little Trotty Wagtail.'

'Pardon?'

'She's like a little bird, that bobs its head up and down as it walks.'

'Oh yes.'

The Samuels must have come in. That's Mrs. Masters chattering frenetically about the Lullingstone villa where they went this weekend I suppose and Miss Evans lamenting the decline and fall of the empire as seen in 4b's inability to decline in the singular. God here comes old Knight, making straight for me. Don't tell me she's going to sit here. Must get away.

'I wanted to speak to you Miss Stevens.'

Caught. 'Yes Miss Knight. I can't be long I'm afraid. I've got some girls turning out the cupboards for me.'

'I'm very worried about your form.'

'Oh?'

'They're supposed to be an 'A' form but they're certainly not making the progress they should. I've been wanting to speak to you about it for some time but you so rarely come into the staff-room at lunchtime.'

'Yes I'm usually caught up with umpiring a match or something. What seems to be wrong?'

'It's their attitude. They don't approach their work in the right spirit.'

'This modern age. Who does?'

'I didn't have this trouble last year when I had the present 4a.'

'But then these have always been rather a problem form even in the second year. They're rather precocious.'

'Rosemary Ellis is positively rude at times.'

'Poor Rosemary, she's rather confused at the moment, going through the stage of questioning all the conventions but she'll grow out of it if she isn't made to feel a martyr for the cause.'

'She's already made up her mind that maths are a waste of her time and she seems to have no respect for authority at all. Her homework is hardly worth my looking at. Really I'm not sure she should be in the 'A' form. When Miss Samuels asks me I don't think I shall honestly be able to recommend her.'

'I don't really see what we can do about it at the moment. If we emphasise it too much in a repressive way we could make her a really hard case which she isn't at the moment.'

'I think children are considered far too much these days, far too much psychological nonsense which is just an excuse for ignoring old fashioned disobedience. I shall be forced to give her extra lessons if she doesn't improve and I shall certainly suggest her going down into a lower group next year.'

'I'm sorry but I must go now or goodness knows where I may find all the stock. I'll see what can be done about Rosemary but I do feel we should be rather careful how we deal with her.'

'Can I help you at all?'

'Thank you Mam'selle that's most kind. If you've finished your coffee.'

'Oh yes.'

And God is love is he? I can see her cycling to the shops on Saturday morning in Beckenham or wherever in the bungaloid growth she lives with it blazoned across her bicycle basket, thinking up ways of getting rid of Rosemary before she takes over the form next year, trying to knock all the independence and originality out of her because it's a reflection on her own pettiness, narrow-mindedness. Yes, look what she did to 4a. Give me 4b any day. At least they're honest and straightforward. She made them sly and mealy-mouthed. 'Yes Miss, no Miss. Do it behind your back Miss.' That's how she'd like Rosemary to be. She's not going to push her out; can't anyway because she's too good at other subjects. Don't think the Samuels would let her either because she wouldn't want to tangle with Mrs. Ellis. Doesn't like getting on the wrong side of the parents. But she might make life a misery for her and she's determined to get the form next term to correct the error of my ways. Why get so het up about it Stevens? Maybe you're more involved than you like to think. Watch it don't let her make you feel guilty just because Rosemary's got a crush on you and you think you might be favouring her. You know you'd feel the same way whichever of the kids it was. Is it because I'm an outsider that I always take the kid's side, side of the underdog? Or is it because I'm immature as they say and can't grow up and accept the authority of convention? See how they confuse you because you know what you are. Guilty, immature, a chip on your shoulder: all the symptoms of the outcast.

'You are very silent. You are angry?'

'I suppose I am.'

'You don't agree with Miss Knight?'

'No, we don't agree. But then there aren't many of the staff I do agree with. That's why I don't go into the staffroom much at lunchtime. I usually go out to a little café with a juke box and lots of bus conductors and schoolboys. You must come and visit me. The eggs and chips is very good.'

'Rosemary is very bright.'

'I forgot you have them for conversation.'

'She asks me difficult questions and about life in France so that the lesson pass quickly. She is very popular with the other girls.'

'That's naughty of her.'

'Yes. But I did the same when I was at school. Only not so much because our professeurs were very fierce. But I would like to.'

'I like the idea of you as a naughty little girl at aschool.'

'Why is that?'

'Perhaps because you look so demure.'

'Like Rosemary. But if you wish to be naughty it is not good to look like it.'

'Oh Mam'selle!'

'Don't you think you should call me Janine?'

'But not in front of the children. Hallo you two. How are you getting on?'

'We've found the missing netball Miss Stevens.'

'Good. I hoped you might. What's left to do?'

'Now we've got to put all the things back in their right place according to the stockbook.'

'Right Sylvia will you put them away while Mam'selle calls them out? Rosemary I want a word with you.'

'Yes Miss Stevens?'

'Yes. I've just been hearing a long complaint from Miss Knight about you. Now don't pull that face. I'm properly in the doghouse.'

'But why you Miss Stevens?'

'Because Miss Knight thinks I encourage you, that I'm not firm enough with you. Now I could hardly tell her that I don't seem to find you particularly difficult. That wouldn't have been a very tactful thing to say. However she is threatening that if you don't pull your socks up she'll suggest to Miss Samuels that you don't go up into 4a next year with the rest because you obviously can't keep up.'

'But she can't Miss Stevens.'

'Oh yes she can. And although I think some of the staff for whom you do do good work would have something to say on your behalf it would all be very unpleasant and unnecessary and might mean Miss Samuels having a little chat to your mother. So, I have decided, that the best thing we can do is for you to show me your maths homework every time before you give it in and for you to try a little harder at it. I don't suppose you'll ever be a mathematical genius but it's a pity to spoil an otherwise excellent record with just one subject. Oh and there's just one other thing. Try to realise that perhaps not everyone has the same kind of sense of humour as you and I, and that not everyone thinks the same way. There are times when one has to say nothing but think the more as they say. It isn't very pleasant for me to have to go into the staffroom and hear that you've been rude to Miss So-and-so. I realise you don't mean it as rudeness but other people don't. If you've got something subversive or revolutionary you feel you must say or you'll burst come and say it to me. I shall probably agree with you anyway. Alright?'

'Yes Miss Stevens. I will try. Honest.'

'Good girl. Now let's see if Sylvia and Mam'selle have finished.'

'There. All is tidy.'

'Splendid. All I need now is someone to tidy me up. I can see I shall have to take on one or all of you to keep me in order. Thank you very much girls. The bell will be going soon. This is the afternoon I have to go to the baths so be kind to your form prefect won't you? No complaints when I get back.'

'No Miss Stevens.'

'Do the children also call you Steve?'

'Oh yes but only when they think I can't hear them.'

'Tomorrow we will go for the egg and chips?'

'If you'd like to.'

'Oh yes.'

'I must dash now or there'll be hell's bells outside the baths. See you tomorrow then. Don't work too hard.'

And does she turn away wondering, a little sad as I am or does she know already and feels the old unmistakable stumbling of the heart? Can't tell. Play it cool. Clutch too desperately and the hand closes on emptiness. The French, the French are different or are they?

Thank God the rain's stopped and this wind drying the pavements, shrug off the school with the door swinging to behind. If this keeps up the fifth and sixth can have their hockey. Wonder why the old girl didn't come along to watch? Knew I knew she'd be along so didn't need to come. Like sending your spirit forth to watch someone instead while you lie comfortably asleep in bed. And his spirit went forth over the waters

Funny to be out in the streets among ordinary people, women mostly, office girls hunting for a bite, weary mums foraging for their families, and 4c kicking up a dust outside the baths.

'Alright girls in you go. I'll mark the register inside. Anyone not swimming today? Right up to the balcony then you two and no noise. And I don't want a great din in the cubicles. We haven't got any non-swimmers now have we? Yes, even Muriel's finally got her foot off the bottom. I'll see anyone who wants to go in for her certificate today. It would be rather good if you turned out to be the only form with everyone with at least the beginner's wouldn't it?'

'Is that true Miss? Would we be the only one?'

'Yes. All the others have got several who haven't started yet.'

'Even 4a Miss?'

'Oh 4a are a long way behind. Anyway I thought you two were supposed to be up in the balcony?'

'Oh let us stay down here and talk to you Miss. Go on.'

'Alright then. You can help me with the certificates.'

And this is what the tadpoles become. The outcasts. Even physically they're not as attractive as the brighter ones. Too thick or too thin; lumpen housefraus or flat-chested and neurotic. No good at anything except games and the domestic things, sewing and cookery.

'When are you going to invite me to dinner again?'

'Did you like that Miss?'

'Best dinner I've had for months.'

'Do you like us Miss?'

'Of course I like you.'

'Yeah, you like us but nobody else does.'

'Miss Samuels doesn't like us.'

'Neither does Miss Evans.'

'Mrs. Parry likes you I'm sure.'

'Yeah but she's married.'

'Well I'm not married.'

'No but you're different; more modern. The others they're old fashioned. They don't like us because we're young and we go out with boys.'

'I hate school. I'm leaving Christmas.'

'Most of our class are.'

'Aren't you going to take your G.C.E.?'

'We wouldn't pass nothing anyway, most of us. What's the use?'

'Why do you like us Miss?'

'Why shouldn't I? You always work hard for me. And you're very reliable and willing to do jobs. I don't see any reason why I shouldn't like you.'

'We're the failures, the chuck-outs.'

'You mustn't think that.'

'We're no good at Latin or Maths or anything.'

'I know what you're good at Cynthia.'

'You shut up or I'll clout you one.'

'Do you three want to do your width? Cynthia, go round the other side and see that they all touch properly.'

Unloved and rejected, behind the bushes with the first boy who'll make them feel wanted, placed in their society; unable to accept what we can offer like putting pork before Mohammedans, pearls before swine except that in some way we're the swine to suggest that our way of life is the real carat and they're only poor donkeys. And that's the mistake of our education all the time that we're telling them that we're better than they are not just because we're older and have seen more, they'd accept that but because we're saying we represent an entirely different way of looking at things, that not only they but their parents were wrong too, that they were born wrong. We want them to take on our whole ethos and discard their own but we don't show them any real reason for doing it. The people who matter to them, the images of prosperity and success they see on the screen and looking out of the pages of the tabloids never read a book or go to a concert or to an art gallery. How can we expect them to be any better or to want to know any more? No wonder they laugh at us because we represent values that no one else believes in, that went out with the fairies. Like dad used to say about poor old Jeremiah trying to convince people they were living in a fool's paradise when they'd never had it so good thank you, in spite of the famine.

'You used to wear an engagement ring when you first come here didn't you Miss?'

'That's right.'

'Why don't you wear it no more?'

'You shouldn't ask things like that Con. Maybe Miss don't want to tell no one.'

'It's not that exactly. It's always a bit difficult to explain these things that's all.'

'Did you go off him Miss? Didn't you like him no more?'

'Yes I suppose that was it really. I just didn't like him in that way.'

'Yeah. I know a lot of boys like that. They're alright to go out with in a crowd but you wouldn't want to marry them or nothing. More like brothers; specially when they're the same age as you. I like boys about twenty-three. They know what they want then. They're more serious like.'

'Cor I know what they want.'

'Cynthia, you're supposed to be over the other side, seeing whether people touch properly.'

'She thought she was missing something Miss, that's why she come round here.'

'Well you'd better get back quickly; there's another lot ready to try.'

We tried, both of us. My last attempt to do the right thing for the wrong reason; to please them. Mother saying, 'Marvellous darling. I'm so happy for you.' And dad thinking of me finally reconciled at the altar. I will go unto: my feet shall stand. Poor Peter. He became more and more bitchy and hysterical as I became more dominant and aggressive. Until that awful morning the telegram came from his mother. 'They found him in his room dear. He'd tried to kill himself. I told him not to work so hard.' And I knew at once that wasn't the reason; that we were the reason together. 'We can't go on with it Stevie. Lying here I've thought it all out. We're just not right for each other.' 'I know Peter. I know. I've been thinking too.' God how young we were; just a couple of kids pressed into the mould by society before our bones had hardened into their individual shapes. 'What are we going to do? They'll be terribly upset.' 'It's our life. I'll think of something.' It was always like that even though he was older than me. 'I'll write and tell you I've decided to go to college after all and that since it's a long time to wait you're perfectly free. They'll say it's all my fault and that I've always been hard but that doesn't matter. I don't care what they say, never have really. Now you go on and take a good degree and don't worry anymore.' Like a child, lying back with his face as white as the pillows and those long lashes, wasted on a boy, darkened with tears. 'You'll write to me sometimes?' 'Yes, of course. Now go to sleep.' Funny though, I missed his mother most.

'Good, that's five more certificates this afternoon. Make sure you've got clean blouses for Friday and you can go up onto the platform in assembly and receive them. Get dressed now girls or you'll be late for your next lesson.'

'Can we have a commended Miss?'

'Go on Miss. No one ever gives us a commended.'

'If you can be dressed and lined up with hardly a sound in five minutes, yes.'

'See you shut your row Cynthy, we want a commended!'

'I 'ent the one makes all the row.'

'If you both carry on for five minutes like that you certainly won't get one. Find yourselves separate cubicles and get on with it.'

Mary'll be along with her lot in a minute. Just about get these cleared in time. Four per cent. Wonder who it'll be out of this lot. They've all got their mates; hunt in pairs mostly; split up at the end of the evening. But they're together all day and God help anyone who tries to come between them. Jealousy, possessiveness. She's my friend not yourn. Doesn't seem to be any physical side to it though, not like boys. Still there's no need since they've all got boy friends as well. Get all the sex they want there and no urge to masturbate either. Might even be Cynthia. She's the most aggressive. More likely someone who doesn't seem to have a boy friend. Cynthy's just a typical working-class brassy mum of the old style. Look at her now with her hair wringing wet still and her skirt held together with safety pins, ladders all up those massive legs. Just the figure for a Willendorf Venus. Must ask Mrs. Masters if she's noticed.

'Well that was quick and quiet. Your can have your commended.

Don't forget to go in quietly past Miss Samuels' door will you or you might lose it as soon as you've got it. Off you go then. Here's the next relay ready to take your places.'

''Ent they sweet Miss. Wish we was still like that.'

'Oh you're not so bad as you are. See you on Wednesday. Be good.'

'I'd rather be clever Miss.'

'Get changed 1b. But no one in the water until Miss Baker says you may.'

Fourteen-year-olds lamenting their lost innocence. Already they feel they've left us behind and when that happens you can't hold them. What have we got to offer them anyway? Sometimes they come back to see you and say they wish they'd stayed on but it's only another verse of the elegy for the golden age that never was when I was a girl. Yet in a curious way they're more innocent than the fifths and sixth. Maybe they're just better integrated. Less conflict between heaven and hell, id and super-ego as the textbooks have it now, forbidden needs. 'It's illegal, it's immoral or it makes you fat.' Their moral code is so much simpler. No real taboo except against hurting other people more than you can help and the law doesn't come into it unless you get caught. That's why they fit into our way of life so much better too, take it in their stride so much more like Jonnie. No feelings of guilt and self torment like our intellectuals, should I, shouldn't I. Only themselves to adjust to not the rest of society as well.

Last game of the season this; last game most of them'll ever play. Exams. start next week, then Easter and when we come back it'll be tennis and rounders. Can't say I'm sorry. Never a game I really took to hockey and this trail up to the heath doesn't help. Wonder how big the audience'll be this time. All the layabouts and dirty old men from miles around. Definitely the last appearance of the Stevens Girls. Fortunately it'd be a brave man who'd interfere with one of our Amazons armed with a hockey stick and a ball as hard as a blackjack. Not that I'd have thought they looked very fetching in those bloody great pads but maybe they're always waiting for them to bend over to pick up the ball.

This is when the real temptations start of course if you're honest with yourself. Not that it'd last or that anything would come of it

65

but they're as old as a lot of the people you'd consider eligible if you met them outside and the situation encourages it, thrown together all day. Not bad looking too some of them and easy to begin picking out the four per cent.

There's Frances Dawson, unmistakeable butch type. Knows what she wants too. Been after Betty Hawkes since her fourth year. Picked the wrong one there though. Betty's only interested in herself. See why she tries though. Really beautiful, another Venus but this one is Ceres or Persephone: corn goddess, Scandinavian beauty, blond hair and china blue eyes. Spends all her time in the staff cloakroom admiring herself in the mirror. Can't tell me she doesn't know what it's all about after three years at art school. Enjoys being admired by someone who can only worship and never soil. That's why she doesn't like going out with men. Afraid the holy shrine will be profaned by rude hands, might put her in the family way and ruin that perfect figure.

Jealous? In a way I suppose I am but I know it wouldn't work. I'd want to muss up that carefully flowing hair, spoil that mouth with kissing. Still maybe it'd be worth it just to lie and look at it. Frances follows her everywhere. You can always find them deep in intense conversation in the corridor. Wonder what little Trotty Cornall thinks of it.

Hilary Ash too, playing in goal, is another one, feminine though. Crazy about Mrs. Parry still although she's nineteen nearly. Often wonder about Mrs. Parry too. Married of course but that doesn't necessarily mean anything. Definitely a masculine type and doesn't do all that much to discourage Hilary. She might make a proper transference to boys of course but she's certainly a very late developer, intelligent too.

A lot of us seem to start like that with what'd be called a crush at thirteen or fourteen still with us when we leave school and no longer calf love. A hitch in the mechanism maybe, a switch that doesn't throw at the right moment but the blueprint was there as a condition of birth and we've only gone on building along the lines laid down for us and when the thing's finished and they find it doesn't work as it should there's no taking the thing apart and starting again if there's a bit that's missing even the headshrinkers have to admit that.

Poor Peter. I was so grateful to him for giving me an exit I even felt guilty about it. Everyone was horrified. 'How can you break the engagement just when he needs you most? I don't understand girls today.' I was right though so right and it was our life. And then mother's disgust when I said I wanted to do something active not sit around for three years with my nose in a book. But I didn't know how it would be.

Tommy could have told me I suppose if I'd been able to ask him. He must have been used to it all at boarding school. Didn't take me long to realise there was something a bit odd somewhere though I hardly even knew the word queer then. Funny when you think back.

Thank God this lot can get on without me. Definitely not with it today. Something's put me right off my stroke. Surely not the little French piece. Janine. Pretty name. Dresses well. Nice legs.

That was when I first started noticing legs, and bodies, female bodies. In the changing rooms and the showers. Fascinated, trying not to stare. Going into people's rooms at night when they were reading in bed and feeling I didn't know what. And the suggestions with a knowing smile until I seemed to be the only one who didn't know. And then when the penny dropped. 'Here come our newly weds. How's the honeymoon going?' Havelock Ellis out of the college library and then anything else I could lay my hands on. And I wanted to discuss it with someone but didn't know how to begin. And then suddenly it was too late for talking. 'I was beginning to think you'd never wake up.'

Face it, face it now after all this time, she used you. It never meant as much to her as it did to you. Just an interlude before marriage because she had to have some release and she didn't want to spoil her chances by slipping up. She never really loved you at all.

Still sore, still the ache. She never really loved me. Can we really love? Or is that the baby we threw out with the bath water? Dare I chance it again? But I was in love with her.

Not again, no, never like that. Only once like that ever. Older now. The smile awry, the slick answer. That's why nothing happens at the club. I know every story too well. Who's been with whom and how often. Have to make a fresh start without the weight of other lives, other loves to drag us down or it hasn't a chance that delicate seedling. Needs light and air and warmth, not hothouse forcing on a diet of alcohol and salt water.

Tired now. Thoughts drag. Not much of an audience today. Weather kept them away. Didn't think we'd be here. Only another quarter of an hour and I can blow the whistle. Have to go back to see the form out. How to evade Rosemary that's the problem. Not in the mood for soulful looks and having to be bright, keeping the child off.

Woman over there with a little girl in a blue mack and wellingtons. Wonder what she'll grow up to be. Easter, what shall I do with it this year? Not home to mother, not this time. Funny how she's got more religious as she's got older, since dad died, and yet while he was alive it was more a social thing than spiritual. Tommy's turn. He doesn't mind going to church. Rather fancies the curate if it's still the one with red hair. I'll tell him that. Give him an incentive.

Chilly standing here. The kids are better running about. Kids! Seem to throw them bigger every year. Must be all the milk and better food as well as the games. Bonny is the word for this lot. Still they'll lose a lot of that when they start trying to live on a grant or a bun for dinner in their hour off from the office.

Have to take the timetable home with me tonight. Thank God there aren't any reports this term except for the fifths and sixth. Must remember to get Janet's before they disappear into the Witch's clutches. She always keeps them for weeks; writes great screeds on everyone. They're a conscientious lot the older ones. Still believe in what they're doing even though it's more of a struggle every year; against the tide. Can't understand either why the kids are so different, old before their time with a false sophistication, why they don't have the same values anymore. Blank faces looking back at you. 'Why not Miss?' Feel the children are laughing at them, mocking. That's when they crack up, in their fifties. Struggling against the waters, building walls and ramparts of sand, flushed away by the chuckle of little waves. The house that is founded upon a rock only maybe there aren't any left. Hope Trotty Cornall looks after her. All need someone to look after us. Time to blow up.

'That's it then. Your last game of hockey, some of you anyway. Have you heard from Holmwood yet Janet?'

'I've got an interview in a fortnight's time.'

'That's good. She's a bit of an eccentric Miss Bowers. Brush up on your uses of physical education. *Mens sana in corpore sano* and all that jazz and look straight at her when you answer and you'll probably be alright. Oh and she's very keen on bare feet. That's where I get it from, and free expression too. The natural approach.'

'Why didn't we have more of that then Miss Stevens?'

'Because I inherited someone else's syllabus and these things aren't easy to alter in a hurry as you'll find. Well another couple of weeks and the mock'll be over and you'll all know the worst. Anyone feel like jumping off a bridge? Good. It wastes such a lot of time. Is anyone going back to school? Would you take the pads and sticks between you then? Thanks. Go straight home and don't talk to any strange men on the way will you? Must rush. Have to see my form out. Did they behave themselves at register this afternoon Hilary? Thank goodness for that. It makes a change. Goodnight girls.'

Tired. Tired of my tongue rolling off the platitudes; attitudes of omniscience and omnipotence; the false front all the time. Roll on the end of term. Get away. Paris where nobody cares what you do or how you dress and the streets are full of individuals. Wonder if Janine is going home for Easter. Take me with you. Flee with me to the casbah. Oh yes.

'Everyone suitably dressed? Goodnight then girls. See you in the morning. Off you go Rosemary.'

'Goodnight Miss Stevens.'

How can I avoid her? Go out of the main gate and up to the bus stop instead of walking to the station. Lord dismiss us. The day though gavest. Evenings are drawing out. Going home in the light. Clocks'll be put on soon. Long light evenings with time to do something after school instead of just creeping home to our burrows to sit in front of the gas fire rocking our loneliness. Maybe Janine plays tennis. The ball singing back and forth over the net. There used to be summers. I remember that first summer at college. No, not that. Don't think about it. Away, push it away. Back and forth, singing. 'Come in darlings, it's time for bed.' Lighten our darkness we beseech thee. O lord nearly forgot the timetable. Have to go back to the staffroom.

There was a thing to walk slap into. Just the two of them and looking as if the Witch had been crying too. A bag stuffed with books to take home and pencil through. Cracking up. Won't make it if she isn't careful. Weather doesn't help. This wind wears your last shreds of energy away. Naked came we into this world. Her face had that pinched tightness; every line drawn fine. Poor dad. God what do we do when we're old?

There's the café. 'Egg and chips please. For you too?' 'Oh yes.' Oh yes, yes please. I've been apart too long. Tomorrow. And then maybe summer again and a white ball singing, swinging back and forth in the long light evenings. Love twenty. Game and match. Come in darling, it's time for bed.

Poor Rosemary. Wonder how long she'll wait. Grow out of it I expect. Somebody else next year or the gawky boy next door. Mustn't let the Knight get away with it, trying to put her down. Mustn't let her be twisted and cramped to fit the mould. Watch it. Getting over anxious. End up like the old brigade; dedicated, dessi-cated. And what if it doesn't come to anything? Does it matter? I'm still alive. God make me chaste but not yet. Better than this half life you've been living. Better than hiding from a memory; too smart to be caught. Faint-heart and the fayre ladye. 'Egg and chips for two please.' Oh yes. 'Both together please. I'll pay.' Whatever the price. Put it down on my account.

Just make the five past if this bus gets a move on, in with the first of the city gents and the last of the school kids, couple of building workers in clayey overalls. All the world going home to tea, seeing a spinster, a school marm with chalk in her hair and if they only knew.

Being now in as great distress as ever our adventurer was once more forced to cast about for somewhat to relieve stark necessity and therefore set forth to visit a certain lady known to her from her childhood, and finding her seated in the parlour with her husband was easily prevailed upon to take some slight refreshment and to entertain them with a recital of her present circumstances, and though it was not in their power to serve her other than with their good wishes and advice yet they did their utmost to convince her how much they had it in their hearts to do what they could.

Sure husband, cries the wife. Here is a poor young gentleman bred to better things and brought down to the sad condition of want you now behold and that through no fault of his own but only through the hardness of a parent's heart and the cruel knocks of fate. Then turning to the poor actor asked what means she proposed for a subsistence giving her to understand that the good man was quite ignorant of her true identity.

Madam, our adventurer answered, I have for so long been innured to the hardships of the mind that I should think those of the body rather a kind relief if they would afford but daily bread for my poor child and self, and truly there is nothing which does not exceed the bounds of honesty that I should think unworthy of my undertaking.

With that the good woman turning once more to her husband began a long apology with many knowing winks and nods as one who would suggest something to a deaf mute by signs rather than words, the purport of which she was at a loss to piece together for some time but arriving at the drift of her hostess' discourse as it were by the back door she repeated her assurances that nothing was too humble for one who stood in need of a crust.

Then said the good woman, since you care not what you do so long as it be honest, which is a sentiment all right minded people must commend in you, I propose that you, my dear husband should bespeak the waiter's place but now vacant at Mrs. Dorr's for our young friend and carry him thither in the morning to wait upon her.

Accordingly it was arranged and the following day they set forth together for the King's Head at Mary-la-Bonne. The gentlewoman was exceedingly pleased at the appearance and manner of the would-be waiter but upon perceiving him to wear a melancholy aspect and understanding that he was well born and bred she began to be fearful that the place might prove too hard for him. For, said she, I am afraid that you will lay to heart the impertinence you must frequently be liable to from the lower class of people who, when in their cups, pay no regard either to humanity or good manners. Such a young gentleman as you seem to be would of a

71

surety do better to seek some less robust employment. I would not for all the world be the means to render you more desperate than your present unhappy condition must make you although in advising you thus I rob myself of an honest servant.

Seeing his new-found position lost or ever it was gained Charles, for so he had been introduced to Mrs. Dorr, begged her not to be under the least apprehension of his receiving any shock on that account. Notwithstanding, cried he, that I was not born to servitude, since misfortune has reduced me to it, I think it a degree of happiness that a mistaken pride hath not foolishly endowed me with a contempt for getting an honest livelihood. I would rather a thousand times prudently endeavour to forget what I have been and submit to the severities of fortune which at this time it is not in my power to amend than perish by haughty penury.

This noble speech so affected the good woman that she manifested her concern by a hearty shower of tears, declaring that the place was his if he would have it and it was agreed that he should begin the next day. In the morning therefore Charles presented himself early and to Mrs. Dorr's surprise soon proved himself a handy creature, and being light and nimble, tripped up and down stairs with that alacrity of spirit and agility of body that is natural to those gentlemen of the tap-tub though as Hob says the house also sold all sorts of wine and punch.

When it came time for them to dine Mrs. Dorr signified that Charles should sit at table with her rather than eating apart or with the other domesticks although this was not her usual custom with her waiters as she hastened to assure him. But, cried she, your manners and behaviour seem to entitle you to that respect and 'tis only with the utmost pain that I oblige myself to call you anything but, Sir.

You are pleased to compliment me, Madam, answered our adventurer, playing her new role as the Man Charles with as much assiduity as ever she had applied herself to the part of Young Bevil or Captain Plume.

It grieves me, the gentlewoman continued, to see one so young and alone in the world.

Nay Madam, not quite alone, Charles answered seeing here an opportunity of forwarding a design she had of not lying at the

House at night but of returning to her poor child whom she was forced to leave alone all day in order to gain a livelihood for them both. I have one blessing; a little girl who is more to me than whole sackfulls of friends were they as rich as Croesus and able to restore me to my former happy state.

What, cries Mrs. Dorr, So young and married. And how old might the child be? I am amazed to hear a young fellow speak so feelingly of a child when the generality of men are but too willing to forget them having begot them, aye and their mothers too if they can. Yet you speak only of the girl. Has she then no mother, though I am sure there are many women would be happy to oblige such a pretty young fellow and take no thought for the consequences, or perhaps your wife is no longer living?

No, he answered, fetching a deep sigh. She died in childbed of that girl ten years ago.

The poor thing! Positively you shall bring her to see me to-morrow. And you too with all the cares of a father and none of the comforts of a husband. How many a young fellow would have abandoned the helpless creature to the harsh nurture of the parish. I understand now that melancholy I first noted in you. It springs from a nature too sensible of the suffering it has endured and one which is resolved to continue in suffering rather than free itself at the expense of an innocent fellow victim.

There is, continued Charles, one way in which you could be of the greatest assistance to me and my poor child.

Do but name it, she cried, And if it be within my small power it shall be done.

It is to permit me to return home each evening so that I may be with her through the hours of darkness when children are most fearful. I will return in the morning in good time. Believe me Madam I should be of small use to you and your affairs with a mind burdened with care for my child left alone.

Do not think of it anymore, the gentlewoman said, I myself would not sleep easy in my bed with such a thought.

Delighted with this good fortune Charles was careful to set all in order before quitting the house and at last closed the door behind him at eleven at night and set out to trudge home. His march extended as far as Long-Acre by which means he was obliged to

73

pass through the thickest patroles of the Gentlemen of the Pad who are numerous and frequent in them fields but by dint of jogging along like a raw, unthinking, pennyless prentice he rendered himself not worthy their attention and so escaped without wounds or blows and came safe home, tired yet content with his new employment.

The next day the child was duly presented to Mrs. Dorr, after being well versed in her part in which she proved as convincing as her mother had been in hers and the remainder of the week passed easily enough until at length Sunday came and our adventurer began to quake in her shoes for fear of a discovery, well knowing the House to be one of great resort and her own face equally well known. However to her violent astonishment, and although she waited upon twenty different companions, there was not one soul among them all that knew her. This was not so greatly surprising since the House was frequented by many foreigners much to the confusion of Mrs. Dorr who was quite unable to converse with them except by signs; which our adventurer observing, prevented her future trouble by signifying in the French tongue that she perfectly well understood it. This was a universal joy round the table which was encompassed by German peruke makers and French taylors not one of whom could utter one single syllable of English.

As soon as Mrs. Dorr heard him speak French away she run with her plate in her hand and laughing left the room to go down and eat an English dinner, having been obliged to dine pantomimically once a week, and when Charles was come down with the dishes she presented him with half-a-crown and sent up thankful prayers to Heaven for her deliverance from her foreign companions.

In the week days when business though good was not quite so brisk Charles employed his leisure hours in working in the garden the further delight and amazement of his mistress, and it was while he was thus busied one day in setting some Windsor beans that the maid came to him and told him that she had a very great secret to unfold but that he must never tell that she had discovered it. Having no great opinion of her understanding or her honesty he was not at first over anxious to hear this mighty secret but on her insistence that 'twas something he might turn to his advantage if he would make a proper use of it he grew a little curious and began to be more attentive to her discourse, which ended in assuring him that he might marry Mrs. Dorr's kinswoman if he would pay his address and that she would like him extreamly for a master.

Here was now a pretty pass and Charles reflected that he had been better to have followed his first instinct and left this mighty secret well alone for had he been really a man the intention of making love to the young woman would never have entered his imagination since she had no one qualification to recommend her to the regard of any thing beyond a porter or a hackney-coachman. However recollecting his state as a widower and father of a young daughter he answered, Though sensible of the honour and advantage that such a match would bring me, nevertheless I have resolved never to enter into matrimony again for the sake of my poor child whom I would not put in the power of a Mother-in-law to use ill and also out of regard for the memory of her dear mother whose loss I still feel as deeply as it had been yesterday.

The maid tried once more to turn him from his resolution, saying he was a fool, and that the greatest in the world if he did not follow her advice but when she saw that he was not to be moved she left him to his own thoughts, and bitter enough they were too, and conveyed his answer to her mistress' kinswoman. Within a few days he was summoned into the lady's presence and to his great surprise attacked with insolently presuming to say that she was in love with him.

Believe me Madam, Charles answered, I never had the least conception that you was in love with me nor have I at any time spoken of such a thing.

No truly; I believe, said she, I should hardly be 'namoured with one of my own sect. At this he burst into a laugh and took the liberty to ask her if she understood what she said which threw the offended fair into an absolute rage. Perceiving that it was all but a forgery of the maid's to them both for her own profit he waited until her anger had a little abated and then recounted how she had come to him in the garden with her mighty secret and in the end brought her to disgrace in vindication of his own innocence.

Yet a strangeness ensued and our adventurer began to grow sick of her place, though Mrs. Dorr still remained incredulous in regard to her Man Charles being a female, and began to cast about for acting jobs, when luckily one presented itself and she left the good woman's service. Yet such is the inconstant nature of the profession of poor player that the small revenue she gained was but enough to keep them in bread and cheese and not enough to protect her from jail or satisfy her creditors' demands. As a help in concealment for the bailiffs were hot upon her tail she took upon her the name of Brown and her friend that of Mrs. Brown, and by coming and going always under cover of darkness our adventurer was able to evade their clutches for several months. The amount of all she owed in the world did not arise to five and twenty pounds but they were as much perplexed for that sum as if it had been as many thousands.

At last however she grew tired of leading such a life of fear and resolved to make trial of the friendship of her mother's brother and sat down to write him a melancholy epistle; earnestly imploring his assistance for the sake of his dead sister to give her as much money as would be necessary to set herself up in a public house. 'I will not put it upon the foot of borrowing as 'tis ten millions to one whether you will ever be paid; and in case of a failure of that nature, I know, I should of course be subject to your displeasure; and therefore ask that you should make me a gift of it if you think my circumstances are worthy your consideration.'

Great was their joy the following day when the uncle returned answer desiring her to take a house at once in earnest of her good intention. Now my dears, she cried addressing her friend and daughter, Here, and she held out the paper, here is evidence indeed that men are not all unfeeling monsters, unmoved by the call of those nearest them in blood, so that we may say with the poet:

How shines a good deed in a naughty world. Let us go forth and settle upon the first house we come upon that I may gallop post-haste to my uncle before his warm heart is cooled by the bitter wind of my family's displeasure and he is driven to repent his kind offer.

Heedless of any warning of haste in matters of business or advice to search any house to the bottom and reveal all its hidden secrets before precipitately concluding and shaking hands upon it, Charles rushed from the room as much elevated by good fortune as he had

been cast down by bad and coming upon a house with a bill almost at once in Drury Lane gave himself not a moment for consideration. It must and should be his and within the half hour was rattling away as fast as a pair of horses would gallop to receive the uncle's golden benediction. Yet as he mounted into the coach, having been granted just enough patience to thank the old man as his bounty truly deserved, he began to think the happiness he now enjoyed was too great and too substantial to be true. Having been so long the slave of misery it appeared like a dream and he was driven to stop at a tavern to count the money and read the note as often as there were shillings in every separate pound.

His first action was to hasten to his principal creditor who had issued out a writ against him a month before but had been obliged to drop the action since our adventurer was not to be found. The man was so good-natured as to hope that Charles would pay the expenses he had been at in his fruitless search, in reply to which Charles assured him that when he could prevail upon a reprieved criminal to pay for the erecting of Tyburn Tree because he was not hanged there, the man should be perfectly assured of all costs he had been at in tenderly endeavouring to confine him in a prison.

Let prudent wives bless themselves that our adventurer was no relation of theirs for with impatient joy he next flew to all the brokers in town to buy the household furniture, gave the asking price for everything he bought and, in less than three hours was thoughtlessly furnished with many things they had no real occasion for. It was after five in the evening when he arrived at the house with an undistinguishable parcel of goods, Mrs. Brown and the children and resolved that they should all lie there that night. Beds were to be put up and everything ranged in order and by the time these matters were accomplished it was near six in the morning, thought of a night's sleep was fled and they had hardly lain down to take their rest than he was restless again, impatient to be spending.

They had not been two days and a half in the house before opened and, as is customary on such occasions, they gave an infinity of ham, beef and veal to every soul who came in for a quart of beer or a single glass of brandy. The faces them they had never seen before nor were ever to see again

adventurer was fully convinced from the number of people that came the first day that they should carry on a roaring trade, though when they sat down together to reckon up the profits they found that they had in reality run themselves out very near seven pounds.

Mrs. Brown sighed a little at this, wondering if it was but the foretaste of the dish to come but Charles was not to be cast down. I shall let three of the rooms so that their rent shall ensure us a profit even though we never sell another quart of beer. Tomorrow I shall find three families eager for a lodging in a house of such good repute.

Three such persons indeed soon came forward but Mrs. Brown sighed again when she saw them for they had little grace of manner or speech to commend them and brought so few belongings that she wondered how they would do to furnish a table. The second great help they had towards getting an estate was their happiness in entertaining several strolling players, out of business and out of money who, since it was so handily placed in Drury Lane used it as a free house. They will ruin us with their continuous credit, she would cry; but Charles was unable to refuse anyone styling himself a comedian. They will pay when they have found something to do, he would reply, not considering that when that happened they might in all probability be many score miles out of reach as indeed proved the case.

I cannot conceive, said Mrs. Brown one night when the uproar from above stairs threatened to bring the ceiling about their ears, How those persons can contrive to be so excessive and frequent drunk when they buy nothing from the house and seem to convey nothing in.

I have myself wondered that of late, Charles replied, And today came one of them to me with nods and winks so I could scarce piece together a meaning, and then later the husband of another with just such enigmatical hints as the first to the effect that some people would wash clouts in beer if it were to be had for nothing and that Mrs. Prickett seemed to find the water too strong or else her legs were weak for he had found her in a heap upon the stairs with her empty pail beside her.

What can he have meant? Mrs. Brown asked. Sure he cannot have meant she was in a drunken stupor and what of the pail?

That we must find out, Charles replied. Bring a candle and we will go down into the cellar and look about us. They descended the stairs and by the candle's light found the beer much diminished and a pail thrown carelessly to one side with dregs still swilling in it where the contents had been drunk upon the spot without the labour of carrying it two pair of stairs to the garrets. Here is the answer to our loss and their riot, said Charles kicking out bitterly at the pail. There is more too. Madam Such-a-One observed to me that it would be very proper to watch the other what she carried upstairs when she went about the house and did I not think she was with child or dropsical that she seemed to be swole up when she passed her going up to her room this morning. We must begin to be a little peery and look round the house to see if anything is missing. Now while they are busied getting drunk as lords on our beer, is the moment for it.

In short their search revealed that the persons had taken violent fancies to their very candlesticks and saucepans, their pewter horribly shrunk, and their coals daily diminished from the same opportunity they had in conveying off the beer. Now, cried Mrs. Brown, I begin to suspect the repeated hue and cry after a thieving dog that has so often been seen by other eyes than mine to have run off with three parts of a joint of meat. Strange that I should never be witness to these phantom beasts and their taking ways.

My dear, Charles replied, we have been gulled and we must find ways to escape from this pilfering crew before we find ourselves in Newgate. Returning to their own room again they sat down with a bottle of claret to decide upon their course. I dare not attempt my uncle again, Charles sighed, with such a tale of foolishness. He will think me a fool in the ways of the world and quite unfit to have a house as indeed I begin to think myself. Nor can we stay and attempt to be rid of them. I see now that they are part of the fraternity of rogues and any threat would bring the whole pack upon us. We must flit in secret and as soon as we may. Tomorrow while they are still sleeping off the effects of tonight I will fetch a cart and disrobe our own apartments of their furniture and all else we can carry away of value so that when they wake they will find their kind hosts have gone.

Accordingly taking advantage of the din continuing above, they began to prepare themselves and as soon as 'twas light and a cart could be found they quitted their apartments and rumbled away to the Haymarket where our adventurer's brother Theophilus was then resident and had just revived the tragedy of Romeo and Juliet. Here they stayed for some months both chearfully and agreeably until Theophilus was obliged to desist by order of the Lord Chamberlain and removed to Covent-Garden Theatre leaving them once again to get their bread as best they could. As for the thieving crew one of them has very narrowly escaped hanging, more from dint of mercy than desert; another reduced to common beggary and lying on bulks being so notorious a pilferer as to be refused admittance into the most abject tottering temement in or about St. Giles's, and the third is transported for life.

Fortunately for our adventurer she was soon offered an engagement with one Mr. Russel, a man of vogue and in universal favour with every person of quality and distinction, who had an Italian Opera at Mr. Hickford's Great Room in Brewer's Street, exhibited by puppets, which she understanding the management of, and the language they sung, was hired at a guinea per diem, to move Punch in particular. This affair was carried on by subscription in as grand a manner as possible. Ten of the best hands in town compleated his band of musick, and several of the female figures were ornamented with real diamonds lent for that purpose by several persons of the first quality.

With Mr. Russel's salary paid every day of performance she was able to redeem all their clothes and new rig both herself and child which made her extremely happy but she was still so unfortunately circumstanced that she was forced to set out between five and six o'clock in the morning, traversing St. James's-Park till Mr. Hickford's maid arose, and for security to stay there all day mingling with the thickest of the crowd at night to get home. However the run was only short, the flowing tide of joy came to an ebb with both Mr. Russel and herself and she heard the unpleasant tidings that he was under confinement in Newgate for debt.

Compassion led her to visit him there though she had not the power to deliver him from that dismal abode but in her wishes. My good sir, cried our adventurer, you cannot conceive with what distress I behold you reduced to this unhappy condition after your great kindness to me, and with your permission I will set on foot a scheme I have at heart which will release you from this place and may perhaps return you to the favour of the town and to your former happiness. You have a humorous piece of your own composing which if you will allow me I will exhibit upon the Hay-Market stage, providing the performers and my own service, and taking the entire management upon myself without fee or reward unless the nightly receipts empower you to gratify me for my trouble, which I do not doubt for the piece has merit and I have ever found you among the most generous of men. As to the money I will have nothing to do with it; both door and office keepers shall be of your own providing, but the people if I engage them shall be paid nightly according to the agreement made with them for I know what it is to stand in want and gape upon promises; and as for me I shall think myself amply rewarded if I can be but partly the happy instrument of your being set at liberty.

What, he cried, here is another come to torment me and deceive me with lies as if they had not already done more than enough. I will not trust them. They smile and smile yet I will not trust them. A little startled at first, she soon became convinced of his growing misfortune and too plainly perceived that he was not entirely in his senses and that nothing was to be gained by further discourse. With real concern she left him to return in a few days hoping to find him in a more settled order. Yet on entering his room it was immediately apparent that from a man of sense he was absolutely changed to a driv'ling ideot nor was there the least consistency in one single syllable he uttered though she at length managed to gather that a person had run away with his only hope of relief.

In about a fortnight after this interview, passing through Newgate, she called to know how he did and was informed he was removed by a Habeas to the Fleet. As it lay upon her way, she stopped there and enquired after him, upon which she was desired to walk up two pairs of stairs and in such a room she should find him. She expressed to the persons who directed her a great concern for him and they as naturally answered 'twas very kind and good in her and desired her very civilly to walk up, which she accordingly did, and after having rambled into several people's rooms through mistake, arrived at that of Mr. Russel.

The reader may conceive a description of our adventurer's surprise quite unnecessary on this occasion when she saw that Mr. Russel's remains only were deposited there, though in a handsome shroud and coffin, but she was for some time very near motionless as the deceased person, until she began to be very angry with the woman who had sent her up without informing her that he was dead.

But, said she when taxed upon this score, I had thought you knowed the poor gentleman was dead, he having been gone two days, and that you was come out of friendship and curiosity to see his sad remains. Nay madam, was the reply, That I did not but am glad to see him provided so well with a handsome shroud and coffin that he is not to be hustled hugger-mugger into the ground. As for that, the woman answered, they are but for shew and provided by a friend, for they must both be taken from him and he put into a plain box provided by the parish, for 'tis the law when a debtor dies without effects or means to satisfy their creditors they must be so interred, for if their friends be allowed to bury them decently the warden of this place is held liable for all their debts if can be proved he suffered it.

'Tis a hard case notwithstanding, our adventurer answered, that humanity should not extend itself even to the dead without hurting them whose principles of Christianity excite 'em to it. Here was one universally admired, and for some time as much the fashion in families as their clothes. But alas! Misfortunes are too apt to wear out friendship and he was cast off in three months with as much contempt as an old coat made in Oliver's time.

How true, said a voice. How well I know those sentiments to be true. And turning she found a young man, an intimate friend of the deceased had entered, whom she recognised from her association with Mr. Russel. I am deeply grateful for your concern, he continued. This has been a terrible affair, made only bearable by some two or three who have shewn compassion for his sufferings as you have done. A man of such sensibility is not able to support such a reverse of fortune and the knowledge that he had been betrayed by the villain instructed to solicit the nobility on his behalf quite undid him. The sum collected amounted to upwards of a hundred pounds which would have more than effected his relief.

And what is to become of his figures? she enquired. I would be willing to take them myself as they can only be an encumbrance to one who does not understand their management. His landlord has them, the young man replied, And has valued them at threescore guineas and the money down. That is the end of my hope then, replied she, For I have not even the hope of that much money in the world. Had I done so Mr. Russel need never have been brought to the state of losing them, his reason and life all together. I do believe you, the young man answered, And may affirm that I stand in the same case as you may readily believe. Thus with many reflections on the cruel malice of Fortune our adventurer took her leave, seriously representing to herself her own situation and that she must hustle if she were not to find herself confined as her deceased friend had been, though as to madness and the losing of her senses she had always had the advantage of Spirits to surmount them for which she devoutly thanked Heaven.

However that may be though my dear, she said when arrived home again, Spirits alone are not enough to supply our bread and clothing for our backs. I will engage myself at May-Fair and thus make shift until the next Bartholomew but then, my family being unwilling to help me to a living and my Father's mind still poisoned against me even though I have often sued for favour and expressed myself a dutiful child, and thus all prospect of advancement in the town closed to me, the girl and I must go into the country to see what we may prog there, and I shall take upon me that dear name of Brown once more, the better to make my way, for if my family conceive that I am gone out to earn my bread their malice will reach out to me even there. But I would not force you to bear company and suffer with us. You have borne enough since you first took us into your house when I was stricken with the fever, and that only out of sincere friendship and an uncommon easiness of temper for sure you could never have hoped for any return of your goodness.

Mrs. Brown however was not to be dissuaded being fully resolved that where her friend went she would bear them company although she was not without some small resources of her own and had no need to quit the town. Their first venture indeed nearly brought our adventurer back again for being engaged at Sunning-Hill in her old part of Captain Plume she found herself obliged to blend it with that of Sylvia, the lady who should have represented it being unable to speak a plain word or even to keep her ground. Yet this was trifling to what they afterwards beheld for there were Emperors as drunk as Lords, and Lords as elegant as ticket porters; a Queen with one ruffle on, and Lord Townly without shoes, or at least but an apology for them.

On one occasion when Mrs. Brown was playing the part of the Queen in the Spanish Fryer, Charles, who was anxious to see how she acquitted herself and himself having no business with her since he was playing Lorenzo, watched from the wings, and found her to speak sensibly but, to his surprise, observed her to stoop extreamly forward, on which he concluded she was seized with a sudden fit of the Chollick and when she came from the stage asked her if this was so. She replied in the negative but at her next appearance, he remarked that she sunk down very much on that side he stood, on which he conjectured her to be troubled with a Sciatick pain in her side and made a second enquiry only to receive the same answer as before. Upon this he desired to know the reason of her bending forward, and fideling so. 'Tis a trick I have got, she answered. Then 'tis a very new one, said he, for I never saw you do so before. But he began to suspect something was the matter and resolved to find it out.

Presently the Royal Dame was obliged to descend to the Dressing Room from the stage, and made a discovery, by the tossing up of her hoop, of a pair of naked legs. Her Majesty having observed Torrismond to have a dirty pair of yarn stockings with above twenty holes in sight, kindly stripped her own legs of a pair of fine cotton and lent them to the hero thinking her own not so exposed to view. Charles let us say was both pleased and angry to find Mrs. Brown's humanity had extended so far as to render herself ridiculous, besides the hazard she run of catching cold. Yet so common was this kind of circumstance that they began to think that going a-strolling was engaging in a little, dirty kind of war, and a very contemptible life, rendered so through the ignorant and impudent behaviours of the generality of those who pursued it, and that it would have been more reputable to have earned a living cinder sifting at Tottenham-court for a groat a day.

In the course of their travels they went to a town called Ciren-cester in Gloucestershire, when an odd thing happened which I will now relate. For three years Charles had suffered intermittently with a nervous fever and lowness of spirits throughout which Mrs. Brown had been a devoted nurse. However when they came to the afore mentioned town he was so near death that his dissolution was every minute expected. The illness came to a crisis which our adventurer survived and began slowly to amend. As soon as he could creep about the house he was advised by the apothecary to ride out if he was able to sit a horse.

There was in the same house a reverend looking elder, about sixty years of age, with a beautiful curling head of hair and florid complexion that bespoke at once both admiration and respect. His temper they found agreeable to his aspect, extreamly pleasing and his company entertaining with which he had often obliged Charles while Mrs. Brown attended her business of a play night. This person furnished them with two horses so that Mrs. Brown too could have the benefit of riding out to take the air after the fatigue of three years nursing during which she never once repined.

After two or three days the old gentleman said one evening, I perceive you grow better. Do you like the horse? Charles answered that he greatly approved it for 'twas an easy and willing animal. Then, said the old man, He is yours and Mrs. Brown may keep the other to ride out together whenever you wish, for it does an old man good to see you both amended by taking the air, only for sometimes I may beg the favour of borrowing him until such time as I can send an order to my estate in Oxfordshire for another for my nephew Jemmy when I send him about the country on business.

Charles thanked the old man heartily and Mrs. Brown happening to come in at that moment he made her aquainted with the old man's goodness. There is yet another thing that I have been turning over of late, the old gentleman continued, that is whether you have ever had thoughts of quitting the stage for in your weak condition 'twould seem to me better avoided than pursued. And on this score I have a proposition which should you think fit to accept it would soon restore you to health and spirits and ensure you both an easy mind for the rest of your days. I have as you know a considerable estate in Brill which I am obliged to neglect to chase about the country on business to keep my stocks supplied for a grazier without cattle is like a sailor without a ship. I have need of someone to superintend my affairs and manage the estate in my absence and also of someone to have the management of the family at home which consists of myself and nephew and about seven or eight servants employed in the husbandry. Now it has come to my mind that you and Mrs. Brown would fill the bill to perfection and if you think proper to quit the strolling life you shall be comfortable as long as you both or I shall live.

Our adventurers looked at each other scarce able to believe their ears or credit that Fortune should smile on them so suddenly and conceiving that the man must be dropped from Heaven to put an end to their miseries. In earnest of my intention, he continued, Here is a trifle for Mrs. Brown as there was never woman yet that could refuse a little adornment; and so saying he drew from his pocket an old-fashioned gold necklace with a lock of the same material which altogether by the weight could not be worth less than twenty pounds, there being several rows and the beads not small.

Charles took it into his hand and having examined it closely desired the old gentleman to keep it 'till they were settled. For, said he, 'twould be a terrible thing if she should lose it in the crush of a play night. Let her put it up herself then, the other cried where she may take it out and look at it from time to time. Mrs. Brown was on the point of agreeing with this and had opened her mouth for that purpose but shut it again when Charles answered that they had no place to keep it but in their boxes which were frequently left unattended and that the elder would give it better care, and so it was agreed at last.

In their own room again, Mrs. Brown demanded the reason for his extreme caution which had deprived her of a valuable ornament. Sure, said he, You would not wear it for 'tis more proper for the neck of a country housewife than a tragedy queen. It's being so old fashioned would make people stare to see an actress so equipped. This mingling of flattery with reason mollified her a little although she continued to wonder to herself whether it would not have suited well with the new clothes she had just received as a present from her relations. The next morning they give warning to Mr.

Linnet, the manager, that they would leave the company at the end of the month. The thought of being so well settled and provided for both their lives was greatly conducive towards the restoration of Charles' health, and their friendship with the old gentleman and his nephew daily encreased.

About a week or so later their new friend, with the utmost ceremony, begged the favour of borrowing the horse and away went the nephew. When he had been gone some three or four days longer than intended his Uncle began to grow uneasy until he worked himself into a downright passion with threats of cutting him off with a shilling for rambling about when he had sent him upon weighty business. Perhaps, Charles suggested, 'Tis the same weighty business that keeps him. He has always seemed to me a sober young man, not likely to be idle in your service. I dare swear when he returns you will find upon enquiry 'tis some grave concern that hath kept him and 'twould be unjust to condemn him without a hearing.

You are right, said the old gentleman, And I thank you for reminding me of it. We are often over hasty to condemn the young for idleness but yours is far the wiser advice. I take it kindly that you should speak for him in his absence where some would be quick to drive the wedge farther between us. 'Tis an earnest of that honesty I may expect in all my dealings with you and when Jemmy comes home you shall have fifty pounds at your service, for honesty should not go without reward. In the meantime you must want for nothing that might hasten your recovery.

However had Charles' recovery depended upon this he might have lain again at Death's door for before Mr. James came back came a sudden order from the Magistrate of the town to insist on the old man's leaving it at a moment's warning on pain of being sent to Gloucester Jail if he refused to obey. In the interim, home comes the nephew with the same charge but they huddled up their affairs in a strange manner and ventured to stay three days longer though very little seen.

The reader may imagine the terrible consternation of our two friends who still could not arrive at the truth of the affair. At length came Mr. Linnet to them almost breathless and with a truly frighted aspect let them know what he had heard from the town's people.

They be both positively gamblers and housebreakers, he cried, and if you are foolish enough to listen to them any longer you will not only be well codded but made innocent sufferers for their guilt, and like to dangle at a rope's end. They have no doubt seen your boxes full of fine linnen and the present of clothes to Mrs. Brown when they have visited you to play cards under show of friendship while you lay sick. As for the old rogue in his venerable beard, others than you have been deceived for he hath been a noted pickpocket, and sometimes highwayman, for upwards of forty years.

O what an instinct for our preservation was mine, cried Charles when they were once more alone together, That I would not suffer you to wear that detested necklace. Had you been seen with it about your neck by the rightful owner you might have been provided with one of a rougher kind and both of us disgracefully exalted for being harmlessly credulous. Let us lift up our hearts to Heaven with grateful sense of its providential care of us and send back the horses at once, for had this wicked man perpetrated his design we might have been made innocent sacrifices to save his horrid life, and branded with the guilt of crimes we should never have thought of committing.

Thus though they had lost their imaginary fortune our friends secured their lives and the little all they were both worth upon the face of the earth, but business falling off they decided to join the company of Mr. Richard Elrington which was then in Devonshire and accordingly set out. They finally met up with them some five miles beyond Tiverton in their more rural retreat, and great was Mrs. Elrington's joy to see them coming into town, Charles and the girl double upon a strapping beast which was of proper size to have rank'd in the number of dragoons and Mrs. Brown single. But the tale she told them of the company's miserable state of affairs was so dismal that had she not rallied her misfortunes with such vivacity that her wit was too strong for their resolution, they should certainly have gone back by the next post.

As they were just entering the town a good looking farmer met them, and guessing what they were by their appearance, asked if they were not comedians. When they answered in the affirmative he cried, Then if you have any pity for yourselves turn back for else by all that is above us ye shall starve of a certainty. This relevation, with Heaven as its witness, threw Mrs. Brown who was not ever the best horsewoman in the world, into such a fright that she dropped her bridle. Her hungry steed seizing the advantage at once made for the nearest meal and run her into the hedge where he dropped her in the ditch.

Let us go back, she cried as soon as she had recovered from her surprise. Of what use even to see the company, better to return directly before we are further engaged. Nay, Charles replied, 'Tis already impossible for we have no more money left to go back and must therefore needs go forward. For better or worse we have elected to join them and join them we must. To this Mrs. Elrington added her own pleas, saying that the addition of two such as themselves to the company would surely change the fortunes of them all and that besides there was a play bespoke which was assured of an audience and must prove a great success; and with all these arguments she was at length prevailed upon to go on.

The bespoke play proved to be *The Beaux Stratagem* but such a version of it as was never seen before or since as I believe nor yet such an audience. In the first row of the pit sat a range of drunken butchers some of whom soon entertained the players with the inharmonious musick of their nostrils. Behind them were seated their sizable consorts who seemed to enjoy the same state of happiness their dear spouses were possessed of but having more vivacity than the males laughed and talked louder than the players.

Mrs. Elrington, who was playing Mrs. Sullen, with such a lovely prospect before her became fearful that Charles, who played Archer might harbour a design of not staying in the drunken scene between Archer and Scrub and accordingly payed them a visit, and taking the tankard out of Scrub's hand, drank Mr. Archer's health and to their better acquaintance. The least Charles could do was to return the lady's compliment by drinking to hers, upon which she ordered Scrub to call in the butler with his fiddle, and insisted on Charles dancing a minuet with her while poor Scrub comforted himself with the tankard.

This absurdity led them into several more for they then took a wild goose chase through all the dramatic authors they could recollect, taking particular care not to let any single speech bear in the answer the least affinity, and while Charles was making love from *Jaffier*, the lady tenderly approved his passion with a soliloquy from *Cato*. In this incoherent manner they finished the night's entertainment; Mrs. Sullen concluding the play with Jane Shore's Tag at the end of the first act of that tragedy, to the universal satisfaction of that part of the audience who were awake, and were the reeling conductors of those who only dreamt of what they should have seen.

I give this as an example of what our two friends were forced to endure yet worse was to come and they dragged on their unhappy lives for some time without prospect of an amendment until they arrived once more at Cirencester, where the manager, Mr. Elrington, took a place in the stage coach for London the very night they arrived, leaving his wife to manage the company. Now came one from Mr. Linnet's company which was then at Bath, desiring our friends to join him there but Charles felt his honour too deeply engaged on Mrs. Elrington's behalf and on her complimenting him with being her right hand he would on no terms leave her but gave her every assistance to take off from her as much trouble as possible since her husband had gone, looking on her as an injured person which doubly engaged his attachment to her interest as indeed she had designed it should.

After traversing through some towns more Mr. Elrington eventually rejoined the company, and they went to a place called Minchin-Hampton, in Gloucestershire whither they were invited by the Lord of the Manor. Here worse befell them, for Charles and two of the men were apprehended, with the connivance of their own landlord, who was in league with a person who had a warrant to take all persons within the limits of the act, and examined almost every traveller who passed through the town before him and extorted money from them before allowing them to pass freely.

The three waited in court, expecting every moment to be called upon and dismissed with a slight reprimand, but eventually they were beckoned to the other end of the court and told that the keeper of the jail insisted on their going into the jail, only for a shew, and to say they had been under lock and key, which was an honour they were not in the least anxious for. At this turn rage and indignation wrought such an effect on Charles' mind that it threw him almost into a frenzy and he very cordially desired his fellow prisoners to give him leave to cut their throats with a faithful promise to do the same by his own if they should be doomed to remain in that place after the trial. However they replied that they were sorry to see him so very much disconcerted but could no means comply with his request, and endeavoured as much as possible to keep up his spirits and bring him into temper. Several times the landlord came backwards and forwards giving them false hopes of their being every minute called upon. The last visit he made, Charles told him all he conceived of him being privy to the affair and a partner in the contrivance to get money from them, uttering several bold truths not in the least to the advantage of his character.

Away he went grumbling and they saw him no more till the next morning. The evening wore apace and now the sufferers heard the clock strike eight which was the dreadful signal for the gates to be lock'd up for the night. From their position they were afforded a view into the pound where were upwards of two hundred men and boys all under sentence of death or transportation. Their rags and misery and the stench of them filled Charles with horror when he conceived that he must be locked up for the night with them. I will offer half a guinea apiece for beds, he cried, Or if not they may hang us out of hand for we shall perish of jail fever if we are to be turned into there.

Now mercifully Providence took a hand in the shape of the young man who was to be their warder for the night, and whom Charles recognised from his previous stay in the town. I am glad to see thee indeed, he cried, For I had thought we must lie on the bare ground tonight. As to that, said the young man, Let your fears be at rest. There be two shoemakers imprisoned for debt in the Women's condemned Hold which 'till their coming hath been some time empty. I will make interest with them and dare answer they will share it with you gladly.

Do so, said Charles, And I will send out for candles and some good liquor to preserve us each from getting an ague in such a petrified apartment. This was done, and the shoemakers willingly aquiesced to share their cell with such gentlemanly company, and though the walls and floor were of flint our sufferers were glad to enter for the two men were extreme neat and their bed entirely clean although one was confined for debt and the other for a design to impose his wife and children on the parish. Nevertheless and despite the good liquor, Charles continued very low-spirited more especially as the hideous din from the felons' chains continued all night long. Now Charles, cried Maxfield, one of the two players and of an odd turn of humour, How often have I seen you exhibit Captain Macheath in a sham prison within walls of canvas and paint and now I have the fancy since we are actually in the condemn'd hold to hear you sing all the bead-roll of songs in the last act that I may have the pleasure in after times when fortune smiles again of saying that I once saw you perform in character. At first Charles demurred but upon them all insisting and saying that 'twould give them all pleasure and help to pass the night, he finally agreed, and striking a pose which after a little he found came naturally enough from the profound effect exercised by his dismal surroundings, he accordingly obliged them all with a performance, and sure never before had the character been more feelingly played or an audience been more attuned to the sufferings portrayed before them.

When it was ended the two actors were admitted to a share of the shoemakers' bed and Charles rolled himself in his boots and great coat within two skins the shoemakers had furnished themselves with for underleathers, and thus secure from every evil that might occur from such a place, except a cold he afterwards got occasioned by the dampness of his bedchamber, slept for about an hour during which he dreamt of all the plagues that had tormented his spirits during the day.

As soon as the dawn of day appeared, he sat with impatient expectation of the young turnkey's coming to let them out into the fresh air, which to do him justice he effected an hour earlier than was usual on our adventurer's account, and let them all look into the yard which was formed in gravel walks, not unlike Gray's Inn gardens, though not kept up in that regular and nice order. I question, said Charles when he beheld them, Whether the first pair were more transported at the view when they first looked on Paradise then I am let out of my cell to this rough yard, and find it comparable to the Garden of Eden.

They sauntered for about a quarter of an hour, Charles deeply immersed in thought, when of a sudden, down came the rattling crew whose hideous forms and dreadful aspects roused in him thoughts of Hell where before he had seen only a Garden of Eden. Why Charles, said Mr. Maxfield, Are those tears I see? Be of good comfort. The morning has come which without a doubt shall see our release from this place. Nay, Charles answered It is not for myself I weep but for these others when I behold how each has his crime strongly imprinted on his visage without the least remorse or tincture of shame; and hear them instead of imploring for mercy impudently and blasphemously arraining the judgement of the Power Divine in bringing them to the seat of justice. See before you how age and infancy are both alike plunged in total undistinguished ruin, and entered volunteers in the service of that being which is hourly preying upon the weak and negligent part of mankind.

At about the hour of eight they received the news that they were ordered to appear in court at nine, and 'tho 'twas brought by the deceiving landlord it was no less pleasing to them for that, and they were removed to the pen. Charles bethought himself of that former occasion when he had been like to starve to death in the Marshalsea had it not been for the generosity of Mrs. Careless and the ladies who kept the coffee houses in and about the Garden who would do all in their power for Sir Charles as they styled him, and prayed Heaven that their benefactor had seen fit to do as much. They had not been in the pen above five minutes however when he was called upon to receive a letter of comfort to himself and friends who although they had assumed a gaiety the night before to restore his spirits, were heartily shocked at appearing at the bar among a set of criminals, the least of whose crimes not one of them would have dared to be guilty of, though but in thought.

However they had the pleasure of being marched out of court just before their cause came on, which ended in a very few words their kind protector having laid the plan for their safety so securely with his interest and power that they were soon dismissed tho' with a bill of different charges to the amount of near twelve pounds besides a quantity of guineas it cost the gentleman who stood their friend in the affair.

After several more months spent roaming the countryside with little profit to show for it, Charles determined to quit the company and against the advice of Mrs. Brown took a house from a friend and, with money from a widow lady living at Chepstow, set up as a pastry cook. At first they met with some success but as soon as their customers' curiosity was satisfied trade suffered a remarkable declension and Charles decided to set up as hog farmer. In his usual extraordinary hurry he bought a sow with pig but great was their disappointment after hourly expecting it to bring forth for three months, during which time it was tenderly nurtured, to find it was nothing but an old barrow, fit only to be sold to the butcher for a shilling or two less than they had paid for it.

Plague succeeding plague they resolved to leave the place, and taking the pastry-cook's utensils with them fled to Pill near Bristol where they set up shop. While the ships were coming in from Ireland in the summer months they had a good running trade, but alas the winter was most terrible and if an uncle of Mrs. Brown's had not opportunely died and left her a legacy they must inevitably have perished.

On the receipt of the letter Charles showed it to the landlord, hoping for a guinea to go to Mrs. Brown's aunt who lived in Oxfordshire and receive the legacy, leaving Mrs. Brown as hostage against his return. But the landlord, conceiving it to be a plot to get his guinea and reward him by running away in debt, refused. Mrs. Brown wept bitterly when she heard it for they had but a groat between them in the world and if a shilling would have saved them from total destruction they knew not where to raise it. Nay, my dear, this will not do, Charles said, To be baulked by the incredulity of a blockhead and kept from what would solve all our troubles and his own too. We must flit, there is no other way for it and that without a word to anybody.

How can we, she cried, When we have no money for the journey and besides you have no hat having pledged it last week at Bristol. How can you set forth all that way without a hat? Notwithstanding, Charles answered, There is nothing else for it. Therefore make up a small bundle with a change of linen and we will go at once.

With Mrs. Brown scarce able to see her way for tears they set off and on their march were met by some of the neighbours who at the sight of them ran at once to tell the landlord that they were gone off. Take heart, said Charles, For at Bristol I will apply to my friend Mr. Kennedy who will furnish us enough to help us on the way. This somewhat cheered Mrs. Brown, though the idea had only then entered his head, and they made good progress to Bristol, arriving there just as the neighbours reached the landlord with their tale. Mr. Kennedy proved as good as expected and they lay that night at a house where Charles was able to procure a covering for his unthinking head from a young journeyman Jemmy Smart who dressed entirely in taste and gladly lent our adventurer a very dusty one of his which had not been worn some time and would therefore not be missed.

Thus they eventually reached Oxfordshire, received the money and returned to Pill, restoring the hat to its owner on the way and redeeming Charles' own. As long as the money lasted he was once again the worthiest gentleman in the land but when their stock was exhausted he was as much disregarded as a dead cat, and it was plain that they must leave the place or starve by inches in the coming winter.

In the succeeding months they were tossed from place to place until they lit finally at Wells where the girl was, she having married some three years before 'tho much against Charles' advice. For the run of six towns they travelled together till at last there came a letter from brother Theophilus saying that Mr. Simpson of Bath had a mind to engage our adventurer to prompt and undertake the care of the stage, and as they were heartily sick of strolling the offer was embraced and they set out for Bath, glad to be away from the insults offered to them both by the girl's husband.

Yet this offer of a position at Bath was not without disadvantage to our friend for it was hedged about with many irksome conditions devised by the family as that she should forsake men's clothes, give up the name of Brown, and not to appear on the stage at all but more especially in the part of Lord Foppington for fear she should be thought to mock her father and brother who were both accomplished in the character. On their arrival at Bath then Mr. Simpson furnished her with money to equip herself in her proper character which she repaid him weekly out of her salary.

From the month of September to March they stayed there but the fatigue of the place was more than her health or spirits could easily support, for Mr. Simpson in his good nature and unwillingness to offend even the most trifling performer stood neuter when he ought to have exerted his right of authority; each had their several wills, and but one bound to obey them all which was Charlotte. This any reasonable person will allow to be a hard task as she was not inclined to offend any of them, and though they herded in parties, she was resolved to be a stranger to their disputes, till open quarrels obliged her to become aquainted with them and she was often made use on as a porter to set these matters to rights. Her proud spirit could not easily brook this, both in respect to her father as well as to herself.

Next she had not, even on Sundays, a minute to herself, and often left fresh orders for the printer while he was at church, either for alteration of parts, or of capital distinctions in the bills without which very indifferent actors would not go on. The rumour was also brought to London that she had been seen in the streets of Bath in her preferred clothes once more, and that friends had requested her appearance in a benefit as Lord Foppington, which intention was frustrate by two persons who each hoped to supply the character themselves though without the advantage of either that ease of action necessary to the part or being able to utter a syllable of French.

To say truth she began to be very angry with herself for ever condescending to sit behind the scenes to attend a set of people none of whom, the principall Miss Ibbott excepted, was capable of discerning any faults she might have in acting. However she determined to finish the season out and would have done so had not the whole business been brought to a stop by an information lodged against the company, the theatre closed and great uncertainty of its ever opening again. Upon this they removed to Bradford to another company and in spite of the entreaties of several of Mr. Simpson's company, including Miss Ibbott, who came to see them play at that town, refused to return to Bath, preferring to travell further and fare worse as indeed they did with several indifferent companies until at length they fetched up once more with the girl and her husband.

Matters here were, as the reader may conceive, no better than before, yet one good thing was to come from it for our adventurer had now made good progress in a design she had of living by her pen and had got half way in a history of Mr. Dumont with which she resolved to try her fortune and never more to set foot on a country stage again. She therefore prevailed on the manager, a good-natured young man, to steer course for London. They were unlucky enough to miss the stage at Portsmouth and were obliged to retard their journey two days, remaining there on expenses which was a terrible disaster as their finances were at best slender.

But had they been much worse Charles was determined to see London and when they at length set foot upon London streets was more transported with joy, though with but a single penny in their pockets, than for all the height of happiness he had in former and at different times possessed.

*   *   *

'About the year 1755 she had worked up a novel for the press, which the writer accompanied his friend the bookseller to hear her read. Her habitation was a wretched thatched hovel, situated on the way to Islington in the purlieus of Clerkenwell, Bridewell, not very far distant from the New-river Head; where, at that time, it was usual for the scavengers to leave the cleansings of the streets, and the priests of Cloacina to deposit the offerings from the temples of that all-worshipped power. The night proceeding, a heavy rain had fallen, which rendered this extraordinary seat of the Muses almost inaccessible; so that, in our approach, we got our white stockings enveloped with mud up to the very calves, which furnished an appearance much in the fashionable style of half-boots. We knocked at the door, (not attempting to pull the latch-string,) which was opened by a tall, meagre, ragged figure, with a blue apron, indicating what might else have been doubted, the feminine gender; a perfect model for the Copper Captain's tattered land-lady, that deplorable exhibition of the fair sex in the comedy of *Rule a Wife*. She, with a torpid voice and hungry smile, requested us to walk in. The first object that presented itself was a dresser, clean it must be confessed, and furnished with three or four coarse delft plates and underneath an earthen pipkin, and a black pitcher with a snip out of it. To the right we perceived, and bowed to, the mistress of the mansion, sitting on a maimed chair, under the mantelpiece, by a fire merely sufficient to put us in mind of starving.

On one hob sat a monkey, which by way of welcome, chattered at our going in; on the other, a tabby cat of melancholy aspect: and at our author's feet, on the flounce of her dingy petticoat, reclined a dog, almost a skeleton! He raised his shagged head, and, eagerly staring with his bleared eyes, saluted us with a snarl. 'Have done, Fidele! These are friends.' The tone of her voice was not harsh, it had something in it humbled and disconsolate: a mingled effort of authority and pleasure. Poor soul! few were her visitors of that description; no wonder the creature barked. A magpie perched on the top rung of her chair, not an uncomely ornament! and on her lap was placed a mutilated pair of bellows: the pipe was gone, an advantage in present office; they served as a succedaneum for a writing-desk, on which lay displayed her hopes and treasures, the manuscript of her novel. Her inkstand was a broken teacup; the pen worn to a stump; she had but one! A rough deal board, with three hobbling supporters, was brought for our convenience; on which, without further ceremony, we contrived to sit down, and entered upon business. The work was read, remarks made, alterations agreed to, and thirty guineas demanded for the copy. The squalid hand-maiden, who had been an attentive listener, stretched forward her scrawny length of neck with an eye of anxious expectation! The bookseller offered five! Our authoress did not appear hurt: disappointments had rendered her mind callous; however, some altercation ensued. The visitor, seeing both sides pertinacious, interposed, and at his instance, the wary haberdasher of literature doubled his first proposal, with this saving proviso, that his friend present would pay a moiety, and run one half the risk; which was agreed to. Thus matters were accommodated, seemingly to the satisfaction of all parties; the lady's original stipulation of fifty copies for herself being previously acceded to.'

Account of a visit to Mrs. Charlotte Charke by Mr. Samuel Whyte of Dublin; Taken from Baker's *Biographiaa Dramatica* (1, p 106), 1812.

sick o I am sick indeep. many waters have gone ovary. words slip wordshift run counter to counterpane. i spy with my fickle eye white walls walz. spray of winter jessamine at the bedside seaside i do like to be beside bedside or is it forsythia. the white walled town with flicker of yellow sunsplash or underwater dance of dazzle of filtered light through the collander of the waves. the flowers burn piercing yellow flames arrowheads through the mind's flesh. enough. they hurt me. turn away.

and on the other side there is the wall only the wall which i am not permitted to pass through. you are walking through the forest where the trees are people and suddenly there is the wall as far as the eye can see. you try to build it quickly as soon as he said it so that it will not be too high as he sits beside the bedside calm with the paper and pencil in his head taking your words down shorthanded the evil little marks pinning you to the pad. take this to mr jollop the chemist. sixteen grains of. the potion to be drunk secretly. oblivion. what is it doctor. you wouldn't understand my child do not bother your poor little head. just rest and try not to worry too much. i have written the magic formula on the paper. behind that screen is my desk where i keep a wingless fly in a phial. when i take out the stopper he crawls across the inkpad onto the paper leaving his little footprints which only mr jollop and i understand. behind his little window of frosted glass he pounds the paper to dust mixes it with blood of a new born child and feeds it to a white rat dropped at the full moon who in his turn secretes it in the form of small pellets which you took away in your hand-bag. untouched by human hand and very hygienic. and so as soon as he says there is a wall you build it very quickly so that it shant be too high because you know in a minute he will ask you to climb it and if you refuse. but it goes on growing and there is broken glass embedded in the top because what is on the other side is forbidden and dangerous. on the other side there is a.

locker with the flowers in a tall slim glass. the yellow flowers burn. i fiori gialli incendono. incendiary blooms. she was like a tall yellow iris against the blue sea and sky. arent you afraid you two girls going all that way by yourselves and you know what the men are like there. yes i am afraid but she is tall and strong and cool in the hot sun her skin smelling of pine needles no one would dare and anyway all the girls are doing it now in their last year. all day we lay on the warm sand or splashed in the sticky salt sea her face dappled with light thrown back by the water. the fine fair hair lying along the sleek brown skin. and at night we would go down to the hotel bar. sit over there marie while i get the drinks. sometimes there were boys in from outside but they were always polite because they were in the hotel. they would smile and buy us drinks and play the juke box. then the day before we left it was we went to see the cathedral and coming out into blinding light into a crowd we got separated and suddenly there were faces all around me dark young men's faces scowling hands plucking at my clothes. wait for me. dont leave me. and voices saying things i didnt understand. pushing me down the steps and a boy with thick lips saying kiss kiss dont leave me. and then there she was pushing them aside smiling and taking my arm walking me on and the boy with thick lips called out something i didnt understand. in the bar that evening sit there marie while i get the drinks there was only one table empty two places and a man leaning back with his eyes half closed watching her go up to the bar in her slim blue slacks tan shirt with the sailor collar and suddenly he said as if we were in the middle of the conversation i don't understand women today what you want is a good. and i didn't hear the rest because i didn't understand and anyway she came back then and he stood up swaying a bit and said i hope you have a very happy love life and then he went towards the door and i watched him the eyes following wondering if hed make it and what hed meant. he was drunk wasnt he. what did he mean. yes he was drunk she said. what did he say. and suddenly i remembered i hadnt heard properly and i didnt understand so i said something about having a happy love life and she laughed and said well that was a nice thing for anyone to wish you drunk or not. drink up and lets enjoy our last evening and we did. and when we got home it was time for her to go off to university and although i wrote she was never a good correspondent and we lost touch. never touched. what do i mean. i didnt understand.

lost touch. gone away. marie youre wandering again. found wandering woolgathering again. maries down among the daisies.

making chains to catch a. youll never catch a boy like that. boys like you to look as if youre interested in them not as if youre miles off in a dreamworld. dont you want to get married. i can see i shall never have a grandchild to push out in the gardens on a fine afternoon and sit knitting tiny doll's clothes for with all the other women of my age. deres a pritty liddle granny's pride an toy. mother i am too young to marry too young to be a bride. used to make me cry in English lessons. the lily the rose the rose i lay. how should i love and i so young until betty howarth told me a lily was a before it was and a rose was a after. doctor bailey beareth the bell away.

but he doesnt stick the needle in because hes a doctor. against the medical code. struck off the list for interfering in your. lie down on the couch and let me examine you. touch of rubber casing warm flesh nearly cried out like. probing. he hurt me. yes mrs pacey i think we can safely say that the needle has had the required effect done its job in fact. let me explain what happens quite simply and then you wont be frightened. its better if youre not frightened. better for you. just relax. dont fight it. let it happen to you. youll feel nothing at first. except the needle. and when we all lined up for vaccination some of the girls fainted. roll up your sleeve to above the elbow. open your eyes. open your eyes. no i cant look.

why cant you look at me. why do you shut your eyes as if i were hurting you. you know i wouldnt hurt you. i love you. yes i do i love you. then why do you if you love me. mother said men were all the same. it was nasty dirty rude words. you wont learn all those common things at a private school. nasty things from dirty boys marie i love you. i want you. dont you understand. yes guy i do understand really. its all right i know you have to. but you dont enjoy it. enjoy it. i mean you dont ever. i dont understand. what dont i. you dont. o whats the use. dont hurt me guy. hurt me. hurt. it was a lie.

i did feel the needle and then.nothing. nothing at all. only lying awake waiting. he didn't do it of course. not put it in himself like that but he made her. the sister. never had a sister. once was quite enough goodness me o yes. youll find out when your turn comes. its not all lovey dovey the dear little sweet thing smelling of talc bite its little bottom having a baby. conceived in sorrow and brought forth in pain. when they first put you in my arms i thought you were an ugly baby you were skinny and red with anger and how should we manage on your father's salary. he was in a safe job of course. a very decent job. i always think when i see those old war films how he helped to prepare the country for all that at his ministry and how lucky we were during the slump. such a nasty word like a woman with a sagging bosom. sit up straight marie. and we used to have fun in those days i can tell you not like youngsters today. visiting cards and tennis though that was a mixed blessing of course in the end your father having that sad accident. struck with a tennis ball right in the place where it hurts a man most and setting off some strange mechanism so that they grew and grew until they were as big as a tennis balls themselves and now he has to have his trousers made specially at extra cost though you must never tell anyone of course like aunt sadie going mad and killing her baby with the breadknife and granny who died with a whisper a growth.

its the second one that does it. sister coming in with the second one that strikes at once like lightning flash a different one this time that sets you free as long as you dont resist it. lets you say wild things you would never dream in your waking or even sleeping.

i hate my mother. i am pushing her into a washtub of bubbling sulphuric acid. the flesh strips from her bones clean bones bleached. smell the good clean smell of bones bleached with our powder whiter than if you dried them in the sun and fresh air. mother you are the skeleton in father's cupboard. daddy daddy what are you doing. dont bother your father marie hes up in his den busy with his painting. what are you painting daddy let me see. come in marie and shut the door. dont let your mother know. its a surprise. its a skeleton daddy. i made it from a model kit. its a female skeleton. you see the wide pelvic bones. they call that the iliac flare. youve got it. yes daddy. its a surprise. you shall help me. yes daddy. you see that little pot of paint. yes daddy. its luminous. i dip my brush in it and i paint these bones carefully so that they will glow in the dark. yes daddy. and then i shall hang it in the coal cupboard so that when she opens the door it will be. yes daddy. a surprise. you see the iliac flare. thats so you can have babies. here and here you see and there and there under your little dress. give daddy a kiss. yes daddy. now run downstairs and dont let your mother know our little secret. no daddy no.

your father of course has always been a very kind man like that.

he has his hobbies and his work. a very kind man like that. what will you do now your holidays are over. you'll have to find a job. what have they taught you at school. a nice post as someones secretary i think. yes mother. with your shorthand and typing. im not very good at shorthand mother. nonsense. youre good enough for them. you have all a managing director could require as a personal secretary. what were you good at at school. English mother. o poetry and drama dreams the stuff theyre made of but no use to you when it comes to getting down to the serious business of living. such pretty things we learnt at school. i used to stand up in front of the class and say them but you forget all about that when you grow up. spelling thats useful particularly for a secretary and punctuation of course and punctuality and a good appearance. you want to make the most of yourself. your typing speed is 120 your figures are o yes very good at figures. mother. and ive always taught you to sit up straight and not let your bosom slump and to walk with your head held high swinging the hips so that the eyes are drawn towards. dont look at me as i walk out of the room. she walks very nicely our little girl and has a very trim little figure. your father is good at figures too he has to be in his job of course. its expected of him. eyes watching you from behind boring into your. not from behind no not the needle. not in my.

only your thigh dear no need to be frightened. no need to turn over. just roll up your pyjama leg. sister. i wont hurt. there did that hurt. no sister. sister is gentle and her hands are. you just relax and close your eyes and if theres anything if youre worried ring for me.

indeep. the flash. flesh. like sunstroke sunflash shift wordshift myshift. thunderflash. falling. where are you. i dont know. yes you do. look around. i cant. i cant open my eyes. the water. its too heavy. open your eyes. its so cloudy i cant see anything. where are you. im at the bottom of a well. my head is heavy i cannot get up the well is cold and deep. do you want to get up. i must. i cant stay here im frightened. there are things around me in the darkness in the mud. at the bottom of a well. it isnt the well its the goldfish pond in the garden daddy's goldfish bowl sunk in the earth. i can see them now. theres one above me hanging in the water just waving its tail like water weed. its watching if i move itll know im here. they eat their young the small fry. you must realise marie that

103

nature is cruel. but why mother. things are made the way they are dont ask silly questions. were as nature made us and we have to keep her rules and nature's rules are the rules of society. if you marry a blackman you have a black baby thats one of nature's rules so society very wisely sees to it that black and white dont mix. cats and dogs do mother they dont seem to mind about different colours. but theyre animals marie you funny little girl you cant compare us with animals. arent they nature we study them in nature study. now youre just being silly and obstinate. you must ask your father hell put an end to this nonsense. why are some of the goldfish red and others black daddy do they mind being different colours. i dont suppose it matters in their world. like kittens daddy. you see that big fat one red hiding its head in the weeds thats your mother and that wicked black one with the gold plates on his back and sides as if he were wearing armour thats me and the slim bright girlfish with the feathery fins and tail is you. there we all are and all quite different. why doesnt mother like black people daddy. theres a girl in my class from ceylon shes a princess and she has a little red dot on her forehead but mother wouldn't let me invite her to tea. your mother knows best marie we all have to agree that mother knows best. whats that at the bottom of the pond daddy. that o thats the eggs of a pond snail i put them in to keep the pond clean scavengers they live off the slime but the goldfish eat their eggs if they dont hide them and grow big and fat on them like the one with its head in the weeds. like mother. but we dont tell her do we its our little secret.

shes watching me if i move shell know im here and shell. but i must get out of the slime the mud or ill never be born. try to move very gently crawl through the slime perhaps she wont. shes coming shes seen me coming down on me dropping through cloudy water. burrow in the slime perhaps shell. help me somebody help me. opening her mouth a dark gaping wound to engulf me. help me help. he wouldnt stop her he didnt help me sister. hush now youre upsetting the other patients. but he didnt stop her. never mind its all over shall i sit with you for a bit hold your hand. try to relax. when i close my eyes im still there in the dark at the bottom. then keep them open. look at the flowers. your husband brought them for you didnt he. think about the flowers.

every friday they had to report the reps coming into the director's office mr carrol will see you now fingering ties spotted with grease beer one with a rent in the seat of his trousers. have you risen on your graph or are your spirits low a descending scale. you must do better young man you are lagging flagging the firm cant afford to pay for your cosy chats with customers unles theyre paying off. brisk you must be or we shall be brusque the brush off. yes sir mister sir with the door on the jar and the outside office all agog and agiggle but the one they were really waiting for was come in mr pacey im the one who sets the and shut the door take a chair and a cigarette. hes going far that one got his sights set high not just anyone out of the typing pool not any common tiddler but a sleek little girlfish all goldfish wholl grace his table and ripple in his. cocksure they all called him. i didn't understand. all combed and powdered they were with their mouths painted in a pout for him to come dashing in throwing his hat to one winking at another joking careless yet watchful waiting for me to come to the door with eyes down and mr carrol will see you now and he would be serious in a moment holding the door open for me seeming almost shy. even mother liked him when he came to tea he had such nice manners and he never once tried to like it says in the back of the books go too far do wrong.

look after her my boy youve stolen the best secretary i ever had mr carrol said and all the others were so mad. i could tell you a thing or two but youll soon find out and i was frightened and fascinated at the same time reading a book i got from church in a brown paper cover on getting married in the train in the mornings and thinking at last id be on my own and away from home and mother couldnt go on at me any more about getting married because id done it all by myself. but daddy never liked him. hes too rough for my little princess and he nearly didnt come to the wedding until i cried and then he said he would but she didnt though i wrote only sent a telegram with love as always and that beautiful wooden dish carved like a leaf and what the hells that supposed to be for he said but i kept it in the sideboard all the same and sometimes in the afternoon id pick it up and feel the smooth-ness of it like the smoothness of tanned skin smelling of pine trees. once i tried to talk to him about her but he said she sounded bossy and not his idea of a woman he didnt like them too brainy anyway and he never knew i had such cranky ideas it was time i grew up and how about a little on the sofa but i wouldnt let him. youre better now dear ill leave you for a little the other patients will be wanting elevenses. sister.

gone away. lost. guy guy guy stick him up high. what do i mean. mustnt close my eyes or im back in the dark. why do you always want the light off. cant you stand the sight of me. all the same you prissy missy private school where you never learnt nothing anything you think i should say but nothing thats what you learnt and thats what you are. should have known i suppose there was a catch in it somewhere they dont give you all that class for nothing make you pay through the nose. you dont like me marie you dont even like me but you wont run to mama and say you made a mistake and can you please come home because you dont like her anymore than me. in fact we understand each other your mother and me though shes a cow she knows what she wants and she gets it and that i understand and right now she wants a grandchild so i reckon wed better get on with it because shes going to win in the end whether you want to co-operate or not youll find yourself with a little pacey for her to dress up and dandle. that first night i thought you were a princess a sea princess sitting there wrapped round in a foam of a nightdress just like dear daddy always called you until i found out id got a bloody mermaid and how do you fuck a bloody mermaid as the indian said how. you hurt me. i provide dont i for god's sake were luckier than most we have a house and a car television washing machine fridge vaccuum cleaner radiogram cocktail cabinet with electric mixer and granny only too glad to baby sit whenever you want to go out dears. but why should i have a baby for everyone else its supposed to be my baby and i ought to say when i want it. its our baby and we say look you have this baby and ill leave you alone i swear ever after if you want it like that and you dont ask what i do well be like brother and sister only you dont ask what i do because a man has to do something. christ what a mess only dont look at me so hurt with those big eyes full of salt tears as if i beat you or something i dont beat you no one can say i do not even dear daddy.

he beat me with a big stick i never knew it was so big it frightened me. and there was only once just once early in the morning when i was still half asleep and i didnt understand what was happening and id been dreaming about her and there we were on holiday like it always is in the dreams lying on the warm sand side by side listening to the water eyes closed and voices drifting by from a long way off and she took my hand but she never did it wasnt true and i started to wake up and he was saying there that didnt hurt did it lying with his arms round me and saying quietly that didnt hurt did it theres a good little princess and the back of my legs all wet and sticky and he put his hand round in front and touched me there and i felt. he never did it again because he didnt have to but he was very good while i was carrying the baby when i was so sick and he got up first in the morning and held me over the washbasin and i thought i dont want this baby but ive wished sometimes since we could have another and i wouldnt mind being sick because he was nice to me then but though ive let him once or twice nothing happened and now we dont bother at all and i dont ask.

and when they first put you in my arms i thought what an ugly little baby you were skinny and red with anger. no mother i wasnt angry only afraid and when they put me in your arms i wanted to stop crying but they wouldnt let me stay there they took me away and put me in a cot by myself and it was lonely and light after the warmth of your body and they brought me a bottle when all i wanted was to snuggle up to you like kittens do to the soft bellied fur of the she cat but you wouldnt let me and i knew then youd never love me. and what about you. i tried i did try because i knew how she would feel my unloving through the warm cocoon of the swaddling clothes seeping like a chill damp into her little bones and she was a lovely baby not red at all but almost smiling and i thought shes mine really and they cant take her away though that was after when the pain stopped. relax mrs pacey theres nothing to worry about you ladies are doing this every day. try to remember the things you learnt at the clinic and your husband can stay with you for a little while theres plenty of time yet. and mother had said youll find out then and they were all so keen on this baby but i was the one who was having it. relax they said everyone has to go through with it theres nothing you can do now and you complained enough these last couple of months about being so fat swaying when you walked like an old crone with the dropsy not the slim warm young girl on the hot sand.

close your eyes in the dark behind the lids there is only pain the flash of exploding suns behind the pressed membrane the load of the loins bearing you down tearing at your flesh a passage for the malformed head the stunted limbs and wizened image of your own anger that will look back at you. the hours pass waiting for pain holding pain sliding down into darkness dragging up steeps into more pain. sister. keep going dear youre doing fine. suppose it doesnt love me like everyone else. but she will ill make her shes mine. why doesnt she come perhaps shes dead already dead inside me corruption slowly destroying me with her corruption. daddy help me but he didnt help. no more no youre hurting me. for god's sake let it be quick now no more please no more help me someone you cant keep calling for sister think of the other patients. but i need her help me. shes busy cant run after as if you were a child still. somethings you have to do on your own somethings other people cant help you with or do for you. time you grew up time you stood on your own two feet time you time. what time is it. still light in the window square but you cant see whats beyond unless you get up out of bed and go across to. but you dont want to get up the limbs weary lie heavy under the pall of the counterpain. only the eyes still move flick from side to side like an adder's tongue questing. the body feels nothing numb. dead. but i did feel something once. that was a long time ago now you only feel pain. why arent there bars no bars. dont they want to keep me in. didnt i. why dont you get up and look out of the window. with the wall she said cutting across everything. and on the other side of the wall there is a. but i cant get up im having a baby. why doesnt it come. the pain again. it doesnt come because you dont want it because youre still a baby yourself an ugly skinny baby red with anger. not anger no mother i only wanted. they put me in a cold hard cot my body is light and small i am become the sheets that cover me iam flowing into space i am becoming air nothing.

why do you shy away why dont you ever. and over the wall there is. i dont understand. you wont face it you mean. relax let it happen. why should i. i dont want this baby its not mine i dont want to be a mother. mother. dont want to be a woman. a woman is pain you hurt me i suffer. the passive voice. passus sum. that Latin mistress we had with the cropped hair and straight back like a centurion. mistress. caesar's lie in silken tents perfumed the white horses stamp in the warm animal dark snuffling the velvet night i lean above him pouring wine my breasts open the spice islands wafted on the. you are new i think from egypt my lord and the scent of her skin distracted me from my parchments the drying ink turned to powder in the horn. my cup was filled to overflowing my lord i am your handmaiden you may use me as you. sit over there marie while i fetch the drinks. and in the fulness of her time she brought forth a.

a girl. trust you to have a girl you knew i wanted a boy. what use are girls to anyone look at you. you knew i wanted a boy. but shes lovely guy look at her. trust you having a girl cant you ever do anything i want. it was you you as much as me you made the baby. but you made it a girl wanting a girl just to spite me. no guy no. dont tell me you didnt think about it morning noon night calling it my little girl little darling myself. not that no. didnt you make a girl child in your mind moulding the wax with soft fingers until the flesh formed so tentacles of thought playing caressing the little body until it was content to stay there instead of thrusting on into the male. not myself no. i wanted a boy.

he wanted a boy but you didnt did you. he was right. in the back of your mind somewhere out of sight hidden behind desire where right and need and the proper way of going about things a boy first and then a girl couldnt reach you hunt you down force you to do again what youd always done what was wanted of you because youre weak you know you are dependent clinging like it says in the books you should be right there you formed the image of a girl child but not of yourself thats why you could cry out thats not true with all the force of someone who says what she knows is not of yourself but of someone to quite different. someone to love me. and what kind of a little girl did you want then that would love you. i dont understand. its time you did. i dont know what you mean. dont you after all i am part of you too as you know even though you havent often admitted me. who are you what are you doing here ill ring the bell ill call sister. and what would she tell you except that i have as much right to be heard as the other one whos always had your ear with an insidious whisper you dont like me because i might say things you dont want to hear or know things you think youve done better without thats why youve kept me quiet all this time. who let you in. dr bailey with his needle. but it wasnt his needle it was hers. who let me in then. i dont know dont understand. you cant go on saying that you know you did when you. no i didnt. you opted out tried to close the door on consciousness and let me in. i didnt know. yes you did youve always known or ive known for you its all the same thing. go away. send me you brought me here shut me up in these walls with you and now i cant get out anymore than you can now youve let me in i can only go out when you do. what do you want. no you cant get out of it that way its what you want that matters thats all i want to know what you really want then i can go. leave me alone for god's sake. i cant you wont let me.

close your eyes. where are you. i am at the bottom of a deep bowl with slippery sides polished darkly burnished. i lie in the thick shadows clustered like lees dregs the walls rising steep above my head around me in the thick dark the shuffle of paws lumber of limbs murmers from twisting animal throats corded with muscle short-necked bull and bear to tear the flesh must get out but the sides are polished i slip back scrabble spreadeagled like a spider against the side of the bath with the snuffling breathing at my back yelp of wolf and hyena. what are you trying to escape from feel around the walls there may be something youve missed.

missed lost gone away never. maries woolgathering again down among the. have you noticed mrs pacey when she walks about doing her shopping shes either just staring or shes muttering to herself poor young man. she just stands there in front of the shop window or the counter staring and when the assistant asks her what she wants she looks at her so strange as if she doesnt know where she is or what shes doing there sometimes i wonder if she knows who she is and then shell say pardon i dont understand or even once i didnt understand such a pretty little thing when they first came to live here and her poor husband it was after the child was born some women do go a bit funny after their first and its no wonder hes never there not that i hold with such ways of going on and enough to drive the poor little thing such a dear little girl they have too and so knowing an old head on young shoulders and seen too much if you ask me. the dwarf women dragging their trundle baskets full of stones and rubble along the pavement galleries of the high street are wispering behind your back as you pass among them in their midget world of treasure trove windows bowing their shoulders dragging their arms from the sockets as they fill their bags with empty tins and cartons plastic flowers papier mache fruit and flesh good only for the eyes to glut on plumping the belly with wind. you have seen them jerking their puppet arms and legs the mouths opening and shutting in the painted wooden faces the sudden sag when you pierce their rag doll bodies with your keen glance and their emptiness trickles out onto the pavement. you have gone home with your basket half empty opening the door into the hostile house which has been waiting for you the furniture malevolently poised to begin the sniggering skitter across the polished parquet behind your back and when you turn there is only the shadow of a movement the chairs stand quite still thrusting their angles at you the central heating gurgles insolently. upstairs the cistern flushes aggressively into the silence many waters have gone. switch on a flickering cascade of light music a spray of quavering notes falling on the dusty reaches of the morning coffee would be nice sit there marie while i but you do not make yourself coffee. you stare through the french windows into the garden where a child has scribbled flowers and grass and the straggling branches of the forsythia or is it jessamine a drowned maiden's hair plants without roots stuck in the ground that die at a rough touch of sun and wind and tumble their leafless skeletons about the lawn only the forsythia persists pricking out its yellow stars in the spring or is it jessamine.

pull yourself together maries down among again and soon it will be time to fetch the child from the nursery. you must prepare the meal guy will be home wanting his tea and the child whats the time. the clock is a liar its hands charge you with ten to three with two hours wandering in the arid garden. the clocks a liar. careful someone might hear you look round quickly did they hear only the house heard you mustnt start talking to yourself theyll think youre think about the tea what did you get this morning. i dont remember. look in the basket. eggs. eggs. eggs will do on toast.

does it always have to be eggs cant your little head dream up something else just once in a while or is it too full of other great ideas to worry about such a little thing like what the familly eats from day to day what goes on in there anyway or am i too insensitive to be told to make even a shot at understanding eggs youll have me as broody as yourself soon. theres a lot of goodness in an egg an egg contains the germ of life and sufficient nourishment for the developing embryo eggs are egceptional. you hear that little girl you hear what your mother says shes the clever one im just dull brutish et tu brute only i bring home the wherewithal to keep her daydreaming down among the here what else does madame want the kids at nursery school the treasure comes in twice a week to do theres nothing to burden you but a little shopping and the tea to get something to think of for tea and all you can come up with day after bloody day is an egg i dont want anymore bloody eggs do you hear dont let me come home to see an egg on this table again not in any shape or form broiled flied blotched or mangled the very sight of one turns me.

im tired guy i cant think of anything anymore. tired but you dont do anything how can you be tired. limbs drag the mind runs down or races out of time tic toc tic toc the blood thickens in the veins stirs sluggish coagulates in the flat arteries lies heavy behind the muddy eyes or pounds under the taut skin sit over there marie on the hot sand. cant we go away guy this year youre always going away but i never go anywhere just this house. careful dont let the words scream stream through the steam whistle kettles boiling. turn that bloody thing off. cant we guy cant we. turn it off. cant we. for christ's sake turn it thats better now what is it you want. go away all three of us this year a holiday a change something new. theres nothing new every place is the same ive seen them all. o i dont know. what do you know youve never been anywhere take it from me theyre all the same. i went to Italy once it was different the warm sand sunwashed walls beside the. yeah you told me its no change for me im driving about all day up and down roads between hedges under bridges its all the same you seen one place you seen them all in this country and who wants to go carting abroad when what i like is to get home sit in the garden in a deckchair sleep for a fortnight knowing i neednt touch that wheel neednt move that lethal machine out of the garage for two whole weeks.

we could go by train you neednt drive we could go south to the seaside beside the seaside you could lie on the beach all day there and sleep in the sun. and how much would a little jaunt like that cost every bit i slave all the year round to save money down the throat of some ginny old bag of a landlady paying a whole fortune to greasy i-tight cafe owners for egg and chips i get every night of the year at home for nix. wont they think it strange if we dont take the baby for a holiday now shes old enough to enjoy it other people do i met the manager in the high street the other day and he said. i know i know what he said because he repeated it all in my ear poured it in he did just as soon as he got the chance emptied the lot how she was just like you and how fond hed been of you the best little secretary hed ever had he should see you now about this place miss efficiency but the child looked a bit pale come to think of it he said you were both a wee thing peaky as if it was my fault as if i didnt give you everything a woman could ask. then youll take us. youre cunning my god youre cunning. but she isnt like me shes fair arent you darling mummy's little golden princess thats why the gentleman thought she looked a bit pale. alright ill take you hell what else can i do if i want to keep my job not to be put down as the cruel wicked father of a lovely familly who doesnt know when hes well off. daddys going to take us to the seaside o we do like to be beside dont we darling and she shall play on the beach and make sandcastles and run into the sea with mummy were going down to the sea like tom shes going to be a water baby down to the sea with the eels and the merfolk and the fishes of the deep the aenemones waving their tentacles the darting shrimps she shall catch in her little net and the scuttling crabs hiding in the weed curtains along the breakwater and you shall build palaces for your delight and watch the sun set over the water and the waves leap.

for christ's sake marie shes only a kid filling her head with all that junk no wonder shes so bloody precocious let her do normal healthy things like any other kid for once you make an old woman of her talk to her as if she were your own age. who else is there to talk to youre not here much. not that again for god's sake were not starting on that one again. you come in for your tea and then you go off out again for the rest of the night every night and i cant even go round to see my mother. we agreed didnt we that was the arrangement and anyway you were eager enough to get away from her and now you want to be running round there all the time. its not that you know it isnt that theres nowhere else i can go why do you make me feel guilty why do you always make me feel guilty all the time.

because you are guilty arent you guy couldnt make you feel guilty if you didnt know somewhere inside yourself that you are what did you do. nothing i didnt do anything. then perhaps you should have is that it. i never did understand. didnt you are you sure about that and now look inside yourself look deep down inside what do you see. nothing theres nothing there nothing happened. and if it had. its full of maggotts like that hot summer the dustbin lid didnt fit properly and when the men had been to empty it i looked inside and there they were at the bottom heaving and squirming alive with them it was. over the wall there is a i dont know i dont understand.

and how are you getting on mrs pacey sister tells me you were rather unhappy at first but you seem to be better now. dr bailey beareth the bell away. im sorry i didnt quite catch that. its a joke something we learnt at school the bailey beareth the bell away only it isnt a real bell of course. what do you think it is mrs pacey. its the weight i seemed to be carrying a great weight about with me sometimes in my head sometimes inside me low down dragging me down but it isnt there anymore at least only sometimes youve taken it away i was frightened of you too when i first came here but im not now. and what about sister. sister i didnt have a sister only a mother i used to hate my mother. and dont you now. no not now. and what about your father. im not afraid of him now either its funny they dont seem to exist anymore. is there anything else. yes theres still something. what is it do you know. no you cant know because if you did you would have to. what would you have to mrs pacey what would you have to do. but you mustnt they wont let you never. close your eyes again relax let your thoughts come slowly drift into the mind dont try to hurry them or let them worry you remember that most of the things we are taught to think of as wrong or are afraid of are perfectly normal parts of ourselves and should be accepted as such.

relax for god's sake. but when will we get there guy soon.

another half hour and we should see the sea then its a long run down into the town and a climb up to the hotel. see the sea hear that darling well see the sea arent you excited. youll have all the sea you want in the next fortnight and mind you asked for it im sticking the wagon straight in the hotel garage and there it can stay if it rains youll find me on tour a crawl round every bar in this town what you and the kid do is up to you just ask for the man with the driest throat. you wont leave me every evening will you guy. not every evening you can come with me sometimes but no questions on my nights out remember the old arrangement that way well all be happier ive done my job ive brought you here and its my holiday as much as yours.

and you were happy there werent you. yes i was happy. the weather was kind sun shone sunsplashed along the sandy beach even guy was kinder. i knew it was a good idea to come. yeah well pass me that suntan oil before im all cooked up say when you look at me im not in bad shape considering. he liked lying there beside you watching the girls pass behind his dark glasses like being at a peepshow what the butler saw and the baby playing in the sand digging and building filling her plastic bucket with sea treasures pale fluted cockle shells and glass gems worn smooth by the abrasive buffing of stone against stone, silver bells and cockle shells and pretty and you ate ices and gritty sandwiches and lay in the sun with your eyes closed feeling the warmth soothing the bruised eyelids the weariness oozing out of your mind draining through your skin into the porous sand flowing down from fingers and toes in little rivulets that trickled into the sea and the waters themselves washed in through your ears the waves breakers through the empty caverns in your head where the air had grown stagnant and foetid leaving them cleansed and rimed with salt that gleamed whitely in the new sunlight fresh shingle coating the slimy floors where you had slithered and lost your footing as the healing waters receded. you lay a little apart from guy your eyes closed against the dark curls that frothed around the bluish skin that crept up his chest and over his shoulders leapt down his arms and spent themselves at the base of his large knuckles.

it was the third day you saw the young man little more than a boy a smooth boy prinking on the sand posturing in narrow striped trunks on the almost skyline behind you where the wind bent the tufts of coarse sea grass and flailed them cat-o-nine-tails across his ankles and he was all the youth youd seen in the expensive art books youd pawed through in the reference library painted and photographed hacked out of stone or moulded in metal david or flandrin's boy crouched his head buried in his arms the vulnerable neck and hair the muscular thighs and ankles you were aware of him before of course a day before you turned to look you lay on the sand not looking over your shoulder purposely not turning your head til your neck ached with not turning but knowing he was there every morning he came down spread out his black towel with white zigzags stretched himself hitched his red striped trunks briefs so you could almost but not quite see but you didn't look went down to dip a toe in the sea exclaimed nodded smiled looked about him for sympathy caught your eyes and swift away you lay back watching the travelling eyes after his every turn ran sparkling up the beach shed-ding water diamonds that darkened the sand with heavy drops like tears draped the zigzag towel about him pouted at the chill and whip of sandthong and lay back the sun glinting a dozen eyegems from the polished skin browning in the light.

guy. yeah pass me the sun oil. you see that boy well not really boy. which boy o that one yeah so what. well. thinks a lot of himself but hes only a kid. yes. you fancy him do you well thats the first time i ever known you to take an interest in by god i could be jealous if i wasnt so tickled to see you perking up at some hairless kid some little show-off ill tell you something about him i reckon. yes guy what. o never mind you wait and see thats all yes you wait and see and you bet im right. but you went on watching out of the corner hes after the girls you thought prinking like that a pretty boy like that after the little girls his own age not an old married woman but im not old really i married young im after all guy does but with a teenager a boy almost young enough to be your and still looking like a girl not even old enough to and so you watch him conscious that you too were standing up to smooth the towel under you taking the child by the hand to lead her along the beach in search of more treasure left high and dry at the tide levels pop-weed and curious driftwood shaped by the knifeblade seas pared and whittled by the rocks rubbed down by fine sand and a slipper limpet for a princess's foot. look darling its like a little pink shoe put it in your bucket lets see if we can find another one to make a pair.

yet no girls came to keep him company they drifted past in twos and threes dawdling giggling waiting for him to call them so they could stop and turn with a what did you say the formal announcement that the game is on but the words were never thrown down he watched them silently turning over on his stomach if they lagged too obviously the defensive eyes shielded by the smokescreen sunglasses on the fifth day you had gone with the child to buy chocices and when you came back there were two of them sitting side by side on their towels chatting and smoking the second boy even smoother and fairer than the first and you were caught off guard for a moment stood still the child's question unanswered. why does the chocolate melt mummy when the inside is still hard ive frozen my tongue. and first there was a sharp pang like an icicle inserted deftly into the soft flesh of the belly and passing straight through the intestines leaving a flush of cold oozing through the neat hole while you thought i could have been his friend we could have said so much now theyll hunt together to give each other confidence youll see when the next pair of girls pass youre an old married woman who cares about you. mummy ive frozen my tongue will it unfreeze again mummy why dont you eat your ice doesnt daddy like ices. you sat down beside guy looking towards the water that had suddenly found a steely glitter under the sun's flat eye and began to strip the foil wrapper from your ice noting with a corner of the mind that it was called gaytime some gaytime i have. i see your boyfriend's found himself a girlfriend at last hes tried hard enough guy sat up suddenly scattering grit and pebbles. dont be silly its a boy. he turned and stared slowly cooly at them well so it is at least its hard to tell whos which out of that pair. im going for a swim coming. he stood up dusting the sand out of the curls on his legs hitching his trunks so that his rose in sharp relief every detail and you looked away quickly hoping no-one else had seen no ill just sit here you go it looks too cold to me hastily closing your eyes and lying back you didn't look at them again.

they werent on the beach when you got there in the morning the child insisting as children do that you should all go to the same spot every day investing it with the immunity of a ritual the magic circle in which nothing could go wrong where the sand must be soft the sun shine a child be good and happy all play long though you had wanted to sit somewhere else not to see them anymore for today he would find someone today courage doubled with his new friend he would hunt down one of the giggling coquetting girls and lie with her beside him on the skyline silhouetted on your horizon.

you didnt want to see you were glad they werent there and when at last they came wandering along the beach swinging their towels and bundles of clothes thonged round with their trouser belts you felt suffocated your mouth full of hot sand bodies pressing you close. here lets sit here again he said giving his friend a push who collapsed laughing into the sand grabbing at his leg to pull him down beside him where they wrestled playfully as you thought only you were aware of a sudden tension that wasnt in the books youd read at school where jones minor punched smith minimus in the ribs and tumbled him in the quad and then they fell back in the sand and lay quite close and you saw or thought you saw fingers touch for a moment and you didn't understand. guy. yeah. those two boys. what about them what are they doing holding hands. i dont understand. hell marie for god's sake dont you know anything theyre a coupla queers. you mean theyre strange in some way. i said queer honey not strange you know pansies homos do i have to spell it men who go with men. but guy how can they. i dont know they just do id have thought that posh school of yours might have told you some of the whys and wherefors you know biology psychology and all that stuff. but what do they i mean. hell how should i know im not like that i could find out if you like the little fair one rather fancies me ive noticed him looking they say they like married men then they can behave just like a woman you know. guy. well you asked me so now you know you get the picture and you thought he fancied you theres the real laugh of it women always like sissy boys they can mother.

somehow the feeling of suffocation had gone you no longer felt hemmed in almost relieved freed in some way though from time to time you looked their way to see what they were doing and in the afternoon when the child said lets go for a walk mummy you were glad to follow her along the water's edge stepping through the warm shallows once you turned and looked back picking out guy from among the other bodies stretched in the sun and you thought thats my husband and i dont care i dont feel a thing i could go on walking along this beach and never go back never see him again and never even think of him and there was freedom in that thought too only the child stumping through the little ripples that splayed out over the ribbed sea-sand carried significance in front of you in the small strong body thats my life my real life you thought and no ones going to spoil things for her shes going to do and have as i never. havent we come a long way mummy you and me all by our selves i cant see daddy anywhere but it doesnt matter because theres you and me here. theres daddy over there darling. doesnt he look little you can hardly see hes daddy mummy do you have to like everybody. not everybody darling you cant possibly there are too many of them. i like you best in the whole world.

stop her your heart thudding at a child's unconscious words she doesnt know what shes saying dont ask it a real adult wouldnt need to but why shouldnt i theres nothing else they took it all away. better than granny and grampy darling. better than anyones else. but granny gives you nice biscuits and sweets. but she doesnt mean it mummy i wont ever have to go and live with granny will i. why should you think that darling. theres a girl in our class lives with her granny all the time i wouldnt ever want to live with somebody else when i grow up i shall always live with you wont i. if you want to. and then when daddy goes away it wont matter. look darling the tides coming in your castle will be all washed away. why cant we stay here always mummy i like it here you like it too dont you youre happy here and daddys here too. we have to go home so that daddy can earn more money and then we can come back next year. but we dont have to go yet do we we have an whole other week first. yes darling another whole week look how quickly the tides coming in now the little waves dashing over the sand further and further in.

whats that mummy what are you drawing its a lady and a man who are they have they got names is it you and daddy theyll be washed away when the waves come the ladys got a funny hat on and the mans got a pipe its granny and grampy isnt it and when the waves come theyll be washed away wont they do you want them to be washed away and then when theyre washed away therell only be you and me and daddy but i cant see daddy hes only a little dot on the sand where we were sitting when will we have to go back to him when the waves come up to here.

and the caricatures of your childhood melted and sank back into the sand under the touch of water flowing on covering and effacing the prints of the past and there was only the barely distinguishable hump that was guy as you took the child's hand and ran together towards him along the edge of advancing water but by some trick of the light falling in your eyes as you ran he didnt seem to get any bigger was just a black smudge against the lighter sand and even as you came up to him and he looked up to you the corrosive words forming in his mouth so that for a moment you saw it full of green acid a trick of the light again from running into the sun even then he didnt seem to grow as you stood there looking down at him a rather too hairy young man who would run to a paunch soon. i see you come running back when you think its time i forked out for tea.

he cant touch me now he cant touch me anymore and you felt free for the first time and the feeling went on growing even when you went home the child silent shut in with the inexorable that the holiday was over. but well come back darling i promise. who says ill bring you cost me a bomb it has. the child's face puckers with misery. dont worry darling if daddy doesnt want to come well come by ourselves you shouldnt upset her shell be sick in the car and then youll be sorry. hey whats this holiday done for you. youll find out youll find out in time. you sat back watching the country fly by the window feeling easy the tension gone out of you. well you look better for your holiday i must say mrs pacey. o i feel it heaps better indeed i do. hey marie where are you going. were going for a walk to the park arent we darling. but what about my tea. o well be home by then and if were not we shant be long and you can wait til we come in or get it yourself. hell what do you think i keep a wife for. i dont know guy really dont tell me later come along darling we dont need coats its still warm enough without. so you strolled in the park together or pushed a swing to and fro in the children's playground laughing at a ragged stray dog making friends with other mothers and children feeding the ducks on the ornamental water and coming home didnt seem so hard to her. its different now mummy why is it different nicer. because we went to the seaside.

you dreamt that night. i am in the garden the garden that was so dry the arid dusty lawn of guy's sunday afternoon in the deckchair of my own empty mornings seen through the grit meshed french windows opening on a desert but now the windows are open the curtains flowing gently easily in a slight draught and i have gone out into the garden because a geyser of pure water fountains in the middle of the lawn streaming up into the sky above my head the water column white with the force that breaks through the crumpling earth like a muscular arm fisting through a flimsy door pane the two boys from the beach are standing hand in hand looking over the fence they nod and smile at me approvingly but it cant stay there in the middle of the lawn someone will notice they will see it on their way to shop the dwarf women and they will stare and point and whisper behing my back. we always knew she was different there was something wrong with her because she would never meet your eyes hooded turned away as if she had something to hide. but i havent we never nothing happened. and now we can see right there in the middle of the lawn and our husbands will see it too on their way home from the station and tonight at the tea-table they will say have you seen the paceys' shush not in front of the children wait til theyve gone to bed i always knew there was something about her though youd never think it to look at her and such a pretty little thing she was when she first came here. i must cover it up ill get a big stone like a paving stone to hold it down and later we can build the child a little playground where she can play ball and no one will know but it keeps comin out round the edges of the stone i pile bricks frantically and as i go to place another a little spurt wells up under my hand and i feel the cool clean water bubble against my palm and trickle away in a brook over flat white stones among shading trees to the river the boys have gone from the fence as i sweat and carry and heap until an untidy cairn stands in the middle of the garden like a heap of rubble stained with the water seep.

you woke sweating but to dream it again and again still you were better as if the dream fountain was itself a release and the child grew and you with her so that you no longer seemed mother and child but two friends. of course you can ask me darling im your friend arent i. guy became a shadowy figure your mother and father no longer troubled you because they no longer existed. she should be wearing little stockings to keep her legs warm in this weather not those socks they dont cover the child's knees. mummy i dont have to wear stockings do i. of course not darling whoever said so. granny said. did she darling i wasnt listening. but you agreed with her you said yes. did i i must have been thinking about something else. she always says things like that. yes i know thats why i dont really listen i think it doesnt mean anything except that she likes to think that she knows best about things still. like when you were a little girl. thats right perhaps ill get like that when im granny's age. but youre not like it now and youre ever so young only sylvia's mother is younger than you.

yes i am young still. but you only said it to make the child give you back the answer you wanted to hear that she thought you were still among the living with possibility before you that there was no great gulf of generation between you. alright i was wrong but what else could i do what else is there. vicarious living you know it doesnt work. yes i learnt didnt i. what else have you learnt. nothing nothing at all i put all my eggs in one basket and the bottom dropped out leaving this mess and im tired of clearing up messes so i said no not anymore and you blame me. is that all. thats all. are you sure why are you keeping your eyes open lie there staring at the white walls the anonymous ceiling the counterpane. counterpain. you cant get away with that anymore youre just making it up you cant fool me i know you too well. alright then since you know it all. we both know but you wont admit it. what are you saying i dont understand. close your eyes let the images come what are you afraid of close your eyes.

youre late tonight darling. we were having a practice. a practice. netball for the match against 2b. but youre not in the team are you. no but im the umpire. i think you might have told me couldnt someone else have been umpire. well you see we didn't know we were going to have a practice till it rained today we should have played them at lunchtime and then it would have all been over but it was raining so we couldnt and miss stevens doesnt think we can beat them because theyre terribly good and mad keen on netball they play all the time because shes their form mistress so we have to practice very hard. how do you know she doesnt think you can win. well because we were playing today and she said wed have to do better than that to beat 2b. she was probably only saying it to make you work harder or perhaps shes a bit jealous and wants her own form to win. o no shes not like that and anyway i think she likes us best you can tell by the way she talks to you. it seems to me you do more than your share of umpiring standing still on a cold windy day like this you ought to be running about more youll be catching a chill you know how you do and then youll have to stay in bed and not go to school and that wont suit you. sometimes i wish youd never passed your eleven plus all you do these days is think about school we dont seem to have any fun anymore like we used to youre either late home or youve got homework to do and you sit up in your own room by yourself reading and im left down here watching the television by myself i shall write to miss stevens and say youre not to do so much umpiring youre to get more exercise and not stand about in the cold blowing a tin whistle. no mummy you mustnt i like it i do much better than playing i want to take my umpire's test and besides if youre umpiring miss stevens comes and talks to you. and whats so marvellous about that. well she says interesting things shes sort of sarcastic but in a funny nice way. do you like miss stevens best then. o yes everyone does and some of her form are absolutely crazy about her i think rosemary ellis makes a fool of herself i think miss stevens likes you better if youre quieter rosemary walks to the station with her when she doesnt bring the car but they dont talk a lot because i followed them once. so thats why youre late home youre following miss stevens and rosemary and hanging about outside i expect to see if shes got her car and hoping rosemary wont be there so you can walk with her instead and who is this miss stevens anyway some stringy games mistress i expect too old to get herself a man and taking admiration from little girls with crushes. o mummy it isnt a crush i just like to talk to her and she isnt old shes about your age i think or a little younger with sort of short crinkly hair. im sick of miss stevens i dont want you to mention her even anymore the kettles boiling its head off you have your tea and go upstairs and do that important homework since thats all that matters to you and ill sit down here by myself all evening again stuck here night after night watching that damn screen til the faces are jumping in front of my eyes whats that. a form for you to fill in miss evans asked us to bring them home. the pta well im not interested i have enough of that school from you. you dont have to go ill tell miss evans you cant come. no ive changed my mind i will go and ill tell miss stevens what i think of all this umpiring and standing about.

the child's face shuts against you and your words no longer reach her but you hear your own voice running on a destructive stream of acid corroding the air between you eating away the bonds of years leaving only the bitter smell of spite the poison of the viper's wound. whats the matter with me what am i saying all this for i dont understand no i mustnt say that mustnt think like that those words i dont understand unlock the door and in comes frisking its tail grinning backing me against the wall until i dont know what im doing or saying any longer like the last time and i retreat further and further down that dim corridor until there are only just the two of us alone in a dusty room where no sound penetrates from outside and even the light comes on muffled paws and i am just a shadow in a room full of shadows no longer marie or even mrs pacey no longer myself. now marie you must concentrate youll never learn to type if you dont put your mind to it ive never met anyone like you you dont seem to make the usual mistakes its your punctuation thats so poor didnt they teach you how to punctuate at school and as for caps and smalls you havent the faintest.

and whats so good about i you wanted to ask why should it be so self-important stalking tall across the page who is this i because it isnt one locked up safely in the brainbox one individual voice i can make my own but now a chorus now a duet silence a child's lonely crying which the i who hears cant comfort being voiceless faceless the self afraid the shadow among shadows in the dusty room alone with the i must understand because if i lose her i shall be alone again shut in myself with the voices demanding contradicting sobbing in my head until i long for silence they recede gone away no never nothing moves the room is empty even of shadows.

what time do i have to be there. half past seven but you wont please mummy. i dont know ill see tell miss evans ill come. you hear the feet dragging up the stairs and you are alone again but this time with something to hold on to a chance. and if i say anything and she never forgives me shuts me out as she did just now better to keep calm it will pass a phase something they all go through and she will come back to you she will always be yours until dont think about that thats in the future years away and anyway she may never but this is now and i have to stop it only i must be clever mustnt let her know mustnt drive her further in make her obstinate like guy there a stronger will than mine his chin must make her think but i need her theres nothing else and weve been happy these last years just when i thought id never be again.

what you doing to the kid marie making her old in the head and so i dont know her my own kid a stranger youll be sorry when you see what youve done in the end. you never come to see us marie i should have thought we have the right to see our only grandchild its obviously the only one youre ever likely to give us i feel sorry for guy sometimes i really do still what you do or dont do between you is your affair that shouldnt affect our position as grandparents anyone would think the child doesnt want to see her granny and grandpa though that may be true of course goodness knows what ideas you may have been stuffing her head with and shes a funny bookish little thing just like you were at her age but i do think now that your father isnt well that she might be encouraged to come and see him you know how fond he was of you as a child and im sure hes just as attached hes always liked little girls better than little boys such a sensitive man.

put on your best spring coat the evenings warmer now stone coloured with the brown velvet collar and perhaps a hat tonight your hair a little dead these last few weeks lacklustre the ends splitting hide it the anxious eyes watch in the mirror from behind the question unasked until you turn and mummy you look absolutely marvellous and so young. thank you darling you dont think ill disgrace you then. outside the house the air is still the lion of march slunk away calm before april tears they break up for easter next week shell be home all day strange to be out of the house alone in the dark guy didnt like having to stay in for once car lights beam past a quieter road now almost an avenue with trees leading to the school a dark sea overhead where branches move gently like weeds in water light from the street-lamps splashing on the sandy pavement tumbling out of the hall windows to lie in pools on the darkened flower beds and lawns push open the door a little breathlessly stand bathed dazzled in the polished bowl of the entrance a wall and two pairs of open swing doors ahead and does it matter which you choose other mothers are entering behind you standing poised as if they might turn and run until a voice reaches out and stays them one of the older girls. can i help you.

move forward try to look at ease after all it isnt the first time youve been here you came for the interview and then again before the first term to hear about rules uniform homework possibilities and you were excited then because it was all working out as youd wanted so why this catch in the throat why is this time any different inside the hall is broken into semi-circles of chairs facing the platform where miss samuels will stand and speak you are placed on the outer horn of one of these marked for the parents of 2a but you hardly notice the nods of the other mother and father or hear the firm words she allows to fall gently into the unrippled bay of the hall you are wondering which she is and how you will know her and if you will have the chance.

tea and biscuits will be served in a moment and you will of course wish to talk to the staff you will find they are all named so that no one can escape the sea of faces ripples evenly but dont turn your head to look for her now there will be time she is there and you will find her. shes an excellent form captain three times now and not a bit affected by it a very steady child is there anyone else you wished to see. we dont take much notice of miss evans mummy shes a bit of an old stick. miss stevens o shell be over there with her own form though i expect shell have finished with most of them now. cross the hall steadily what do you expect stand behind her for a moment while she finishes with someone else a tall father with greying hair now shes free and will turn and look at you feel you there and turn to face you. eyes catch the name pinned on your coat.

mrs pacey you must be linda's mother havent you had any tea yet or would you prefer coffee sit over there mrs pacey and ill fetch you something to drink. turn away stumbling sinking into the chair offered you the words the words beat in your head like surf the white light-washed walls spin as you drown green water closes over you. mustnt not here what would they all think mustnt and anyway its not the same quite different dark and she was what does it mean steady now breathe deeply there she is her back to you again just as linda described her a little younger than you and with short crinkly hair then why memory drowning i dont i dont.

i brought you coffee now what did you want to see me about though i think i can guess you want to know how shes getting on at games because if i remember correctly i was about the only member of staff who didnt write a glowing report for linda last term. it wasnt a bad report. no but it was nowhere near as good as she had for all her other subjects this is terribly difficult there are some girls who just arent any good at games arent the athletic type by nature and linda is one of them it isnt that she doesnt try doesnt work hard she does very but im afraid she will never be in a team of any kind the only thing she is any good at is swimming she has a very steady stroke not fast but quite staying this is why im so pleased shes taken an interest in umpiring lately because it gives me something positive i can say on her report you see its very disheartening for a child and particularly a sensitive girl like linda to feel that shes doing her best trying as hard as she possibly can and not getting anywhere in fact still taking home a bad report.

but the words are flooding over your head and youre not listening for their meaning only to the waves of sound breaking on a distant beach setting an echo booming in the empty caverns of your head you have left so long unexplored unvisited and the sting of salt in old wounds sets your flesh on edge the hair rising on the scalp pricking of sweat in the palms a million silver fish sport in your veins leaping and twisting and the trapped dolphin of the heart thuds its blunt snout against the bleached rib-cage.

murmer something in understanding the words you would have used are dried and rattle like stranded popweed above the high water mark nothing you can do or say now except a polite thankyou and turn away cross the stone-coloured parquet floor of the hall through the righthand set of doors into the entrance past miss samuels' room out into the dark where the wind has risen a little and the branches toss against a sky spumed with cloud look back at the hall a blazing liner run aground with a wrack of wallflowers at its bow and turn into the night. i cant go home i cant go home yet but why not why cant i and why cant i understand i must get away and think.

how long did you walk you cant remember but later you were calmer the tide receded leaving you exhausted in a street not far from home and you drifted through the gate up to the front door somehow found a key opened it and went in where they were both waiting some instinct making you glance quickly at the clock and it was only half past ten a possible hour two faces one anxious the other a yawning discontent. how do i look i wonder not too. the winds getting up its quite wearing just trying to walk against it how have you got on did linda cook you a nice supper. just like you to be back at the last minute to make me miss my nightcap. o i dont know if you went now youd just make it. youre getting bloody smart on the licensing laws. he grumbles to his feet shuffles into a coat the door slams to behind him. mummy you didnt i mean. what darling miss stevens yes i spoke to her she was very nice and explained it all to me now im very tired and i think ill go to bed you should be in bed too.

sleep didnt come as youd known it wouldnt you lay in bed and listened to the wind heard guy come in wondered at the tension that held you rigid in the cold sheets as if some cover holding down a tremendous force were about to be thrown into the air releasing the charge buried in your own flesh suppose tonight you should when guy came up for once but the image of his body and the knowledge that he would make it something hasty and meaningless pushed the thought away it had never worked before why should it now he sat downstairs for a long time hes brought something back with him you thought before he came clumsily up to bed undressed breathing heavily and fell into his bed and asleep you were alone with only his occasional grunting in the dark.

i wanted to understand then for the first time and i tried turning it over how had i looked what had she thought of me just another of the foolish clucking mothers getting on in her thirties with dead hair and eyes. not very bright obviously hardly seemed to understand what i was saying. but im not like that not really i went to a good school i was fond of music and poetry i could have gone on to a training college too only and once i went abroad went south to the sun and all day we lay on the hot sand or splashed in the and she said sit over there marie while i but i dont understand was it the building i mean being at school again that made me think of her and where was she now teaching perhaps in a school like that or married a university wife like those you read about in the papers with two or three children lost gone away no never nothing ever happened.

in the windy morning after theyd both gone i went out of the house following guy's track to the station and bought an excursion get away from it all by train hardly knowing even the most familiar name thin black letters on a white ground vacant although we went there every year now and it might hold a key an answer as it had once before but stepping out of the station i realised i had made a mistake for there was no comfort to be had from the blank eyes of boarding houses hibernating through the off season shuttered fish cafes peeling signs that beckoned in the wind to desolate amusements chained and shrouded until their easter awakening yet the beach must be the same i thought i would walk along the beach and turned against the wind better to have it with me coming back.

what did i really want i forced the question out against the stream of air hurtling along with spray on its lips knowing that i was talking aloud but i didnt care there was no one to hear me and there was an exhilaration in thrusting my words in the teeth of the force that whirled them away in a cloud of sand only to return for more i felt as if i was on the verge of understanding as if the phrase that had echoed in my head again and again pushing me beyond the edge of reality was going to be answered as if i was strong enough to grasp the answer at last and my strength came from this battle with the wind on a deserted beach but not quite deserted ahead was a man with a dog and they too were part of the problem and the answer.

and then nothing came though i struggled on beginning to feel cold and hungry and tired there was nothing that was my answer nothing for me somewhere id lost my chance when i hadnt even known what it was and now i was just an insignificant figure pretending to battle with forces that didnt care or know i existed at some vital point i hadnt understood hadnt known and it had gone away from me and would never come back linda was no longer the child she was herself id seen that yesterday she existed in a world quite apart from me one that would get farther and farther away as time went on and although she was all i had she had to get away from me or i should be repeating the old pattern all over again guy and i no longer existed for each other there was no one.

what happened next. i came to the spot where the two boys had lain those summers ago and i stopped waited while the wind shoved its shoulder in my chest stood there trying to understand what had happened why i had suddenly felt lighter that day i hadnt understood but id got better id been able to go on all these years on that one moment i hadnt understood should i understand it now was that what i was here for. and did you understand. theyre a coupla queers do i have to spell it out for you men who go with men. but i still cant see why it should have made any difference to me why the school should have upset me so much and that teacher except that i was jealous of her i suppose mother losing her only chick. then why did you. there was no answer i turned away back along the beach the magic beach which had failed to free me this time. it wasnt the beach it was you who should have freed yourself the answer is always the same we have to do these things for ourselves. but sometimes we need help someone like doctor bailey or sister and there was no one. all they can do is show you things that you already know inside you but because they understand and accept them you can do the same. i know that now but not then at that moment there was nothing i couldnt see anything.

wherever i looked down the years there was nothing and behind me there was nothing even to remember i might not have been born and i was no longer alive as i had been while i was living the child's life linda had taken her own life on herself and she needed every bit of it if she wasnt to be overcome as id been. you didnt think of what would happen to her if you werent there. i only thought of what might happen if i was that i would find myself in that dusty room again at the end of the shadowed corridor only this time she would be trapped with me and become a shadow too in my nothingness i had never done anything for her except given her a life and then lived on it like a parasite now i would go away and she would grow up strong.

the sleeping tablets were still there in the drawer from when id last needed them i got a glass of water from the bathroom poured them into my hand sat down on the edge of the bed and took them systematically one by one without any feeling of despair or pain only of being already at a great distance from what they call reality then i lay back on the bed and fell asleep.

i wake to this room. when i open my eyes i shall see the flowers no longer burning fiercely beside the bed and the sunsplashed walls of this little ward the white counterpane and the window opposite. who am i lying here in the narrow bed with the world going on outside the window how did i get here and how long. im Marie and I haven't been well. Marie and I are the same one myself lying in the bed looking at the flowers and out of the window. But I cant see anything except a patch of sky with clouds. Why don't I get out of bed and look out of the window? Because there's a wall there isn't there and on the other side of the wall there is. Turn back the covers slowly sit on the side of the bed. Very weak still. I must have been here some time. Slippers under the bed now hold on and ease yourself gently towards the window on these cotton wool legs that are threatening to let you down at any sudden movement. Panting a little lean against the wall and look round the curtain. There's the wall. But it isn't very high I can see over it quite easily and on the other side there's a sort of wild garden with bushes and flower beds rather untidy and paths that wander off out of sight. There's somebody there digging in that bed. It's a woman. Now she's resting looking up at the house, leaning on her fork and looking up. Is she looking at my window? Can she see me? Now she's gone back to her digging again. She looks very content, the fork going in easily under her foot, bend and heave up a chunk of earth, thresh it a little to break it down and then in with the fork again cutting a neat line. It would be good to be out there alone digging or just walking in the garden by yourself looking at buds thrusting through their skins, wallflowers too. Where did I see them last? At the school only it was too dark to see them very well and they were still wind-bitten. Those must smell lovely. What was it I wanted to get away from? The emptiness, I remember. The flowers by the bed, forsythia or is it jessamine I never know, anyway they don't have any smell and the flowers are like bright yellow wax under my fingers.

'Goodness Mrs. Pacey, I wondered where you'd gone.'

'I've been looking out of the window. There's nothing there except the wall and that isn't very high and a garden on the other side with someone digging.'

'That's Miss Birk I expect. She drives the ambulance sometimes and looks after the garden for us. Do you think you should get back into bed now? We don't want you to catch a cold.'

'I've been ill haven't I but I'm beginning to feel much better now.'

'Good. I've brought you some tea and a couple of tablets to take Mrs. Pacey and then you should try to rest quietly til supper time. Dr. Bailey will pop in to see you later on. He'll be pleased to see you're feeling so much better.'

'Is she still there?'

'Miss Birk? Yes she's still there but you mustn't keep getting out of bed, you're not strong enough for that yet. Perhaps Dr. Bailey will allow you up for an hour tomorrow to sit in a chair but you mustn't overdo it at first.'

'The flowers by my bedside.'

'The ones your husband brought?'

'Guy, yes. They're starting to drop.'

'I'll take them away then shall I?'

'Yes, please. Sister?'

'Yes dear?'

'Is thirty-three old?'

'Of course not. Good gracious at thirty-three I'd hardly begun to live.'

'That's how I feel.'

'Now I have to go and take the other patients their tea.'

'Sister how did I get here?'

'Your husband came home early from work to pick up some things and found you unconscious so they brought you here.'

'I'm glad he found me.'

'Will you promise to stay in bed when I've gone and not stand at the draughty window?'

'Is she still there? As long as I know she's still there and I shall see her again, as long as there's time.'

'Oh there's plenty of time before you go home.'

'Home? I don't want to go home yet, not til I've thought it all out, till I've understood completely and know what to do.'

'Dr. Bailey will help you to do that. Now try to get some sleep Mrs. Pacey and promise me, the window?'

'I promise. Sister. My name's Marie.'

'SHE was, oh I don't know, how would you describe it?' said Matt. 'I remember thinking when we were at school together that she was like a tender unopened flower. Do you mind me telling you all this?'

She smiled a little. 'No, why should I? It was all over and done with long ago, long before I knew you.'

'Long before I knew too and there was nothing on her side of course except ordinary friendship. I used to think if any man takes her and hurts her, breaks something so delicate and vulnerable, that was the word I remember now that I used for her in my mind, I thought if anyone does that and I could feel a kind of rage rising inside me and still I didn't know why I should feel like this, not til much later when I got to college and found so much of it there and started to take stock of myself. And then she sent me an invitation to the wedding. I didn't go of course. Now I suppose she's a typical suburban mum with two or three kids a brick box with all the latest gadgets and a commuter husband and the thought of me never crosses her mind. Why should it? I sometimes wonder?'

'What do you wonder?'

'Whether you wouldn't be happier like that.'

'But I love you. If I'd been desperate for that kind of life I could have had it over and again.'

'All your past lovers madam!'

'But I didn't love them, not enough to marry them. Mostly I could see it was something else they were looking for anyway not really me and I didn't want to be a substitute.'

'Still you went to bed with them.'

'Not all, only some, two or three.'

'How many?'

'I don't remember.'

'I thought women were always supposed to remember these things.'

'Men like to think so of course.'

'I wonder if you'll remember what it was like with me.' He said it, he heard himself say it quite deliberately knowing it would hurt, watching the hurt come into her eyes, saying it not to hurt but out of his need, trying to make her say what he wanted to hear her say, to wound her into some defensive answer that would do him for the moment, carry him along a little further. Yet at the same time he thought that it was worthless a reply forced out like that as if he'd twisted her arm and childish of him to need it. 'I've learnt nothing,' he thought, 'still a kid crying out for mother-love. Why can't I stand up by myself and not need to be reassured, given lollipops, and anyway you know you won't get them there, you know you won't so why keep on trying.' He took a step forward and put his arms round her, holding her so that her head rested against his shoulder. 'I'm glad I'm taller than you, that you're only little. What time did you say we'd be there?'

'If we get there by half past eight we can get a seat near the band. It's not so noisy up there.'

Blades of light scythe through the dark air mowing down the night in swathes that fall blackly from the lamp-path, lying thick in the gutter and at the roadside. Inside the car is warm and drowsy with the scent of her body. She puts a light hand on his thigh and he is conscious of them both rushing under dark branches, cut off from the rest of the world by a thin skin of glass and painted metal, hurried along together in its soft upholstered belly. He winds down the window.

'No wonder the advertisers exploit the car as a womb symbol.'

'Oh there's too much of that.' She withdraws her hand to light a cigarette, making a small glow that comes and goes in the blackness like the fading and blooming of a blown ember. 'Everything's a symbol of something else. What happens when you get to the something else?'

'How do you mean?'

'Well draw a car and it's a symbol of a womb, draw a womb and what have you got?'

'Motherhood I suppose. Except that wombs are pretty unprepossessing things, rubbery and clinical like pigs' hearts in a butcher's window only really signifying surgery and pain and death unless you express them in abstract terms. You know figurines like the ones in Blegen's *Troy*. They puzzled me for a long time, trying to see them as representations of the mother goddess without arms or legs like a mutilated Aphrodite. I didn't see why they should have made them like that. After all they had eyes. They knew humans had arms and legs so why not whatever gods or is total anthropomorphism a late decadent development. That can't be because the neolithic ones are closer to the original human shape and they're earlier. So they must have progressed towards greater abstraction. Those little blobs on top of bigger blobs are too crude for failed females, if you see what I mean, for people who lived in walled cities and made fine pots and bronzeware. But if they were abstractions, symbols of a desired fertility what would they mean to an ordinary little woman touching the rough stone with a sort of fierce reverence to bring her a son. It would be the essence of womanhood surely, her own womb with the child in it. That's what I think they mean.'

'But a womb isn't that shape is it with a child in it?'

'No, but then they wouldn't know that unless they went in for cannibalism which there isn't any evidence for. I mean they wouldn't have seen inside a human body. Animals yes but even then not animals carrying young. They were very selective in their slaughtering as far as we can tell from the bones. They soon learnt about killing the goose that laid the golden egg. A newborn child or calf must look rather like that particularly if it's born in a caul which is traditionally supposed to be lucky. So I could be right, though I can't really prove it of course. It comes under the heading of beliefs and ritual and you know how the old die-hards hate that, shy away from it. That's the trouble with so many of the interesting things, you can't prove them and I'm not even in a position to try.'

'Well.'

'Oh I know it's my own fault but there we are. We've been into all that and it's entirely my own choice but it doesn't stop me thinking even if I'm nothing but a greasy mechanic all day. Anyway you're the sixth drawer of chamber pots in the country so one of us is making a contribution to the total sum of knowledge. The cause goes forward. Funny it should have been just that I found in the wood and it was before you got this job too so I couldn't have been influenced. The female symbol to represent them all. But you don't believe in all that of course.'

'I've heard too much of it. "You are walking through a wood and suddenly you come upon the utensil. What is it?" I take it with a good big pinch that's all. Did you know I've got a diploma from an institute that says I'm an expert in these things?'

'I've never seen it.'

'There are a lot of things you haven't seen yet. I'll get it out and show you some time.'

'So having been through it you end up thinking it's a lot of old eye-wash?'

'Not all. There's something there of course but they make a system out of it, wrap it up in fancy words, and then it gets into the wrong hands, the unqualified, trading on the fact that it's a field where everyone tries his hand a little just in the course of everyday life rubbing against other people, you know.'

'See that silly bugger can't wait, has to nip in and cut me up; about six inches between him and that lorry and he'll go home and tell his wife what a good driver he is, how smart. I'm doing just over thirty so what was he doing? Come off the by-pass I suppose. Thank God I don't have to use up my aggression that way. There we are? a perfect example of what you were just saying.'

'You use yours other ways.'

The suggestion prickled the hairs at the back of his neck. 'You're a bad girl when I'm driving.' He heard her smile in the dark inside of the car, with a low sound in the throat, and knew how her face would be though his eyes never leave the road. The car runs out from under the intricate vaulting of plaited branches the bare flanks of the common drop back from the pressure of marching houses outcropping from the core of the city, sprouting from the tarmac skin along the radiants. He took his right hand from the wheel and gestured. 'The urban sprawl they call it but what's the use of kicking; we belong to an urban civilisation and we might as well accept it and use it. You know I often imagine all those hundreds in their tiny bedrooms at the top of the parental mansion in Lugton and Bigthorpe and Bumpstead Major making the great decision about themselves and throwing their battered suitcases on the narrow beds, packing slacks and pullovers, shirts and socks with clocks, bought secretly and only worn in their own rooms, taking a last look in the mirror, a last look round at the cell where they first came to consciousness that they could never grow into the pattern set for them, feeling their desires running out over the edges of the mould, slopping out their parents would have said if they'd ever dared to tell them, or just knowing themselves made of a strange alloy that would never gell at the normal temperature, the die not take, never be stamped in the resistant flesh; sleeking back their hair and murmuring to the sallow features in the glass, you are, yes you are different, and turning and snapping the locks to on the case, taking hold of the handle, opening the door and shutting it firmly behind, going down the stairs with the memories, the demands, plucking at a sleeve whispering in an ear and falling back as the front door closes; down the road, no one can stop me now, and caught up in a train hurrying South or East to a life they've only dared to imagine between sleep and waking.'

'But will it be dreams when they get here? Do they really have to come?'

'Not if they're like you perhaps. If the war hadn't moved you, you'd have probably still been there, married to a bank manager with a nice house and a couple of children, but people like me and, say David, what could we do against the pressures of a small-town closed society? Our only answer is to up and run, lose ourselves in the shelter of the city.'

And the train pulls in, draws its length along the platform kerb, brakes wheezing with the effort, doors flung open, watch that door, opening on the foam of fairy seas, breaking against the barrier white surf of faces, all your tickets please, and the station booming like the public baths with echoes of feet, voices, slamming metal bouncing off the glass and girder roof. A female voice amplified as if the deity speaks from the throat of some brass idol sends its commands flying in scattered fragments of sound incomprehensible as the delphic oracle to strike the inattentive with apprehension and trembling. Step through, give up your ticket, all tickets please. Where do we go from here? Up to now it's been easy. Get on a train and the machine will make all the decisions, carry you across country once you've set its wheels in motion, and spill you out of its tired belly at the appropriate time, a little late perhaps as the timetable shows but time enough for you with nothing in front of you. Almost as you draw through the suburbs you would hold the wheels back now with a braking will but set going like a sentence half spoken and regretted there's no drawing back and now you're on your own, beyond the man in uniform taking away your pass to security the decisions are all yours; resume responsibility for the feet that move you into the dour entrance hall, the place of transit where even the tramps and the meths drinkers, the hooked at the end of a visionary high who clog the benches for a little, are only passing through though they sit humped, motionless as statuary, limp hands crossed, or shuffle uneasily in their stale clothes, migrants brought down on this draughty perch by a sudden squall of down on your luck. Leave them; continue up the ramp and pause at the top of the steps. At your feet thunders the river of the Euston Road. You stand on the bank, held above the flood that sweeps along cars, buses, lorries; straws, leaves, logs whose waters are the dark waves of hurrying taxis. Go down, immerse yourself in the stream that can hide your past in the anonymous swirl of its waters until you no longer even remember yourself, the hurts soothed, the edges smoothed away.

'Taxi Miss?'

She shook her head and began to move aimlessly in any path that her feet would take, down the row of parked cabs with their drivers reading newspapers, a fat man leaning in at a window in sidelong furtive talk, and down towards the street, the roar increasing with every step and breaking over her as she passed through the ungated portal, blanketing out all thought, all ability to decide anything until she was brought to a stop again like a stupefied hunted animal and leant against the wall, holding on tight to the case and breathing quick and shallow.

But it's no good, she thought, I can't just stand here, must move, get somewhere. The address, find the address. She dug in her pocket, wanting to put the case down and search properly but what was it they said at home? Never put your case down in a London street or they'll whip it away from under your nose before you've time to look round. So she hung on and struggled, aware she was wearing too many clothes and it wasn't as cold down here. Still I couldn't have packed them anyway and they had to get here somehow. I can't imagine them sending anything on.

It came out at last, the scrubby back of an envelope where she'd written it down as Babs had given it to her. 'There's the Y.W. of course,' she'd said, 'if you're really stuck or the cops will always find you somewhere but I always try to keep clear of them. Well you never know do you? Not that I ever but anyway that's all over now and I'm a respectable married woman. But you, what're you after down there? I mean you're not the type. You're clever? Funny how we hardly spoke at school and now I'm telling you all this.' 'I've no one else to ask and you promised not to tell them anything.' 'And neither I won't. Besides it's a big place London is. They tell me there's like eight million there and I can believe it. You'll see when you get there. Like looking for a French letter on Hollheath. What you going for Cathy? Won't you ever come back? You will, you see, just like me, when you're ready to settle.'

Southgate Terrace, it said, Bayswater. She looked up at the buses but they were bowled along in the stream and none of them said Bayswater on the front, not even in the smaller print and they might be going in the opposite direction. Best to walk on the way she was going until she came to a policeman or to another station and it was a good day for walking even with a suitcase heavy with all your life up to that point, and a bit of a sun shining although far away through the haze of fumes and smoke and everyone seemed very brisk and busy as she passed a huge building site where men in orange tin hats drove tractors, mixed and poured concrete or simply walked about with plans and schedules clipped to bits of board looking purposeful under the raking shadow of the giant crane that lowered a ton of steel girder as gently as a woman picking strawberries. 'Aye, they're always building summat down there like kids with a box of bricks but dammall we get done up here and where would they be wi' out us any road?' she heard her father saying and she would have liked to have stopped on the observation platform, provided by the company for the amusement of passers-by with a bird's eye view, among the smart poster men in their bowler hats that she'd thought had all gone long ago apart from the picture house since foremen had given up the fashion and her father had put his carefully away in a brown paper bag at the top of the wardrobe.

Then, across the road, she saw the station, Warren Street it said, with people coming and going like ants from the nest on a summer's day and she crossed the road waiting first for the stream to be dammed by the red light. What does this remind me of, this going down a hole in the ground? How do I know where to go? That's where you get your ticket, phone boxes, a map. You are here. Now if I stand here and just look through all the places eventually I'll find it. There's the river Thames. Would it be North or South of that? There doesn't seem to be much in the South. Nowhere in the middle; they're all famous names. The Right will be the East End and it isn't there. Somewhere near the park, she said. Which park? Hyde Park? That's the only one I know of. There ought to be an easier way of doing this. Supposing I get lost among eight million people. Well I just find a station and try again. Hyde Park Corner, Marble Arch, Queensway, Bayswater. There it is. Now how do I get there? Go back to square one. You are here. I'll write it all down so I don't forget. From here to Tottenham Court Road, then the red line, where's the key, that's the Central to Notting Hill Gate, then the yellow line, that's the Inner Circle to Bayswater. Go West young man is the answer.

Her voice sounded high and strange as she asked for her ticket and she put down half-a-crown and pushed it towards the man thinking that would be enough if she didn't understand what he said. A dark skinned girl in the official uniform clipped her ticket, the first time she'd seen one off the screen though she thought they had them in Bradford, and she stepped on to the moving staircase, all luggage dogs and perambulators must be carried, and they had one of those in Bradford too in a big store. The platform seemed very narrow and the drop on to the glinting rails almost enticing so she drew her eyes away and looked at the other travellers who were all shapes, sizes and colours as she'd noticed up in the street. Well among all of them who'll notice me; eight million and all looking so different like hundreds and thousands or dolly mixtures.

The journey was long and nerve-racking because like a sailor at night she had to continually check her course by the points 2f the compass and by the fixed star of Bayswater. Emerging into daylight again she felt tired and hungry, the case too heavy, and she still had to find the road. Once again she was bewildered by the different faces of the crowds hurrying past. No one looked like a resident, someone who could be trusted with directions. Like the people in the station they seemed to be just passing through. Then she saw the policeman waving his arms at the traffic and dragged her case across to his island. He brought out his little book and thumbed over the pages. 'You'd have done better to go to Queensway.' Her mind staggered and then steadied itself to concentrate on the directions. He seemed fairly cheerful about her prospect of getting to Southgate Terrace and carried along by his optimism and her first communication with another human being in this city, she walked down two streets, changing hands on her case at every sixth lamp-post and turned Right into a row of high white houses with late classical porches at the top of shallow steps.

'How long did you want it for?' the woman asked staring at Cathy round the half-open door.

'I thought perhaps four days.'

'Nights; we go by nights here. A guinea a night, twenty-one shillings, in advance. Alright?' The girl nodded. 'You look very young to me. Not run away? I don't want no trouble, no men in your rooms after twelve o'clock.'

'I'm nineteen.'

'That's alright then. Long as you're over age. I'll show you your room.' She opened the door fully, let the girl step past her into the hall and shut it again after her. 'How did you find us? Someone recommend you?' She led the way upstairs.

'I was just passing and thought . . .' She had decided at once not to mention Babs. From her own account she'd led a pretty hectic life while she was here and who knows why she'd left or whether a friend of hers would be welcome. The woman paused on the half landing; pushed open a door. 'That's the lounge and breakfast room. Breakfast is at eight if you want it.'

Cathy wondered why she shouldn't want it having paid for it but suspected that she might find the answer next morning. She had noticed a strange smell as she stepped into the hall, a smell that grew stronger as they climbed until it seemed concentrated in a solid mass behind a curtain on the second landing. Again they paused while it was drawn aside to reveal a small gas cooker, a vintage model like they had at home which seemed to be hand-made in wrought iron, its enamel surfaces pocked and lined like a lino cut, its black metal coated with brown grease that would cling against all assaults of hot soda water, vim and the scrubbing brush while leaving the water with a thick lees of rust and mud. 'You can cook any meals you want here.' She picked up a pan half full of some rich sauce the origin of the strange aroma. 'Curry; the Indian gentlemen use a lot of it. Students. Don't care for our food much.' She put back the pan, drew the curtain and led the way on up to the third floor where another door opened to her push. 'This is the room.' She crossed to the window and drew back the curtains, letting light in.

It seemed to be clean and there was a wash basin in one corner. The coverlet on the bed was well washed too. Cathy put down her case and dug in her pocket for her wallet. She hoped she had enough without rummaging about in her case in front of the woman for the extra she'd put aside. 'And you must never let 'em see how much you've got or they'll have it off you before you can say knife.' She heard her father's voice and remembered the strange expression with which he'd leant forward on that last word as if it were a blade unsheathed in his hand. She held out a five pound note.

'Oh thank you dear. I hope you'll be very comfortable. I'll give you your change later; I've nothing on me at the moment.' She folded the note carefully and put it away into the side pocket of her crumpled green slacks. 'The bathroom and W.C. are just across the hall. Baths are two and six and I must have warning in advance. The front door's open all the time, just turn the handle. I always say I've got nothing to hide or steal. There's a bolt on the inside of your door in case you think you need it. Some do, some don't. The sheets are clean. I always change my sheets for a new person. If you decide to stay longer you'll let me know as soon as possible won't you? I can always let my rooms; turn people away all the time. There's no prejudice in this house. I find the coloured gentle-men most agreeable mannered.'

The door closed behind. I don't know her name, Cathy thought, but I don't suppose it matters much. She sat on the bed and looked round the room. Then she got up, slid the bolt into position and sat down again. All at once she felt sick with weariness and reaction. I must have something to eat or I shall be howling my eyes out. Go out and find a cafe that's it. Ought to unpack really but that can wait. I wonder how many other people have sat here like this on this bed, and if there were many like me. There doesn't seem to be a key. What do I do about my money? Take it with me I suppose.

She put the case on the bed and unlocked it. As the lid sprang back from the expanding clothes inside, she paused and turned. Behind her was a dressing table with a mirror. With slight variations the room was almost a replica of the one she had left that morning and for a moment she felt the walls closing in to stifle her again, as if she had never left, never travelled two hundred miles into the afternoon. But there was no bolt on her door at home. Will they know yet? Will they have found the note? Well, there's nothing they can do. I'm over age, whatever she meant by that, anyway too old to be brought back even if anyone cared enough to try. Don't you like it here with us? she used to say, and now it won't matter anymore. But I'll have to be careful with my money. It won't last long. Tomorrow I'll look for a job; not libraries though, something quite different. After all if I don't like it I needn't stay. No one will know; no one'll say that three jobs in three months is a sign of bad blood somewhere but then you never can tell what you've got to contend with when they're not your own. No one can say that again or if they do I'm not there to hear it. Among all these eight million people there isn't one who knows or cares a damn. I suppose some people would find that lonely but I don't. If anyone does come to know or care it'll be because they want to and because I want them to not because they have to or feel they do. That's what I want; that's why I'm here.

She shut and locked the case again and stood it neatly beside the wardrobe. She counted the money that was left. It had taken her a year to save at a pound a week out of her small salary and it had seemed a fortune but she knew how expensive London was. Hadn't he told her? Spend brass like water down there. Don't know how ordinary folk get by except they must earn a deal more than us and do a damn sight less for it. Such a fortune it'd seemed that she'd spent five pounds on clothes, on a three-quarter length donkey jacket and a pair of navy jeans with fly fronts, going all the way into Bradford to buy anonymously in the big camping and sportsgear shop, and smuggling them home when she knew the house would be empty. Then as a last useless gesture, a meaningless blood price since they weren't of her blood, a niggardly conscience money for how can you ever repay them for taking you out of that home and bringing you up as you were their own, she had tucked two five pound notes into the envelope she'd left on the hallstand. The fare had surprised her, taking a huge bite out of what was left.

'Return?' the man has asked.

'No single.' She'd wanted to add, 'I shan't be coming back,' but it had sounded too much like tempting fate and she found herself suddenly superstitious. Now she had about twenty-five pounds left. At seven guineas a week plus food she had less than a fortnight and then? Panic ran acid in her mouth and churned in her empty stomach. A job and a room, she thought, or should it be the other way round? Now which way do I go to find something to eat? Back towards the main road and the station I should think. Must remember which turnings I take so that I can find my way back again. What about that then? La Pasta. Menu in the window. Let's see how much. Yes that'll do. Just like the one at home only a bit more plush and only sixpence up on every price which isn't bad considering. She wished she'd brought a book but the few she'd brought with her were still packed in the bottom of her case. Even a paper so that she wasn't forced to sit and stare round. Like a gaping provincial though they're an interesting enough collection. I wonder what they'd think to them at home. But I mustn't keep on wondering that as if what they think really matters when I've come all this way just to find out whether it does or not, whether their way's right and the only way to get born and grow up, get married to the boy next door and have children and that's that, the cycle complete and your life only to be lived in theirs ever after. The terrible questioning year after year: what's wrong with me, am I the only one, what do I really want and then when the answers began to come and all the parts of the equation resolved themselves to a^2 on one side, nicely finished off, and y on the other. But no that won't do. Perhaps it should be $a + b = a^2$ and where do I find someone to make the square? Must be light headed thinking like this. Let's hope this is mine coming now before I float right off the chair and out through the door. Imagine the headlines in the paper. They'd say, must be our Cathy she always was a bit strange. I'll have one of those rum baba things after from that trolley over there and then two cups of coffee and I'm ready to start taking things in.

Over coffee she took up the problem again, spooning the layer of froth into her mouth like icecream and watching the people passing the window through a bead curtain of condensed steam. The first thing to do was to buy a map of London like they'd had in the reference library, then she needn't have this continual horror of getting lost. Tomorrow she must look for a job. How do you begin? The evening paper I expect and the local labour exchange so I'll have to find the nearest public library where I can read the papers with all the other down and outcasts and ask where the exchange is. But not today. Today I'm going to have to myself to walk about. I'm free at last, don't have to be home for tea because it's been cooked for me and it'll spoil if I'm not there on the dot and that'll be another sign that I don't belong, that I'm not one of them because he's always punctual to his tea, you could set your clock by him, and where would I be any road since I haven't a boy friend that they know of though if she had we'd be the last to hear you can be sure of that. There I go again thinking along the same old track and what's the use of coming all this way just to do that. I'll save that other coffee til later; go out now and find some shops, get a map, walk about, maybe go to the picture house, anything, anything I like.

The streets seem friendly and the air alive. She is bumped and brushed past but she doesn't mind and wanders on taking a different turning to find herself at another station. They'll have a map at that bookstall I bet, then I'll find somewhere to sit and sort out where I am. She turns away from the station mouth and sees across the roar of traffic a wall and above it the moving arms of trees veiled lightly in small green leaves and the suddenness of them in that place maker her more aware of this coming Spring and its possibilities than she has ever been of any changing season before.

Pretty, how pretty and I never expected it not here. So often they said to me how lovely the moors were with their changing colours and sunlight and cloud shades passing over them and how I didn't appreciate the beauties of nature, wasn't natural they meant, and I couldn't see what they were getting at, to me they were just waste, wasted on you they said, miles of rough moistureless-looking grass in various tones of beige and putty with the black outcroppings of stone. You ought to like it they said, after all you're named for one of the characters in a great book about these parts, but they hadn't read it and if they had they'd have known there was never anyone less like her than me. Heathcliff now that'd be more like it. All those wild speeches he makes to her about how if she'd only had faith in her love and dared to flout convention instead of betraying it for pretty clothes and parties are just the kind of things I might say to someone. The dark outcast, cuckoo in the nest, where do I find my Cathy?

Here, here it is, the Bayswater Road and on the other side Kensington Gardens and Hyde Park. Which way shall I go? Over into the park and walk about among those trees? No, I'll save that, just knowing it's there is enough for now. What happens at the end of this road? Marble Arch and Oxford Street. That's the way then. Shall I walk or take a bus. There seem to be long queues. Must be nearly the rush hour. They have that in Bradford too. Walk then, you're warm enough. Catch sight of yourself in one of those windows. Don't look so bad either the jacket and jeans. Glad I bought them now though it was a bit of a wrench at the time parting with five whole weeks savings in half an hour. And nobody turns to look. Have you noticed that? At home I wouldn't have got twenty yards up the high street without all the wives and the lads turning, screwing their necks for a good eyeful. And how much more sensible they are on a windy day like this, hint of rain up there too. Look at those clouds and the blue bits between just a bit overbright. Those girls in their full skirts and long thin legs in nylons and a couple of straps for shoes must be fair starved. Funny to be walking past buses looking in at all those faces and not one I know or who knows me. Not many bikes either, all cars with one person in taking up half the road and moving at a snail's pace. There goes a lad on a scooter passing them all. Good lad, that's the way to do it. No sense in hanging back with that lot.

It's farther than it looks on the map; still I must be getting along now, uphill too. All those squares and streets with trees on the left must have been very fashionable once. It must have been easier living in those days, easier to disguise yourself and go away where nobody knew you. Heathcliff for instance, went away and made his fortune in America and came back to claim his Cathy, only she'd given him up, never really believed he'd do it, and now he had all the girls after him. What was it they called it in that book: wish fulfilment and so I suppose not really true. But it's a nice thought all the same when you've been starved of . . . of what? What was it they didn't give me? Affection? No, not really, at least no less than a lot of children. Appreciation, that's it, appreciation of myself, of my individuality, what I am and can do rather than what they want of me or think I ought to be.

What's this now, the whole road opening out into a square with traffic tearing round at a tremendous rate. How do I get past this lot? That must be Marble Arch itself over there. I see: if you can't go over you go under, down the subway with all the other ants and up the other side into Oxford Street. And then what? Another cup of coffee I think and then the pictures and an early night. Enough for one day. I've got plenty of others.

The picture was foreign, the seat pneumatically comfortable and expensive. When she came out a little dazed from trying to follow the colloquial French and the erratic sub-titles at the same time, the street seemed just as full of people and cars, light fell in great washes over the pavement from the plate glass windows of the big stores. Cathy ate an egg on toast in a snack bar and then walked slowly back the way she'd come, surprised to see that the sky above the park wasn't black or even blue but glowed a sombre red as if the whole city were on fire. Hell some people would call it, she thought, but I like it. It gives you a feeling of warmth and excitement, and all these people walking about as if it was a summer's holiday whereas at home at this time its as dead as wakes week with everyone glued to the little box, shut up in their own living rooms like they were boxed up already and waiting for the hearse to cart them away. That's what they'll be doing now. They'll have worked out what to tell the neighbours and relations about me to save face and now they'll be sitting there able to watch what they like without feeling my silent criticism seeping over the edges of my book and gathering in a corrosive pool on the best carpet. Oh it's best for all of us I'm sure of that at this moment when it's done and if anything I should be beginning to feel lonely and that it's all a terrible mistake.

As she turned the handle and stepped into the hall the smell of cooking was even stronger than before and climbing the second flight she saw that one of the other residents was busy at the stove alternately stirring the contents of two saucepans with a wooden spoon. He turned towards her as she reached his level, bowed with his spoon and held out a thin brown hand.

'Good evening. You are new here. I am Nala. So pleased to meet you. How do you do. You are staying long? You are English? Do you like curry? I make very good curry. You must come and have supper in my room.'

Cathy shook hands with him, mesmerised by the flutter of questions and wondering which, if any, it would be wise to answer.

'You are hungry? You like some curry?'

'Thanks very much but I've just eaten and I'm rather tired. Another time perhaps.'

'Next time I shall insist. Tomorrow. Good night. Sleep well. I am very pleased to meet you.'

'Most agreeable mannered,' she thought as she closed and bolted the door behind her, but I wonder how you say no.

Finding a job turned out to be easy. It even suggested itself. At breakfast there were only two of them, herself and what looked like a middle-aged business man who'd made a dreadful mistake in coming there and was leaving at once. The cornflakes were stale and took on a tough rubbery consistency as she poured the milk on. The egg too had been left to keep hot and lose all flavour in the oven while the meagre slice of bacon shrivelled beside it. The girl who served them swore at the hot plates, plonked down a plateful of hewn hunks of stale brown bread and slopped the tea on the cloth. She seemed barely awake, hair uncombed, red feet in soiled mules. There was no sign of Nala or any other of the gentlemen, perhaps being students they didn't get up too early.

Cathy was glad to get out of the house and into the air which was colder this morning and a little stale as if it had been up all night. It needs a shower to give it a good wash, she thought, still it's better than in there. I don't think I care for curry with all my meals but if I've paid for them I feel I ought to eat them just to make my money go farther. Shall I take a bus or walk? The eternal question here when you don't know how far you might be going. I wonder where the public library is. I doubt if it'd be much good asking Madame What's-her-name. I shouldn't think she spends the long evenings with a book. Here's the station again and there's a bus. What's that on the side of it? Join London Transport as a driver or conductor. Why not? Hey it's off. Where do I go to join?

'So you start your training tomorrow,' the man in the peaked cap said. She nodded. 'Subject to your being satisfactory of course you'll be running up and down stairs like nobody's business in a couple of weeks. Do you think you'll stand it?'

'Oh I'm used to being on my feet all day.'

'Good girl. We'll see you in the morning then.'

And now all I need is a room and I'd better be quick about it for I shan't have much time for looking once I start work. I wonder how you go about that here. I think I'd like to be somewhere not too far from here. It's such a big place this London you could go on looking for miles til you were dropping in your tracks and your shoes walked through to your socks but I've fallen here and I'd like to stay here. Funny that they always said I was rootless, would never settle to anything but I want to settle here where I suppose there must be one of the most shifting collections of people in the world, people like Babs and Nala. I wonder if she found them agreeable-mannered. That's something she won't have told them at home, and then coming back and marrying that little wisp of a chap that'll live and die a moulder in Bilthorpe's.

He must have been waiting for her, she decided, waiting for her to come in. There was a soft scratching at the door, and when she drew back the bolt as silently as possible and opened it Nala was standing there smiling.

'Have you eaten yet? I do hope not because if you remember we have a date. You have promised to eat curry in my room this evening and it will be ready in a very short time.'

She didn't remember promising but she nodded her head and asked him the number of his room. Perhaps he could tell her where to find somewhere to stay or at least how to begin looking and he seemed very friendly. She remembered something about the

Colonel's lady and Susie O'Grady being all the same under the skin but wasn't sure how it fitted this particular moment.

'Come in please,' he called to her as she reached the open door. She stood just inside for a moment, not sure what to do next, watching him flit about the room with light quick movements. Darting at the bed he plumped a couple of bright scatter cushions which didn't wince or give in their tight jackets and waved her into position on what had become an eastern divan with one graceful gesture of his hand. 'Please sit down and make yourself comfortable. Here is a magazine. If you excuse me I go and finish my cooking.' He laughed, bowed and was gone.

She sat down obediently on the bed and opened the magazine. It seemed to be full of people talking in groups and turning to smile at the camera, attending garden parties, reviewing troops, opening huge modern buildings that looked like hospitals or colleges, and everywhere the sun shone, hands were raised in gestures of benediction, faces smiled while keeping their repose and dignity, and the shadows were steep and black. Then came a series of pictures showing a lot of obviously poor men sitting in a rough circle on the ground listening to a very serious address from a man in a very light western suit; old men talking together gravely, a little girl with wild straggling hair and thin twig-like limbs barely supporting the potbelly of malnutrition, her eyes showing only the apathy of hunger, and finally a group of doctors preparing for an operation. After this there was a splendid shot in colour of an elaborately carved temple in red stone and then another garden party. The women, she thought, looked particularly beautiful with their calm faces and sad eyes above the bright painting of their saris.

'That one is my father,' Nala had come silently into the room bearing two heaped platefuls of rice and sauce. Would he shut the door? Cathy wasn't sure whether she wanted him to or not. With it open anyone going up or down stairs would see her sitting on the bed eating but once it was shut she had a feeling that the situation would develop too rapidly in the close intimacy of the small bedroom. He put the two plates on the dressing table and closed the door. 'You see, that one there. He is a very important man in our country. My father sends me this paper always when he is in it. You have not eaten curry before?' She shook her head. 'You will find it very hot therefor I am giving you a glass of water to take with it. Also I have a bottle of wine for us to drink.'

'But I thought you didn't drink anything intoxicating.'

'Oh that is only the religious people and the Moslems. I am not religious. It is very terrible for my father because he is a very religious man. He fasts and he does not live with my mother but searches for his true self. But it is not too bad for him after all because his religion teaches him that the wheel spins and I too will be old and religious one day.'

'So he's just like all the fathers then.'

'Oh exactly, the old men are all the same. They land us in a pretty mess and then they say, one day you will be like us and you will understand all the difficulties we have had. I have written all these things to my father and he has answered me that I am very young and too much influenced by the ideas I learn from my western teachers at college. You like the curry? It is very good. Because it is your first time of eating I do not make it too hot. Also the wine is good with it. Let me fill you up. It is good for you. I see you are rather pale and it will give you a good colour in the face.'

'It's strange to think of you disagreeing with your father all those miles away.'

'Oh that is why I came here. One day I said I am going away to learn what they do in other countries about all these problems and so I came here to be a student at the London School of Economics.'

'And he didn't try to stop you?'

'Oh no. Really he is very proud of me and it is good for him to be able to say my son is studying economics because that is what we need more than anything else. You see this picture? That is a most terrible thing that it should have to be. Because there are so many people in my country and every year more children, too many mouths to feed and everywhere hunger in the streets now they have a big campaign for sterilisation. Here you see they are talking to the poor people telling how much the government will pay them to have no more children. And all this is because they have not thought of all this a long time ago. Here is a picture of a temple.'

'It's very beautiful. All those carvings; every square inch of it covered.'

'Yes they are very fine but it is a good job that you can't see them very well too close because they are very frank carvings of the old ways of the religious legends.'

'I've seen some of them. *The Karma Sutra* we had it in the library on the closed shelf of course, not for the general public except on request but I thought a lot of the pictures were very good.'

'Ex-actly. They are very good for those who understand them but when there is no understanding . . . Now it is the fashion in my country to say among the educated and the middle class that they are very bad and we are becoming as narrow minded as the old lady Queen Victoria. Now they say we must be like my father and not sleep with my mother and we must all practise the karma yoga which will liberate us from the tyranny of the body like Christian monks and nuns. But of what use is it to say this to a man who must work very hard all the days for a little rice and only have holiday on a feast day of the gods when he will remember the old stories of the loves of Krishna and sleep with his wife because that is the only happy moment in his life. For too long the rich, old religious men have despised the body and its vital life and it has grown unchecked until now it will swallow them and all their prayers all together in one great hungry mouth. So I write my father.'

'And he was angry?'

'No because it is a terrible thing to be angry. You must not be concerned with such trivial matters for it would only be your pride that makes you angry and that is bad for you. And so you see nothing is done. Then one day all the poor men who have any strength left in their weak bodies will become communists and kill them all and take over the country and they will die with very surprised looks on their faces. Oh yes I see it all ex-actly how it will be.'

'Are you a communist then?'

'Good gracious that too would be a terrible thing, very terrible. I would not dream of such a thing. Excuse me, I talk too much about these things and I will bore you.'

'Oh no I think it's all very interesting. It all seems very obvious to me the way you put it.'

'That is most kind of you to be interested in my problems. But that is another thing; the women of my country are still not altogether emancipated. Some of them yes but not many to whom I could talk as I am talking to you. It is so pleasant to sit like this and have intelligent conversation with a charming young lady. In my country this is not possible. Oh you can't imagine how good it is for me to have someone to talk to like this. Mrs. Hardcombe is always most willing of course but she is a little too old and she frightens us.'

'Frightens you?'

'She is like the man-eating tiger. She would devour us until there are only our shoes left. I have been so lonely but now you have come and everything will be alright. I am such a Romantic. It is because of my name. Nala was the name of a great king in one of the stories who suffered much for love. He fell in love before he had even seen the most beautiful Dalmayanti. Have you enjoyed the curry? Now we shall finish the bottle of wine and you shall talk to me. I am longing to hear all about you. Excuse me one moment while I wash the plates.'

She wondered whether she should offer to help him but there seemed so little to do and the wash-basin was so small that she decided it would be safer to stay where she was or even to get up and walk around the room, look at the magazine again, the few books and pictures while watching Nala at the same time, the light graceful movements that fascinated her with their subtleness and femininity. Yet although he was slight and no taller than herself, his hands as slender as a dancer's, his eyes large and fringed with long fine lashes, she realised that he was not at all girlish and would have been very surprised to think that she had ever considered him so for a moment. The other men in the magazine all looked the same yet they were so potent that mass sterilisation had to be initiated to stop the population devouring itself. She remembered an old book they'd had in the library called *Mother India* which was all about the miseries and pains of Indian women, and the sad calm faces at the garden parties, the harems and the child marriages. There had been periods in English society too when the men had seemed almost effeminate. They'd read the *School for Scandal* as a set book for 'O' level but, she thought, they'd been periods of great sexual excitement with woman as the quarry and a double standard for the sexes since it was always the worst rake who married the chaste though witty heroine while the women who'd been his prey and comfort throughout were thrown on the scrap heap. Behind the façade of the fop lurked the same self confidence in masculine superiority enjoyed by the Garsley lads as they roared through the town on Saturday night, greasy hair whipped into rats' tails, plastic leather jerkins shining black as a stormtrooper's jackboots or slashed against the wall beside the British Legion at closing time. Not even Babs who had nothing to lose would pass there without an escort after half past seven. It would take her a long time to get over this feeling of freedom, Cathy thought, walking the streets of the city at night without the continual fear of being emotionally molested, set upon by catcalls, shouted invitations with the terror that one day she wouldn't be able to hurry past fast enough looking straight ahead, and an arm would shoot out, catch her, bring her close to the grinning face, the breath stained with nicotine and beer.

'You are deep in thought. And by your face these are not happy thoughts.'

'I was wondering how long you'd been here.'

'In this house or in England? It is both the same since I live here ever since I have arrived. That is two years ago.'

'I need a room. I wondered if you could tell me how to set about finding one.'

'But why? You can stay here. Why should you look for anything else?'

'Oh it's much too expensive. I couldn't afford it.'

'Mrs. Hardcombe will make an arrangement with you if you are staying a long time. We all have arrangements with her.'

'It isn't just that. I want somewhere of my own where I can cook and invite friends and do what I like.'

'But you can do as you like here. There are no rules. In many places you cannot have men in your room that is if you are a girl but there is nothing like that here. All is completely free. And you haven't met everyone yet. There are some very interesting people here whom I am sure would be pleased to meet you and you would like them too. Don't say you are going now you have only just come. My heart is broken. First I find you and then suddenly you say I must lose you the next day.'

'Oh I don't suppose I'll find anything as quick as that.'

'It is always the same when ladies come here they do not stay. They are like beautiful birds resting for the night and then in the morning they resume their flight. Before you are up even they have flown away following the path of the sun and we are left here with an empty heart knowing they will never return.'

'You shouldn't get up so late then.'

'Oh yes, you have the proverbs about the early bird we learned in school just as we learned to play cricket and now you are playing games with me. You light up my life for a moment and then you become cruel like all the rest when you see how it is with me.' He moved towards her. 'Will you not be kind to me to make up for it?'

'I'm afraid I have to go now. You see I'm starting a new job tomorrow and I'm worried that I won't wake up in time without an alarum clock.'

'What is this new job? Why do you need it?'

'I need the money of course. I'm starting on the buses so I expect I'll get rather tired at first.'

'Still I do not understand. What is this need for money? I have plenty of money. You can stay here with me in my room. We will share it and make the arrangement with Mrs. Hardcombe. She is most understanding in these things and when I tell her how unhappy I shall be if you go away everything will be alright. You cannot work on the buses. That is not work for an intelligent girl like you and I do not think you are so strong either because you are very pale. You will be unhappy on the buses and it is not right for us both to be unhappy. There is no sense in this.'

Cathy felt her brain growing numb under the persistence of his arguments and realised she would have to get out of the room quickly before she found herself with no answer and her silence taken for acceptance.

'But this is daft. I hardly know you; we only met yesterday. Do you always work this fast? You don't even know my name.'

A hurt look crept over his face. 'What does that matter when two people like each other at once as we have done. Alright you wish to be unkind to hurt me. It is perhaps some kind of test. I shall let you go now then to show you I am not afraid. Tomorrow we shall talk about this again when you have been running up stairs and down all day like a servant and this foolishness will be forgotten. All foolishness.'

'I know you mean it kindly Nala but you don't know me; you don't know anything about me. Suppose I turned out to be a thief or something.'

'You have not the face for a thief and anyway that is not important. I know what my heart tells me and I know I will die if you are not kind to me.' He turned towards the window and stood looking out and she wasn't quite sure that he wasn't crying.

'I'm sorry,' trying hard to keep herself from going up to him but realising that this would be a dreadful mistake. 'I have to go now. Thank you for the curry. I liked it very much.'

He turned to face her. 'Just one thing, tell me one thing only to show you do not hate me.'

'Of course I don't hate you.'

'What is your name please?'

'Cathy.'

'Cathy?'

'That's it. Goodnight.' She opened the door behind her quickly and was outside and halfway to her room before he had realised what she was doing. He turned to the half empty bottle of wine, poured himself another glass then went down on his knees and pulled out a portable record player from under the bed, selected a record from the full rack on the mantelpiece and put it on the turntable. Then he lay back on the bed with his glass in his hand, staring up at the ceiling and letting the sadness of the music flow over him.

As she undressed she heard the music begin above her head, a wailing of strange instruments she couldn't even begin to indentify to a light drum that tapped out an incessant time like the muffled thud of a heartbeat, and then voices took it up sometimes in chorus, sometimes a solo, rising and falling slightly or dwelling on the same note as if analysing and displaying the most delicate subtleties of human emotion.

Well, and what would Garsley think to this lot? The funny thing is I don't dislike him at all, in fact I rather like him as a friend or a sort of brother. He says all the sort of things I'd want to say, that I'd rehearse in my head, if ever I found the right person.

I'd want to be just like that, walk straight in and sweep her off her feet. There, it's that old Heathcliff again; keeps coming back does that one. I'm not your Cathy. What was it she said? 'I am Heathcliff.' Anyway one thing's for sure: he's not going to help me find anywhere else and I need somewhere even quicker now. Tomorrow I have to let Madam know if I'm leaving and I want to be able to say yes. And how the dickens am I going to wake up in the morning? First thing I must do when I've a moment is to buy an alarum clock. Try banging your head on the pillow; you used to think it worked when you were a kid.

It was cold, raw cold, going out in the morning and it hurried her shivering along. The banging on the pillow had worked. It had kept her in a half-conscious state all night, surfacing through sleep in a panic with sick fear in her stomach, a glance at her watch and then a rapid descent to the bottom, every couple of hours, and after the last at six she had lain there holding herself just below the surface until she was worn out with the effort and dragged herself out of bed to dress and sit bolt upright on the hard chair until it was time to let herself out of the house which was sunk asleep still as if it would never wake.

'You look worn out before you start kid,' said Ted her instructor; not at all like a bus conductor, she thought, with his big blond head, curly beard and pipe. I doubt they'd have had him on the buses at home looking like that though I don't reckon it'd worry him much with that great laugh he's got to him. 'Did you have any breakfast?'

'They don't serve it at our place before eight, where I'm staying.'

'In a hostel are you? Terrible places those. Run your life to a clock if you let them. You want to get out of there pretty sharpish. Well now, think you can get something inside you in quarter of an hour before we get cracking? Let's go down to the canteen. I can tell you a few things while you eat. Could do with a cuppa meself.'

She learnt a lot that first morning just by watching and listening; how heavy and messy the ticket machines were with their smudgy ink and paper rolls that always ran out at the worst moment or jammed with a full load in the rush hour; how the coppers weighed you down and grimed your hands with their metallic deposit and the hours were long on the feet and the stairs on the muscles of calf and thigh, and the schedules were crazy and the public but she knew all about the public from working in the library, and she was very glad when their first real break came and Ted pushed open the door into a small clean cafe where other crews were constantly coming and going. She liked their driver Stan too though he didn't have much to say. Stan was getting on to retirement and had learnt to save his energies for rush hour driving so he ate and drank slowly and rested behind the football results, turning them over slowly in his head as he worked a fibre of mutton out from under his bottom plate.

Ted showed her how to make up a waybill and how to set the ticket machine. 'Tomorrow morning you can have a go. We'll let you in lightly today.'

'Will I have time to buy an alarum clock somewhere? I don't think I could stand another night like last night worrying all the time whether I'm going to wake up or not.' She heard her father's voice saying, Never be late in on your first morning or your last. You can set your clock by me I always tells the young lads.

'There's a few shops round the corner, a jeweller's too I think. You'll have plenty of time. What you really want to do is find yourself some lodgings or you won't last a month with no breakfast.'

'Oh I know. I do want to but I don't know where to begin.'

'Just come down here have you? Well you want to start with the cards in the tobacconist's window, things like that. They're the best or the local paper. Don't want to get hooked by one of these agency places and the big papers are no good for what you want. Have a wander round this evening when we knock off. You'll sleep better too with that off your mind.'

The afternoon dragged a bit although she tried to keep her mind on watching Ted knowing she would have to do most of this herself tomorrow but she knew too that she had absorbed as much as she could without getting down to the hard facts of experiencing it herself. And she was beginning to feel very tired although the thought of the alarum clock she'd bought locked in the little cubby hole under the stairs was very comforting as it ticked away the hours until she was free to begin her real search.

'See you in the morning,' Ted said, slapping her on the shoulder, 'and tomorrow I'll have a nice easy day dinging the bell and seeing the customers on and off while you have fun with the tickets. Here, don't forget your clock.' He tossed her the box which she caught with her heart jumping in fright.

Tea first and then along to that main road and look for a window with cards in it. Good job the shops stay open later here than in Garsley or I wouldn't have a hope. Here's a little cafe says it's open at seven in the morning. I could get breakfast here in the morning. One thing about the uniform it's a passport to anywhere. You can wear trousers all day and nobody turns a hair.

After tea in a huge mug and egg on toast everything seemed much easier and she wasn't all that surprised when she found a newsagent with one side of the window full of all shapes, colours and scripts with everything for sale, wanted, small removals, lady will baby-sit, lady will, repairs undertaken to electrical installations, let us quote you a fair price for a fair job, all the rag and tag of the district displayed and among them half a dozen or so suit two business gentlemen sharing, good home and food for working man, no coloured, quiet house and finally bed-sitting room, own cooking, use of bath, suit single, £3-10-0 p.w., apply inside.

'No dear, it hasn't gone to my knowledge and anyhow it's always worth a try. Just round the corner, 26 Dorset Crescent, Mr. Gregory; he's a very pleasant gentleman.'

'There are two things first I must tell you why the room is so cheap. That is because it is right at the top of the house and is a very small room. So far up I do not go up there very much myself so you are not troubled with a nosy old landlord only when you come to me and say something is wrong. Now do you wish to see this room or have I put you off? We go up then. The lady who have it before tell me at first is terrible, and then after three weeks she find herself running everywhere she is so strong and healthy. You work on the buses then for you it is nothing because you are all day up and down the stairs.'

'Oh, it'll be the other way round with me. I've only just started so it will be good training.'

'There is one other lady up here and you have the bathroom between you. Excuse me if I stop a moment here. It is the terrible thing of getting old and fat that you must count every step and every breath you take. That is better. Now we are nearly there.

This is the little bathroom. Here you may put a little washing as you arrange with the other lady. She is very nice. She is a kind of nurse at the hospital but not quite. She takes the pictures of the chest and other part of the body.'

'A radiographer?'

'That is it I think. This is the room. You see, each one has its own yale lock so inside it is altogether private and your own business. As I tell you, is very small.'

But it was very bright too she saw at once and although the furniture wasn't the very latest from *House Beautiful* it was the kind she was used to and there was plenty of it including a very useful cooker top with a grill and burner, a good quality Axminster on the floor and cheerful matching curtains and bedspread.

'I do not supply bed linen only the blankets nor also the crockery, pots and pans, etc.'

'That's fine. I like it very much.'

'You will take it then?'

'Yes please.'

'And when would you wish to move in?' She hesitated. 'You can come at once if you wish. We begin the rent from Friday, one week in advance so you give me one week's notice when you want to leave and you pay nothing that week.'

'I'd like to pay you two now if you don't mind but I've paid for my room where I am for tonight so I think I ought to go back there, and anyway my things are there.'

'That is very wise. Give nobody the money you have work hard for for nothing, not even me. I give you a receipt for the two weeks though one would be quite enough.'

'Oh I'd rather, then I know where I am.'

'And you will come tomorrow? I give you the key to your room and to the front door.'

'Thank you very much. There's just one thing.'

'Yes?'

'Could I bring my case in at half past seven tomorrow on my way to work. I don't want to take it with me and I don't particularly want to go back for it.'

'But of course. I shall be up but that doesn't concern you. Just leave it in the hall. Don't bother to take it all the way up to your room or you will be tired before even the day begins. If there is anything you want to know anytime you ask me and I am happy to tell you that is if I know the answer of course. You come to me you understand otherwise I do not bother you. Goodnight.' He held out his hand for Cathy to shake.

Well I've done it now, a room and a job in no time at all. To-morrow! Thursday and I've got Saturday off as it's my first week so I can go shopping on Saturday morning and buy a few pots. Must remember to get a pair of sheets and a pillow case tomorrow in the dinner break. Only tonight to get through and then I can really start living in a place of my own. That'd surprise them at home to think of me so eager to put down a few roots. What did he say she was? A radiographer. Maybe she'll be able to tell me. No I won't even start thinking about that. It's a case of physician heal thyself first. Later maybe when I've sorted myself out a bit, perhaps found someone else like me I can talk it all over with, I can start to think of that again. What shall I do about Nala? I don't want to go through all that again tonight; it only hurts us both. Try and creep in without his hearing me and if no one's up in the morning I can leave a note for madam, after all I don't owe her anything; in fact she's never given me my change back.

Strains of sad music mingled with the smell of curry as she stepped into the hall, silently pulled the door to until the lock clicked and slowly climbed the stairs. If she didn't make a sound he wouldn't know she had come in even if his door was open unless he was actually sitting on the third flight waiting. She turned the bend, saw there was no one there though the music was growing louder, eased herself gently from tread to tread, saw the curry bubbling like a mud pool on the stove, got her hand on the doorhandle, turned it, was inside and shot the bolt. Feet moved across the floor above her head but didn't come out onto the landing. She began to undress in the dark, putting her things down as quietly as she could.

All at once the whole thing seemed ridiculous. This is my own room and I've paid for it so why shouldn't I do what I like. I don't have to see anyone if I don't want to. Otherwise if I'm going to be hounded and made to feel responsible I might as well be back at home. She put on the light and began to pack the few things she'd bothered to take out of her case. Then she wound and set the alarum, took off her uniform and got into bed, pulling the lazy switch above her head like a shutter over the day.

It must have been the getting into bed that did it. There was the sound of feet on the stairs and a soft knocking on the door. Cathy didn't answer. She heard the handle turning. 'Cathy, are you in there? I know you are because the door won't open. You have bolted it.'

'I'm very tired. I've gone to bed.'

'You see, I told you that job was no bloody good for you. Now will you listen to me. I will look after you and you will never have to work hard again. Won't you answer me? I will stay here all night until you agree to what I say. You are very unkind. I have been so lonely and now I must be lonely again. It would be better you had never come, I had never seen you to suffer like this. I am dying for you. You are killing me with this silence. Cathy.'

'Please go away. There's nothing for me to say. I'm leaving in the morning and I have to be up early. I'm sorry if you got the wrong impression but I don't think it was really my fault.'

'You don't like me because I am coloured, that is it. You are like all the rest of them but we are Aryans like you and if you lived in a country of sun instead of all this damn fog and rain every day you would be like us.'

'You know perfectly well colour's got nothing to do with it. It's just that . . .' What more could she say. The unfairness of it struck her. She had to lie and listen to him, to anything he might say to her and she could say nothing in reply.

'You see, I am right. There is nothing you can answer, nothing at all.'

Cathy lay silent then and after a little she heard the feet dragging upstairs again and the sad music wailed louder through the ceiling. How would it have been, she wondered, if she'd been different? Was she really different? She imagined his brown body naked in the room and found it less disturbing than her father stripped in the kitchen for his evening wash down. It was nothing to her and stirred only a vague envy. If you only knew I'd swop you the colour of your skin for everything that goes with it. There was no excitement just a pity for pain that she couldn't ease. She felt no shock either at the speed with which things had developed, partly because it amused her to think how Garsley and particularly her parents would have reacted with a gossiping from yard to yard, heads shaken and a descant on the wickedness of the times as dismal as anything on Nala's whole stack of records yet she knew of dozens of families in the town where the birth of the first child was dangerously close to the wedding day among the parents of her friends, and others who were a legacy from the camps on the moors the soldiers and airmen of all nationalities who had never come back. There'd even been one or two black ones she'd heard from Babs but they had disappeared into homes in the cities so that Garsley could still present a uniform face to the world.

She was falling asleep lulled by Nala's music, a fantasy forming in her drowsing mind which had something to do with the radiographer who was her new neighbour. Dimly she heard a soft voice calling her. 'Cathy, Cathy, I am dying for you.' But it merged with her dream to become a girl's cry. Wish fulfilment again, she thought, with a half smile at herself and sank into deep sleep.

Inevitably as the days pass she becomes a unit in the complex structure of the city which is forever changing and expanding, thrusting out a part of itself which will break away from the main mass to begin a separate existence as satellite town or suburb with its own nucleus; casting off dead cells only to replace them as dust is swept into the orbit of a star, the sweepings of distant places drawn irresistibly to its magnetic centre; the outer skin constantly renewed as buildings crumble, streets are bull-dozed away, new blocks rise. Each cell has a life of its own yet is part of the total life of the city. All day she performs her function within the corporate body only when work stops does she break away, withdrawn into herself, lies quiescent, storing up her resources for as yet the city does not nourish or refresh her. She is not completely integrated. It gives her freedom but nothing more. There is a working arrangement between them only and the relationship goes no farther because she is not yet involved. The central problem remains and now at last she has time to concentrate on it; all distractions removed it stands before her in a paralysing simplicity. What can the newcomer do? She is free but now her freedom begins to taste a little thin and bitter. She is still alone; no longer distracted by the meaningless demands of a family to whom she has no true relationship, her day to day economy taken care of, she exists now like a character by Henry James isolated from the comings and goings of the rest of society, concerned only with the infinite subtleties of emotion and introspection, like Nala's music but she will not see him again. She is more apart than women in purdah or the mediaeval lady shut up in her castle and like them she is in danger of obsession.

At night and on her days off she wanders the city, peering into amusement arcades where the lost play pintables, fruit machines, stare through sights out of alignment for a bull's eye, top score, jackpot, the answer that comes when the bell rings, lights flash, the world comes crowding to see the tarnished silver leaping into the cupped hands, overflowing onto the floor among the fag-ends, blown paper, dust, or dive clubs where children of her own age dance bound together, caught up in the present, seeing nothing while the music holds them. She walks swiftly like someone with a destination but she is searching. Somewhere there must be, they are here I know, there was that article. Never believe all you read in the papers, catchpenny, catch you too if you don't look sharpish. Once on a tube train a woman stared her down, the eyes full of question; once she followed a couple through the streets until they disappeared through a discreet door and she caught a brief glimpse of steps leading down, heard music and voices laughing but it closed against her and she hadn't the courage to push it open again and walk in. She searched the faces of crowds too, dreaming of the small incident, the sudden happening that would unlock her isolation but the miracle never came. All around her were signs, hints, a way of walking or speaking, a style of dress or gesture, the question in the eyes but they were as indecipherable as a tramp's message scratched on a gatepost, understood only by the fraternity.

For long hours she stood beside the river watching the windows of the great hospital. Ambulances, visitors came and went. Up there perhaps they were operating. Shadows passed like the play of silhouettes behind a screen. Yes sister, no sister. Even that they had kept her from. What do you want messing about with the sick and the dead. It's a long hard training and poor pay at the end of it. Just some romantic notion like some kids get stagestruck. I can see you sticking to it when you can stick to nowt else. There was a life she could be part of but not yet. Perhaps next year when she knew more, was certain. This must come first, she could do nothing til then. Physician heal thyself but how do I even begin, she thought. It was nearly May. Spring would soon be over and she had done nothing. After the deceptively easy start her progress was at a standstill.

As Nala had prophesied the work wasn't easy, it was often very tiring, but it had its compensations and she had been brought up to look for compensations in a job rather than positive fulfilment. She liked George who eventually formed the other half of her crew and the backchat and innuendo that went on between the others, particularly the married old-stagers of both sexes, didn't worry her much; it was stock dialogue in almost every occupation varying only in expression from level to level not in basic content. But she made no close friends. Ted continued to treat her like a dutch uncle as Garsley would have put it but the others kept their distance. With George she seemed to strike an immediate chord though, perhaps, Cathy thought, because we're together so much, see such a lot of each other although when I come to sort it all out I don't really know anything about him at all except that his parents are elderly and have a mania for television.

They were sitting in the small canteen behind Cargrave Square supping tea and gossiping lazily of this and that, whiling away an odd half hour when it happened. A little group of actors had come in from the nearby theatre and were talking loudly, still acting through their break. George turned to watch them. 'Look at that one. I bet he's as queer as a coot.'

She felt her colour rise. 'How can you tell?'

'Oh with him it sticks out a mile, besides a lot of them are in the acting profession. The girls, too, like all these film stars the men get all hexed up about.' He turned to face her and instinctively she knew what was coming and the answers began to take shape and dart about in her mind like mayflies over the surface of the pond on Garsley Green. 'You know what they say about you Cathy? They say you're a les.'

She looked down into her cup and automatically stirred the dregs. 'What makes them say that? How can they possibly know?'

'We've had one or two before and they were all like you.'

'What do you mean like me?'

'Well you can tell when you start chatting a girl up if she doesn't come back with the smart answers leading you on, means she isn't interested that way. If she's married it may be that she's still in love with her old man though generally the married ones are the worst. If she's single she's either flashing a great engagement ring and her ears are too full of bells to take in anything else or you're always hearing about who she was out with last night and where they're going tomorrow. Then the single girls or a lot of them still live with their mums but the others they live by themselves if they haven't got a girlfriend. And another thing look at your uniform.'

'What's wrong with it? It's the same as everyone else wears.'

'Ah but you don't wear it the same way. You're always so neat with a sort of shirt and tie under the jacket, and those flat shoes and men's socks.'

'How do you know they're men's socks?'

'They are though ent they?'

'Anything else?'

'Yeah, you walk like one and look at your haircut and no make-up. But it's mainly the lack of interest that gives you away, and the way you drop your eyes of course if you think anyone's getting too near.'

'So you've all made up your minds. What happens now?'

'Nothing much. Someone might pull your leg about it sometime soon that's why I thought I'd better show you the old red light.'

'Thanks very much.'

'Now don't be like that. I'm trying to help you.'

'I shouldn't bother. I mean if you're right there's nothing in it for you is there.'

'I thought we were mates. The trouble with you is you're too prickly, spiky as a pair of running shoes, trampling all over people who want to do you a bit of good. I don't think you're very happy like you are that's your trouble.'

'Oh I know that one, I've heard it before. Come to me and I'll cure you. All you need is to hop into bed with someone double quick and all that nonsense'll be forgotten.'

'So you are then.'

'Very clever. Yes I fell for that one didn't I. Well there's only one thing to do now and that's find another job.'

'Now don't be so daft, go and fly off the handle like that. I said I wanted to help. Honest Cath I meant it but I had to know for sure that you were. Straight up though you're not happy are you?'

'I'm not unhappy. I try not to think about it too much. I mean I'm better off than I ever have been. You can't expect everything to come at once, turn up on a plate just like that. Things don't happen like that.'

'Have you been to any of the clubs?'

'Clubs?'

'Yeah, where all the girls go. Don't tell me you didn't even know.'

'That's the trouble if you're really interested. I don't know anyone or anything. As far as I'm concerned I might be the only one in the world. How do you meet people? Just to find someone to talk to, to know I'm not the only one.'

'You poor kid. All this time.'

'How do I find them these clubs, at least I think I did find one. I followed a couple but how do you get in? Can anyone just walk in?'

'I dunno. Look there's a pub I go to on Friday nights. There's some of the girls get in there sometimes. Why don't you come with me this Friday? You don't know, you might get talking to one of them though it's not like us. I always think they're more cliquey so I suppose that makes it more difficult, stick to their own little gangs more.'

'You said "us".'

'Well. How else would I know? I'm not saying I'm all the way mind. I've been with girls and maybe I will again, least I kid meself though they say once you're in you're in for keeps. One of me mates did get married the other day. We're all waiting to see how it works out and how long before he's doing the rounds again. Sometimes I think about it or about marrying one of the girls but I dunno.'

'Will you really take me? What shall I wear?'

'Well there again they seem to be different. You know more divided into butch and femme I think they call them, boys and girls like. You'll see some of 'em in suits, what they call full drag. I'm just warning you so you don't stand there gaping like a provincial. You'll come then? It's all fixed.'

'George?'

'Yeah?'

'Does anybody know about you at work?'

'I don't think so. Hope not anyway. I never mix business with pleasure see. This job don't matter to you Cath, anyone can see that who's got a bit of common. You're better than this job and you could go out and do something else tomorrow. Oh I'm not saying you don't do it well, better than most, but I reckon you as a grammar school girl and that you're only doing this while it suits you, while you find your feet. Me, this is the best I'm ever likely to rate and I want to hang on to it. That's why I'm careful not to let the word get round, put up a big front with the girls, and in future if anyone asks me I shall say you're not neither, that you come from a good home and you're not used to the old backchat, and you're waiting to go to college or something and that's why you're different. You see if I seem to be too matey without telling a bit of a tale they'll begin to put two and two together, think we're tarred with the same brush, and it's still against the law for us you know.'

'Yes I know that. You can tell them I'm going to be a nurse and then you'll be telling the truth. You know just talking to you I feel better already. What's this place called?'

'The *Sweet and Twenty*. Funny name for a pub ent it?'

'It comes from Shakespeare.

> 'Then come kiss me sweet and twenty,
> In delay there lies no plenty . . .
> Youth's a stuff will not endure.'

PUSH open the door, shoulder aside the curtain of smoke, the malt savour of spilt beer that hangs before the threshold thick woven with the tensions that are already strung across the evening so that the walk to the bar becomes a bat flight between taut wires that bounce back their warning signals as you draw near. Eyes swivel, robot antennae housed in the rigid metal masks that encase the soft, vulnerable core behind each drawn face, querying each inswing of the door that eddies the curtain, sends waves of hope humming along the wires for the loved one or the desired, the young man who comes with an apple in his pocket, the golden apple of immortality to renew the flush in dried cheeks, set the blood flowing in the flattened veins.

Who's here tonight? Who's in, who's out? Early yet, the main body of the saloon still empty; a fringe of solitary drinkers clings to the bar; a group or two chatters by the platform where drums and piano beat a kaleidescope of shifting sound patterns into the air. A tall queen passes by on her way to the gents, shoulders slightly hunched, stardust gleaming in her set hair, unsmiling, impassive. And this must surely be the place where the differences show up best, under these too bright lights that rain down from the ceiling, semi-naked bulbs at the end of spider-leg contemporary chandeliers, unlike the House of Shades where anonymous figures drift together in the undersea twilight. This is a place that would echo sunlight, tanned young men on a beach in light classical colours, gossiping hand on hip, waiting to wrestle or run. Women's rites are more ancient and secret, the virgin goddess who is another face of the earthmother, old Hecate herself honoured in the halfdark where form is indistinct, curved and flowing.

'There's David over by the band, he's early, and Steve too. Better grab some seats while we can. What'll you have? You go and sit down. I won't be a minute.'

What would Mr. and Mrs. Everyman think, I wonder, suddenly out for a quiet drink one evening and dropped in here. First look round wouldn't notice anything unusual, then as the time wore on, more and more were pushing open the doors, staring round as they cross the floor, appraising, a voice pitched too high, the camp gesture, a mouthful of conversation overheard, slowly digested. 'A fine one she is. Where'd you get your handbag darling? Get you!'

'Come on Elsie. Let's find somewhere else. Can't stand all these theatrical types.'

'Oh is that what they are. I wondered. Very nice looking aren't they. Still I suppose they have to be in that job. Well dressed too, not like our Derek and his friends with their long hair all over their collars and their terrible flash clothes. I must say these look like nice quiet boys, sort of clean like you get in the *Woman and Wife* our Joy buys every week. Make some girl a lovely husband some of them would.'

'Wouldn't make pussy a husband between them, this lot.'

'Oh I don't know. They're bound to be a bit sensitive. It's their job.'

'Shut up for Christ's sake. You don't know what you're talking about. Finish that bloody drink and let's get out of here. They give me the creeps.'

The strained silence that comes from things which must never be said, never mentioned as if at the naming of them the whole order of society would crumble, the streets be filled with howling wolves welcoming the fall of civilisation, resurgence of the beast, drives the wedge further between them as they get up to go, she thinking, it's always the same when I'm enjoying myself, and he, Bloody women they don't know nothing. And that's how the misconceptions get perpetuated from generation unto generation, Matt said to himself, putting down his money and picking up the two glasses, until it's as ingrained as a pottery style or a method of working flints and takes aeons in human terms before anyone sees the need for a change or the sense in it. Imagine the poor devil who first thought of chipping off flakes from a prepared core instead of just using the whole flint. What they must have thought of him trying to get half-a-dozen for the price of one, and how long before he could make them see they could all use it to their own advantage and the advantage of the tribe as a whole? There must have been hundreds who were tucked away in their little gravel beds still maintaining it wasn't right and that was why the Ice Age was coming.

'What are you looking so worked up about?'

'Hallo David. I was miles away I'm afraid, fighting an entirely imaginary battle with the common man and his ignorance.'

'You'll never change people, at least not in our lifetime.'

'Oh I don't know. The signs are there. I think we're on the move. Besides it's no good giving up. You have to keep trying even if you are banging your head against the same old brick wall. I reckon with the progress in psychology . . .'

'Don't talk to me about them. I was listening to a programme the other day where they were talking about this new cure they reckon they've got where they give you an electric shock and make you vomit every time you have a pleasant thought about another man, and it made me sick just to listen to them. I mean how can you do that to a human being. You must be very convinced you're right to use a thing like that.'

'Who's God for this week? The trouble is you can use the same method to make anyone do anything for a time: make criminals out of honest men, inverts out of normals, communists out of American soldiers, so where are you. You haven't really established the validity of such a cure and any results you may get prove nothing except that the human mind can be made to respond to stimuli associated with certain states of feeling regardless of the value or possible morality of those feelings, which we knew anyway. It's the kind of method they use to train an octopus to only take food out of the trap when the light comes on.'

'Most of the time you don't feel you're sick, you kid yourself you're part of society doing an honest job and your private life is your own. Then you hear something like that and you realise that there are a whole lot of people in positions of importance who regard you as no more than an animal to practise vivisection on.'

'The funny thing is when they read about German doctors doing experiments on living people in concentration camps they all throw up their hands in horror but this kind of tampering with the mind they hear about while they're eating supper and never turn a hair.'

'Hey you lot, pack it in will you. This is supposed to be a jolly evening and you're sitting there telling horror stories giving us all the jumps. What's the matter with you anyway tonight Matt?'

'Not enough alcohol in my system I suppose. I'll get better as the evening progresses.'

'While I remember Matt, can I borrow Rae for an evening this week?'

'What is it, firm's dinner and dance come round again?'

'That's it. Thursday, should be a good meal this year; they're trying somewhere new.'

'They'll be asking you soon when you two are going to get married. Don't they think you're a bit slow?'

'They think I'm a dirty old man and bloody lucky to get away with it. All the married men wish they could do the same. I tell them about the parties I go to, the weekends away, the holidays abroad with just a bit of embroidery here and there and their eyes are popping out of their heads. I suppose that's one of the compensations; we enjoy ourselves more.'

'The psychologist'd tell you you're immature. You ought to be happy sitting at home with the baby in the evenings instead of gadding off out with us lot.'

'What happens when you're too old to enjoy it?'

'I don't reckon we're any worse off in old age than anyone else. In fact if anything the record evens up a bit. I mean if you're normal married your children have grown up and left you by then whereas we've learned to do without them. We've got our jobs like everyone else and we've got more friends than most because we live a more social life than other people. We might be frightened of the wrinkles but then hundreds of marriages haven't got much more than companionship by then if that. How many happily married people do you know.'

'Two or three couples for at least a dozen who aren't but who rub along somehow.'

'So you don't reckon we've got it so bad then?'

'It's alright for you; you're not illegal. Still there's a few here who'd miss the excitement if they were. Might even make them normal.' David looks across at the opposite tables filling rapidly with the regulars who will perform for us later. The compère is already beginning to fuss over his opening number, trying to persuade a boy in a smooth grey suit to follow him. But the boy is unwilling. It's too early in the evening. He hasn't got into the mood. Who'll hear him. His best song, almost the International of the gay world, would be wasted on this handful.

The talk swings predictably to and fro like a captive stoolball. Matt has heard it all before and will hear it many times again for there is nothing new under the all-seeing eye that can be said on the level of polemics about the problems of minority groups, the poor, the sick, nothing that will convince either side since they both speak from their own needs their own stage of development, rationalised experience and until they are ready to go further golden words fall on their ears like lead. The same questions and answers, the same for and against are repeated all over London in flats, round dinner tables, in clubs and pubs, in homes and restaurants until the mind thrusts them off into a no-mans-land, the ears continue to hear but the brain no longer receives. Yet they will be given because they must be given, the messages are still sent even if the earphones have been laid aside because apart from the facts that must still be stated until they become commonplace, something in us needs the release of this kind of conflict as an affirmation of our stated selves.

He looks at Rae fingering her glass and wincing at the too-loud voice of the hearty young man who has been reared on community singing and is inviting the world to consider itself at home. 'You don't believe in all this do you; this discussion, argument call it what you like. To you it's immature, a waste of time.'

'I can only see a lot of people exhibiting their egos, each trying to shout the others down, and I just won't take part in that sort of thing. That's why I keep quiet. People are themselves and that's what you love them for.'

'Have you two had a row or something?'

Matt laughs, knowing he has to. 'No, it's just that we don't agree. I don't even mean that really. I just don't understand, let's put it that way. I keep on hammering at the same point with all the reasons, the abstractions, the isms and ologies while Rae just steps straight into it, and deeper, lives it all and beyond, leaving me still shouting about, finding a system, a scheme that'll fit it all in. It's the old, the traditional difference, I suppose between masculine and feminine ways of approach, both necessary, complementary but irritating to each other. You think I can't see. It's so easy to you. You simply get on with it. The problem of whether it's right or wrong, a good life or a bad one doesn't even occur to you. It is, it exists. I can see all that but at the same time I know these things have to be said, made articulate, otherwise how will anyone else ever know about them. And people suffer unnecessarily because of a lack of knowledge. It's all very well for the little groups of people with their own private vision living it out in their own lives but there are millions wandering around in a half light, scared and often ill. Don't you see it's not good enough? We all have to rise in the end, not just one or two who were smart enough, had will enough for their own salvation but all the halt, the maimed and the blind of us which is most of us.'

'I know, I do know.' Pained by his attack she takes up this strange weapon of words to defend herself whose normal speech is through hands, through understanding, through a hundred simple acts and gestures. At the same time she doesn't resent the attack, admits his right to make it and the validity of it.

'Do you always let Matt cross-question you like this?' Steve asks bending forward to deaden the noise of the band.

'Oh yes. Why shouldn't I? I know she's only trying to get at the truth, to put things clearly in order, and I should be able to answer.' She turned towards him where he sits listening, the muscles of his forehead clenched to make two deep vertical lines from the bridge of the nose. 'I can only see two problems: first that parents don't realise the tremendous effect they have on their children and that if there is any blame to be attached to anyone for the ultimate result then it must be largely theirs, second is the attitude of our society which makes them feel as if they're doing something wrong.'

'And neither of these are fundamental problems but things that can be changed by time and more education in the real sense.'

'That's it. There are dozens of problems, divorce for instance, but the people involved don't sit down in a group of only divorcees and complain about their state, and ask each other whether it's God's fault or their parents' or their own. Everyone has problems but they resolve themselves gradually.'

'Surely we're more like a different race?'

'Negroes in America you mean? Even that's only a matter of time. Look there's young Eddie just come in, up at the bar buying a slimming tomato juice but which of us thinks, "She's Jewish," as soon as we see her? She's just Eddie, a nice kid, and the fact of her Jewishness is just an extra something interesting like David being from a Welsh mining valley. A generation ago that wouldn't have been so and you can still see its effects on an older Jew so that I know one of our friends who doesn't even let it be known because her father had his windows broken before the war and she's never forgotten it. Then there are the ones who still want to play the sad, sensitive Jew and can't get on with the Israeli because they're so extrovert and vigorous but it's all passing, as Rae says, a matter of time. I think Eddie's even better adjusted to being queer because of it.'

'You won't get people to change as quick as that.' David looks down at his hands fighting off the impulse to crack his knuckles, the bones showing whitely through the thin skin. 'How do you get a change like that?'

Steve laughs a little then, 'My father could give you an answer. Through suffering, he'd say, accepted and comprehended suffering like the Jews have done, and the Negroes are now.'

'Is he queer?'

'I think so. We've never discussed it.'

'You must admit the attitude of organised religion has improved a lot quite recently.'

'Well, so many of the parsons were queer themselves they had to do something about it. I mean, let's face it, the oldest joke in the book is the one about the vicar and the choirboy.'

Rae sees Steve's face withdrawing behind its accustomed mask. 'Eddie's coming over, find her a chair David.'

The evening is filling up. Tommy the compere begs for more quiet for the singers but the conversations continue, punctuated with jerks of laughter, drinks are downed more quickly. Then all at once focus is on the stage. Suggestions are thrown from the thickest press of standing young men, whistles, catcalls. The singer pitches a voice to a ringing falsetto.

> 'When I have a brand new hair-do,
> With my eyelashes all in curl,
> I float like the clouds on air do,
> I enjoy being a girl.'

His gestures and expressions take on a coy, provocative effeminacy yet seen in repose at work or walking in the street he would pass as a handsome boy, a good catch in the marriage stakes.

'You'd never think to look at him . . .'

'Oh that one, she's all bitch.' David answers delightedly. 'You should see her husband, a great thumping Irish navvy.'

> 'Animus and anima
> Agreed to have a battle
> For animus said anima
> Had spoiled his nice new rattle.'

The words parody up and down Matt's head. For all my talk there's something in me that doesn't quite accept or accepts only certain aspects, jibs at, cavils over and yet who am I to question. It's just a way of not looking at myself. As long as we can find a mote who sees the beam as I expect Steve's father would put it. There's a love hate relationship if you like. She can take the mickey but don't let anyone else touch him. Rae saw it too; that's why she changed the subject. Who are the two over there I wonder. I've seen him here before I think but she's a new face. Looks very young and scared to death. Trying not to show it but daren't look up or round. What's she drinking? Half of bitter. Intelligent face but rather white and strained, anxious yet defensive. What do you do about people like that? Anything? He's looking this way, saying something to her. Lifts her head for a quick glance. Down again. Seen me staring. Mustn't stare it's rude, besides you'll frighten her or she'll think you're interested and she's an obvious butch, so far anyway though she might change later when she gets into the swim more. She's young yet. Funny how I couldn't fancy her physically but there's an attraction there. Narcissistic I suppose; myself when young about eighteen. The exchange of like minds. Carl. Carl? No answer. Only that once and what was it called you up then? The place or my need. Never before or after. All is changed, changed utterly; a terrible sameness is born. Supposing I went over and spoke to them? Isn't that Jill over there with a little group I don't know? Just come in, working her way forward, looking for someone. Me? What comes next?

A young man with shining cheeks and hair slicked back like a baby after its bath mounts the stage attended by an acolyte whose face is seamed with concern, the vicar's warden bearing the trappings of the ritual. It is the fire-eater. Loud applause. He sweats a little under the lights as if he has already sucked fire into his belly. Drums and piano play softly in a Persian market. The drinkers are quiet now watching. The acolyte stands beside him holding the tray with the lighted candle, paper torches, heaped white drift of cotton wool which the magician begins to stuff into his mouth, sometimes lighting it at the candle flame, snorting and blowing to keep it smouldering in his cheeks. The music builds him to his climax, he throws back his head and vents a dragon breath of sparks and smoke. We hear the flames crackling deep inside him where the banked furnace must be. The drum rolls, the piano crashes a final chord, the audience laughs with relieved delight and applauds. Next he takes paper torches from the tray lights them and passes the roaring flames across the bare flesh of his forearm as a cook singes a leg of pork. He treats the fire with complete disrespect, licks it like a child with an ice lolly, bites off a piece and chews it down. The audience are leaning forward caught like children at a Punch and Judy show, gasping in the incredible. Now he will walk on broken glass for us, the cruel blades prickle the soles of our feet, make the air gay for us with strings of bunting flown from his mouth, swing full beerglasses high above his head and return them without a drop spilled, hack a rope in pieces and join it again with a pass of his hand. He is our shaman, taking the edge off our fears, freeing us from the compulsion to play with fire and sharp toys, to wound ourselves in secret drawn by the nature of the thing itself to dare it to prove ourselves. There is nothing to it. It is so easy as he does it that we no longer need to try. But his body is not like other men's stuffed with animal entrails, shambles, viscera, organs that beat and contract and secrete: his body is a vast dark cave, half-lit by smouldering fires, the floor strewn with cut glass, the living walls hung with pennants.

We deal in illlusion. Matt looks round at the children's bewitched faces.

'Whatever must it be like going to bed with a chap like that?' David wonders.

The fire-eater is bowing and smiling now. The acolyte fussily arranges the spent remnants of the dream. The magician becomes simply a very pleasant young man with a boy's smile. But for Matt the mood is unbroken; not having succumbed to the enchantment, the end brings him no release. The others are gayer, the talk rises higher, someone gets up to sing and they join him in the chorus but Matt feels the evening closing about him.

'Hallo then.'

'Hallo, I saw you come in. Who are you with?'

'Don't look directly or it'll know we're talking about it. You see the very good-looking one in the black sweater. She's marvellous, really it this time. Ring me up and we'll have a drink and I'll tell you all about it. Must go now. Very jealous. I've told her all about you. Give me a ring, don't forget.' The crowds part for a moment and then close again absorbing her. He sees her reappear beside the unknown group and stand waiting for a crumb beside the tall figure in black.

It was right of course and inevitable. He had known it would come and that he must be freed from the tentacles of their past, that he must go on and create again, bend his mind and will to it, but he was tired, needing the touch of illusion which was no longer possible for him since he was no longer a child or even an adolescent. It was he who had grown old on their failure not Jill. He would always love her as they had been. It wasn't something that could be wiped away. He couldn't say no it never was so, I was deceived or I deceived myself. He must admit to himself that what had been had been and what had been true then was always true. He knew the danger period was near with Rae, saw all the signs in himself, the urge not to face the problems of adjustment, the transmutation of physical passion into something more, but to go out and look for some new diversion, he felt the old restlessness, the roving eyes and then he looked down the months and then years at the misery, the anguish and deception that would follow. Not again, he said to himself, not all that again. Where would it ever end? It has to be done this time. It has to be done and she wants it too. He looked across the table to where she talked with David. She looked tired, older. That too is my fault, he thought. I only bring destruction. He stood up.

'What would you like to drink? Have something different. Something special. I did well on the tips today. Have a Tia Maria if they've got one.'

And this deprived fringe-life he asked her to lead didn't help. It doesn't help, he thought pushing his way to the bar, not that we starve but the spirit starves all because of some besotted clinging to a principle that begins to seem pale, without substance even to me. It's not so much that I earn far less than I would if I even made some attempt to get into my field, it's the never seeing anyone, the never doing anything, the lack of contact with minds that aren't circumscribed by this one problem; no pleasure, no real pleasure in the Wordsworthian sense, that's it.

The feeling that he had pinned the thing down at last even though it did not mean a solution or even a respite, cheered him a little. He found himself half consciously joining in the singing, grinning at the compère, able to look across to where Jill hovered at the elbow of the black sweater without feeling it a total denial of all they had professed. Indeed he hardly felt at all finding himself more and more drawn towards the two figures he had noticed earlier. 'You see those two over there,' he leant across to Rae and David. 'What do you think?'

'He's a regular,' David peered through the smoke, 'comes in here regular though I don't think he's with anybody. Not bad; wouldn't mind a go myself but I've never seen the girl before.'

'She looks very unhappy, very unsure,' Rae blew a jet from her cigarette and used it as a dissolving screen to watch them through.

'Shall I try one of my charming smiles?'

'You try and put one in for me.' David laughed. The young man smiled back.

'Now we don't know whether it's you he's trying to make a pass at or if he wants something more.'

'What more is there?'

'I'm going over to speak to them. See if my guess is right.' Matt pushed back his chair and worked his way towards them turning over his first words in his mind but there was no need. The young man spoke first.

'I'm glad you've come over. I was thinking I'd have to come and shove me way in soon.'

'I wasn't sure but I thought it was worth a try. I'm Matt.'

'I'm George and this is Cathy. I brought her along tonight hoping she might meet some of the girls. You see she doesn't know anyone or where to go or anything and this was the best I could do.'

'Yes, I thought it was something like that. Would you both like to come over to our table and meet the others? I mustn't be away from my drink for too long.'

'You see I feel sort of responsible, wouldn't like her to get in with a bad lot or get hurt.'

'It's alright George. I know what you mean. This isn't a pickup. That's my wife over there. Besides Cathy and I are too much alike for anything like that. I think we understand that straight away.'

David's face shone with excitement for a moment and then took on a cool ease as the introductions were made. There's two who won't be cold tonight, Matt thought as Rae made room for Cathy and began to draw her out. Matt looked at the two heads bending towards each other to shut out the noise of the bar around and felt relaxed, almost happy. Something positive had been done against the common darkness and loneliness. Perhaps it was only the beginning of the ride on the merry-go-round that whirled them up and down, round and round faster and faster, throwing them against each other and then away again while the music brayed raucously, drowning all sense of time and meaning except that they must cling on and be carried round while the faces beyond blurred into a mist and earth and sky reeled together yet that after all was only one way of looking at it. This child might do better than the rest of them. At least she must be given the chance. What would Steve's father say about suffering? She had suffered already. It was on her face. Now she needed to know that she was not alone. After that it must be up to her.

Above the din he caught some of her words to Rae '. . . to be a nurse.'

'You know about the Nightingale of course.

Dearest, very Dearest—Very precious to me is your note. I almost hope you will not come tomorrow: the weather is so cold here. St. Mary's expects you and next do I. Be sure that the word "trouble" is not known where you are concerned. Make up your dear mind to a long holiday: that's what you have to do now. God bless you. We shall have time to talk.

F.N.'

'Did she write that?'

'Yes to one of her matrons. And there are dozens more. You could say it was just Victorian emotionalism of course. Lytton Strachey said it was the beginning of softening of the brain. He should talk but I suppose he didn't want to recognise it as years of sublimation and repression coming out in the form of passionate, and pure of course, relationships with young nurses. That's the only way her whole life makes any sense.'

'Does it matter,' Rae said, 'whether she was or not? Does it make any real difference?'

'Not in some ways of course but in others yes. You see unless we begin to understand all the springs of human conduct, all the manifestations of the human spirit how shall we ever keep up with our tremendous technological and scientific advances. What else have we got to offer on this side of the fence that's comparable in importance?'

'Do you always see things in this way?' Cathy asked.

'How do you mean?'

'Well so big and weighty.'

Matt rubbed his eyes and brought his hands down over his mouth while he thought. Then he took them away and said, 'Yes I suppose I do, don't I darling? I'm a terrible pain in the neck really and an awful bore to live with. It's my job you see, seeing things on a time scale instead of just what's happening here and now with no before and after.'

'What do you do then? It must be very interesting.'

'Me, no. I work in a garage. I'm a fraud too you see. What'll you both have to drink?'

'How do you feel? As you're driving . . . ?'

He looked into himself and considered, took his pulse, examined his reflexes, 'Alright, I'll just have a half then.' Once more he thrust himself forward into the mass that broke, yielded a little before him and suddenly he seemed to have been doing this all his life, thrusting against the press towards an imagined end and coming back with an easy answer to hand, a short cut to release, forgetfulness soon downed and the same trip to make again, arrivals and departures that lead nowhere from nowhere, phantom journeys giving an illusion of movement even of progress but when he looked out of the window the view was always the same. It's that child, he thought, so sure, knowing what she wants quite clearly, bringing out a something in me that's got buried so that I'm saying things to impress. Not that I don't believe them when I stop to think about them at all these days. I seem to be coming to one of those points where all the lines converge, gather into one that rounds the corner and there it is stretching straight in front as far as you can see. Even Steve looks different tonight, less wary, gentler. Eddie's her usual self. Cheerful and solid. David seems to be well away with George. Interesting to see the very first moment of an affair. Be good not to be in on the last for once.

'When shall we go away?' He looked down at her as he handed

her the slim glass. We must give the child the possibility of love, he thought, even if we most of us lose it, betray it, and are we any worse than the rest of the world after all except that we admit defeat sooner, go back to square one.

'Soon.' She smiled as if she had lifted her glass to a toast. 'Let's make it soon.' Turning from one to the other Cathy thought that it was possible then. Even if she never came again, didn't meet anyone for a long time she had what she needed now. She found herself clenching her palms tight so that something almost tangible shouldn't slip away. No need to search the faces in the crowds. If she wanted them she would know where to find them. Tomorrow she would fill in the forms and cross the road into the park.

They stood outside on the pavement after time, the voices still calling in the bar behind where the lights were almost out. David suggested a further call at one of the boys' coffee clubs. George turned to Cathy.

'You go,' she said. 'I've got things I want to do in the morning. Thanks George, thanks for bringing me. See you tomorrow afternoon. Don't be late.' The boys walked off down the street already moving together as if they were lovers.

'Can we give you a lift?' Rae asked.

'No thanks. It's not worth it. I'll just hop on a bus over there.'

'Anytime, you know where to find us.'

'I'll remember.'

'Good luck. See you.'

'See you.'

They watched her cross the road to the stop and join the short queue.

'She'll be alright won't she?'

'Oh yes.'

'Not a bad evening.'

'Not bad at all.'

As they drove home through the half lit streets she asked, 'When shall we go?'

'I'd say go tomorrow. Just put a couple of things in a case and off.'

'Why don't we do that?'

'Where would we go? I haven't really thought about it yet.'

'I have. We could go to Lexbourne.'

'Good God, why there?'

'I've got a friend who runs a hotel there. I'd only have to ring. It wouldn't take long by car. I could ring in the morning and we could easily be there by lunch even with Saturday traffic.'

'Who is this friend?'

'Stag. Oh I've told you about her before.'

'But not by name. Some butch character out of your past by the sound of it.'

'Wait and see.'

'Why there particularly?'

'It's convenient and she always treats you very well.'

'Treats you well you mean.'

'I think you'd find it interesting. I'd like to see you there.'

'Okay then, we'll go. I'm due a Saturday off. Old George can whistle for me for once. Pity it's not warm enough for a swim yet but we could drive out into the forest for a walk. I'm tired of streets on streets for one time in my life. I want to see green instead of grey, rest the eyes. What's she like Stag?'

'Oh I'm not telling you; I want you to make up your own mind.'

'They'll miss us down the club.'

'Why do you call it the *House of Shades*?'

'That's what it is for me and most people down there.'

'Why do you keep going then?'

'I feel I have to, as if I'm involved. It's a sort of Orpheus myth in reverse.'

'How do you mean?'

'Well you following me down there. It should be the other way round though I've often thought the traditional explanation would bear some looking into. Psychologically the bit that makes the most sense is the end where he's torn to pieces by the elemental passions he's denied. That's just neat Freud. I don't know. I suppose I have some crazy metaphysical illusion that I'm doing some good by going there, because I know, and so many don't know, what it's all about. They're so busy living it they can't stand back and look at it. Then sometimes I think that I'll just clear out and leave them to get on with it like some people do but before I do that I want to be sure that I'm doing it for the right reason not just ducking out in order to conform, to get my share of the cream like everyone else. In a way it's like grubbing about among the roots of buried towns, you never know what you might turn up, like that kid tonight. To be open that's the thing and to be involved on all the other levels not just the personal. Do you understand?'

'Yes, I think so. I mean I'm coming to understand more as you explain. It wasn't easy at first.'

'Poor darling. I'm sorry. Sometimes it's so clear to me I forget you aren't used to the way I go on. You deserve a weekend away among civilised people, a chance to see your friends instead of always having mine thrust down your throat. You ring in the morning and if it's alright we'll go. And the rest must do without us for once.'

So it better be time and a half too, dragging us in here like this on a Saturday morning, dragging us out of our nice warm beds, making us do without our little bit of Sat'day lie in and the only time we do get a little bit of the old how's-your-father these days with Jonnie always so tired working her guts out til all hours every night just so's we can live a bit near the mark, a bit like normal people, all them Joneses we're supposed to be so hot on keeping up with like they're always stuffing us with on the screen, the goggle-box like Matt says. And what was it she said now, she said we love it and hate it, love it and hate it sitting there night after night with only Mitzi for company the little darling, must bath her tomorrow when Jonnie's home to help me cos she struggles like a little demon for all she's only a scrap, nothing of her at all when you come to pick her up but she does her little best snuggling up to me so's I won't be too lonely as if she knew somehow and we sit there hour after hour loving it and hating it because there's so many things I could be doing about the flat if only I could tear meself away but I seem so tired somehow so gawd knows how Jonnie must feel and it's wrong of me I know to take it out of her when she comes in, but I can't help it, making up to her, smooching round her for a little bit of the old you-know and feeling all aggrieved when she turns away only wanting a cup of tea and a sit by the fire and I can see it going through her head what have I been doing all evening but she's too tired to come out straight with it so it's never brought out in the open for an airing, only I see her looking round at the dust you could write your name in on every flat top and thick enough to grow carrots along the ledges and me still sitting there in me old slacks like I just come in from work, with me hair a mess of tangles and me face gone all blotchy from the fire. Oh I see when I go out to put the kettle on, catch a sight of meself in the glass and think what a fright to come home to. You watch it my girl as mum would say or one day she may not be so keen to come home.

It's them lovely women on the telly that do it though, I mean spoil you for yourself knowing you can never be all smooth and glossy like that even if you used wonderful pink olé for a lifetime and laid in a bathful of it till the cows come home because you just wasn't born right somehow, behind the door when the good looks were given out, not that there's anything wrong with your face when you take it to bits and look at the nose and the eyes and all that separately. They're all there for a start, not like them old tarts you hear of been on the bash too long and start dropping apart like leprosy and how they must stink. I don't know how Jonnie could. And it's not as if you'd got a blinding great wart or something on the end of your nose or your eyes was crossed but it's just that you was behind the door, backward in coming forward for once so you'll never make one of them lovely women smooth as drinking cream like Rae for instance. She's got it and I see just what Matt sees in her like one of the filmstars in the picture annuals, not a modern face like the bits of kids you get down the House but more to it somehow so that she could never look common even if she tried and that's why some of 'em don't get on with her because she's a cut above them and sits there quiet, not that she'd even think it because she's not like that and one of the nicest people to talk to if you can get her on her own and you've got troubles you want to get rid of on someone. But she's got it by nature, born with it and you wasn't and that's all there is to it and it's not that you begrudge it to her but it makes you kind of despair knowing you're not even a starter in the beauty stakes as they call it on the box when they have that Miss World contest and they're all lined up in their next-to-nothings so a lot of dirty old men can slobber all over them like the slave markets you see in them Biblical pictures.

Look at her down there now working away so all I can see really is her curly black hair with not a grey one in it yet and I'll make her touch it up as soon as they start showing cos I'm not having my Jonnie looking old even if it is supposed to be distinguished. All the filmstars die their hair men as well as women so why shouldn't others and it does you good makes you feel younger if you look it and she's got such a slim figure still, looks real handsome in her best suit not like some of them fleshy butches you see about and even Matt's starting to put it on a bit though maybe that's the winter like that programme on bears I saw where they put on pounds to see them through hibernation and there's a big word for something I wouldn't have known except for the box so it's not all rubbish they put on there though I should have known it from school I suppose if I'd paid any attention or had any brains. And that was something they didn't teach us in nature study only about the birds and the bees and only then how to get a baby and what happens to it inside of you though we knew all the rest anyway from each other and who had seen their mum and dad having it away and whose big sister was expecting but what I've needed to know since they never told us, don't suppose they knew theirselves some of them though looking back there was one or two of the teachers I wouldn't be so sure about knowing what I do now with that Steve and the others who come down the club, still if they were they never let on to us. That's why I didn't know when the girls started calling me names and just because me and Sheila was friends and didn't run after the boys like all the rest. After all we was only kids of thirteen and how the others knew there were such things I don't know cos I'd never heard the word before and even when I did I went running home to ask mum what it meant and even she a married woman and dad was never finicky with his language still she didn't know.

'What's that bloke doing in among all them girls?' that man in the blue suit wanted to know when the foreman showed him our shop. Laugh though I went a bit hot and cold at first wondering if the others had heard and what they'd say but funny they never said nothing cos they seem as if they take Jonnie for granted. Being in the army so long I suppose they think makes her a bit different, a bit strange and the foreman he never says nothing neither cos he knows she's the best worker in the shop and don't waste no time chinwagging with the others and always keen to do a bit of overtime. Gawd knows how we'd manage otherwise with the lousy wages they give you here, and the rent of the flat but she would have it we must have a decent home although now I've got it I hardly know what to do with it being dragged up to newspaper on the table and hardly a stick of furniture cos he'd never give her anything towards it, food money that was all and not much of that and the few chattels we had were chuckouts from the neighbours like the clothes to our backs was handmedowns. Still we had a bit of fun in them days when he was out of the house til he come home knocking our heads together and clouting her round the earhole til she fell against the scullery wall and her face was the colour of dirty sheets not so much because of the pain, no not so much that though he hurt her we could all see more than he hurt us but for the hurt inside and the foul language that seemed to stick to you and thick the air like an open sewer. Seven colours of shit that's what he used to say he'd knock out of us. Played on me mind as a kid so I was always imagining it and making me stomach throw up and I imagined other people could see it too, the kids and the teachers at school so they'd turn their noses up at me and point. 'That girl's . . .' Oh it doesn't do to think about it too much even now how we lived from poverty to poverty in them days.

Maybe that's why Jonnie's so good to me now, gives me everything I could ask for, cos she knows what it's like. She's seen hard times too but she's come out different being more like a man I suppose and not so easy upset though I reckon she understands better'n any bloke could. Only one ever understood. 'What do they mean by it Larry?' 'It's hard to put it Sadie. I mean I don't know what to say.' 'Go on tell us. I want to know.' 'Well they mean you, you'll never get married. Yeah that's it, that's what they mean, you'll never get married.' 'Gawd is that all—what's so terrible about that. Lots of people don't get married. My cousin never has. He's always stayed with his mother. He's not lonely or miserable. He has his mates come round the house. And our Georgie's not married either though it's different for him I suppose being in the army. Still he might when he comes out.' 'Oh I don't reckon. It runs in your family by the sound of it.' And that was all there was to it then. We went on being friends, going out together but he never touched me except sometimes to put his arm round me and I liked it like that. Then it was his turn to go away and I was so lost without him I thought hell why not. After all I'm going to work now and everyone else does at my age. What you think you know at fifteen. So knowall I thought meself all tarted up for me first real date with a boy. He said would I come to the pictures and now I can't even remember his name. Wouldn't have been a bad picture *The Old Man and the Sea* but he never let me see it in peace, had to be all the time messing about and then when we got outside and we was walking home he said could he kiss me goodnight and I said yes thinking it'd be like me and Larry used to be sort of nice and gentle, friendly and suddenly there he was feeling me in the hatshop doorway and his mouth open on mine with his wet tongue I could feel poking between me teeth til I thought I'd be sick all over him and serve him right the dirty little devil at his age.

There now I've done it, gone and made a mistake, made me hand shake even after all this time and there's one'll have to go in the can unless I can rub it down a little on the other edge to even it up. Funny how you can bring it all back and what happened, nothing really, just what's normal for kids that age but it wasn't normal for me and I sat on my bed and cried when I got in, rubbing me mouth with me hanky til it was sore, half afraid I'd get a dose or something just from a kiss. Silly little bitch I was then. That's better. The numbers are coming up right now. Slip it in with the rest and no one'll know the difference. Now you try to keep your mind on your work my girl stead of rambling on through what's over and done with and no good crying over unspilt milk. If that was what you wanted you could have had it, still could now come to that so where's the need to get so worked up. Funny how you can get excited just thinking about sex, any sort of sex, but when it comes to the pushover then something doesn't click as it should and stead of going all weak at the knees you feel sick, sick as a dog right down through you, a real griping gutsache if it's a man. A woman's different though. That Matt now that time in them leather pants with that little purse slung from her belt in front. When we danced and she held me I could feel it hard pressing and the leather like another skin and I could have, right there on the floor I could have if she'd asked me. And she knew it too. Don't tell me she didn't know and strong that one, all butch not like some of these halftime change ends and wanting you to kiss their fanny and things no real butch should want a girl to do. And that's another thing I like about my Jonnie. When she wants you it's a woman she wants not a little boy; playing winkles together in the boys' lavatories and all the girls giggling round the door. 'I'm telling sir of you.' 'Go on, only jealous cos you haven't got one.'

Get us all working away for dear life. Poor old Edna can hardly get her belly under the bench. I must say she's hanging it out to the last gasp this time. Wonder if she knows who the father of this one is. I lose count. There's the little girl her mother looks after for her and then there was a boy and I think another little girl who were both adopted and this one'll go the same way; bound to. You'd think the welfare could do something for her so she didn't keep having them like putting a tanner in the slot and an ounce of jelly babies drops out. Still I suppose she's not bright enough to take care of herself and it's a terrible thing to think of an operation. However many would she have had if she kept it up til she was fifty and high time to retire then though I have heard of some go on that long. Remember reading about a woman who's had twenty-six and that was the record. Well at least they can't say we leave babies lying around all over the place for others to come and pick up. Seems a dreadful thing to give your own kid away even if it is best for it in the long run. I'm glad our mum didn't do that though she had cause enough. Bad as the old man is he's still your father and there's blood there between you thicker than water and anyway I reckon if I'm honest I'm more than a bit like him. And it upsets a child, don't care what you say, to feel that right at the beginning somebody didn't want it and look how many down the House are adopted, that shows something. Nature's way of birth control that's us though I'd like us to have a baby if you could pick one off the shelf. It's the pain that puts me off. First he's got to put it in and they say that can be bloody painful and then there's the baby coming and that can be sheer hell though Edna reckons it's no worse than having a tooth out and Sheila said she felt everso sexy when her Tina give her last shove.

What was it Matt said about me being frightened when I was a kid and I'd never thought of it as a reason but it does make sense when you dig about a bit. As soon as she asked me I remembered. There I was it seemed standing in our front room and mum saying to go round the corner shop for a large white cut. Out I run and as I'm passing the Mackies Brenda calls me in. 'Stay with her while I go for the doctor. It's coming,' and pushes me into their bedroom and slams the door to behind me. There was a hump in the bed and their mother's face peering at me over the sheet that she'd screwed up under her chin and her hair all sweaty and strewn about the pillow, peering at me but not recognising me I could see and suddenly she lets out a screech like when you tread on a cat's tail and thrashes about in the bed as if she was having a fit. I want to run away but I can't and I stare at her and she stares back wildly crying and groaning for what seems hours and I'm so frightened I can't move or even close me eyes to shut it out. Then she went quiet and I thought she might be dead until suddenly there's a man's feet and the doctor's voice booming over me head and he goes over to the bed and turns back the clothes and I see or think I see something wet and black and she crys out again so that I let out a sound with me hand over me mouth in fright and the doctor swings round and says, 'What's that child doing in here? Get her out at once.' And Brenda pushes me through the door. Funny I went on and got the bread almost as if nothing had happened in a short of daze, sleepwalking until I got in our front door and mum said, 'And where do you think you've been all this time?' Then I cried, sobbed and sobbed and she couldn't get no sense out of me for a while. Out it all came at last 'Will she die mum? Will she die?' 'Die, not her. She's as tough as an ox and had all that tribe already. Don't you think about it anymore.' Oh but she was wild though, hopping mad that a child of nine should see such things and so she went round and told Mrs. Mackie as soon as she was better. A right royal row they had over it and we never spoke to the Mackies for years after. Yes I can remember that as if it was yesterday and that's why Matt says but knowing don't help, don't make no difference. I still feel me stomach turn when I think of it; that wet head I suppose it was when he turned the covers back.

Oh the time drags; think it was running backwards when you weren't looking. Seems like hours gone and gawd the morning's hardly under way yet. They'll be swinging down the rise now to the market. Not too many yet, just enough to make a bustle and give you a feeling of, oh I don't know, what would you call it? A sort of excitement as if you was all going to a big party. I miss my Saturday morning. If it wasn't that we need the extra, that you got to take every chance when it's offered cos what they pay you come the end of a normal week ent enough to keep little Mitzi in biscuits hardly, let alone pay for Jonnie's new suit and paper and paint for doing up the sitting room. Then there's the holidays coming along and nothing in the kitty for that. No holiday at all last year just kept on from day to day cos we wanted to move so bad from that basement with the walls all running water and all the work she put into it, those hours every evening when she come in just so much you might as well have gone out in the gutter and poured down the drain. It wearies her I know it does, not so much the actual work but the coming to nothing and the starting all over again.

Going shopping now, that's what I'd be doing with a pocket full of money and Jonnie egging me on. 'Go on, get it if you want it.' And then back home with the bags stuffed to bursting and we'd stand emptying it all out on the kitchen table and gloating over what we've bought. Oh I'm an extravagant bitch I know but it does you good a treat of a weekend and I love looking in all the windows like when we was kids me and Georgie only we couldn't buy then. Wonder how he's getting on and who his latest affair is. They're not like us though the boys, don't seem to stick for long most of them though when I get down the House sometimes and you don't know who's going with who this week cos you missed a couple of Saturdays I start to wonder about us and how long we can last. Four years this June which is pretty good going. And think I might never have got started if I hadn't decided to leave home and take that job at that holiday camp in St. Brigid's Bay. Still, as I said to Matt, if it's in you it's got to come out and if it isn't it won't. Look how I fought it for months, saying to Larry, 'I'm not like that, no I'm not,' but even with him and I was fonder of him than anyone I was trembling before we even got to his bedroom door. And then he just turned and said he couldn't. Couldn't force me he meant cos he was fond of me too.

All because of them two I saw in the pictures, never forget it.

Give me their tickets she did and as I was showing them down the centre gangway with me little torch she asked if they could sit in the back row. That was it; asked if they could sit in the back row so I found them a couple of seats. Then I'm swinging me torchlight along a bit later to see if there's any seats going spare and I catch them in it for a second and I see they're holding hands. I can see it now; their two hands joined and I flicked the torch off them quick and leant against the wall at the back shaking and ill with shock I suppose. I felt I couldn't go past them again I was so frightened. I opened the door and went out into the light. Just stood there a minute taking deep breaths when up come the manager and asked me if I was alright. It all come out in a rush, always does with me, just like me dad. He laughed. 'So what. They won't hurt you. Just a couple of leses.' And it hit me he was using the same word the kids had shouted after me at school. Was that what it meant? No not me. I wasn't like that. Yeah that was it and how I come to ask Larry. I have to laugh when I think of it now.

Wasn't funny then though and not even good for a giggle when I found I couldn't make it with Larry. Even me own test I couldn't pass. Still I thought I'd be alright cos I didn't know anyone like that and I couldn't ever imagine meself starting something with someone. Thought I'd go right away and forget all about it. Get a job by the seaside where I could go dancing and to the pictures and no one knew anything about me. I'd be safe there. That was the biggest laugh of all. Lovely rooms we had in that hostel, overlooking the bay and with everything you could want. Lived like one of the guests, better in fact, and I got on alright sharing with Myra at first. She showed me round and the ropes of the job and we went to the pictures and made up foursomes for the dances with a couple of boys who were friends. Then things started to go wrong. She didn't seem to want me around anymore, made excuses when I suggested taking a bus into the next little bay along and going swimming there with the boys, didn't fancy the pictures and when it came to the Friday night said she was going into the next town with Mariette a new girl who'd just been taken on. It was Mariette all the time now. How bloody miserable I was, stumbling around in the dark and not knowing why. I didn't go out with the boys anymore. It'd been fun the four of us but I wasn't interested in seeing the one who was supposed to be mine by hisself and they didn't want me hanging around when they went out together. Most of the time I just went up to our room, had a bath and lay around on the bed, mooning about mum would've called it. The end came when she asked me if I'd mind swopping rooms with Mariette. I can remember that oh so clearly, looking across the room at her and saying, 'Why, don't you want me any longer?' And she looking back at me as I lay on the bed with a strange expression that I didn't understand, 'You don't know what you're talking about. Why can't you just do what I want without any questions? Why do you have to make it so hard?' 'I don't want to go. You can't make me. It's my room as much as yours. Why don't you go if you're so keen?' I might have been one of the girls in the adverts, the ones their best friends just don't want to know. She shrugged, 'Alright it's as broad as it's long. If I go in there her room-mate will have to come in here.' 'Suppose she doesn't want to move? Why should she? Why can't we stay as we are? I wish she'd never come. We were alright together til she came. What's so special about her that there isn't about me?' 'You asked for it don't forget, you wanted to know. I didn't want to tell you. What do you think it's been like sharing a room with you and having to behave as if we was all girls together, seeing you walking about half naked, sleeping in that bed like a baby?' 'What do you mean? What difference does it make if she's in here?' 'She knows darling, she's like me. If she's in here we can sleep together, get it? Oh for God's sake, I'm queer you little fool. Now do you understand?' 'You don't like me.' 'Can't you see, I was getting to like you too much and you being so innocent made it so hard. When Mariette turned up I spotted what she was straight away and so did she. You know, like calling to like and all that jazz but there's something in it. Rubbish recognises rubbish I reckon.' 'You don't have to go. I mean I don't want you to.' 'Yes I do. How can I put it so you'll understand. I can't stick it in here any longer with you. It's making me ill.' I turned over to the wall, feeling the tears coming and still not knowing why. 'Don't cry baby, for God's sake don't cry on me.' I felt her cross the room to the bed and stand looking down at me and suddenly that was that and all I'd ever wanted.

Don't think about it. What's the use raking all that dead old story over. All good things come to an end and you're happy enough now. Shouldn't think about it at all really, sort of disloyal in a way but they say you never forget your first, being a sort of puppy love I suppose and all the pain of a kid in it still. Funny, my luck she should turn out to be bi. Don't expect it in a butch but it do happen; you hear of it. Sometimes wonder how butch she was. With me of course but what about with Mariette. Said she'd never loved anybody more than me. I was silly enough and young enough in them days to believe it. Still I wouldn't go back to her now not if she turned up and begged me on bended knees cos Jonnie's worth a baker's dozen of her. It was different, not real somehow like one of them holiday romances they're so fond of in telly plays, all kissing on the beach just out of the sea with the water still running off them and then he lays her down. How they ever find a beach where you can find space for a sunbathe let alone private enough for that I can never fathom. Maybe it's different in the South of France or wherever it's supposed to be though what I've seen it's just as crowded there even if they are all starlets and princes.

That's what I'd like to see; a play about us. Not one of these prison dramas, all Eton crops and jolly doings in the cells and not a documentary either as if they were talking about some desert tribe and their funny old ways of going on but a bit in one of the serials treating it like it is, just something that happens everyday with a bit of romance thrown in. Reckon I could cast all the parts too if I thought about it. They want me up there. Directed by Sadie Knowles. Look rather good on the credit titles. Think of the letters they'd get and then I could be interviewed and explain the purpose of the play and how I hoped to entertain as well as instruct. Hallo they've wheeled in the barrow. Break for coffee Miss Knowles only it'll be Amy's filthy tea out of that urn I swear she scours round with carbolic every day. Where's me biscuits? There's Jon just gone up for hers. Wish I could go and talk to her. But there you can't have everything. In a minute she'll get out her paper and bury her nose in that for ten minutes, then fold it neatly away and get stuck in again til lunchtime. Wonder what she thinks about while she's working. Bet her thoughts aren't running all over the place like mine are or she'd never get through the work she does. I've always had a good imagination though, least that's what the teachers used to tell me. Don't think I'll take me tea over to natter with that old lot. Tired of hearing about their kids and their old men what they do and don't do. Gets a bit boring when you can't put your oar in too. I could tell them some things we do'd make their eyebrows curl. Never go up West from one year's end to the next, some of them never been outside this hole in their lives except to Clacton for their holidays every year, and never will neither. You'd think it was all a den of vice and sin to set foot there to hear them talk; all paper talk too what some smart journalist thinks they want to read about for a bit of a thrill and he's right too. They make me so wild sometimes cos they think they're so right and that's all there is to life and anyone who doesn't think like them's a bit touched in the head. Coming here every day's the only life some of them see. Oh I wouldn't be like that, wouldn't change places for all the tea in China when I really come to sort it out. Sometimes I think I'd like to be like them just to be able to talk to them without putting a guard on me tongue all the time and then I think it's not too late and any time you really want to try it you can go out and find somebody cos you're only young yet and time enough to change if you really wanted to, if you could put up with the bed side of it and they ent found no way round it yet though they keep trying with their test-tubes and babies in little glasshouses so I suppose it's only a matter of time like landing on the moon and then we shall get some peace maybe when everybody's having it for fun and anyone can order a baby from the laboratory. Jonnie and me could have one then. I'm not against babies after all, never have been, only the way you got to have them. What was it that little niece of Jon's said once, 'You could be a mummy and Jonnie could be a daddy.' There was knowing for a four year old. Just goes to show kids aren't born with these ideas. They get them banged into them by their parents and by the other kids like calling me a les at school. They must have got it from someone cos you don't come into the world with your head full of them things and I didn't know what they meant by it cos mum didn't I suppose which just goes to show.

Nearly finished their little tête-à-tête. Wonder who they've been taking apart. Here comes Nan's little mob back from their smoke in the lavatories. Not very nice really having to go in there everytime you want a drag. There ought to be a restroom where you could smoke or else time to get to the canteen stead of drinking your tea chained to the bench. Notice the blackies all stick together when it comes to a break. Always reckon that big one's butch. Looks just like that one who gets down the House, the one Matt asked me if I could fancy. Like I said I don't mind, I mean the world's big enough but they don't attract me; don't think I could go with one. I like fair people best even though Jon's so dark. Myra was mousey really though when we'd been swimming a lot that summer and lying about in the sun it got a sort of golden tint in places. Interesting though when you think about it that it don't make no difference the colour: there's them like us in all races. Fancy them harems too and all the men thinking it's such a sexy idea dozens of beautiful women just sitting about all perfumed and painted waiting for the lord and master to crook his little finger and say, 'I'll have you tonight,' and all the time they weren't waiting at all. Wonder what happened if he found out or perhaps he didn't mind. After all they go in for little boys a lot in eastern countries I heard somewhere so maybe they take it all for granted. Must have been rather a comedown having to put up with a fat old man if you was used to someone younger and better-looking. You'd have to think of it as just a job to earn your keep like the pros do and if there were enough of you it wouldn't come round all that often.

Back to work; there's the foreman getting out his little whip to get our noses to the grindstone. I'll save them last two biscuits for our cup of tea when we get in. Mustn't eat too many or I'll be getting too fat and then Jon will be wild. Besides no one'll want me if I get the size of a house. They ought to have telly in here to keep your mind off things while you're working, I mean just in the breaks so you don't go thinking too much and upsetting yourself. That's the trouble with having a good imagination you can be miles away and all caught up in what you're romancing about that's why I'm no good going shopping without a list. I get carried away so easy and don't come back with half I should. That's why I like it best when Jon comes too cos she never forgets what we're supposed to be out for and I can enjoy meself and talk and laugh and make up stories without worrying I'll get home and find I got nothing in me bag for our dinners. Oh she's like a rock Jon and just what I need. 'You're too fly-by-night by half,' mum would say, 'and I dread to think of the poor devil that's got to keep you.' Maybe that's why she's so fond of Jonnie, sees how good she is for me and asks no questions, doesn't care so long as I'm happy and in a home of me own, getting some nice things together which is more than she ever had from our dad.

France, that's where we'll go this year if I can talk her into it. I bet there isn't one in this whole shop that's been to Paris say though Nan put it about they was flying to Majorca last year she and her husband. Full of it she was for weeks and then suddenly she went all quiet and we never heard no more so I don't reckon they ever got there. But you can have some stunning times in Paris; lots of the girls go and you can get a list of the clubs there from those who've been and have yourselves a real ball. They're more broad-minded in Paris, used to all sorts, artists and people so who'd notice us. Make up a foursome that'd be best with someone who speaks a bit of the language, and then I can just see us strolling along by the river and sitting out on the pavement to eat, wine with every meal, a different club every night. Trouble is you wouldn't be content with just once, I reckon, as a taster; you'd want to be going back there again and again and this hole'd seem even worse after a holiday like that as if you'd wandered into a film by accident. Still that's life for most people without even a chance to get away like we can. If I can only talk Jon into it. I'd be so good you'd think I'd grown wings if I thought at the end of it there'd be something like that, and I wouldn't sit about and mope when we come back so you needn't be afraid of that. I'd be so full of new ideas, things we'd seen and done, you wouldn't know the place or me. I'd need some new clothes though. That old red moiré's getting a bit past it for evenings out if you're really going places not just seeing the same old mob who'll think yes that's Sadie and no more. Going among strangers is different and the Parisians are supposed to be ever such smart dressers I wouldn't want Jon to be ashamed of me always being so neat and handsome herself. I'd need me hair done too before I go with a new tint to it; this auburn lights is nearly grown out. What about Mitzi? She'd have to go to the kennels. Mum'd be glad to have her but I wouldn't trust him; come home boozed one night and tread on her he would. Oh there's a lot to think about if you want to branch out, see the world before you're too old to enjoy it.

197

It's alright for Jon; she's been about a bit. Join the army for a life of adventure only from what she tells me the kind of adventures they had weren't the sort the government had in mind. Now there's another thing they never had on telly: women in the forces. That'd make a smashing play. Still if they told the truth about what really goes on there'd be a riot with hundreds of butches all queuing up to sign on. Fancy them officers searching through your kit when there's a raid on. What do they think they'll find? Letters and photographs mostly Jon said and there's a liberty when you think of it quizzing through people's private things. Oh I love it when Jon tells me about her time in the army cos you can just see her when she's telling it in that uniform so confident and cool. Never had no worries Jon; no am I or aren't I and what did I ought to do about it. Just took it all as a matter of course. Like when Matt asked her if she ever did by herself and she said, 'Yeah I might if ever I was without a woman for long enough but I never been without a woman for long.' Made me go all cold and wanting to have it there and then straight away except that we'd got people in to tea and I've never cared for some of these tales you hear about all in together girls nice fine weather girls. Now I think that is perverted if they like.

The story I like best is the one right at the end when she'd sent in her papers for her discharge and they posted her to a new camp cos she'd been in hospital and they closed her old one down while she was in there or something. I never get that bit quite right cos I'm dying for her to get on to the next where she gets to this camp and finds the whole place is full of it and they call the dormitories married quarters. Then what happens? Oh yes she won't get mixed in it because she knows she's going out any time now and besides she's already got a girlfriend and troubles enough of her own there. A sergeant she was then and they'd asked her to go for an officer but she said no cos her girls like her and bring all their worries to her but they wouldn't do that anymore if she was to become an officer. So practically as soon as she gets to this camp the top brass gets a whiff of how things are and a big blitz is on with pryings and pokings and everyone up on the mat in turn. Comes Jon's go and she stands there to attention. 'Easy sergeant,' says the brass and explains what they're after Has she any suspicions although they realise she hasn't been there long. Haven't they searched the kit she wants to know. Oh yes they say. Then you know more than I can tell you. But we thought you might have heard something that could help us in our enquiries. I'm afraid not, says Jon. Then they start to get tough. Those who are found will of course be dishonourably discharged. It would be a pity after fourteen years sergeant and with a record like yours. Are you sure you're not involved yourself. Quite sure, says Jon. Why are you so sure? Because none of them attract me, says Jon. Surprise on all their faces. Do you mean that you are admitting to homosexual practices? Yes, says Jon, but not within the camp, though I'm not saying it mightn't have been different if I'd liked any of them. You're very frank in your comments, they say. Why shouldn't I be? I've got nothing to lose. I'm going out anyway. It's just a matter of time before the papers come through. So you won't help us then? I'm afraid I can't. You'll never stamp it out you know, no matter how much you try. If you stop it here it'll come out somewhere else. It's only natural, says Jon. Well, we shall see about that sergeant and we shall certainly have to consider your case very carefully in the light of what you've said. And then they dismiss her.

Oh I'd give anything to have been there, to have been a little fly on the wall and seen it all. But they left her alone after that cos she'd shown them she didn't care and spoken out Jon reckons, though the blitz went on and they did catch one or two and discharged them. Jon knew too much after all that time about the whole set-up and about the officers who were involved cos a lot of them was as bad or as good as the ordinary privates. When the time come she found nothing had been said and she'd got her honourable discharge after all. A bit after they closed that camp and separated them all up. Never stamp it out Jon says and you can believe it when you see all them butches from the barracks come down the House sometimes though she thinks it's a shame on some of the kids go in knowing nothing and then find it's either that or the little soldier boys from up the road as if you was one of them floozies used to follow the army round in the old days like I see in that serial where the young captain didn't know which to marry: the beautiful young lady he'd left behind or the dark gipsy-looking girl who'd looked after him when he was wounded in battle.

Lovely that was and really something to look forward to every Sunday just as it got dark. Course they never said that's what she was cos of family viewing but anyone with a grain of intelligence could've worked it out in a flash.

She's been about has Jonnie and that's one of the things I liked her for when we first met; took it all so cool instead of getting all het up. Still we'd never have got off the ground if she'd rushed it too much cos I swore I wouldn't have nothing to do with no one not ever again not after that blonde butch taking me home when I was plastered so I never know what I was doing or what she was up to neither and still couldn't remember when I come to in the morning except that me nails was all broken and there was bits of skin in them where I'd clawed at her back. She showed me the marks. 'Look what you done,' she said and I said I was sorry. 'But what was you doing to make me?' I said. 'Don't you remember? Then it couldn't have been nothing too terrible.' And there was that thing, like the one Jonnie and me made once only it didn't seem much good maybe cos I never been with a man, and it was all broken. 'You didn't use that on me?' She laughed. 'Well it must be your fault if I scratched you. There must have been some reason for it.' And she laughed again. Real rough she was, sadistic and I swore I'd never go with anyone again. Kept it up too for nearly a year til Jon came along. Sore I was for nearly a week and I'd warn anyone against her if I thought she was after them. Was she got me drunk too though I haven't much of a head at the best of times and it's always then that me and Jon have our little set-tos. Wasn't I crying all over Rae last time we had a party and telling her all me troubles, how Jonnie didn't love me no more and it was all me own fault. Sat there and listened all serious she did, ever so nice, though you can see just by looking at her that she'd never been used to drunks crying in her lap. Still she manages Matt and they say she likes a few though I've never actually seen her real drunk.

Must say the second half's going a bit quicker than the first and needs to too. Shan't be long now and then home and see what Mitzi's been up to left all alone on a Saturday morning. I'll pop along to the Seafry and get us some fish and chips for dinner. That'll be quickest then a bit of shopping for tomorrow, back for tea and a few minutes sit down then it'll be time to start getting ready for this evening. Rick's going to pick us up in the car so I can wear me light coat since we won't be standing freezing at the bustop. Better too when Jon's got her best suit on in case someone gets too nosey though they can't tell as a rule til she opens her mouth. It's the voices give them away and then people start to look cos they don't know what to make of it. We been lucky though, never any real trouble, beatings up and things like some have. That Tony's face was a mess the other week behind them sunglasses. I couldn't stand to see Jon get bashed about. I'd clout 'em with me handbag if they started on her. Makes me feel sick to think of it, violence. Like our dad. Animals that's all they are. Always the young ones, the teds and what are they afraid of that's what I'd like to ask them. I wouldn't go with them if I wasn't with Jon. That's what's so stupid. I mean if Jon turned into a man I'd have to leave her. Oh it'd be terrible. She'd like it though. I know she would cos she said once she doesn't think of herself as a woman. That'd be a dreadful choice. What would I do? Still it isn't likely now after all these years so I won't think about it. No sense in worrying over something that'll never happen. It's a shame for Jon though. I mean think of the money she could be earning, the jobs she could have with her experience if she had've been born a boy stead of working her guts out doing overtime to make it up to the lowest wage the old boy on the broom gets paid. There was that once she brought home thirteen pound at the end of week. That was a lovely week. She'd rather I only came on part-time I know and so would I but we couldn't manage with six pound a week rent even if I screwed and scraped like mum used to. You can't do it these days. It's seeing all them lovely things on telly make you discontented so you're struggling and striving all the time for that little extra. Maybe we'd do better on the pumps like Matt but you're out in all weathers there, it's got to be on a busy site to bring in the tips and you can be turned off anytime and then where would we be? Out on our ear if we couldn't pay up at the end of the week and there's the few sticks of furniture on the never-never to be kept going somehow. Bloody funny we'd look standing in the street with all our goods and chattels and nothing to feed Mitzi. Like a Victorian melodrama and very amusing I'm sure, a great big laugh from a rumbling belly.

There you go again imagining the worst, making up terrible tragedies to frighten yourself to death with, wasting your time when you could be thinking something nice and cheerful to pass the rest of the morning. No wonder Jon gets wild with you sometimes. But I wish she wouldn't go all silent, wish she'd up and tell me straight out what she's thinking or even give me a good clout round the earhole. I mean I could understand that better but when she just sits there saying nothing I forget we're not speaking, me thoughts go running on and before I know where I am I'm singing some song or starting to tell her a story as if we wasn't in the middle of a blazing row if you can call it a row when nobody's letting out a word in case it's just the wrong one. And it's always me who's the first to make it up. Not that I mind. I like it better like that cos it shows she's stronger than me and that's how it should be. I don't think you can have respect for anyone who gives in to you all the time. I get frightened when I'm in one of my paddies that I'll do or say something, something I don't mean, something that'll mean the end of everything and then what would I do? Would Jon take me back? Say I went off with someone like that blonde butch and everything cos I was miserable? That was the only reason last time cos I'd been on me own since Myra went and I thought who cares anyway what I do? Who'm I saving it for? Was it before or just after I lost me job and had to get out of that room? Not that there was anything to miss in that miserable hole, more like a morgue than anywhere for the living. That was why I went home with her I remember now. 'Come home with me darling,' she says all sweet, 'if you haven't got nowhere to go.' And all the time she was buying me drops of gin and orange and I was drinking 'em down like a silly bitch not thinking til I was so sloshed I couldn't see out of me eyes. She was ashamed in the morning though I could see that, didn't feel so bigsy then. That's why she let me stay on though I never let her touch me again. Went down the House most evenings to get away from her and just sat in a corner by meself. One or two tried to get friendly but I'd had enough. I told them no go.

And then I noticed her come in. Oh I love remembering how it was. Late in the evening she come in first and I didn't think nothing of her trailing behind that woman. How she could and if I'd known then the things she's told me since I'd never have let her come near me. Might have picked up all sorts of things. You could see what she was just looking at her even though they do say she's got a heart of gold and'll always help out anyone who's a little down on their luck. Oh I knew, not all of course, and wondered what a nice-looking butch like Jonnie was doing tagging on. All them bright colours she wears and she's no chicken. I like a bit of colour meself but not them low necklines almost slipping off her to go with it. I don't reckon she's got anything special to show off anyhow. Mine's as good as hers any night of the week but she's got all that cock-sureness from being so long on the game I expect and she don't care who knows it. Jealous that's what you are Sadie Knowles cos she got there first even if Jonnie swears blind she didn't, that it wasn't like that but she wasn't crying out for it when she picked you up, was she now and what was it she said about never being long without a woman?

Stop it. You're spoiling the story. Remember how it was properly without all this getting in between. Only another half hour to go and then you're free. Maybe this afternoon when we're sitting having our cup of tea, maybe if you're good and Jon isn't too tired before we get changed so it don't mess me all up again. Who knows? Don't let there be anyone else, please God not that. There you go again imagining things. And if there was it'd be your own fault for letting yourself get scruffy the way you have. You want to buck your ideas up. Stop all this dreaming and pull yourself together. And then what happened? Come on now, tell how it was. Well a couple of days after in she comes again only she's by herself this time and I'm sitting in me same corner making one drink last the evening. It's a Sunday evening and things are beginning to liven up. I watch her out of the corner of me eye because she looks different, looks nice and as if you could trust her, not like some and she stands there talking to a couple of friends, watching other people dance and making up her mind. I see her look across at me once or twice but I don't make no sign cos I'm tired of it all, don't want nothing to do with any of them. Suddenly, she decides, throws her fagend down on the floor, puts her foot on it and walks straight over to me. We take a few turns, swop names. Where do you come from? Are you by yourself? Then it's a twist. Oh we twist lovely together and she really enjoys it you can see, with her eyes flashing and me I shake and quiver til the sparks fly. We sit down again in my corner and she gets us both a drink. I tell her a little about the family and then I find meself talking away as if I'd known her years. She's nice to talk to, listens to what you say and you don't feel it's just because of what she's wanting out of you afterwards. Charlie calls time to go and we arrange to go to the pictures next evening. I walk back to the room I'm still sharing, feeling it, hating it worse than ever though she's been so nice to me since it almost hurts.

The next evening I'm there on time and she doesn't come. It's raining and wind that blows through you like a knife. I walk up and down to try and keep from freezing to death and I'm just giving her up and deciding it's a damn good job I haven't built nothing on it and how they're all the same people not to be trusted when I see her hurrying along towards me and I'm so glad to be getting out of that perishing street that I hardly bother with what she's saying about how come she's so late. We go in and she's not like some she lets you watch the picture and she never makes a move to hold your hand even. I like her better for that cos she's treating me as a human being with feelings not just a lump of meat in the butcher's window, something to be gobbled up to satisfy your appetite. When the pictures come out we go to a coffee bar and have coffee and them Danish pastries cos she says I look half starved. I tell her about losing me job and having to get out of me room and how I've got this job but the money isn't brilliant and I'm trying to get enough together for a week's rent in advance before I look for a place of me own. Then there's a misunderstanding cos she thinks I've been living with this butch and I'm just looking for out so I have to tell her all about that night and she goes very quiet so I'm frightened she thinks I'm just a tart and she won't have no more to do with me but it seems she's only picking her words careful. 'You can't stay there,' she says. 'You can come and stay with me for a bit if you like. No strings attached and I won't lay a finger on you til you really want me to. That's a promise and I don't break my word.' I didn't know what to say. I looked at her all dark and serious sitting there opposite me and I thought I'll risk it cos I can't be much worse off. 'I'll go back and get me things,' I said and she said she'd come too and wait for me outside because she didn't want to see that other one for fear she might get wild knowing what she'd done to me and she'd learnt one or two tricks in the army that could hurt so it wasn't worth the risk.

She didn't want me to go the other one when I got inside and she said again she was sorry and couldn't we give it another try. I said there never had been nothing so how could we give it another try. I put me few clothes back in me case and away we went. I never speak when I see her down the House cos I know Jon'd go wild. It wasn't a bad room with a bed and a couch and she slept on the couch so it was just like she'd said. I kept it up for a fortnight and everyday I loved her more and I wanted her to want me til I couldn't stand it no longer and thought if she didn't I'd have to go cos it was making me ill. At last she come back from the House one night when I'd been egging her on to get us quite a few drinks to screw me courage up and when it's time for bed I say, 'You can come in here if you want.' 'You sure?' she says. 'Oh yes, I'm sure,' and I put the light out quick and lie there waiting me heart going crazy til I think I'll choke and I feel her get in beside me and then I put me arms round her and . . .

God make it soon. God let it be alright. Not too late. Don't let there be anyone else. Never too late to mend, mum'd say. All his fault the old bastard, never give any of us a chance, but mine too for not knowing when I'm well off. How could she go with a woman like that after the things she's told me, things it makes you sick to think about, my Jonnie? Swears she never had her but how could she be in the room while she was doing all them things for them men all standing round watching and afterwards not do nothing? But I mustn't say it, must keep me big trap shut or we'll be rowing and the evening spoilt since she won't hear a word against her as if she was the bloody queen or Lady Muck herself. Gawd help me to keep me mouth to meself and hang on to what I've got with both hands til I know I been crossed, hear it from her own lips. Move round the hands of the damn clock the last five minutes. Some of 'em sitting back already, packing it in. Poor old Edna looks as white as a ghost. Be lucky to see her in on Monday morning. Well that's one thing we're spared, and all this about what'll happen when you're old and alone, I don't reckon we're any worse off than anyone else. I mean how much will her kids care for her then? Besides who makes their life as if they was laying up for their old age? It's enough just trying to get by from day to day for most of these so where's the difference? See you soon, Jonnie, meet you outside and we'll walk to the bustop together. Can you hear me Jon? Soon be home with Mitzi jumping all over you, glad to see us back. And I'll try, I will try to keep me and the place looking decent so you need never be ashamed of us, never let you down. She lifted her head up then just as if she could hear. Laying her things neat like she always does. Nearly time. Wonder what's on this afternoon while we're having our dinner. Nothing but sport I suppose. A lot of silly schoolboys chasing a ball about. It's films I like best. Old films though all them lovely women do spoil you for yourself. Have to find something to cheer meself up after sitting here all morning. Maybe there'll be something later while we're getting ready to go out before Rick comes with the car. Unless there's anything more interesting going on. But I won't think about that, won't bank on it and then I can't be disappointed. Hallo Nan's had enough, jacking it in, first on her feet. Now the others all following suit, all standing up, pushing their chairs under the benches, stretching, the tongues unloosed starting to wag. Who's for home then eh? Open the cage man, we're coming out.

It is early evening. Judy is at her toilet. All day has been devoted to the preparation of her exquisite body. This morning she got up late after an hour of conscious relaxation in the soft arms of blankets and mattress, slackening the muscles of eyelids and throat where the first wrinkles will appear. For today is Saturday. All week she goes to bed early, sleeps alone but tonight she will bring back the devotee who will be permitted to worship for one night and then sent away dazed before the neighbours are up in the morning. Rise slowly; there is no hurry. Hurry breeds carelessness, neglect. You have all day before you. She stands naked in front of the mirror, unpins her hair, wipes the remains of youthifying nightcream from her face with a tissue and surveys her country, turning from side to side to admire the contours; right hand on hip, left knee bent in a little; swing to left hand on hip, right knee bent. Not bad. Not bad at all. She touches her breasts with delicate finger tips. The nipples have thickened a little, grown darker, two shadowy circles blurr the white skin. She remembers when they were small and quite pink but many lovers have taken airy nourishment there, moulding them with their lips. She sighs a little. Even admiration, homage has its disadvantages and must be taken in small doses. She picks a matching set of underwear in coffee lace from the dressing-table drawer. Every day has its colour. Tonight she will be muted, subtle, whisper sadly in the shadows, decline to dance. She goes towards the bathroom, switches on the heater, runs the bath, begins to clean her teeth, spitting pink foam accurately at the plughole. She adds cubes and essence to the bathwater, swirling it with her hand until the fragrance dissolves and rises in a cloud around her then steps in and squats letting the warmth and steam absorb her. The water creeps over her ankles and rises up her thighs flushing her with hot pleasurable sensations and darkening the ginger fur. She wonders whether she should trim it or whether it will do for today, tonight that is. The water reaches waist level. Time to lie back and let the legs float detached from the submerged trunk so that the eyes can look down on them from above the coverlet of suds, deliberating the delicate questions of toenails and calloused heels, where to cut and how much and then what tints to lacquer on. Soon she will rouse herself to soap and smooth, to cream her armpits and brush the pads of her fingers over the thrusting prickles on her calves. They must be scraped with an abrasive mitt and the skin fed with skinfood to keep it soft. She must search it for black-heads and squeeze them out between sharp thumbnails. An hour later, clean and sweet, the water thickening and cooling, she steps out.

It would be delightful to follow Judy step by step through her day. It is always interesting to be in on the secret preparations behind any rite whether it's a coronation or a simple tonsillect-omy, a visit to the city hall or a trip round the brewery but there isn't time and besides certain details of Judy's day might be meat for the prurient. We would like to be told how it's all done but we will let Judy keep her mystery inviolate until one day comes the all-mastering lover who will desecrate the holy places, refuse the command to leave with the light, move in on her hallowed bathroom and drop his clothes on the bedroom floor. We see her bending to pick them up, the priestess become a handmaiden.

Now at last she is at her dressingtable. She will be here for two hours, lighting candles at her eyes, anointing herself with unguent, sending up the savours of incense, and then the ikon itself must be retouched until it glows with rich colour, every detail of the face picked out, enhanced until it seems a true portrait of the goddess, the skin layered with flesh tints, cheeks and mouth vermillioned, the eyelids shaded with green, lashes brushed thick and dark. Pope's young madam Belinda arraying herself for the fray was no better supplied with bottles, and wares, from the four corners of the globe than Judy. There is no need to describe them for you when they can be seen in any chemist's window or displayed to perfection on the cosmetics counter of your smalltown Harrods. It is the number, the variety and the quality brandnames with the French flavour that would surprise you on a typist's salary. The hands that perform the rite pound mindlessly five days a week in the typing pool for all this. The hands, the hands that perform the rite are the hands of a serving woman, of the sink and the scrubbing bucket. They are never used to make love for Judy only receives. She never gives. It is her lovers who are the blessed and who inherit her kingdom on Saturday nights.

She is ready. One last look to be sure then she rises from her stool, picks up her blue suede jacket and throws it almost carelessly over the silk shirt. The pockets are loaded with all she will need, purse, cigarettes in their sealskin case, comb a little greasy from the bright blonde hair, lipstick and a dash of powder if her face should begin to shine in the hot twilight of the House where she twists and beckons. She carries no handbag, her hands swing free from the shoulders or dive deep among the objects in her pockets. Other walkers turn and stare as she moves through them to the station, wondering who she is, what she's doing brightening the dingy streets, where she's going. Young lads nudge each other to call after her but their voices fall short, without conviction. Some instinct tells them she's not for them and though she bristles with hatred for their clumsiness, their rough male lechery she doesn't answer. Tonight perhaps will come the dark severe butch whose jacket and trousers we have foreseen on the bedroom floor. But she doesn't know this yet. Judy is going out.

THEY left London under grey skies that seemed to drain the colour even from the branches of cherry and laburnum clustering their pink and yellow blossom in the suburban gardens that edged their route to the West.

'There's something about the quality of our light,' Matt said as the road swung them out into more open country. 'It's denser, almost a substance in itself. I mean if this were the approach to Paris now we'd be driving straight through an Impressionist landscape, Pissarro say, a froth of fresh Spring pastels and it isn't that he's exaggerating, it really is like that; I've seen it but our light is thick so that you always get that Constable colouring. It's the damp I suppose that makes the atmosphere opaque instead of clear.'

'I may be quite wrong of course and it may simply be the illusion of childhood. No let me start again. What I'm trying to say is that I don't remember it always being like this when I was young. I remember clear bright Springs, crisp winters and long hot summers when we seemed to spend every day on the beach. My uncle, who wasn't much older than I was, made us a sort of truck that you pulled along.'

'Like a modified version of the little carts made of a soapbox and two pairs of pushchair wheels that we used to drag each other up hill in so we could run down the other side?'

'Yes, that's the kind of thing and they'd load it up with the tent and picnic basket and buckets and spades and spend the whole day on the beach because of course living on a peninsula we had beaches on three sides. I used to join them after school. I suppose it is just looking at the past through rose coloured glasses.'

'No, I don't think so. I think you're quite right. As a matter of fact I read an article about it the other day in some scientific journal. Apparently our climate really was warmer during the first forty years of this century, the culmination of a warming up process that started very slowly at the end of the seventeenth century after a very cold snap of a couple of hundred years, you know when they held an ice fair on the Thames and roasted an ox. Then the Middle Ages were different again, warmer. I always wondered how they managed to grow vines out of doors in this country and produce native wine. Then I used to worry about them in those draughty castles, what Keats said about aching in icy hoods and mail. He was living in a cold snap too of course. Really they weren't as badly off as we imagine. The interesting thing is that we all think the climate is static. We know about the ice ages of course and the periods of tropical forest but we think that's all in the past, that since the advent of recorded history anyway the English climate has always been the same, one of the great immutables, and that our national characteristics are as they are because of it and therefore, by imputation, immutable too. The climate of thought doesn't change because the geographical climate doesn't either. It's all part of being English and must always be so, amen. In fact the climate is open to quite an amount of temporary variation and I begin to wonder whether the national temperament is too. How much of the laissez-faire attitude of the upper classes and the alternation between attempted violent action and apathy of the poor in the early part of this century was encouraged by the good weather? And why was it characteristic of the Middle Ages for Englishmen to be as passionate and highly coloured as any Southern European? Anyway the point is it ought to teach us that ideas we've held as unassailable truths are as vulnerable and subject to change as anything else.'

'All this from Uncle Henry making us a trolley to take our things down to the beach.'

Matt laughed. 'Not really. It's because I read that article and, oh yes, because I heard a talk the other night by an eminent man of science about the history of various scientific premises and it occurred to me, after listening to him on how bogged down they were for a long time over the question of whether the atom was the smallest particle of matter and that having once accepted as a law that it was it became in a sense a barrier to progress, I thought that the scientific mind isn't as flexible and open to new ideas as it might be and this is one of the dangers of empiricism.'

'Yes?'

'Well I think this is inclined to bog us down in archeology too and in other fields, like the division between psychiatry and psychology which just shouldn't exist. It's the tragedy of the division of the cultures. The ideal mind would be a combination of the scientific and the artistic and I think you do get this among the leading men in every field but it isn't applied enough to other levels, the mythical man in the street for instance. Our present education doesn't teach it. It teaches compartmentalism and a vertical scale of value instead of a horizontal one or, even better a combination of the two. It's no good just putting forward facts without some attempt to interpret them. That way they just don't become accessible to society for its use and improvement. What does your friend Stag think of this kind of thing?'

'You'll see. I'm going to watch this weekend with great interest.'

'I hope you won't be disappointed.'

'I don't think so.'

Matt smiled to himself, sure in his own mind though he did not quite understand why that this was some kind of test; it wasn't just circumstances that set them on the road to Lexbourne. He felt it had been in her thoughts for some time. He was about to be measured against some yardstick though this he knew was only his own crude way of seeing it. Hers would be more subtle so that if he'd said, 'Why did you do it?' she would have answered, 'Do what? What do you mean?' And when he had explained, 'But it wasn't meant to be that. I didn't think of it as that.' And she would be right too. In his process of over-simplification he would have distorted as he so often did. On the other hand her responses to situations seemed to him so subtle and complex as to be incommunicable. He knew his own limitations. Unable to accept anything that was inexpressible in ordinary human terms he sometimes found himself at the brink of wondering whether she loved him at all. 'Do you love me?' he would ask and when she answered with a simple, 'Yes,' he would be disappointed, left wondering what she meant by it, with no apprehension of what it was like to love him and therefore no real conviction that this state really existed. He was forced to guide himself by her actions like a blind man feeling round a wall. Still I've learned something, he thought as he drove, I don't nag at it any more as I did with Jill so maybe there's more hope, maybe I shall grow out of it, not to care, simply to accept things for what they seem to be without question. 'That's the difference between us,' he remembered saying once, 'I don't like not knowing something. You don't mind do you?' And she'd answered, 'A little mystery is always intriguing like a present I haven't unwrapped. I like to turn it over and look at it. I know I shall know what it is in the end.' He could have said then that she had a security he didn't feel in her. He would probably never know, was what he felt but now he didn't voice this as he would have done once. He added it to the store of things he was learning that one had to do without, realising the childishness of roaring for the moon.

Briefly, as they drove along the front through Lexbourne, the sun patched the sea with light and then was gone again. 'There's a car park at the back of the hotel. We can drive straight in,' she directed him. Latham Court Hotel stood a little on the other side of the town in its own grounds, facing the sea. It had been built earlier than its neighbours when proportions were still important and there was a fancy for wrought iron balconies and elegant verandas on which to take the maximum of sea air with the minimum of sun so undesirable for a delicate complexion.

'Stag owns this does she?' Matt looked up at the immaculate frontage and round at the beautifully kept grounds.

'She has three more now I believe but this is her favourite perhaps because it was the first. They're none of them large.'

'But rather exclusive I should think and expensive.'

'I suppose they must be. I've never thought about it.' He realised that she had simply come and gone as a guest without it ever occurring to her to ask who paid. He hoped silently that they would accept a cheque knowing at once that he hadn't brought that sort of money with him. He took their small case out of the car and followed her into reception where the attractive girl behind the desk was smiling and chatting, obviously an old friend.

'This is Irene, Kay's secretary.' He shook hands wondering who Kay was.

'She's put you in number seven. If you'd like to have a wash and then go up.' Rae nodded and moved towards the lift.

'We'll see you later Irene?'

'Oh yes. I'll be up for lunch.'

'Who's Kay?' he asked as the lift carried them up.

'Stag of course. Stag's only a private nickname. We don't actually call her that to her face.'

'The bed looks alright anyway. Thank God we haven't got to huddle together in a single. Much as I love you it's nice to have a bed that's big enough to get away. And the view darling, look at the view. It's as if there were nothing between you and the sea.'

She opened a door. 'Here's our private bath.'

'It's nice to lie in clover occasionally.' He wondered whether to mention the cost but decided against it. 'I wouldn't mind staying in this room for the next two days with you. Could we have our meals sent up do you think?'

She laughed. 'I'm afraid we've got to sing for our supper. Let's get tidied and go up to the studio. That's what Stag's private suite is called. Because it's right at the top I suppose and would make a splendid workroom for an artist. I'm hungry.'

'You mustn't keep calling her that or I shall forget myself. Will you tell me the origin of it sometime?'

'I don't think I'll have to unless I'm very wrong about something.'

'Should I put on another shirt?'

'No, not now. Save it for later. Shall we go up then?'

The lift took them right to the top this time and they stepped out into an entrance hall where Irene met them again still smiling gently and led them towards the lounge. As she pushed open the door a woman got up from the long low sofa and came towards them crying out some words of greeting that were lost on Matt because at that moment a huge herring gull planed across the expanse of glass that was one wall, sobbing and mocking until the whole room was full of its sad demented laughter. He shook hands and began to take stock. Stag was dark and handsome with a startling white streak bleached into her hair above the forehead. She was immensely at ease; her very tone of voice calculated to impress with firmness and control. The formal words of welcome dropped neatly from her lips in clear rounded syllables. He felt an urge to stutter and shuffle his feet and it wasn't just the difference in age although he judged her several years older than Rae. For the first time he knew the smell of wealth, not money which is tangible and carries the reek of all the palms that have handled it leaving a little of their feverish sweat imprinted on it but invisible wealth untouched by human hand and with the fresh smell of uncut pages in a book, a leather wallet just out of its tissue paper wrappings, new carpets. As his feet moved through the thick pile on the floor to stand before the fire wrapped in a silky white fleece he felt himself surrounded by an audience of unruffled faces which were gazing at him with slight amusement and suggesting that he should perform. Desperately he pushed down the childish obstinacy and rudeness that kept rising in him and accepted a drink. Why should I feel like this? he wondered.

Stag dispensed the drinks from a gleaming bar in the corner of the room. He forced a compliment on it in an effort to find something to say.

'I'm glad you like it. I'm rather pleased with it myself.'

'Kay actually made it,' Rae explained. Matt doubled his compliments while thinking that it had been a meaningless labour consonant with Churchill's rockeries and swimming pool built with his own hands when the streets swarmed with unemployed; a rich man's indulgence perhaps because he felt himself out of a job. What is the matter with me today? Why should I carp at everything like this?

'Are you hungry?' Stag asked. 'I thought we could have a cold lunch and then if it stays fine go for a trip in the boat this afternoon. I know Rae likes that. Irene, hand round some plates and things will you. I hope you like lobster. I'll open some champagne. I always have it with lunch as a kind of pick me up after the morning. I take it like a tonic.'

Oh I know your trouble, Matt thought to himself, it's just rank jealousy. Champagne and lobster, and trips in the boat. Why didn't she warn me it would be like this? Maybe because she knew I wouldn't have come. Well you'll have to get over it somehow my son because there's a hell of a lot of weekend in front of you and jealousy isn't a very becoming emotion however romantic the opera tries to make it.

'You know I envy you being able to wear what you like.' Stag looked down at Matt's slacks and then up at the dark blue sweater and open-necked shirt. 'I have to compromise such a lot because of my work. That's why I like to get away in the boat as much as I can. I think the weather's going to be kind to us this afternoon.'

'I don't suppose it really matters, the clothes I mean except that all clothing is a kind of mask. You know the theory behind the use of masks of course: that the mask, once you've seen yourself in it, works inwards upon the personality until in fact you become what you see yourself as; I think it's the same with all clothes. The opposite is also true of course: that you choose the mask you find expresses what you see yourself as or want to be seen as.'

'That's very interesting. Do you really think it's as complicated as that. Couldn't it just be that one likes certain clothes and feels at home in them?'

'I think you're probably both saying the same thing in different ways,' Rae put in, carefully spooning stuffed olives on to her plate. 'Matt is perhaps taking it further back and trying to explain why one feels at home in them.'

'I don't think it mattered so much when clothes were more similar, when everyone wore a version of the tunic and the cloak for instance but having a more complex and fragmented society has made our clothes like it too so that we not only have sexual differences but class and occupation as well all expressed in what we wear and how.'

'Surely there isn't as much variation as there used to be before the war for instance?'

'I think it's more subtle but the classifications are still there. Given half a dozen people in a line-up one could still more or less pick out their status and background from what they were wearing and I don't think there would be many mistakes. The other interesting thing is the number of people who complain because they find it harder to tell than they did as you say before the war. Readers' letters to the papers are full of it and so are the more pandering articles in the tabloids. They like to see the distinctions clearly because they prefer to respond to other people as types rather than individuals. Take this business of working class boys growing their hair long in imitation of their favourite pop groups. It upsets people for two reasons or even three. One because they can't tell them from girls and so there's a sexual confusion and an implication of softness and homosexuality among boys, and they might even get deceived themselves and find they've been attracted by a boy by mistake. Then too how can they maintain their own position of superiority if men look like women. Secondly longhairs in this country have always been considered intellectuals and artists and that for most people means anarchists and layabouts. From this they expect them to behave in an anarchic way and so they do, as witness all this fighting and ganging up on each other in the seaside towns. The third thing is a class confusion. It's always been the prerogative of the upper classes to wear their hair long in this country particularly when going through a phase such as being an undergraduate and now fifteen-year-old teaboys on a building site are doing it. Funnily enough you can reckon that anyone who wears his hair long almost certainly isn't queer. He'd be too vulnerable so I've never seen so many neat heads as among David and his friends. The blow wave and the shampoo and set but not a hair out of place. It's fear and insecurity of course that makes people cling to their rigid distinctions. I was in a pub the other day when the draymen came with the week's delivery. One of them was a tall slim muscular boy of about nineteen with long golden curls. A fat little man in the bar who's been telling a few blue tales and throwing his weight about a bit spotted this boy rolling barrels and when the carman came in with the invoice and the others all walked through into the public for their drink he asked the foreman if he'd got girls working for him now. The foreman turned round very quickly and said that the boy was one of the best workmen he'd ever had, extremely strong and likely to pick the fat man up by the scruff of his neck and pitch him outside if he was annoyed although normally an easy-going lad and well-liked by his mates. The little man tried to bluster and carry it off, looking round for support but I'm afraid he didn't get any and least of all from me.' He paused, realised he had been making a speech and that no one was applauding, went to the bar and helped himself to more champagne though mentally registering that he didn't like it anymore now than he had the first time he tasted it at somebody's wedding but that he had better stick to it and not mix his drinks in case he was expected to drive anywhere. He found Irene at his elbow offering him pickled walnuts and smiled at her gratefully wondering how she fitted in to the set-up. Obviously she was in the know or she wouldn't be there. Perhaps she was Stag's little bit of overtime; a variation on the secretary on the boss's knee. That's bloody coarse, he thought, but then I feel coarse. He would have liked to have taken Irene away to some quiet spot and made love to her. Now why is this, he wondered again, and looked across the room to where Stag was talking quietly and earnestly to Rae. That's it, that's the answer. You want your own back. You want to prove something to yourself, that she's not just with you because for some reason she can't have Stag: simple sexual jealousy of someone who knew her before, who knows the shape of her body, its feel. Who's made love to her and knows what she's like when . . . He gulped at the thin fizzy wine.

'Have you known Rae long?'

'About eight years I suppose. She met Kay in the army didn't she?'

'I don't really know. It's all a mystery to me.'

'What are you two talking about?' Stag called across.

'You as a matter of fact. We were wondering when you met and where.'

'It was the army wasn't it?' Irene looked at Stag for confirmation. She's in love with her, Matt thought, Stag can do no wrong there that's obvious.

'Almost the end of the war wasn't it? Rae signed on at the last minute didn't you?'

'And got out again as quickly as possible when I realised what a mistake I'd made.'

'I'm surprised you ever went in,' Matt said.

'Oh I was very young and wanting to get away from home. I hadn't really gone into it deeply. Besides we'd almost come to accept war as a condition of being. There didn't seem anything strange or immoral in it to someone who'd been brought up in it. It clouded all our thinking. Then they dropped the bomb of course and that made it impossible for me ever to see things in that way again. It made nonsense of any talk about human rights or which side was God's or humanity's. Anyway that's how I felt. I hated army life too which didn't help.'

'Rae was rather disappointed in me I think because I stayed on a little longer.'

'But then you liked the life.'

'Oh yes. I didn't mind it.'

'Kay was an officer. It was rather different for them.'

'I think you'd have liked it Matt.' Stag poured herself another drink.

'I don't think you know Matt well enough,' Rae suggested. 'It wouldn't do at all.'

'I'd love the chance to wear a uniform and parade around of course, at least part of me would but the whole business is so contrary to everything I believe that I'm afraid I'll never get the chance. By nature I'm inclined to be militant, even violent at times, but I can't kid myself it's a good thing, that there's any virtue in it so I can't indulge myself. It comes out sometimes when I've had too much to drink. Then I'm inclined to beat my wife, aren't I, but on the whole I try not to.'

'In that case we'd better take your glass away now,' Stag laughed. 'What about clothes for this afternoon by the way? You might get a little damp. Can we lend you something?'

'We brought jeans and canvas shoes with us,' Rae answered, 'so we should be alright.'

'Did we? That was clever of us.'

'I packed them thinking something like this might happen.'

'Hoping you mean. If we've all finished then we might as well change and get down there before the weather alters its mind. The trailer's all hooked up ready. I did it this morning. We'll go in my car shall we? I expect you've had enough of driving for today.'

They drove down to the harbour with Stag's gleaming toy trundling behind them over the sullen grey flagstones of the quayside that was already alive with visitors and fishermen although the holiday season was hardly under way yet. But there is something about a harbour that draws a crowd to compose themselves into a brightly coloured picture against the natural background of sea and sky and old stone walls. The fishermen were genuine enough humping their flat boxes of evilly grinning dogfish out of their boats, barefoot in their navyblue, across the cobbles to the little fishmarket. The visitors too, children hanging excitedly over the sea wall pointing and exclaiming as boats came and went while their parents stood back a little observing quietly, happy to have tired minds and bodies rested by the different images of bobbing boats, and inexorable cloud drift, by the shifting patterns that broke and reformed of people who existed more as shape and colour than as complex entities demanding a response, but looking round at his own group Matt felt complete phoney. There was no other word for it. He had always despised what he called 'the floaty-boat types' with their loud voices and tortured diphthongs, their fanatic devotion to tiny details of positioning fenders and boathooks, their theatrical comings and goings on mysterious and vital errands so that the watchers could admire their gaily expensive anaraks and Norwegian sweaters. He hated them for making a business of pleasure and for flaunting their good luck in front of people whom they would despise for taking trips round the lighthouse on the *Marybelle*, and now he was one of them.

The speedboat was unwrapped from its coverings, the trailer unhooked and run down to the water's edge where Rae was helped into the boat while Matt, Stag and Irene held it steady. Stag climbed in and started the motor while he and Irene fended it off the slipway.

'Aren't you coming?' he asked as she stood back She shook her head.

'I'll take a line from you when you come in.'

The boat was now a little way off. Stag signalled to him to get in. There was nothing else to do but to step into the freezing water to his knees and clamber aboard beside Rae. The motor roared as the gear was let in and the faces dropped away from them behind. They raced through the inner harbour towards the outer where Stag turned parallel with the shore and slowed down sufficiently to turn her head and hold a shouted conversation with them against the wind.

'I like to get out here away from everything. I find it very relaxing just to cruise up and down out in the harbour. If it isn't too rough you can take her beyond the wall out into open sea there but it's a bit choppy for that today. We'll do a few bumps shall we? You're not seasick or anything?' He shook his head. 'I know Rae loves it.'

Matt saw her smile behind her sunglasses and then they were off bounding across the tops of the waves, heading straight into them at speed so that they hit the boat with a dull vicious smack that seemed as if it would smash the bottom to fragments. The boat bucked and fell between the crests with no attempt to avoid them. Back and forth they planed, the slipway shrunk to a blur with distance, the coastline a satisfying curve of sand and clifftop and waves creaming towards the beach. 'Would you like to have a go?' Stag called back. He shook his head.

'Yes, go on,' Rae urged.

'It's quite easy. You can't go wrong.'

Suddenly he found himself in the position of being unable to refuse without losing face and yet he had no desire at all to drive this flimsy plaything anymore than it would have occurred to him to take the wheel of Stag's expensive saloon. There was no pleasure for him in it only the fear of making a costly mistake. He was glad he had insisted that Rae should wear a lifejacket. Precariously he climbed over into the bows and tried to attend while Stag explained the simple controls. Then she took his place behind with Rae so that the bows would lift better and he was on his own.

He felt his way at first and then encouraged from behind went a little faster, managing a couple of dull thuds but constantly aware that he was going at half-cock, putting up a very tame show beside Stag's earlier performance.

'Take her a bit faster, you get a better bump.'

It seemed to Matt that the water was getting rougher and the sky darkening as he turned to run along the coast again this time at fuller throttle. Once, twice he smacked successfully through and then the third time the boat caught the wash of a small cargo ship that was heading in to harbour, staggered crabwise, throwing a heavy curtain of spray over the stern. Looking back to apologise he saw that Rae was soaking, her dark hair plastered in wet strands against her cheek. She laughed back at him to show that everything was alright.

'Sorry,' he shouted, 'that was a bad one. It seems to be getting rougher.'

'It doesn't look too good,' Stag said, 'I think we'd better take her in. I'll come over shall I? You needn't come back into the stern.'

Expertly she swung the speedboat round and headed her towards the quay. The figures drew nearer, resolved themselves into separate colours bounded by a distinct shape, became people watching and last Irene waiting to catch the rope Matt threw. The boat drew in towards the slip. Irene pulled on the bow rope while Matt grappled with the boat hook. Then he let himself down into the cold water and heaved the boat up the slip til it rested in a couple of feet of water. Stag jumped over the side and turning to Rae before he had a chance to intervene helped her on to the gunwale and then on to her back and carried her ashore. Irene ran the trolley down into the water and the speedboat was half floated, half pushed back into its moorings. Between them they hauled it up the steep, slippery stone ramp and hooked it on behind the Jaguar.

'That's the easiest I've ever known it come up that slope,' Stag said.

'You never had me on the back before that's why,' Matt laughed though feeling that in some way he was re-establishing himself. 'What about a cup of tea in that café over there before we all start to shiver.'

'A good idea,' Stag said. 'Irene and I often do that if it's been a chilly run.' She led the way. As they went Matt spotted a stall selling shellfish and half out of bravado, but also because he could never get enough of them in town, he stopped to buy prawns and brown shrimps and cockles, entering the café with them triumphantly and persuading the rest to try some with their bread and butter and cups of strong tea. The woman behind the counter smiled at them benevolently not seeming to care that they were eating someone else's delicacies on her premises.

'Now we'd better get home and changed before we all catch cold.' Stag stood up, paid the small bill and led them out to the car. 'You drive Irene, I've had enough.' She gave her the keys and then sat back watching the girl's profile as they flipped through the clean, wide streets.

'What about your hair?' Matt asked when they were in their own room again. 'I'm sorry about that. It caught me off guard. Will it be alright?'

'Oh yes. Don't worry. I'll give it a rub, comb it and push it back into place.'

He took her in his arms. 'Are you cold? You'd better get changed.' But he did not let her go at once and she made no move away. 'I love you.'

'I love you too. Now I must get out of these things. Don't watch me will you?'

'I'll try not to or you might never get dressed again this evening.' He turned his back on her and began to peel the sodden jeans from his legs. 'I'd better put these in the basin to soak or the seawater will ruin them.' He went through into the private bathroom and amused himself steeping his old pants in the elegant shell-pink basin. Then he wandered back into the bedroom in his underwear.

'I love your legs. What a pity you can't walk about like that all the time. They're much better than Stag's but that never was one of her strong points, most attractive features I mean.'

Matt stood in front of the long wardrobe mirror and looked at himself, positioning his legs in various stances to get an all-round view. 'What do you like about them particularly?' It was curiosity rather than vanity that made him ask, part of his long search for what attracted her, what she responded to in himself and others, and, from this, what went on in that hidden country behind the eyes.

'They're so strong, muscular and furry but not too much so, like the boy in Flandrin's picture. They're just right somehow, very much you.'

'I like yours better.'

'So then we're both satisfied which is how it should be.'

'It's not fair you know. If I can't look at you, you shouldn't look at me.'

She laughed and took a towel from their case. 'Will you rub my hair for me?'

He pulled her towards him, conscious of her warmth and the smell of her wet hair. 'Now you're just being deliberately provocative. They ought to lock you up. However, I refuse to be distracted or we shall be late and then I'll be blamed.' He towelled vigorously and unsentimentally. 'There.'

She shook her head. 'You've almost taken my head off.'

'Serves you right for trying to seduce me. Go and get dressed. I'm nearly ready.'

'You don't have as much to do.'

He went to the window and stood staring out over the sea that had grown rougher still since their return and ran in sharp corrugations the colour of molten lead across the sweep of the bay. 'So you and Stag met in the army. Like Jonnie always says it must have been full of it. Were you worried when it first happened?'

'No, just curious. I was involved in a rather hit and miss way with an R.A.F. boy at the time and so I was a bit surprised at first but I never had any moral scruples if that's what you're after. I simply thought that if it exists then it exists so where's all the fuss. Besides I was among people who took it for granted without a lot of heart-searching and that always helps.'

'Like the fairy story of *The Ugly Duckling*?'

'Yes, that's it exactly. As soon as he got among others of his kind he stopped being miserable. There was a whole crowd of us and anyway these things didn't matter so much when everyone was living with questions of should they get married and should they have children, and this may be the last time we see each other and so let's have what we can.'

'Would you say it was an immoral time?'

'Well war is pretty well always immoral isn't it? You'd agree surely? People just go on as best they can under those circumstances, making the decisions that seem right to them.'

'You were very young. Didn't you ever feel you'd been 'taken advantage of' is the phrase I believe?'

'Good heavens no. You see it's so difficult to explain how differently one looked at things then. Most of the girls were sleeping with their boy friends and nobody thought anything of it. In fact you'd have been thought hard and self-seeking if you hadn't, if you'd insisted on security, marriage and a home first.'

'Were you sleeping with the R.A.F. lad?'

'Yes.'

'And then you went off and slept with Stag?'

'Yes.'

'And then what happened?'

'Oh I was very unhappy for a long time after that. Then I got engaged as I've told you.'

'And did you sleep with him?'

'You know I did. I've told you all about that.'

'Then that broke up and what did you do?'

'Oh next comes my long list of gentleman friends of various ages, professions and states. But I didn't sleep with them; that's before you ask.'

'The post-war reaction was well under way by this time. Must have rather hampered your style. You know you make my chaste youth seem very dull. Makes me wish I'd sewn a few more wild oats in my time. All those lovely women I'll never go to bed with.'

'Oh they're not all that fruitful, wild oats. The point is as I was telling you, we never thought much about them.'

'Still you must have some exciting memories; all those lovers. Does your life now seem dull by comparison?'

'Not particularly. After all I must have been looking for something rather different from what they offered me or I'd have stayed with them.'

'When you say a whole crowd of you what does that mean?'

'Just what I say. There were ambulance drivers and medical people as well as those who were in the forces. There's rather a nice couple I'd like you to meet who live quite near here and before you ask I haven't slept with either of them. I thought we might drive over tomorrow afternoon and see them. I wonder if Stag sees much of them. She used to be very friendly with Billie at one time. They're quite a bit older than us but very lively and Feathers is a great character. You'd like her. She's been an actress, not straight but variety, that's where she got her name from one of her acts. I always think she's a little like Hermione Gingold, same voice and mannerisms; her generation of course. There, how's that?'

'Worth waiting for. You look marvellous. Let's go and astound them all.'

'I thought we could go out to dinner,' Stag said when they joined her. 'We could have it here of course but I do get rather tired of my own food. So much of it has to be good plain cooking because that's what the customers like best. It doesn't upset their poor old stomachs. Most of them are getting on and like to be pandered to. I sometimes think I'm running an expensive geriatric ward instead of a hotel except that they can all get about and can up and leave when they like. Most of them don't, thank God. There comes the day when they feel they're getting too feeble and then they transfer to a proper home or else go and live with their relatives but they mostly like to stay on here as long as they can so I suppose they must be satisfied. The trouble is one gets rather tired of the foods one ate in the nursery, however wholesome and well-cooked one knows them to be. Sometimes I think I'll give it all up and go and do something really valuable though it's getting a little late for me to become a starry-eyed idealist.'

'You still go on buying them though. How many have you got now?'

'Just the three still though I am vaguely interested in something in Scotland at the moment. I'm not sure yet whether it will do but it has definite possibilities properly organised and with a bit of money put into it. You'll be able to go for fishing holidays and it's good for walking and shooting too.'

'Perish the thought,' Matt said. 'I should die of boredom after a couple of days!'

'Fortunately for me not everyone feels the same. I've booked us a table or at least I believe you did Irene, for seven. I thought we'd need to eat early after that light lunch and the fresh air. What about a drink first? There's rather a nice little pub down by the harbour.'

'I was hoping someone might mention the magic words. Whose car?'

'Oh mine I think then we need only take one. I'll drive there and Irene can bring us back. You can't get too tight on Cinzano.'

Stag beat him to the bar on the first round and before he'd had time to savour the long pint she was on her feet again lining them up. He sank the second without really tasting it and there was a third in front of him, this time keeping company with a double scotch. He began to long for seven o'clock and reflected a little hazily that he'd never enjoyed a drink less. Once again he was at a disadvantage, forced into a position of dependence by being unable to buy his round, and plied with drink while everyone else stayed sober, all under the assumption of hospitality. He wanted to get up from the table and walk away down to the quay and watch the unmoved, ever shifting waters unfolding on the beach but he knew that he must sit it out for Rae's sake. She had brought him here for reasons of her own and a pretty poor showing he was making of it. Well it was her own fault and if she regretted it now, regretted him it was too bad, there was nothing he could do. He was on foreign ground knowing neither the terrain nor the rules of the game, aware only of the hostility between himself and Stag. There was only one thing for it. He would have to go out the back and ditch the lot if he was to make it through the evening. He got up and nodded to Rae to excuse himself. Now he was on his feet he reckoned he'd have little difficulty in getting rid of the problem. His mind was quite clear now. Remembering the boat bellyflopping across the outer harbour would help.

When he got back there was a movement towards the car. No one seemed to have remarked anything and if Rae had noticed, knowing him so much better, she said nothing. His head was clearing; soup and bread and a careful eye on the wine should see him into that state of objective detachment that follows an early evening drunk as if the body has built up an immunity after an overdose, withdrawing the senses to leave the mind in a state of depressed clarity.

It was certainly a good meal. Matt concentrated on building up his resistance, choosing tagliatelli verdi to lay down a solid base and then chicken with rice. 'Let's have an Italian wine for a change. I always think they go better with Italian food.'

Stag passed him the wine menu. 'I'll leave the wine to you then.' He began to feel a little more cheerful. The evening might not turn out to be such a shambles after all.

'What shall I have?' Rae asked him. 'Choose something for me. I don't know what half these things are. I'm not used to having to decide for myself.'

'How do you mean?'

'Well when you get taken out to dinner it's usually all done for you.'

'Poor darling. It just shows how rarely I've been out anywhere decent in the last few years. I've forgotten how to behave.'

'Oh I'm not complaining just I'd rather you said that's all.'

'Let me see then. It depends how hungry you are.'

'So-so. You know, not starving but just healthily hungry.' He suggested a clear soup with egg and little bits of toast bobbing gently in the liquor, and to follow escallopes of veal in marsala.

The waiter was a rather dour man. Matt saw straightaway that he was in a mood to be irritated by the vacillating English and that Stag's patronising attempts to make him join in the party were making things worse. He became slow and boorish, refusing to explain or answer questions except with a shrug and an indifferent spreading of his palms. 'I'm damned if I'll come here again if he's going to be like this. I've been a good customer here and I expect a bit more cheerful service than this.'

Privately Matt thought that even money couldn't buy good humour. He leaned forward. '*E troppo lungo il giorno eh? E stancato lei?*'

The man smiled. '*Lei capisc' Italiano signorina?*'

'*Sono stato sei mesì vicino Roma. E una bella città.*' He smiled at his own mistake, reflecting that the Romance languages were even more inexorable in matters of sex, but the man took it to himself and smiled back, whisked up the menus and set off for the kitchens. 'I think we'll do better now.'

'What did you say to him?' Rae asked.

'I asked him if he were tired and said it was a long day. Then I said I'd spent six months in Rome and that it was a beautiful city. I think that cheered him up though he's from the South himself.'

'What were you doing there?'

'Digging. It was outside Rome actually. Mostly Etruscan stuff, at least that was what we were after. I was a carefree student in those days.'

'And what did they think of all this?' Stag said. 'Ah good, here's the wine.'

'Who? The Etruscans? That's just what we don't know of course. It's exactly in the fields of thought, beliefs and feelings that we've made the least progress in archeology because they don't leave much visible trace and what there is we don't know how to interpret yet. There ought to be some means of comparison based on a semi-statistical approach such as Ventris used in deciphering linear B but it's so much more difficult to do and overflows into other things like anthropology and ethnology. It would need someone with a terrific breadth of knowledge to lay the bones of such a system.'

'Is it really worth doing?' Stag raised her glass. 'Cheers everybody. I mean does anyone care?'

'No, I don't suppose they do but they'll have to learn to care. We can't go muddling on as we have done, in the areas of knowledge that deal with the human mind I mean. The more we can find out about how it evolved the more we shall understand about its present condition. You know, we've pushed material progress so far that in America anyway they're talking about the day when machines and the passive witnesses who sit and watch them will take over almost all the everyday jobs humanity wastes so much time doing. When that happens we have to be ready for a tremendous liberation of mental energy that will have to be employed some way if it isn't going to sink into apathy or turn in upon itself or even frenetically extrovert in some hellish science fiction fantastic, except that it isn't fantastic any longer but just around the familiar corner ahead. You see we go on as if all the simple theories that we think applied to primitive man can still apply to us and we can kid ourselves with this because we don't really have any idea what he did think. We're just about as deluded as the people who swooned over the noble savage idea in the eighteenth century. We imagine a society in which men were men and women were women and never the twain did except for one thing; you know all those caveman jokes about his dragging her off by the hair and she loved every second of it. That was healthy and natural and that's about as far as popular ideas about one of our most fundamental problems go. As far as anything to do with psychology most of us are still living in the dark ages. Our grasp of modern developments, inferiority complex and terms like that, is a not very subtle version of the theory of the four humours.'

'You'll find education a long and difficult process. Do you honestly believe that people are capable of assimilating ideas like you're suggesting because I don't. Even among the people with an education, my residents and their relatives for instance, I don't suppose there's a ha'pporth of understanding of our kind of problem and I certainly shouldn't like to put it to the test to find out. I'm quite sure I'd find myself with four very empty hotels in a very short time. I'm curious to know though whether you think things have ever been any different for people like you and I.'

'That's very difficult. I think there have always been outstanding women, mostly rich of course because we don't hear so much about the others. I mean if you were a queen in your own right you could do a great deal without anyone batting an eyelid and some societies were quite used to being commanded by women without anyone thinking they were stepping out of line except perhaps the enemy. Imagine us with a woman sealord or a gcneral. We're just beginning to creep into politics. Take someone like Boadicea with a dead husband and two children. I think one of the things that really caused her to raise a rebellion was the fact that the Romans had treated her as a woman rather than a queen and she simply wasn't used to it. Raping her daughters and whipping her like a slave showed exactly what they thought was the position of women. But here was a presumably more barbarous backward nation who didn't think in this way.' He took a sip of wine, looked round at them and wondered whether he had them, whether they would listen. Seeing their faces a little flushed now, receptive with the good food and drink he decided to risk it. After all what was a feast without a story. He sipped again leant forward and began . . .

Then the queen spoke; shook out her bright spear before all the hosting; long tresses in the firelight as beech drops its leaves in fall, burnished copper from the smith's hoard hidden in the dark earth. Strong her voice in the ears of the princes, snarl of the wounded she-bear, said What shall we gain now by stillness under oppression? The harsher shall be our burdens as we bear them with patience. In the days of our fathers one king ruled his people. Now two are set over us: the governor to let flow the streams of our life blood, the procurator to leach us of our lands and goods. And all is the same for us the downfallen if they strive with each other or ally against us. The centurions of one and the slaves of the other heap injury on insult. Nothing is safe from their greed and their lust. See now my bruised body striped by their rods.

In battle the spoils are won by the bravest. Spear, shield and sword go to their master but our homes are torn from us by cowards grown soft with rich living, in the name of the Emperor. Sold into slavery or ravished our children; the warriors conscripted to fight for the enemy and only our own land are we unwilling to die for.

Let us look at these conquerors who have trampled us under. They are only a handful compared with this hosting. Others across the sea saw this and cast off the yoke with only the narrow waters of the river between. We have the wide sea, grey gull's road. We shall fight for our country, our wives and our parents while they fight but for greed and soft living. Now while our gods keep the governor in exile on Mona we take counsel together. Let us carry our spearshafts forward against them, not fearing the outcome. Bold be our warring. My stripes be your banner.

So said the dread war queen, towering before them. Like a goddess her stature in the flicker of torches. Heavy the twisted gold at her throat and the folds of her mantle; her tunic many coloured as the sky at sunset when nightfall stains the blue with purple. Proudly the warrior rides forth to follow her from among all the kingdoms. Lifted up spears with a great shout, set forth to reclaim their own.

Then fared they South past fenland and forest through the land of the Iceni. Forts fell before them; word was carried to the enemy. High in her chariot rode the queen. All men obeyed her. Brave warriors she chose before the people; sent them forth secretly to lie in ambush; hold the way of rescue. Princes of the Trinovantes were her cupbearers till they came to Camelodunum.

Now they halt before the city, dwelling of the haughty, hated of the nations; the ancient seat of kings made a reward for the slayers of brave men. Fallen their Victory in the market place. In the wide waters of the estuary the colony is seen to burn in blood. Women run crying in the streets, Doom is upon us. The ebb tide leaves the prints of corpses in the sand.

Defenceless it lies before them without rampart or palisade and only the temple of their gods to serve as stronghold. There they make their stand; a hated handful against the hosting. Fire took the city. It burnt in blood. Strongly they fought with flame on every hand. For two days and nights they strove, backs to the wall. Many were the deeds of valour, lasting the glory.

On the third day the queen shook forth her spear, said, Now let it fall. Like a rampart of sand at the sweep of the sword wave it crumpled before us; the walls of the temple like a rock taken by the tide. None were left living. There died two hundred soldiers sent to assist them; the priests of the temple in their greed and rich robes. Of all who had betrayed us, Roman and Briton, not one escaped; women who had lain in the laps of the conquerors, children of treachery.

The queen said, Let the city be built again on the site of our fathers below the hill where the ways meet. We are not Romans to live in fear on the hilltop. She drew with her spear the line of the earthworks. Ditch and rampart they dug where the kings had known them below the ashes of the enemy city. Men may see them still.

Word came to Lindum where the soldiers sat at meat. Our triumph was told to the legate. Then he answered, Let us set forth at once and chastise these rebels in the midst of their boasting. They went forth in their thousands with trumpets before them, both horse and foot. Great was the noise of their going; sad their returning.

Like the grey mists of the morning we rose from the marshes as she had directed the wise one who sent us. Useless their horses and the weight of their armour. Breastplate and helmet fought on our side; bore them down beneath us. The hands of the marsh spirits drew down their heels. Only the horsemen escaped from that slaughter; fled from our long swords following their leader. We rose up as many as reeds in the river and cut them down like rushes the women gather to trample under the feet of warriors. Two thousand were slain.

The queen spoke, said, The way is open. She rode before us to Londinium, her mantle streaming in the wind of her passing like banners of the sunset. As we went the nations threw off the yoke of the conqueror; left the fields unsown to join us in our triumph. Fear took the procurator, hated of the people. He fled overseas.

The governor rode to Londinium fresh from the slaughter, the massacre of our priests on Mona. Far in the West he heard of our victory. Bitter was his triumph. Threading the valleys at the head of his men where all faces turned towards him were hostile, came to the city before us. There met him the merchants and tax-gatherers, hated of the nations, entreated him with tears to defend them, knowing they were come to judgement. Steadfastly he turned from them, rode out again northwards, taking all who would follow him.

We camped before the city; our fires thick as stars on the hillsides. Then said the queen in council, Now there is no returning. The general has fled from our swords. She the wise one saw all. I dedicate the city to Andrasta our lady of the dark groves. We are not Romans to barter for prisoners or search for riches among the fallen. All shall be sacrificed to the goddess that she may give us victory and new life after.

A great shout rose as we went forward in the morning. To Andrasta. There was no wall to hinder us. The dark goddess received them. No man stayed for booty. Their bodies were hung up in the sacred groves. None was left alive, and in the evening we feasted.

Yet as the bards sang of the victory a shadow fell upon the queen; sat silent amid the feasting. Her eyes looked on the future. She rose from the table, the mead cup untasted. No man dared to follow her. Tall before the warriors she went forth.

In the morning we left the city still smoking, marched northward to Verulamium, following their legions. This too we burned. There was no turning back now. All things Roman had grown hateful to us. We would make the land anew. Wherever she went in her chariot at the head of the host she drew all men after her as it had been the great goddess herself. Said, Let us show them they are hares and foxes who would rule over dogs and wolves. Even their emperor fears our power. Let us hunt them down; force him to leave our shores forever, flee like Julius; surrender the lands to those they belong to. So the host rolled still northwards by nations together, wives and children also in the waggons to see the end of the tyrants. Yet many were hungry and cried to the mothers who had nothing to give them. Wherever we came the granaries were burned, sweet smell of baking but no bread for our bellies; cattle driven off and the animals of the forest fled at our approach. No meat in our wallets or mead for our throats; only streams as we crossed gave water for our thirst. Yet we sang as we marched the songs of our triumph and the tales of our forefathers, north along the old ways, over the ridges into the lands of the Coritani, where the forests gathered about us and the winds moaned among the branches at night. He, the enemy, the cunning one drew us as Eloquence draws men after him on chains of gold. There at last we caught up with him on ground of his own choosing and there the battle was joined.

The queen spoke, shook forth her spear before all the army, rode before the nations in her swift battle chariot whose wheels flashed blades of sunlight, her daughters riding up with her, the sun bright on breastplate and hair, burnished as the smith's hoard, said to each of them, Often of old queens have led you to battle but I fight not as your queen descended from mighty forefathers, eager to avenge my stolen riches and kingdom. I fight as the least of you for my lost freedom, my bruised body striped by their rods, my daughters broken to the lusts of the Romans whose greed no longer spares either old or young. The high gods shall give us vengeance upon them. Those who opposed us we slew in their pride. The rest lie skulking behind the walls of their forts not daring to face the thunder of our thousands, stand to our charge or meet us face to face. We have come forth in our numbers thick as stars upon the night sky and now there is no returning. This day brings either victory or death. That is my resolve taken as a woman. Let the men live to be slaves if they choose.

The enemy stood before us. Their backs were to the forest; upon a hilltop with the plain before them. The warriors of the nations were like sand upon the shore. Their women fought beside them or watched with their children where the waggons were drawn up behind us. So we came on crying for victory as the hounds bay the boar. At bay he stood waiting our coming as we rushed the long slope; held back his javelins until he felt our breath. Bellicicus stood forth, challenged their warriors. A spear took him. None among them was brave enough to meet us sword to sword.

At the word of their leader they let fly their javelins. Like hawks they hovered and plunged to the kill. Useless our shields heavy with their weight. We cast them from us. They let fly again, birds of ill omen. Many a warrior fell beneath them. The lashes of the women were wet with their tears.

Then as one man they moved, drove through our ranks as the boar through the hunters, dividing us from each other; turned again to rend us. The wings of the enemy beat down from the hillside, fell upon our flanks. Seeing our agony the war queen led forth the chariots. Again and again she rode to our rescue. Yet we could not prevail. They fought not as warriors fight when brave man stands to brave man, when long swords clang together before all the nations but as cowards cling together, safe behind a shield wall, stabbing with the short sword as wolves hunt in packs.

All day the battle swayed this way and that. Many were the deeds of arms; many the warriors won lasting glory. Weary in the evening they closed in upon us, cavalry and shield wall. Their bowmen loosed deadly rain of arrows, kept off the dread queen, the succour of chariots. Our backs were to the waggons when they made an end of us; slaughtered women and children and the beasts in their harness. Only the fortunate fled from that field.

Shattered the hope of the Britons. Vanquished her warriors crept home by hidden ways through a land weeping to the kingdom of the Iceni; waited the coming of the conqueror, doom that should fall.

The queen spoke for the last time, said, Come now my daughters. Let us not grace a Roman triumph to be dragged through the streets at the scorn of slaves. Our bodies they have already broken but our spirit never: As I spoke before the battle let the men live in slavery. The gods withheld victory but not honour. We are no less than Romans; it is easy to die. I am heavy for my people. I see the time coming when they must pay for their boldness in fire and in blood. Let us go forth together without fear and without shame.

So spoke the war queen, last of her line. Drained to its grim dregs the goblet of death. Weary lay down, her long spear beside her; sad for her people sighed out her soul.

Many days the Iceni mourned for her going. Wept for the dread queen; warriors kept watch by her. Then in her chariot they carried her far, bore her secretly no man knows whither. Laid her in the earth, wrapped in her mantle; her spear beside her, twisted gold at her throat. Last of her house took with her the royal treasure; her chariot also. Went before her people. Broken the goblet, shattered the spearshaft.

The Romans came seeking her with sword and fire. Punished the people for their silence; laid waste all the country from Durobrivae to the sea. A long and terrible winter. Hunger walked among us because of the grain unsown, the ears unharvested. There was no mercy for those who surrendered. A proud, harsh man he, the governor took vengeance as the queen had foretold it. Yet we resisted through the lean months and in the Spring driven North to a bleak shore fell upon his ships as they lay upon the beach. The gods drew back the waters, delivered them to us with all their men. The smoke of their burning was good in our nostrils.

Waste the land, broken her people. The sword grows rusty hidden in the earth. Romans rule over us. They offer us slavery and call it peace. Limbs grow bent and weak under the yoke. Old age comes upon us. We are weary for death. New governors succeed and plant their cities amongst us. Our children learn new ways. As for the dread queen, last of her line, no man can say where she lies buried, hidden from the sight of the enemy. Crumbled the chariot, tarnished the breastplate once bright as the smith's hoard. Leader of princes gone from her people; last of her line . . .

'That's fine, fine,' Stag said, 'but what does it mean?'
'Nothing, nothing at all if you don't want it to, can't see it I

mean.' Matt leaned back in his chair, a feeling of palpable depression centring between his eyes. Somewhere along the line he had lost them. Recreate the whole thing for them and they still can't see, hear only the top layer of the story with the surface of the mind.

'I don't know,' Rae said, 'but I think . . .' She was used to him, used to his way of thinking. Irene too looked as if she might have understood. Perhaps it was only Stag. 'I think the point is,' Rae went on, 'that there was a woman doing all these things and being completely accepted for it. In a sense she became Andrasta for them and yet she never stopped being a woman and probably was more successful than a man would have been. Like Queen Elizabeth I. She was another one who used all the undertones of being a woman to sway people.'

'Why isn't it possible now?' Irene drew a diminishing spiral on the table cloth with her butter knife. 'It's partly Christianity isn't it? St. Paul always upset me at school I remember. He made me feel as if the original sin was to be born a woman and there was no absolution for that one. Didn't the Gnostics say that women would become men before they could inherit the kingdom? That was supposed to be one of Christ's sayings wasn't it?'

'To be understood like "Except ye become as little children," I should think. It was becoming a patriarchy with God the father that did for us.'

'But it still wouldn't make any difference to you and me would it?' Stag looked across at Matt. 'We wouldn't want to be women even if we could be rulers, generals. At least I wouldn't because I just can't think of myself in those terms. I know a lot of people can and are quite happy to do so but I don't, can't. I imagine you're the same. The only thing I would be if I weren't myself would be a man with a wife and family, a doctor. Not that I worry about it. One of my girlfriends said to me once, 'The only difference between you and a man is that you wear a deodorant.' And now men are taking to those so that lets me right in. What about a sweet? I'll have some cheese I think and let's get him to bring us some more wine.'

'Try a zabaglione,' Matt suggested, 'I think you'd like it.'

'I'll have one too,' Irene said.

'Three zabaglione,' Matt ordered.

'*Tre?*' the man said as if the others no longer existed and the two of them had a linguistic conspiracy all their own.

'*Si e formaggio per la Senora.*' It seemed ridiculous to call Stag '*signora*'. '*E un altra bottgilia di vino.*'

The waiter bent forward, whisked away plates and unused cutlery, flicked his serviette over the cloth, smiled at Matt and hurried away to return at once with another bottle which he un-corked with a grand gesture, poured all round, and was gone.

'Cheers again everybody,' Stag said for the fourth time raising her glass though she and Matt were now drinking most of it between them. 'Where were we?'

'Just deciding that if you and I weren't what we are we'd have to change sex altogether. What I look forward to is a time when we can all be what individually we are and nobody gives a damn. They don't already of course in some groups. I find when people know you first and then you tell them they usually accept it.'

'I don't think I have any compulsive need to tell anyone.'

'Oh I wouldn't call mine compulsive. It depends how close a relationship you want with someone. If it's going to be anything above the level of nodding acquaintance, friendship with the usual communication, you've either got to get it straightened out or lie or evade, which is a form of lying. Choose either of the last two and there's the end of the relationship. This is particularly true I find with a man. In fact it's amazing how much sex or some aspect of it comes into our everyday conversation. All the fertility pre-occupations of the days of primitive religion seem to have to be lived out in our own lives all the time now we don't externalise them anymore.'

'That's true.' Irene dipped her spoon into the smooth froth of zabaglione in its glass dish. 'I noticed it particularly when I was working in offices. The whole of one's conversation, day after day, was tinged with it whether it was just among the girls or the sex war that lit up every time one of the men came in. I wonder if we really are more conscious of it than our parents' generation?'

'Oh I think so. You were quite right,' Rae said turning to Matt, 'this is very nice. I think it's all much more open now and there are dozens of reasons why when you think about it; wider education, development of psychology, mass media like television and newspapers, the fact that people have more leisure to think about things and aren't simply concerned with where the next meal is coming from, oh and many more.'

'It's a phase we're going through of course, overawareness like kids who are just finding out how babies get born. It's funny how we seem to have to go right through the natural process of growth even in the dissemination of new ideas. I'm afraid we've got a painful amount of growing up to get through before it all becomes so much a part of common knowledge that no one takes much notice of it anymore and we can get on to the next stage whatever that's going to be.' Matt finished his wine.

'Coffee and liqueurs all round?' Stag asked. 'I'll have a brandy I think. What about everyone else?'

'Brandy for me too. Rae?'

'Just coffee.'

'And for me.'

On the whole he was very glad he wasn't driving, he decided when the waiter had bowed them out into the night air. He was happy to sit back while Irene took them safely home. The lift shot them straight up to the studio, the bar was opened and music began to spill into the room from a gleaming radiogram. He found his way to the bathroom, slapped his face hard and doused it with cold water to bring back some feeling and then stood for a moment staring at himself completely alienated in the mirror above the wash-basin. You fool, he whispered to his image, you bloody drunk fool. Who are you? What are you doing here? Letting yourself be taken up and patronised like some little snotty-nosed, ragged-arsed foundling from the workhouse and only because you've no confidence in yourself any longer, because you've identified so much with the shades, with the dead that you're only half-alive yourself. Is this what Steve's priestly father would mean by suffering? Is this why Steve won't accept it? The audacity of you to think you could suffer like that, be submerged and still keep your own identity. Don't you understand, there's nothing you can do this way because you're no longer even making real choices, there's only the negative choice to go on and that's become mere habit. You listen to your mouth talking and no longer believe it though you know the words are true. But they don't mean anything, are just thrown off

237

from the top layer of your mind because underneath there's an emptiness, nothing, a vacant tomb. The dead have possessed you, dead hopes like children in limbo, every vital feeling a ghost of itself; the face of a zombie looking back at you from the glass. He pulled down his bottom lids one after the other and the sockets showed yellow and bloodless. Then he shrugged and grinned at the mask in front of him and turned towards the door.

As he came through into the studio he saw that Rae and Stag were dancing, pirouetting and swooping as if on a ballroom floor and went to stand before Irene. 'Would you like to dance?'

He knew only one way to dance as they danced at the House of Shades, held close, the fingers of one hand slipped through the tie of Irene's dress behind so that he could let her ride slackly in time to the music or draw her to him their loins moving together. In his present mood any other kind of dance seemed decadent, gutless unless it was done for display as animals and birds do, and the smooth conversation of foxtrot and quickstep irritated him with its urbanities and posturing. 'To coin an old phrase, what's a pretty girl doing in a set-up like this?'

Irene looked up at him and unaccountably her eyes were pricking with tears that made her even more attractive. He watched her hold them back and then he said. 'What's for you here? You're not happy are you?' He felt drawn to her by their common age-group and by their dependence although his was only temporary. To-morrow he could drive away if he wanted to. 'Stuck down here in the country what life do you see? Who do you know that you can really talk to?'

'No one. You're quite right of course. We don't see anyone and everything has to be kept quiet because of the business. Kay's hotels are all in healthy, bracing, narrow-minded places. If the air and food are good and they get good service they're content to lie there or amble through the countryside or along the front.'

'Prolonging a cocoon life, wrapped in silk and imagining that one distant day they'll spread their wings and fly away to heaven to be butterfly angels for eternity.' He had made her laugh and she was even more tempting when she laughed through the tears. He imagined her throat under his lips and shifted his grip on her belt.

'The music's stopped. Perhaps we ought to.' He let her go. Finding his way to the bar he poured himself another drink and turned to survey the room. He felt anger against Rae rising in his gorge. Why was he here? They didn't enjoy the same things, the same people; she would never dance properly with him in public feeling that it left her naked to other people's eyes he supposed. He knew he was very drunk but he felt that it was her fault. The weekend away was being a terrible failure. But then isn't it always when I try to run away from something. This time I'm not going to run. Suppose I got Irene to leave Stag, to come to me, what would it mean? Only another running away that would deceive me for a while til the first flush was over and then I would wake to desolation with nothing solved and another heap of ruins around me. I have to find another answer, there has to be some way out of all this.

Aware that someone was speaking to him, he focussed his eyes, trying to keep them off the angle of wall and ceiling that wouldn't stay in place but tried to catch him out by wandering up and down. 'You know I've been thinking,' Stag was saying, 'perhaps what I need is someone like you to travel about and keep the managers on their toes, particularly if I buy this place in Scotland. It'd be too far for me to get up there very often. You have a car and can drive. You could decide which one you wanted to live in, live as well as I do, everything found, petrol off the hotel account, all your salary to yourself.'

He wondered for a split moment whether he'd heard right, decided he wasn't that drunk and said thickly, 'Thanks but I have a job. Shall we dance?' He turned to Irene. As he began to move he heard Stag say, 'Come in here a minute Rae, I've got something I think you'd be interested in.'

When he turned again in the course of the dance he saw that they had disappeared and drawing Irene to him he let himself bury his face in her throat, breathing in her perfume and moving his lips against her skin. 'Sing to me. I like women to sing to me while we're dancing.' She allowed herself to relax and then he felt her body grow taut, attempt to draw away but he held her there guessing that the others had come in to the room, and only let her go when the music stopped. His grasp of the evening receded. He moved and spoke like an automaton, answering like an intelligent parrot. Only when they were back in their own room, a little feeling returned and it was anger that rose again, rose and choked him until he was down on his knees before the shell-pink pan throwing up his pain and misery until his whole body was torn and empty. Then he heard himself crying out bitter words against her, words to wound and claw while she stood there silent. At the end she said quietly, 'Thank you. Thank you very much.' He fell into bed and asleep to waken again and again with his miserable body demanding water for its shrivelling flesh or that he should drag himself back into the shell-pink bathroom and sit there with his head held in his sweating hands. Towards morning he slipped into a heavy sleep that was like a coma and which left him with a foul mouth and a slight fuzziness of vision but more than anything else a sense of shame. He wondered what he should say to her and looked at her still sleeping beside him. He let his mind play over the evening finding great gaps in his memory that he filled with terrifying actions and guilty words. Why should she love him? What was there to love? He put out a hand and touched her and she laughed quietly in her sleep and moved closer. What would she remember when she woke and what would she say to him?

'Was I too bad last night?' He had fallen asleep again and wakened to find her getting out of bed, swinging her feet quickly to the floor as she always did and slipping them out of sight in the soft grey moccasins. She went into the bathroom and he sat up, reached for his clothes and began to pull on his socks. By the time she came back he was half-dressed and ready to face the answer.

'You were obviously very unhappy.'

'Yes, but did I say terrible things to you?'

'I didn't really listen because you didn't really mean them and I was a bit hazy myself, so I let you carry on and then sleep it off. Poor Matt.'

'You know I can't remember much. Did I do anything awful? I mean did everyone else know how plastered I was?'

'I don't think so. Everyone was pretty far gone. You made a pass at Irene, kissed her or something.'

'My God, did I really? Oh hell that's torn it.'

'I don't think anyone took it seriously. Anyway it was all Stag's fault. She always overdoes everything and she hasn't much idea about people's feelings because she's too busy being the LadyBountiful. She just doesn't think and it seems to me the more money she has the worse she gets, more divorced from reality, insulated in a sort of golden dream blanket. There's no need for it all. Why can't she just be herself. With all this drink and easy money she won't have a thought in her head soon.'

'I thought you liked it rather.'

'You are silly. Why do you think I left her?'

'I don't like to think.'

'She lost my respect.'

'Yes, but you like nice things, and food and all that. I don't give you any of those. That's why she makes me so on edge I suppose because she makes me feel inadequate, that I don't have enough to offer you.'

'And now you see. I could have had all that if I'd wanted but it · isn't any use without other things. You have the other things.

'What was she like, you know, in bed?'

'I don't really remember. Now don't say it. I don't.'

'That's not much help to me in curing my insecurities.'

'You mean "who's the prettier fellow and wears the braver dagger"? You are funny you know, just like little boys.'

'Well?'

'I'm here aren't I, with you. Now are you happy?'

'Better. You honestly don't remember?'

'I told you, no.'

'Then it couldn't have been so good. Do you think you'd remember me?'

'You're you. That's different. I love you.'

'But you thought you loved her?'

'Yes, I suppose I must have done but it wasn't like this quite. I can't explain.'

Matt gave a mock sigh. He was up against the impenetrable barrier of the feminine mind again but this time he didn't care so much, it didn't drive him to exasperation.

'How do you feel?'

'I'll be better when I've had a good solid breakfast. My stomach's flapping on my backbone and I've got a mouth like the bottom of a parrot's cage. Tea that's the thing, several cups. What do we do about breakfast here?'

'Ring I should think.'

'You do it. Those bells put the fear of God into me. I feel as if I'm pressing the burglar alarum and there'll be organised pandemonium. I'll have everything that's going but most of all tea, buckets of strong tea.'

'What shall we do today?' Rae asked when the maid had gone. 'I gather we're on our own, till this evening anyway.'

'What would you like to do? You know this place better than I do, what is there to do? I feel like fresh air, apart from that I'm easy.'

'Shall we go up into the forest then? We can have lunch somewhere and perhaps call in on Feathers and Billie if you haven't had enough of my past life by then.'

'I think I can take a little more provided no one wants me to drink champagne by the quart. I've had that. Too deceptive for a beer drinker.'

'Billie's a beer drinker, at least she used to be and I can't imagine her changing much. Feathers is like me, probably a couple of martinis will do for her.'

'Right. Do you know the way or should I look it up?'

'I think I do but you'd better make sure and anyway we want to wander a bit first, don't we?'

'I always feel this is very old country,' he said as they drove out. 'You get the impression of its years pressing down on you or is it pressing up from the earth into humps of barrows and earthworks everywhere.'

'Like those in the field over there?' She pointed across at the collection of grassy hillocks and ridges rising unnaturally out of the level. 'They could be just odd formations I suppose?'

'Oh they could be. I wonder if anyone has tried to find out. It's difficult when they're on somebody's farmland. Those horses'd be upset if you came along with a spade and wanted to dig up their paddock. How far before we get to the forest proper?'

'Just keep going along this road for another mile or so and we'll find ourselves in it.'

'The greed of kings, clearing all these hundreds of acres of their inhabitants just so his majesty can go chasing after other animals whenever he's the fancy.'

'Still it's turned out quite well in the long run because it's left us all this open space. And it's a beautiful morning, one of the best we've had this year. You see, we're into the forest now without noticing. Slow up a bit. There's a clearing along here on the left where we can run off the road. This is it.'

Matt bumped the car over the uneven turf and pulled up. 'This do? It's more like a heath than forest, proper forest with trees like Epping.'

'There are trees, great stretches of them but there are these heathy bits in between. See, over there, trees. We can take the rug; the sun's quite warm. There'll be more people out this afternoon but we're the first. We can have it all to ourselves.'

He took the coloured rug from the back seat, locked the car and followed her across the coarse hair mattress of rough grass and heather. A skylark, a speck against a blue so bright it hurt his eyes as he tried to catch it, dropped down the scale shedding its clear notes over their heads until he lost it behind a clump of hazels. They passed out of the light, under tall trees whose boles were deep in young bracken, the tips of the fronds still curled into tight green snails. It seemed dark under the roofing branches as if he had followed her down into another world away from the sunlight.

She stopped and waited for him to catch up. 'We'll find somewhere off the track where we can lie in the sun.'

'Isn't it fantastic how the year's been getting on without us. You just don't notice when you only see streets and houses every day. You come out into the country and suddenly it's summer and you've hardly even noticed winter's over.' His voice sounded strange as if he should be whispering in the shadowed aisles of the forest. A patch of sun falling between the boughs onto a bank of fronds a few feet from the path made them glow a vibrating green.

'There's a gap over there. Let's see if that'll do.' She led him on to an enclosure walled with thick-growing bushes with a single silver birch whose leaves trembled a little in the still air. 'This is fine. Put the rug down there.'

'You sure it isn't damp?'

'A bit I expect but with the bracken and the rug we should be alright.'

He stretched it over the bending stalks. 'You'll have to sit on it or we'll never flatten them down. That's it.' He laid himself beside her and watched while she lit a cigarette and let the smoke curl straight up into the air. He was grateful for the rest. A lethargy had come over him; he wanted to lie there in the warm sun and doze the morning away. Under half closed lids he watched the silver birch and turned his head to peer into the insect world of giant stalks at eyelevel. A few midges began to dance above them, 'Smoke up, the enemy are coming.'

She lay back and blew a smoke screen over their heads that eddied and thinned in the strong light. Watching it he fell asleep, the sun falling hot on his face. When he woke she was lying beside him, eyes closed. He felt warm and strong. Even the taste in his mouth was different with a tang of iodine that comes from sleeping in the open air. He picked a long furry grass blade and began to tickle her neck with it and she smiled but didn't open her eyes.

'You're not asleep, you're just shamming.' She opened her eyes. 'Do you think we ought to be moving?'

For answer she reached up a hand round his neck and drew him down on top of her. He felt the fire jump between them as their lips met and his hands began to move over her body. As they made love she seemed to be drawing him down into her and when the climax came he cried out like a sudden death pressing his body deeper into hers as she twisted under him. He seemed to feel strength go out of him and lay there, covering her, exhausted, for what was only a few moments but felt to them both as if ages passed. Eventually he lifted his head and kissed her. Then he sat up, thinking that if all the world had gathered to watch they wouldn't have noticed. He bent over her and caressed her with his lips. 'You're a wicked woman, leading young lads astray in the woods.'

'Love you.'

'I could start all over again but I'm getting hungry and we ought to go if we're going to find anywhere to eat. Come on now.' The woods seemed even darker in their noon stillness as she led the way back and the heath, when they came out onto it again, was drained of colour under a milky sky. Looking round he felt a different person from the one who had followed her into the trees that morning, stronger, more sure of himself though why this should be he couldn't decide and anyway they were soon on the road again, running along beside the heath, once glimpsing two gipsy caravans, a tribe of ragged children and two dusty-coated horses who didn't lift their cropping muzzles as the car spun past. They had lunch at a pub, set back from the road, where the beer was still drawn from the wood and they could put away pasties and bread and cheese while a few locals talked horse sense in a corner under the dart-board. A notice in the window had said 'No Gipsies', and Matt would have liked to have gone on but time was running out if they wanted food. The couple behind the bar seemed cheerful obliging people and he wondered why they had put up such a notice. Perhaps it was the customers who didn't like gipsies or perhaps there was something about them, fighting when they'd had a few too many or not washing over much. He felt his old indignation rising but knew there was nothing he could do in this context. 'I don't get it. There aren't many of them and they're fairly harmless apart from petty crimes. What do they represent for us that makes us so afraid of them? Is it their nonconformity, finding an echo in us so that we become frightened that we might chuck everything up and go native as they used to call it. I remember as a child they used to come round selling, the old women with baskets of flowers and clothes pegs, and I was terrified of them because they were so different. Witches I suppose.'

'I've always rather liked them, and thought I'd quite like that way of life if I'd been born to it. In the same way I'd have liked a bargee's life on the river, the freedom of it and being outdoors most of the time.'

'Instead of which you sit in a little office drawing pots all day in smoky old London. But they're dirty and irresponsible.'

'Are they? I don't know any so I couldn't really say except that it's the life that appeals to me. Why can't people be allowed to be individuals any more?'

'Is it because we're outside society in a sense that we find it easier to think like this than the average man who's got everything to lose or thinks he has if everyone doesn't keep the rules. Funny how the word dirty always gets tacked on to the outsider whatever he is: Jew, Irish, queer, black. Perhaps it's the old idea of the scapegoat loaded with the sins and filth of the whole community before he's driven out into the desert?'

'If so it's a relic of the primitive people ought to be taught to recognise before we all do ourselves harm. But how do you ever teach that kind of thing?'

'Just knowledge, knowing more and more about ourselves and making sure that knowledge gets down to the level where it can be used. You just have to keep on even when people say you're mad, obsessed. Progress just isn't made any other way. Come on, let's go and see these two friends of yours, find out if they've got anything to add to the puzzle.'

She looked at him questioningly. 'What does that mean?'

'I can't explain exactly. I feel as if I'm gradually piecing something together that'll push me along some new way. Not a final answer or anything starry-eyed like that but a direction, something that answers the moment. Growing pains I expect. I'm about to become adolescent so watch it.'

'Something I never quite understand.'

'What's that?'

'How you seem to yourself.'

'Maybe you only see what you want to see?'

'I don't think so because then I'd be proved wrong in the end and that doesn't happen, at least not very often. I just wait and take things as they come as you know and usually it comes round to my way, in its own time and style of course as you have to know things in your way not in mine.'

'Can people know something in different ways and yet it still be the same thing, still be true?'

'I believe so.'

'And what about Stag?'

'She's hidden any faculty she had for knowing in any way at all. It needn't have been so but there you are, she made her choice. Look we're coming to the kennels now through those gates. You'll see the house at the end of the drive.'

He heard the dogs even before he drew up at the door and switched off the engine. 'My God, I wouldn't fancy any burglar's chance of creeping in here unnoticed. What a racket! I hope they're all well-fed. I'd hate to end up as a dog's dinner even if it does have a pedigree as long as my arm.'

The door was flung open and a horde of small brown sausage dogs dashed itself at their feet and legs, recoiled yapping and snarling and bounced back to the attack. 'Kiki down, Mim be quiet, damn dogs, down! Rae darling, it's marvellous to see you. Franchie! Where's my stick? I heard the car, or rather the dogs heard it first of course; they always do my dear. Kiki! Do come in, if you can get in that is. They'll settle down when they get a bit more used to you. Have more than one dog my dear and they become a pack, believe me.'

'This is Matt.'

'And I'm Feathers darling, everyone calls me that. It's stuck so long now I can hardly remember what my mother used to call me. Bill's out in the garden somewhere. You know what she is Rae dear. She'll be in later and we can have some tea. You will stay won't you? We see so few people stuck out in the depths here but it's the only thing you can do if you're not going to be fighting law suits with the neighbours all the time, just don't have any my dear, at least if you want to keep dogs. You see they're settling now, provided you don't move your feet or stand up or anything they'll be alright now they've got used to you. Rae dear you look marvellous. What have you been doing with yourself? You must tell me all the news. You'll excuse me being in these old slacks and my hair done up like a pudding in a cloth but, as I say to Bill, what's the use of trying to look like Dietrich when you're nothing but a damn kennel maid. You know me Rae, I like to look smart. It goes right against the grain when I think what I've been and done in my time but here I am. She's got her way and buried me in the country. Not that I'm complaining. After all they're my dogs. Stop it Kiki! You're staying with Stag I suppose. How is she? We never see her you know even though she's so near and such an old friend of Bill's. Our worlds just don't touch. In fact my dear, the only person we do see much of is Sally Wilmot. She's doing a lot of showing you know. Done frightfully well too with some of her dogs. Got a small riding school too and shows for other people. Absolutely raking it in. Must be worth a fortune and hardly spends a penny except on the animals. Still what is there to spend it on down here.

We go into Lexbourne sometimes but they're not really my kind of people. You know me Rae, I like a bit of fun, a few high kicks. Well I'm used to it but that place is as dead as Manchester on a wet Sunday and I've seen that a few times I can tell you. By nine o'clock they're all tucked up in their bathchairs in the lounge watching television. And the others, the crowd Stag runs with, all business and money, they're not my kind either so there isn't really much life if you know what I mean.

After all, by the time I was seventeen I was working non-stop in variety at Leicester Square and what I didn't learn about life, abortions, queers, prostitutes in those four years my dear just wouldn't fill a sixpenny programme. That's where they first called me Feathers, after the act as you might say. I used to go straight home and tell my mother everything and she'd gasp with horror and say, "Keep away from theatrical parties." You remember my mother don't you Rae? She was very hard you know; a will like steel and used to throw hysterics just to get her own way. I never had her love, not up to the day she died. I fought her for it, begged her for it, even went and nursed her for months hoping there'd be something at last but there wasn't a word. She knew what she was doing all the time too but that was how it was between us. When I was a kid, you know, I often used to think that maybe she wasn't my mother at all, I mean what natural mother bundles a child off to a convent in Scotland at three? I wouldn't do it to the dogs, even Bill wouldn't and she's not as soft about them as I am. She's out there concreting you know. Mucking around with shovelfuls of sand and cement and buckets of water just the same as ever. Something about it must give her a feeling of security I suppose. Damn useful in this game I can tell you. Don't know how I'd have managed if I'd had to employ men to come and do it all. Now she's building a new shed for the next batch of pups and every bit has to be perfect, absolutely bloody perfect. You'll have to excuse my language, I swear like a stableboy these days I'm afraid, cut off from civilisation out here. You know when I first saw her I said, "Don't tell me anything about yourself. I know all about you. You ought to be in a garden growing cabbages and things." I could see it even through the uniform. You were just a child in those days Rae, I don't know if you remember. She's made this house and everything beautiful, laid the paths built the conservatory and everything has to be bedded in concrete my dear as if it had to last for ever. No sentiment, no romance.

You remember how we met? Stag had all the army, at least that's what it seemed like when I walked into that huge lounge her mother had at Oak Lodge. Lovely rooms they were you know and some gay old times we had there. So understanding her mother, didn't give a hoot about convention. She was pretty good to me too when I was so ill that winter. Flu three times my dear and the last time I collapsed on the stairs and came to at three o'clock in the morning in an absolute bath of perspiration with my poodle licking my face. The doctor didn't come for hours and when he did he told me I'd a temperature of a 103, probably had it for days. The poor old devil was rushed off his feet, it was a shocking winter, everyone went down with something. The war I suppose. Anyway he dropped dead of a heart attack a week or so after so I couldn't really blame him for taking his time. Why am I telling you all this? Oh yes, so there I was weak and lonely, apart from the poodle, and along came Bill as the song goes or was it Jim? It was terribly romantic at first, the uniform and the war and all that. We used to go to the House quite a bit in those days. It was rather sophisticated with a piano and tea at little tables. Then the last time we went it was full of youngsters in teddy-boy suits and a jukebox in the corner going wah, wah, wah and I said to Bill, "Come on," I said, "this is no place for us," and we've never been back since. Well darling someone who's auditioned for *Maid of the Mountains* as a mezzo soprano finds all this modern noise absolutely hideous. I might just as well go out to the sheds and listen to the dogs howling for all the sense it makes to me.

Course it was about that time that the penny dropped when I was working at the London Coliseum and auditioned for *Maid of the Mountains*. There were two girls in the front of the house who'd had a bet about me for fun and they took me to a night club. Well it opened my eyes I can tell you, in fact the first couple of times they were coming out on stalks my dear. Eventually I got asked to dance by various people and curiosity killed the cat. Then like the green kid I was I thought I'd made a marvellous discovery, something absolutely new and I ought to go home and write a book about it until some woman told me I was a snob and threatened to black my eye if I asked her any more questions. Fortunately one of the girls who'd had the bet saw I was fascinated and heading straight to make a damn fool of myself before I was very much older and she took me under her wing, mothered me you might say and I lapped it up like a kitten on cream. All those years at boarding school and no affection from mother made me an absolute sucker for anything like that. Not that I didn't have a relationship at school but there was never anything physical in it if you see what I mean. It was all very spiritual and emotional.

I think I've told you the story before Rae. I suppose I was about five when it first happened. It was St. Patrick's night. We little ones slept in a dormitory with a long corridor leading off. It must have been a laird's castle at some time, a great big old house with panelled walls and dark recesses and ceilings that, as a child, seemed miles above your head. I hadn't been in that dormitory long. Before then I slept with the other babies but a few weeks before this night I'd been put up into one of the girls' rooms. Being a Catholic convent there were a lot of Irish girls there of course and in the middle of the night, or that's what it seemed to me, pitch dark, the most terrible din woke me and I found the room full of hooded shapes, all screaming and clashing metal basins and spoons together like weird instruments. One of them bent towards me. I leaped out of bed and ran across the room out into the corridor with them all after me, and I saw one of the senior girls standing under a light at the end of the corridor, looking absolutely calm and beautiful. I ran towards her and she went down on one knee and stretched out her arms to me so that I went straight into them. And I felt safe, perfectly safe. Everything I did after that I did for her. I was in love with her. If I danced it was for her. We were very idealistic: Liszt, art, music and passionate relationships all around us. I wanted to take the Catholic religion too and become a nun but my father wouldn't hear of it so I left the convent at sixteen and went on the stage.

My God when you think of it, it was a hell of a contrast and I damn soon forgot about becoming a nun and fell for the pianist who was only a boy not much older than I was. He was very frail and feminine and we never even kissed but I still keep his letters.

He was a marvellous pianist. You know I met him again ten years later, three years running in the same show together. He was the bear and I was the fairy. Can you imagine? We looked so different it was frightful. Then I gave up the stage and took a restaurant with my friend and I was perfectly happy for thirteen years even though she was having meetings with different women behind my back. Not that I knew my dear though I did suspect once and threatened to pack the whole thing in, including the business. In the end she met someone else and let me down completely. I thought, that's that, never anymore. Well do you blame me? I'd been absolutely sold on her and I took a very nasty knock. I was left with the cottage and that was all. Of course I had to have a solicitor to sort everything out and one day he rang me up and said he knew I wanted to let part of it to recoup a bit and asked me if I had anything against coloured people because he had a friend, a married woman, who wanted somewhere to stay. Should he send her along? Well you know me Rae dear, being in show business and all that I've no prejudices of that sort and anyway we're all supposed to be the same in the eyes of religion so I said let her come. And she came and she seemed a very nice woman, respectable, not terribly black anyway and rather attractive, Indian or Anglo-Indian so I couldn't see where the fuss was and I told her she could bring her things along. The next thing I knew there was a knock at the door and when I opened it there she was in slacks and motor-cycling kit with a bloody great bike leaning against the kerb. "Oh God," I said, "not another one. I swore I'd done with all that." "I'm afraid so. I thought you'd guessed," she said and that was that.

I thought I was so damn safe with a married woman, shows you I must have been pretty green even then, and the first thing I did was to fall flat, head over heels, and I've never enjoyed myself so much. She was my sort, quite mad of course, and I've never been so alive. She'd wake me up in the middle of the night and say, "Come on, we're going to see the dawn." And out we'd go. I saw things then I've never seen since. Once there was a tremendous storm and we got up and went out with macks over our pyjamas and sat on the common with the lightning flashing round us and the rain streaming down our faces. I wonder we weren't killed. Oh lots of things like that I remember. Well my dear you have to fill your mind with something while you're being nursemaid to a brood of pups that look just like little rats and you think to yourself, at least my life wasn't always as dull as this. Not that I don't love them of course. Look at them lying there just like four little pigs. These are the favourites; there are lots more out the back but only these allowed into the house or we should end up like the Irish living with their animals all in one room. She was always like that, so alive. But it was short and bitter not short and sweet I'm afraid. In the end it turned sour and all that life got twisted. She accused me of terrible things; went for me with a knife one night. She had the most terrible temper and she'd be quite beside herself while it lasted. At last I said it was enough and I kicked her out. "I've had enough," and she went, and that was that, and I cried myself sick. She came round one night a few months later. You never knew that Rae did you? She asked me to go back. You know I've always been psychic, always been interested in spiritual things. I'd had a dream the night before and woken up hearing this motor-bike roaring away in the distance, and I knew then it was her in the dream. I was sitting there the next night quite late, and suddenly I heard this bike exactly like my dream, and I went to the top of the stairs and called down, "Come on up." She came up into the light, we had our sitting room upstairs in the cottage, and said, "My God, how did you know it was me?" I didn't answer that one. Then she asked me to come back but so many things she'd done had left a taste in my mouth, and besides she was bi-sexual and I've never been interested in that. I'm truly what I am dear as you know and all that's never appealed to me. So messy, especially contraception. Imagine feeling all romantic and having to dance round the room looking for a contraceptive in the middle of it. The very thought of it's enough to put me right off. Oh I was lonely after she'd gone of course that's why I was so ill, and then as I said along came Bill and she's been just like a rock to me so I'm not complaining. We live our own lives, hers out there and mine in here and we get on pretty well. But she doesn't know me. I'm a very old soul, about two thousand years I should think, and to me she's just an adolescent. Now, just as if there isn't enough to do, she's taken on the odd jobs at the nursing home you can see over there, just beyond that wall. Goes and digs for them. Between the two gardens we're practically self-supporting. They're mostly mental patients, voluntary you know, but I often wonder who's sane and who should really be in there when I look round at the people I meet from time to time. I'm a dreamer that's my trouble. I can listen to music and have the most beautiful love affair in my mind. The great thing is of course that it can't fade whereas the other sort, what some people would call the real thing, will always fade. I've learnt that much anyway.

You'll have to forgive me talking like this, chattering on and not letting anyone get a word in edgeways. I'm not always like this, am I Rae? But we see so few people and it tends to get all bottled up inside. You take out the cork and out it all comes with a whoosh. Look it's going to rain. She'll have to come in then. How strange those trees look with the storm light on them, like witches. The first word I ever said was tree. That's Bill's favourite that big oak. The old man she calls it, and the silver birch is the lady. But she doesn't like that. Says it's too feminine, just a weed that ought to be rooted out. That's where we're different because I think it's beautiful and anything that's beautiful is an end in itself to me. That's just the difference between us. I'm an idealist and she's a materialist. The things we have most in common are the dogs I suppose. Bill adores them but I have all the looking after to do. Sometimes I think hell, give it all up and get back to the bright lights and then I think what would happen to these four, I don't care so much about the others, and I know I just wouldn't be happy. I think dogs are wonderful people. A dumb animal is the only thing that's really faithful to you, that really loves you. I had my poodle thirteen years you know and when it died Bill and I found we were going around talking to a dog that wasn't there, so I said, "Oh come on darling, we just can't go on like this. We'll have to get another dog." We decided on a dachs this time so we rushed straight out and got one from a breeder Sally Wilmot knows. That was how we got Kiki. Then it didn't seem right to have only one. We thought it might be lonely after being with all the others. Next day we got Mim. I won second and third showing them and someone suggested we should breed so we kept the first two pups, that's those two, Franchie and Miss Woo, and that's how it all started. Then of course we had to buy this place, miles from anywhere because of the racket, and now we're completely surrounded with dogs and in so deep we couldn't even pull up and go if we won a fortune.

Well I don't know when I've talked so much and I always could spin a yarn as Rae'll tell you. Look at it out there. It's absolutely falling down. Here comes Bill. I thought it'd be too much even for her. I'll put the kettle on now. You notice we haven't got round to a tweeny in a cap and apron yet Rae. I'm still cook-housekeeper only now I have to be kennel maid as well. We've got visitors Bill. Rae, and what was your friend's name again?'

'Matt.'

'Oh yes my dear, and I've absolutely talked a hind leg off a donkey. It's been marvellous, such a relief. Bill do go and change. You look like the gardener. I'm just going to get some tea.'

'Does she really always talk as much as that?' he whispered when she'd left them and Bill had ducked her head in at the door and out again. 'Wow, I feel as if I've been brainwashed. Still it's all good stuff and you don't have to sit there drumming up something to say. You can just lie back and let it flow over you. She makes me look like a non-starter and I always think I talk too much.'

'Wait til she gets on to matters spiritual. Bill takes a bit of time to get used to people. It's not that she's shy it's just that she's sizing you up to see whether you're worth the effort. I believe she quite often decides people aren't and goes back to her concrete.'

'How long have they been toegther?'

'About eight years I think.'

'Does everyone get the full life story?'

'Oh no, at least I don't think so. I learnt a few details today I didn't know before. Feathers always assumes I know it all because I was around for part of it.'

'Here we are then my dears. Do you like this cake? I made it myself. God knows when I find the time to do all these things but there I must have known you'd be coming. Not that I got a message. I mean I don't usually get those unless something absolutely catastrophic is going to happen, the whole kennel running with dysentery or something ghastly. Bill's solicitor came to see her the other day and as he was just going I said to her, "Tell him to be careful driving back there's something wrong with his left wheel at the front." "I can't tell him that," she said, "he'll think you're pooped." "Alright," I said, "but I know. I've told you." Damn me his tyre blew out on the way and put him in the ditch. Thank God it wasn't any worse or I'd never have forgiven Bill. I can tell you it's not very nice having a gift like mine sometimes. It can be very uncomfortable especially when you can't do anything about it. I felt like that poor woman in the legend, Cassandra wasn't it? The one with the second sight that no one ever took any notice of. I'm just telling them about Mr. Burcott Bill.'

'I wish she wouldn't get these things. Don't see that they're any use if you can't use them. Look at that business last night. What use was that? Just means your hair's looked a mess all day.' Bill took a cup of tea and a plate and went to sit by the window.

'My father's passed over now you know Rae. I see quite a bit of him but this was quite different. I was sitting there, where Bill is now, last night, putting the rollers in my hair because you know my dear I have to do it every night or it just looks a frightful bird's nest in the morning, and all of a sudden something took me and threw me on the floor, right down there, as true as I'm standing here. And I said to Bill, "Don't touch me just watch what happens." And as she watched I changed in front of her eyes. Didn't I Bill? I went all black round my mouth and I had a hooked nose, and withered like a very old woman. Someone must have been trying to get through but God knows who. Perhaps they had a message but they didn't say anything and gradually I changed back again. Anyway after that I was so exhausted that I couldn't finish putting in the rollers so I'm as you see me in this pudding cloth. I've been thinking about it on and off all day til you came and I still can't think who it could be. I just don't know anyone like that. I don't dabble in it now like I used to. After my second affair I made a real study of it. Lots of people told me I was doing a dangerous thing because I did it by myself not in a circle but I've seen so many phoney circles. My mother used to belong to them. I used to put myself under a trance and sometimes it was a bit frightening when I knew I was out of the body or saw a spiritual person standing in front of me but I had such faith in my religion I couldn't really believe any harm could come to me. And then once I came face to face with death. That's another story though and I won't go into that now. I just wanted to prove something to myself and now I've done it I don't bother any more. More tea?'

'How's Stag?' Bill asked when the cups had been filled.

'Very well,' Rae stirred her sugar carefully.

'Still got that damn great car drinking up the juice? What is it miles per gallon or gallons per mile?'

Matt laughed. 'What's yours?'

'Oh we've got a Hillman Estate so we can fill it up with dogs and bags of sand. Looks like rations for an army when we come back from town. She treating you alright?'

'Too well.'

'Matt got the champagne and lobster treatment yesterday.'

'You see I prefer beer and I can't really take all that thin stuff. I don't know where I am, start drinking it by the pint. Then I'm in trouble.'

'She will do it. Piece more cake Feathers please. I always take my own when we go to see them. I like guinness, always have done but I know it's no good expecting anything wholesome like that there. Tell you what if you're not rushing back we could have a couple before you go. We don't see many people. Feathers gets a bit lonely and I don't get out all that much not with someone who likes a drink though we've got a local in the next village that isn't too bad.'

'That sounds a good idea. What do you think?' He turned to Rae. 'We don't have to be back early do we?'

'No, no of course not.'

'What were you thinking of Bill?'

'Thought we might take them to the *Drover*. Interesting pub. The gypsies go there regularly. Sing a lot of their songs. Turn Rae's ears a bit blue. Feathers is used to it.'

'My dear, it's no good being squeamish in this game I can tell you. We took Mim over for a mating the other day and the time we had would have turned my mother bright pink all over. It was a place we'd never been before, thought we'd introduce a drop of new blood and Sally Wilmot had recommended them. Well when we got there we knocked at the door and explained to the woman what we'd come for. "Oh yes," she says, "Father does all that. I'll bring you in some tea." And before we could say no thank you very much, she'd shown us into the room with father sitting in his chair smoking his pipe and a very fine dog there too beside him. "Where's the bitch then?" he says. "We left her in the car." "Well we won't get our bit of business done with her out there and him in here. Go and get her." So Bill went and got her, carried her in and put her down and we both made a move for the door. "Where you going?" he says. "We thought we'd wait in the car." "Sit yourselves right down," says father. "How do you know what you're getting if you don't stay and watch. I could palm you off with any old dog and you'd be none the wiser. Besides Bessie'll have made tea now." So there we had to sit and make polite conversation while the two dogs got on with it. Then damn me if there wasn't a tie and you know once that happens there's not a thing you can do without damaging one of them. Kept it up for half an hour if you'll pardon the expression while we drank cup after cup of tea and talked about the weather. I tell you, Rae, I've never been so glad to get away from anywhere. Let's only hope it's come off after all that. Last time we mated two of them and they didn't take, had false pregnancies both of them and not a pup to show for it.'

'You ought to tell them,' Bill said. 'They're losing us money. You can't run a business that way. You hear that you four? No more of it now or we'll sell the lot of you.'

'Oh you wouldn't Bill. Look at their little faces. Don't you take any notice of her darlings. Mummy loves you. She won't let her send you away.'

'Potty on those dogs I tell you. We're not taking them with us tonight. It'll be too crowded for a tribe of dogs under everyone's feet. You go and get yourself ready or we shan't get a seat.'

They drove through twisting lanes where the evening sun dipped under the branches pouring its light through the leaves so that they glowed with rich colour in every shade from pure pale apple to the dark moist moss of the farthest banks of bracken. The inn when they reached it after half an hour's fast drive, was a low ceiling'd brick building with stone flagged floor, wooden benches and tables and a deeply recessed ingle nook with stone seats where two or three men, obviously the gypsies, were sitting smoking and drinking pints of mild.

'What'll you have?' Bill turned to them.

'I'll help you carry,' Matt said and followed her lean figure in

257

slacks and a light raincoat up to the bar. She was obviously well known, had made herself a place where she was treated with respect, accepted as herself. Exchanging remarks with the landlord, she seemed absolutely at ease and looking back he saw that Feathers was bowing and smiling at one or two of the customers, unbuttoning her coat and gesticulating largely as she chattered to Rae.

'My God this is an original,' he whispered to Rae. 'I didn't think there were any places like this left anymore. Those men over there too actually look like gypsies, dress like them, silk scarves, battered hats and all. And their faces, as if you'd chipped them out of a block of wood. They wouldn't do for D. H. Lawrence though, too old and tired.' He turned to Bill. 'The pub we had lunch at had a notice saying no gypsies. I gather they don't feel like that here.'

'Oh no. They're one of the star attractions. You'll see when the singing starts. That's Fred going over to the piano now. He always has a bit of trouble at first, some of the keys are loose and he has to pad them with bits of matchbox.'

Fred played a few trial notes, lifted up the back and peered in, fiddled inside, then tried again and seemed more satisfied although to Matt's ear the difference was a very fine one, and struck out firmly with *Lily of Laguna* which the whole bar eventually took up. From that he led them through a maze of old favourites, mostly musichall, Feathers' voice standing out clear above the rest. 'Used to be a mezzo my dear but ruined it with smoking. Now I croak like an old frog.' Gradually they warmed to the music, self consciousness dropping away, hands and heads swayed in time, and at last a man's voice emerged singing different words to the same turn that brought shouts of encouragement from the rest. 'Go on Sim, give us one of your own.'

He got up from his place at the fireside and came forward to sing them the originals of songs they might have learned in school or heard from ballad groups about pretty little misses who lifted their skirts and farmer's boys and sailormen who were there to see. Then his place was taken by one of the others who sang another in the same vein. 'Now sing us the sad one,' one of the customers called and he began on the tuneless chant of the true ballad that rambles from phrase to phrase as the words take it in tragic understatement.

'What's this one then?' Matt whispered to Bill.

'Just one of the songs. No one knows quite what it's all about but they seem to like it.'

> 'I am a man upon the land,
> I am a seal upon the sea,
> And when I'm far and far from land
> My home it is in Sule Skerry.'

'Do you know it?' Rae asked when the singer had finished.

'I think so. If it's what I think, though his dialect got in the way sometimes and some of the words are a bit odd because I don't think he knows what they mean himself, if I'm right it's a version of *The Great Silkie* about a woman who has a child by one of the seal people. They're quite common, songs and stories like that where human beings get mixed up with creatures of another world, mermaids are the same idea. It always ends tragically for someone, usually the creature because Christianity taught that they had no souls and so they couldn't win. The seal people were supposed to change on land into ordinary human beings, well more or less. If you could find their skins where they'd hidden them under rocks and steal them then they could never return to the sea. They were supposed to have the gift of second sight too so maybe Feathers is a seal princess.'

'Not me darling. I can't bear the sea, at least not round these coasts. It has to be warm as a bath before I even dip a toe in.'

'I wonder if we ought to be going soon. I don't know how good my navigator is in the dark.'

As they got back into their own car outside the house the dogs were in full yap inside. 'Come and see us again,' Bill said as she stuck out a hand.

'Yes Rae dear, don't leave it so long next time. You can stay with us you know. We've tons of room upstairs and the dogs'll soon get used to you. Remind Stag of our existence out here won't you?'

'What did you think of them?' Rae asked as they drove back towards the town.

'Oh I liked them both. The funny thing is, lots of people would say they were eccentric, a bit quaint but I don't know. To me they seemed better adjusted than most.'

'You don't want to worry about what Feathers says about being stuck in the country. Actually she looks better than I've ever seen her. Who do you think it was trying to get through?'

'Some part of herself I expect, something she's suppressed or some hidden fear. She didn't really have much of a start with a mother like that did she? I reckon she hasn't done too badly.'

'You went down well with Bill.'

'Did I? How do you know?'

'Oh she liked you. She doesn't come out as much as that for many people.'

He was pleased with this bit of information as she'd known he would be. It helped to make up for Stag, made him more confident in his own eyes, less of an unhappy little boy. 'I feel we could get on quite well together, you know as drinking companions, something I haven't had since Carl died.' He said the words quite deliberately, naming his loss to pin it in perspective at last and free himself from it.

'Yes I thought so.'

'How did you know?'

'I just knew.'

'It won't happen of course because our lives won't cross that often but the possibility does something for me. It could be. I can't explain. Do you know what I'm talking about? Still, why ask? You always do. Even that worries me less tonight.'

'There'll probably be a summons from Stag when we get back. We won't make it late tonight though because of getting back in the morning. Will you do something for me?'

'What's that?'

'Don't let the antlers clash too much.'

'That rather depends on her.'

'It's you I love after all. All the rest was over long ago.'

'Alright I'll try but don't blame me if it doesn't come off.'

Irene met them in reception as they went in. 'Have you had a good day?' she smiled.

'We've been to see Feathers and Bill,' Rae answered. 'They took us out to a pub where the gypsies go. Have you been? It's rather interesting. You'd like it.'

'I've heard of it. We keep meaning to go but somehow we never seem to get there. Kay wondered if you'd care for a farewell drink. She probably won't see you in the morning. You'll want to get away early.'

The lift whirled them up to the studio where Stag was waiting beside the fluorescent bar ready to dispense confusion and forgetfulness. 'I'd like a beer,' Matt said, 'if there's any going. It doesn't do to mix them and we've already had a few tonight.'

'I think there are a couple of cans in the fridge Irene,' Stag began to pour three glasses of champagne.

'You've been to see Bill. What did you think of them?'

'Fine.'

'They're tremendous characters don't you think? I've known Bill for years even before we were in the army together. She's a splendid person, absolutely reliable. Oh good, you managed to find them. What about some music? What would anyone like?'

Matt took a can from Irene, punched it and began to pour, determined that he would stay sober this evening. Stag and Irene began to dance. He looked across at Rae and grinned. Then it was his turn to dance with Irene. 'How are you today?' he asked her. 'You must have been the only one sober last night or should I say this morning. I don't think I remember much after we got back here.'

'You carried it off pretty well then. I wouldn't have said you'd had that much.'

'Do you remember all that happened?' he asked her jokingly.

'Oh yes. I always remember everything.' She answered so seriously that he felt apprehensive, wondering what she might be thinking and how much he might have said. When the music finished she thanked him formally, gravely and he took her back to the bar where Rae and Stag were standing together looking down at something on top of the bar. A vase of flowers stood there, the petals beginning to drop in the warm atmosphere; hot-house roses, pink and white daisies and delphiniums. Stag had pushed the boat-shaped petals into a design which puzzled Rae but set the hairs at the back of Matt's skull upright with a life of their own. Afterwards when he tried to reconstruct it in his mind, to say which petal had lain where signifying exactly which part of the female complex, he never could, only at that moment as they approached and Stag, taking a slim blunt unopened bud began to thrust it at the heart of the open petalled mouth below the curved delphinium spur and said softly to Rae, 'What do you think of that then?' he felt anger rising in him and as she turned to take up the bottle again he took two large rose petals and laid them across the white daisy lips, breaking the symbol into a meaningless design of dying flowers. For perhaps thirty seconds he had contemplated sweeping the lot onto the floor to be ground into the carpet but held himself back, knowing the action would be inexplicable and seem merely petulant. Now he was glad he'd resisted this first impulse because it was quite clear from Rae's questioning expression that she'd understood nothing of the sequence. He would explain later but smiled reassuringly and asked her to dance. He felt stronger again as if he had beaten Stag at an invisible game that only they two had known was being played. If she had known. He would never be able to prove it. Perhaps it wasn't a conscious gesture but something that the depths of memory threw up, a last reaching out before it let go forever and what had been sank out of sight so that like Rae she would no longer even remember what was once.

'Why did you do that?' she asked as they danced. 'What was it all about?'

He shook his head. 'I'll tell you later.' Her lack of understanding drained the last bitter anger from his blood leaving it free to run calm and warm in its narrow courses. What did it matter? They were going home in the morning. 'Isn't there a language of flowers?' he said.

Irene was leaning against the bar watching them while Stag spoke quietly in her ear. 'You look tired Irene,' Rae said as they finished the dance. 'I think it's time we all went to bed or we shan't want to go in the morning.'

'Why not a day off? You know you're very welcome to stay here a week, fortnight if you like.'

'Unfortunately we have to go back and make some money. No work, no eat as the old Chinese proverb should have had it.'

'I think I'll go and have a bath in that marvellous pink tub. I'm sorry to break the party up but I really am tired. It must be the air here or something. Feathers perhaps. I always find her exhausting. Thank you for the weekend Kay, it's been a lovely change.'

'Well you must come again when you feel like getting away.'

'I'll say goodnight too if no one minds,' Irene said. Matt looked at her. She seemed weary, a little sad. The goodbyes formed formal patterns on the air.

'What about one for the road if Rae's having a bath?' Stag said when Irene had gone.

'Suits me.'

'You won't be too long because of the morning?' She looked up at him a little anxiously.

'No, not long. You have a nice bath. I'll be down soon.'

'What'll you have, something a bit stronger?'

'Since the road is so short, I'll have some scotch.' Stag half filled a tumbler. Matt helped himself to water.

'You know I feel women have come between you and I and it's a pity because I like you. I didn't first of all but now I know you a bit better . . .'

'Wasn't it inevitable in our situation?' he wanted to make it easy, to make it seem a fault of circumstances rather than the fundamental conflict of personality it had been. 'After all it was a difficult situation for me. You having all this even though it means nothing to you. You must expect the poor brethren to be a bit touchy; isn't it what they always say that they're too proud, won't be helped? Then there's the past of course.'

'Women always make trouble. Bill says the same. After all a woman like Rae, all she wants is someone to lean on and I didn't want that.'

'And Irene?'

'Oh she's absolutely faithful, always would be no matter what happened. Besides I don't let her get too close. That way I'd lose everything. What's she like in bed?'

He felt himself stagger again under the heavy hand but he refused to be angry this time. 'Very good, excellent. I mean what does one say? It's not something you can give marks for. One man's meat and all that.' He wanted to say, 'Don't you remember?'

'Yes, she would be. It isn't everything though.'

'No. But it helps. At least it's important to me. Still I've often been told I make too much of it so there we are. Once again it's a matter for the individual.' He was careful to play it easy not wanting an argument at this stage.

263

'So I can't persuade you to take this job?'

'Oh I don't think so. There are lots of things I could do if I just wanted to make money. Unfortunately lots of other things interest me more though sometimes I think I ought to earn a bit more for Rae's sake. I don't mind women leaning on me.'

'You know I rather envy you. Maybe that's another reason why we didn't really meet. You see in a sense you're all the things I'd like to be. I wanted to be something once. Rae would have helped me, did help me but it was too late. I did crazy things, went about everything the wrong way and then in the end I had to give it all up. It beat me. You could say that circumstances beat me. My mother was ill and I was confused about various things. And then I got ill. By the time I was better everything had changed. I bought this place and it went well. I have a good business sense you know, almost a flair for making things go well on that level. In a way it's a pity perhaps. Now I have all this and nothing I sometimes think. That's why I envy you because you still have all the possibility. You've managed to keep your life fairly straight.'

'It often doesn't seem like that to me. Though I do think it's probably the only thing to do, make it all of a piece, so that life isn't departmentalised, fragmented; try anyway.'

'I'd like to be friends if that has any meaning for you.'

'A lot; too much. I'm willing to try but I think your money and position will probably always get in the way. That's as much my fault as yours of course but there it is. You see there isn't anything I could do for you, that you'd let me do and that makes the whole relationship unbalanced. When you can come to me and ask me for a bed for the night then we might try again. I'm willing.'

'I know what you mean. I do know, I can see it. We can only ever meet on terms of equality, that's it, isn't it? And I'm not used to that. Well here's to us anyway.' She lifted her glass. 'Now we can only wait and see.'

'What have you been saying?' Rae asked when he opened the door. She was sitting up in bed, reading and smoking. He began to undress, repeating what he could remember as he took off his shirt and trousers.

'That was all. I did the best I could. Look the Furies have been after me.' He turned his back to her, pointing out the big red weals

264

that covered his back and arms like pursed mouths. 'Some on the back of my legs too. They itch like hell.'

'What is it? How did it happen?'

'Mosquito bites. Have you got any? No, there's your answer. They had a meal off me while you and I were busy this afternoon. I think you must be in league because it was you who kept me there, distracted my attention while they got on with it. The evil eyegoddess who has her lover's blood spilt in the act.'

She laughed delightedly, holding out her arms to him. 'Poor Matt, caught in the act.'

'Bloody good job it wasn't with my pants down or I might have been ruined for life and then you'd have been sorry. You'd have had to find a new one, another pretty boy all young and eager. Tell me madam, is this the way you usually dispose of your lovers?'

'Come to bed.'

'I don't know if I'm safe. What am I going to do about these bloody bites tonight? Suppose they keep me awake?'

'Oh I think I know what to do if they do. Come to bed.'

GOING down the road feeling, going down the road feeling, feeling bloody terrible after a weekend of booze and talk, people, things, symbols, people as ideas to be absorbed, sucked down for the mulching, munching process to begin, things not to be taken hold of, that are only embodiments of abstractions until you are going down the road like the man in the picture, going to work all blurred and furred at the edges with too much light, bombardment of sun particles that dizzy the eyes. Stagger as a drunken man going down the road.

Hell and a weekend like that is no incitement to the ordered life, the life of dedication, of the little man nine to five, to the years ahead looked at through the wrong end of the telescope, diminishing to a pinprick, to an itch under the wrinkled skin for what will be never, diminishing. Leaves you with muddy of emotions unsettled, cloudy so when the old man says, as he will, make no doubt of that lad, says where the red, white and blue blazes were you yesterday you must make a big effort, and an effort it will be, to answer the gentleman nicely with your pat lie, please sir I was ill sir, knowing his bite is non-existent, his bark doesn't last for long and the mechanics laugh at him behind his back and half to his face even, the smirk averted rather than an outright insolence that would make even this worm turn.

'Morning George.'

'And where the bloody hell were you on Monday, to be precise yesterday as ever was?'

'Had a bit of a stomach upset, couldn't make it I'm afraid. Caught a chill I reckon.'

'Chill be buggared. Boozed all the weekend and couldn't get up. Good job for you I'm a fool, a soft simple old fool, and a good job you weren't late this morning or you'd have been out of here quicker than say knife. You can help out on the forecourt this morning. This afternoon I want some parts collected from Newley's at Beaconsfield.'

'Not this morning?'

'No. Sid's got the truck out on tow.'

Into the hut where Alice'll be brewing up. Never go in to work late. Better not to go at all then they can't prove anything, can't stick anything on you. To be late is to be lazy, slapdash, sluttish, uncaring, reasons are only excuses and your stammered excuses give them power, the power of the employer that can make you shit your pants with fright, the sweat of an idle hand that closes on emptiness at the end of the week. Is it good for me to feel this, the fear that harries millions? Haven't I felt it long enough so the edge is worn down, no longer has the bite to wound, become a commonplace?

'Morning Alice.'

'Morning. Feeling better?'

'Yes thanks. Had a bit of a chill on the stomach.'

'Oh we know. That bloody draughty forecourt. One thing I'll say for this job, you're never short of an excuse and you'll never be so healthy again. I haven't had a cold since I come here. Must be the wind nips them all in the bud, even the germs die of exposure. Facing the common too, that's a big thing, all that fresh air can't but be good for you. That's why we huddle in here, keeping up a good fug whenever we can. Quiet this morning aren't we?'

'Don't think I'm quite recovered yet. Toss up.'

'Your call.'

'Heads.'

'Heads it is. My first patient. Here have you ever thought, blood transfusion that's what we do, a shot in the arm? Makes it more interesting. Here we go. That's the bell for kick-off.'

A good soul Alice, salt of the earth and all that with her skinny sickly old man and two thin kids like bundles of sticks. Look at her sometimes when she isn't doing anything except sitting there on that box, her mind gone far off, and wonder whether she's thinking, what about, or the thoughts just lying quiescent, content to let her body go slack, her eyes cloud. Think about her body too, let my mind slip questing, finger, flicker delicately over the forehead and temples, in the sockets of the eyes where the furrows begin to crease the thin white skin, over the cheek ridges down to the mouth, the lips thin but not drawn, the soft line of chin and sweetness of throat where the tongue seeks out the hollows. And what would the hands be doing all this time? Busy with their own world, putting aside, so gently aside the coverings, lifting and peeling away until there is only the fruit exposed ready to taste, to bite. My hands caress the ripe rounded fruit of breast and belly, smooth the curving back, cup about the silken buttocks. Mouth follows hands.

She doesn't know of course as she sits there, gone far away, her head full of her children running through fields, along sands in the sunlight that she pays for with her days in the cold and stink of oil. How much of the diesel reek clings in her hair, grimes her nails at night when she swings her legs into bed beside him? Not that they bother anymore now the children are there and they've done all that was expected of them. Thoughts like that are for the strong and the brave and they took his meagre ration of both and poured it into the celluloid figures that dance for them in the evenings. Now he no longer has to be brave or strong except by proxy, his courage and strength united with thousands of others' to produce the superman who fights and loves on his behalf, dies in her arms and rises smiling, god-like, hymned and haloed against the sky in the last reel. Two or three times a night they can see that, seven times a week, a thousand times a year. So she never knows what I'm thinking as she sits there.

What is it about a woman, what is the stuff they're made of that they're so penetrable, receiving you into their soft depths? Sugar and spice and all things nice, and their smell quite different from the manstench of armpit and spilt sperm overpowering. Every part of a woman has its unique savour, varies with time and mood. Breathe it in mingled with her perfume, nuzzle it in her neck, inhale it neat from between the thighs, the odour of sanctity. You're hot this morning. Got out of bed too quickly and run to work with the night sweat not cooled on your limbs. There's the bell and a wind out there'll chill any ideas, desires still lingering, put them in cold storage til this evening.

'Yes sir?' The touch deferential; might be a tip from this one, not much but as the old lady said every little counts, mounts. 'Three of the best. Oil and water alright? I'll just check them for you. Could do with a pint in here, getting a bit low.' Poor devil looks as if he could do with a pint in himself, a shot in the arm as Alice says. What existence does to some people, don't call it life for God's sake. There's only one life and this isn't it. Ring up three gallons. Insert nozzle into hole provided and fire. Fill her up with the life-giving juice that puts fire in her belly like a long ejaculation. Withdraw slowly so's not to spill a drop. 'That's eighteen and elevenpence halfpenny please sir.' Good he's waving a greenback.

'Keep the change. Student are you? Not much of a job in this wind. Goodbye.'

Not a bad old boy. Funny how they all think you must be a student as if you wouldn't be studying if you were at this time of year. Maybe Oxbridge has finished by now, gone down as they call it. Shall I go back in the hut or hang about out here a bit? Jump about. Well that's the first one over and not bad as a promise for the day, a bob to start with. Soon get rid of me hot pants out here. Good job I'm not a brass monkey. Poor old devil he looked half frozen in the firm's car. Won't make retirement if he goes on like that. Somewhere it must be different surely, somewhere I've dreamed of men walking tall and upright through spacious streets, not bent and worried through their grey lives. That's my trouble I suppose, a latter-day Victorian believing in progress at heart, an incipient do-gooder, who'd like to see everyone fulfilled and creative, and won't accept things as they are in this sad dog-eats-dog old world of our today.

There goes the old lady with the gulls' breakfast. They know she's coming, wheeling and mewing high over her head and won't drop down til she gets back on this side of the road. Goes over there with part of her turkey for them on Christmas day she said. God knows what they mean to her. Wonder if she watches them out of her window. Remind her of something maybe, in her childhood. Can't be travel. Don't reckon she's been farther than the end of Brighton pier all her days. Hallo, here's someone going to have trouble getting in. Alice's turn. Stand back and watch. Just made it. Another hairsbreadth and the display stand would have gone for a spin. Knows it too; her face flushed, wondering who saw and what they're thinking. Are they thinking bloody useless woman driver? Not been driving long and borrowed the old man's car. Hell of a racket if she puts a dent in its glossy hide. Wonder if she'll make it out? Nervous now, right rattled. Good girl Alice, flagging her up a bit. Should be easy past that curve in the mount-ing. There she goes, way up the road, glad to be free. Here comes a joker in a minibox. Mine I think. On guard.

See it in their eyes, the question. What is it? Meaning how should I react, which of my faces'll cover this situation, can hide myself behind? Whether to be cheerful man-to-man, slightly patronising of course because while he's got that thing stuck in my car, I've hired him so to speak, paid for him, or whether to be what's a pretty girl like you doing a dirty cold job like this for? Why don't we get together and work something out? I could show you a thing or two, you don't want to play around with that thing when you can have a real live warm son of a gun of your own. Not who is this person but what, relating to it not thou as Buber saw. Little men with their fragment of jealously-guarded knowhow, mugged up on the spot and clutched close against all comers, I am a challenge to them, to their assumptions and the life they found on them, on sand.

Wasn't it always like that? Whenever was the golden age that you can look back on and say then it was different? Illusion. But it exists, is held in the minds of men as they hold galaxies, the universe with only an intimation of what they mean, an apprehension. What happened to our golden age that put a foot over the threshold of the twentieth century? It was swallowed up by greed and disgust, corroded by two wars that nobody won, that spread their poison like mustard gas, blinding and leaving a legacy of old men run down before their time, coughing up their lungs, just about able to cosset themselves in a chimney corner til they die in blood and phlegm. How many of my own family are like that with the fire gone out and their only concern to be comfortable and nurture the little life they walked away with from the battlefields of the world; bringing up children to do the same, to lie quiet and take whatever's going because your father paid for it and it corrupted him. Conformity, smell of mortality. See it on the face of the man in the minibox as he roars his meccano-size engine into the millrace, ratrace of traffic, uneasy behind his tiger-skinned miniwheel so the first chance or half he has he must tear up the tarmac overtaking on the inside, shouldering other cars into each other's lanes to reassure himself. Time to get out of the cold, join old Alice in her hut.

'Funny they should be playing that. Got a cup of coffee Alice?'

'Thought you'd be in as soon as I made meself one. What's that then?'

'That song on the wireless. Listen.'

'What's it all about? Folk song isn't it? What's a silkie?'

'It's about a girl who marries a seal. Listen.'

'What's so special?'

'I heard it on Sunday. A gypsy was singing it in a pub we went to.'

'You do get to some funny places. She's very popular that girl, American. I've heard her on here before. Sings one called *The Streets of Laredo*, cowboy song, I remember on the wireless when I was little. My brother used to sing it too. Imagined himself in a stetson and high boots I suppose. Well it makes a change. How could she marry a seal though? I mean what did they do?'

'Well in those days they believed that seals became men on land. Actually she didn't marry him, she just had a baby and she didn't know who the father was, what he was called or where he lived. Then he turns up one night and pays her for looking after the child and says when it's older he'll come back and take it down to the sea and teach it to swim. Then, he says, she'll marry a man who's a very good shot and the first time he goes hunting he'll kill both the silkie and his son with one bullet.'

'Don't really seem worth it.'

'He must have thought so.'

'Yes, but what about her? What did she get out of it?'

'She was well paid and she got a hunter for a husband in the end. So she wasn't too badly off. The interesting thing is that it says the father wasn't good-looking, in fact he was rather ugly but she didn't seem to mind. Still perhaps she only saw him at night.'

'Oh well that's alright then. He left her with the kid though. Just like a man.'

'He came back to fetch it and paid up.'

'Then he was better than most. Honest this job is enough to put you off men for life. You'd think me with a great thick wedding ring and a diamond like a lump of glass they'd leave me alone, I'd be safe enough but it don't make a scrap of difference. There was a bloke come in yesterday wouldn't take no for an answer til I told him me husband was a bouncer for a gambling den. Always after the same old thing and when you tell them no they think you're playing hard to get or something. Why don't they get themselves wives then they can have it legal on tap. Oh I tell you if the hours didn't suit part time for the kids coming in from school I wouldn't stick this a minute. I don't know why you do when there's other things you could be doing.'

'You sound like Rae.'

'And aren't we both right? Think about it.'

'There's the bell. I'll get it if you like. You finish your coffee.'

A big Wolseley. Have to watch these for air bubbles. Was she right I wonder? Why does that song keep going through my head? Because I'm half and half I suppose like the silkie. Funny how the women don't seem to mind but he has to be punished in the end for daring to step out of his element. There was a bit more place for the outlandish though on the fringes of society; comes up in a lot of myths and ballads so long as society hadn't too repressive a hold. Then it just ran wild of course, witch hunting for instance. Oh we wouldn't have stood a chance in that time; sure sign of a witch to love your own sex and look at Joan of Arc who's a transvestist with a strong mother fixation. She made herself a place, put heart into a whole nation like Elizabeth or Churchill and they burnt her for it as soon as they could do without her. Oh the motives behind that

271

stake are so complex if you look into them, a moment when a society becomes like one mind complete with all its fears, repressions and neuroses. Hitler did the same with the Germans, made them a reflection of his own psychotic personality until the cold analysis of steel sheared them away bit by bit and he was left with just his own megalomaniac circle. Have we learnt I wonder, that you can't sink your personal responsibility in the collective? Or is that what I've been trying to do, involved myself so much in the problems of a group that I can't see straight myself any longer? Is this the suffering Steve's father means and is there any end to it, meant to be any end to it? Is there a point where you can say, 'I've suffered enough. Now it's time for a resurrection.' Death has closed over me. I've been in the place of the tomb too long refusing my house among the living until I've become like a shade myself, adrift on the dark sea of the underworld. Maybe it's a mistake to sink down so far. Orpheus never recovered after all. The world of the living tore him to pieces in spite of his music. Wonder if anyone's ever pointed out that the lyre is shaped like a bull's head? Graves maybe but I don't seem to remember it. That would make him another of the young god lovers of the goddess, in fact the most perfect example of the lot when you come to work it all out. That's something I've never seen explained in psychological terms. Graves always said she'd come back of course, the goddess, that we neglected her at our peril, had gone too far the other way with our patriarchal society. He meant in the mind I suppose or perhaps even more than that.

Animus and anima agreed to have a battle, but it's anima that loses most of the time. Sometimes I wonder how many men really can appreciate a woman or whether the old sex war has gone on too long with too much money invested in it for there ever to be a truce. Yet, they'd say, how can you love women like this and not accept yourself as one. But you don't love yourself unless you're Judy, you love what you're looking for, your opposite, complement. Why should I love me, the mind that can stay detached, ambition, ruthlessness, violence all the things I know are there, see in the faces of men behind their wheels, their calculating eye? What was it Rae said once about feeling friendly towards the masculine, loving it and that's what I can't do, can't feel friendly, warm, towards it

272

because I know it too well from inside. In spite of all the books say about accepting facts, not living a fantasy, I can't make myself feel feminine, only other people can do that, and then I feel outraged as if they were insisting I was someone else and must live out my life like that. That's where we're different from David and the other boys, at least people like Jonnie and I are. The boys wouldn't change, wouldn't like to be women even if you could wave a fairy wand over them but we would because for us it wouldn't be a real change, only a simplification. Oh it isn't true for thousands I know. We're the odd ones out even there but it's no good everyone falling over backwards to say we don't exist and that it's more realistic to say, 'I'm a woman who loves women.' That's fine for many but not all and that's where even we become intolerant though we ought to know better, to have learnt the pain of isolation and find acceptance for each other whatever the brand and tribe.

Penis envy, the feeling of having been castrated perhaps that's at the root of it all like those dreams I have where I've got one six feet long, a fine big fellar almost too heavy to lift but it's only the male who thinks there's no substitute, women don't mind as long as they get their climax. I'm the one that feels the lack not Rae and neither did Jill, like animals really, happy to be stroked and fondled. Somehow for me though it's incomplete unless there's penetration though there are different ways of loving for different moods and situations. Maybe that's the answer: that there is no one answer and we shouldn't try to force one on the moment but let the moment dictate its own. How many times you've thought about it in the open air, even tried it once or twice, and then suddenly the other morning it was the right moment and you didn't have to think about how; it just happened. Is that something else a woman has almost by nature, being receptive to the moment, the creative kind of passivity? That's something you can't teach yourself either; it's there or it isn't. No there's no way out lad, no point in pretending to be what you're not. There are dozens of ways of being queer and you have to find what your kind is and then make something of it even if the answer leaves you a kind of little half-chick, a natural eunuch, the stock figure of fiction. You have a choice. David and the boys don't have a choice because they're outside the law anyway; a negro doesn't have a choice because it's obvious and no hiding the colour of his skin except in very rare cases. But no one need know as far as you're concerned and yet the only real barrier to their knowing is your pride or fear. The choice is yours whether to side with conformity and pretend that there's only one way of being a human animal or to stick your neck out and say no, there are millions of ways, all elements in the kaleidoscope, shaken together we make the pattern. The pattern is alive like a living cell seen on a slide, changing, vibrating with colour. Civilisations fall. A hand shakes the tube; the pattern crumbles and reforms. Whose hand? Our own.

That's one thing about this job of course, you don't have to give it too much attention, can let the mind run on as long as you remember to say yes sir, no sir, what can I do for you sir, ring up the number, count out the change. They always come in a rush so they're queueing up for pumps and then, slack, sigh a bit as if you've been holding your breath, stand and look out across the road towards the common and those birds. Rest your mind on the dip and sail of wings, gulls' wide white wings carry the ache away up with them and loose it on a banked turn. Aren't you hiding though here? Aren't you doing just what you condemn, fragmenting your existence, refusing your part of the pattern? Here's a man asking for upper cylinder shots. That means a trip into the repair shop where the mechanics'll be sitting having their break, the confraternity of oily brethren, and the laughter will ripple as you turn your back. That hurts doesn't it? You almost hear the joke that sets it flowing as you fill the cylinder. There are too many variations on that theme. It hurts. It hurts because there is no defence, nothing you can say or do. You can't even hate in return because you know the fault isn't theirs. They're only doing what they've been told, been taught. Like the time you felt the fists thudding into your body. Even then there was nothing you could do except cover your face with your hands and crouch into the wall. Their own ignorance was a weapon and a shield you couldn't counter because it left you without anger against them only against the nebulous, faceless shadows behind them which you knew that physical blows wouldn't harm, would only give greater substance. Yet in play you fight on equal terms. Remember the day you found the secret, the difference between the way men fight and the way women fight. Women fight without conviction even in fun; men fight to win. You were running over the heath, half a dozen together, students out for a romp, the girls already squealing and dodging, the boys catching at their clothes and hands. It began as a walk, a serious peripatetic through the grounds before Sunday lunch at the big house used for weekend seminars on modern poetry and the evaluation of history on scientific principles, and suddenly in the sun, up the long grass slopes, someone gave a little push and it became a Spring rite. You found yourself stranded between two swiftly developing attitudes, not knowing whether to hunt or to run. Every instinct told you to hunt but you knew you were expected to run. The game moved quickly, chasing across the turf like a pack. Then one of the girls was down, crying for pax, mercy, struggling like a kitten held up in the air. The boys hooted and bayed. You tried to shear off but Kevin was coming after you, his long legs covering the heath like the football pitch. When he caught up with you and brought you down with his arms locked round your legs you should have screamed and laughed but no sound would come. No trigger instinct opened your mouth except to grunt and puff a bit and then he began to pin you to the springy grass. You struggled a little as girls do and then as you felt yourself held, the moment come when you should give in, go limp, the muscles refusing to resist anymore, something snapped inside and you twisted with all your strength under him, not caring if it hurt, if the flesh bruised, flung yourself sideways and up until you were free, driven by an instinct to win, to be on top. Now you held him down trusting in your thick muscular legs, knowing your arms were thin and undeveloped, and took his wrist and twisted it bending the thumb back. You saw the amazement come into his eyes. 'You fight like a man.' And you laughed and let him go because you were fond of each other and he had taught you a secret. When one of the other boys approached he said proudly and because he didn't want them to try and discover what he knew, 'Don't touch her. You'll have taken on more than you bargain for.' You laughed at each other and ran on and when it turned to horseplay among the boys with Kevin challenging as you understood he must to restore his position among them in the male chain of being, you stood a little way off, watching them, seeing that the moment came for them all when they must either put forth their strength or give in like a girl, and that in that moment they didn't care if it hurt. They found their bruises later and compared them, complaining cheerfully, all part of the game. But you'd learnt not only the secret of that moment but something about yourself: that the instincts you should have had weren't there and that you could no longer play the games other children played because the rules that governed them excluded you. From now on you would have to play among your own kind or not at all because that kind of rough and tumble is based on sex.

Is that true of all fighting, except large scale organised warfare of course which is part of power politics and economic pressure? Though, when you think of it, by the time it comes down to individual men fighting each other the propagandists have to introduce a sexual element to really get their blood up, make them feel the other side are sexual rivals, or perverts or effete. Not so much the primary propaganda of ideas, we're right, they're wrong, but the underground whispers of rape and mistresses, physical tortures, orgies; all the tales we believed about the Germans as kids while they probably heard about the shocking doings at our public schools, le vice anglais, and our degenerate aristocracy. Even with Rae and Jill it came down to a physical struggle in the end so that, in the last resort, they knew who was boss I suppose, and all the husbands and wives I know go in for some kind of sexual rough play even if it's only with their tongues. It's not just that you want to be boss: you get a real excitement out of it so the natural thing to do is to make love after. Carry it too far and you'd end up with rape or necrophilia. De Sade was the boy for all that of course but it's interesting to see how it works in everyday life to a lesser extent. Suppose I rushed wildly into the hut now and threw poor Alice down on the floor and set about her; that'd make the eyebrows shoot up all round. Oh if she did but know it I'm as bad a lad as all the rest who don't care whether she's got a ring on her finger or not except that I keep it to myself, don't go shouting about what a virile beast I am, what Judy calls the look of the predatory male in my eye.

Glad Alice got that little Hillman; swines to fill they are; slop it all over the floor, your feet too if you're not careful and then George blames you. Not a bad smell, petrol. You get used to it after a time so in the end you hardly notice it. But that diesel reek, no I'd never get used to that if I was here til doomsday. Gradually, as the day runs down, you find your thought getting slacker too with lack of stimulus until it's just ticking over like an idling engine, stalls at words more than a couple of syllables long or an idea that's more than a simple fact to be grasped, something to be done. And that's what's happening to a good half the population every day; women shut up in their own homes with only small children and big mechanical gadgets to occupy them; men tied to their mechanical masters til their minds are stupified with repetition, in, out, pull, push. There's no dignity in that kind of labour except what a man puts into it of himself and the same applies to a woman. What makes the difference then? Isolation? Yes that's it. At one time people worked in groups, gangs; women banged their mats at the street door and gossiped or, earlier, slapped their dirty wash together on the flat stones by the stream. We were more a community; it's the terrible corroding loneliness all day until in the evening you seem to have lost the power or will to speak, or simply there's nothing to say and you sit in your isolated units in front of the box that feeds the private dream, finally does away with any need to communicate so that when you go into the room people look up dazed, almost angry at being broken in upon. I wonder if we have this compulsive need for company, for The House of Shades, because our isolation is more conscious, more realised than other people's. We pity ourselves, tell ourselves it's because we're outcasts but in some ways we're no worse off than anyone else, better perhaps because the consciousness forces us to go out and look for others like ourselves while the normals, as David would call them, sit alone in their own front rooms once they're married, thinking they're doing the right thing like everyone else and not junketting round the town, looking for the bright lights like feckless people do. 'We're homebirds.' Where did this idea of two people locked up in their own little cell with all their soporifics around them ever come from? Look at Alice and her husband, the comfortable, vegetable life and yet it isn't their fault, you can't despise them for not knowing better when nobody's ever told them, taught them only the virtues of hearth and home, made thorough little introverts of them. Isn't there a thought there somewhere? Haven't we got something to give if we could only see it, something that's needed I mean, instead of hiding in the shadows like pigmies confronted by a technological civilisation? We keep ourselves too much apart instead of making a place for ourselves and taking it.

Where did I get this Blakean vision from? Surely you're not born with that kind of thing, glandular secretion, chemical make-up. But then they don't know enough about that yet to be able to tell us anymore than they can say for certain what makes a queer. Does it matter? I'm beginning to think it doesn't, that the things that really matter are what comes later. Maybe some people will never to able to accept themselves or others until they know for sure how and why but in the meantime they're wasting valuable lives. Look at the power station chimneys down there towards the river belching black smoke. Master William would have had something to say about that. Nearly two hundred years and not much sign of the New Jerusalem, the rebirth of Albion yet, and plenty of dark satanic mills still around. If he'd known that things would get even worse, plunge right down into the valley of the shadow of Dickensian London, Orwell's mining slums, and his words sung meaninglessly by ladies in comic uniforms, what would he have said then? Mad of course like everyone else with an obsession, vision, call it what you like: sufragettes, abolitionists, C.N.D. all mad. So they peered through the garden hedge and saw him playing Adam and Eve with his wife in their birthday suits, and that proved it of course. After that he could be laughed at, his ideas ridiculed, his poetry dismissed because it was driven into strange symbols, became more and more obscure as the horizon darkened. Oh I remember the anger I felt, can still feel it now, when I first discovered the *Songs of Innocence and Experience* and realised he'd pointed it all out, well most of it anyway, all that time ago, and yet it was still happening all around me. Then I felt like the tiger and the man with the bow of burning gold. What happened? Why did I change? It wasn't just getting over the first adolescent rash of idealism surely. Something sapped me at the root, right deep down, taught me to withdraw and be fearful. My own failure; Carl dying; the shadows closed in.

The morning drifts by like that smoke. What have I done?

George is having an early lunch today. Still if he goes now he'll be back in time to give me the spares' list. Not a good day for tips after all. Hope Alice has done better than I have; she needs it more only working half days. Soon be lunchtime. Then there's the afternoon, this trip over to Beaconsfield, needn't bring them back if I last it out, they won't be touched til the morning, and so home. Must have a shave this evening. Just about get through today without anyone noticing but won't do for tomorrow. That'd give the mechanics something to grin about in their off moments if I came in with a quarter inch of stubble.

Wonder if Alice is brewing up again now old George is off the premises. Makes skivers of all of us this kind of job. It isn't even that George is a slave driver; it's just the rules of the game. No matter what good intentions you start off with you all end up dodging the column just the same.

'At it again I see; thought I'd catch you if I dropped in now.'

'What a lousy morning, need something to cheer me up. Never come across such a lot of tight-fisted, mean-faced little worms behind a steering wheel in me life. Look at that lot. All halfpennies and threepenny bits. If farthings was still currency they'd have dug a few of them out of their pockets too. Just about buy the kids a quarter of sweets each. Do you know one miserable sod had me check his oil, water, top up the battery and the air pressure all for tuppence. I felt like slinging it straight back at him.'

'Never mind darling, you can knock off in a few minutes. I've got an afternoon to get through yet.'

'Listen to that. There's that bloody bell again and I've just poured me tea out.'

'I'll get it.'

'You're a friend. I could fall for you. I'll pour you out a nice cuppa for when you come back.'

'Don't tempt me or I might forget myself one of these days.' Sampson and King's lorry. That'll be on account I expect.

'Morning.'

'Morning my love. Sorry, thought it was the other young lady.'

'She's having her tea. Did you want her for anything special or can I do it?'

'Oh she knows me. I always try for a little bit of special but I

279

don't get it. Tells me her old man's a bouncer somewhere but I reckon she's pitching me a yarn. You a student? Thought so. In fact I thought you was a bloke at first. Just can't tell these days. My kid's got hair as long as yours or did have til I took his mother's shears to it last week and give him a short back and sides. Looked like a nancy boy he did, not a boy of mine. Didn't half holler. You'd have thought I'd cut his tail off if you see what I mean. I'll have four in the tank and ten down on the book as usual. We always split fifty-fifty me and the other gel so I'll do the same by you. Oh and you can put me down for a gallon of oil. I'll take half. That way we pick up a few bob each and no one's any the wiser. Let me have the book and I'll sign for it. You're not very forthcoming are you? Cat got your tongue as my old mother used to say? What's the matter, don't you like me? Maybe you're one of them don't go much for men eh? You just don't know kid, ent seen nothing. I could show you a few things.'

'Don't worry mate I've seen it all.'

'Now don't be like that. Here give me love to me girl friend. Tell her she better be on next time or I'll come and sort her out. I don't go much on little boy-girls. I ent kinky like some.'

Hold on to it, that anger sticking like a fist in your gullet so you can't breathe. Remember it isn't his fault; he doesn't know any better. It's your fault for being here, for putting yourself in this position at the mercy of ignorance and brutality. And what can you do about it? What can you say from down here in the mud? Nothing. Take it, swallow it down, all the filth they care to throw at you because you've earned it in your own obstinate sweat and gall. If this was your honest job and you didn't know any other then you could answer, give it them back in their teeth but you can't because you're a sham, a fraud, playing at being something you're not out of fear and pride until now you've lost your way completely, whirl round and round like a scarecrow on a stick with every puff of hot air a fool cares to blow at you. Remember how you used to be, how you held your own, stood up tall and proud that summer in Italy? And you were only a kid then, a kid who knew nothing. Remember in the hotel bar ordering the drinks when that man suggested? You didn't care. Nothing told you to be afraid or ashamed then. Now you hurry through the shadows with your head down in case someone should see you, notice you scurrying like a rat through the wasteland, and send their blunt missiles of words thudding into your flesh. Stand up for Christ's sake. Hold your head up and look around. You don't have to have money like Stag. Crawl out from under this stone into the daylight even if it blinds you for a while.

'What's the matter? Thought you'd gone for good. Here I put a saucer over your cup or it'd have been stone cold. You look as if you've swallowed sour milk. Somebody tread on your toes?'

'One of your boyfriends left you his love and this.'

'What's that then? A quid.'

'Sampson and King's lorry. Apparently, the man says, you've got some arrangement with him.'

'Oh yeah. That's right, on the account. They all do it the drivers. When I first come here I was a bit took aback but it's been going on so long and all the garages do it when they can so I just fell in with the system. Anyway it's yours since you served him. You don't blame me do you?'

'No, I don't blame you. Still, you have it. I mean you should have been out there and you need it more than I do. Go on.'

'Thanks Matt. I'm grateful, honest. Here, have half a dollar; buy yourself a drink. No don't argue, put it in your pocket. Soon as George gets back I'm shoving off. In fact I'll go and see if he's in now. Did that bloke sign the book alright? See you tomorrow.'

'If you're lucky.'

'Meaning what?'

'Oh you never know.'

'Well that's true anyway. You never know from one minute to the next, never know your luck. I might get home and find the old man's come up with three draws at last. Still you don't even have to wait for that. Like I said this morning, think about it. See you and if I don't, good luck.'

Oh Alice, Alice who never went through the looking glass or into wonderland, whose whole life is compounded of the commonplace, Alice I love you and you'll never know it. I love your refusal to admit defeat because for you there was never any chance of winning, never any possibility that your life would stray from the straight and so very narrow yet you can still see it for others, urge them on into places you can only guess at, without malice or envy.

Might as well go for me own lunch in a minute. There she is over there talking to George. Now she's gone back into the hut. Must've forgotten something. Looks like this big chap's coming in here. Another bloody Wolseley. No sign of Alice. I'll just get this one then and I'm off. George can look after his own pumps til the other girl comes on. Jacking it in I am. Alright mate, I'm coming. Watch out for the bubbles.

HE TURNED the key in the lock and pushed open the door, took two steps across the tiny windowless hall and opened a second door into the workroom. She was bent over the board, touching up a drawing with pen and Indian-ink, adding a little to the hatching to give the pot greater depth, a fuller curve.

'I'll be with you in just a minute,' she said over her shoulder.

'How would you like to do that on site?'

She didn't answer at once, didn't even look up. There was only a hardly perceptible pause in the rhythm as she applied the fine pen strokes and then she went on as before. He watched her as he always did, admiring the deft movements. After a bit she said, 'What do you mean?' and put down her pen.

'A chap came in in a big Wolseley today, very last thing this morning just as I was getting ready to go along to the workman's for a bite to eat, I'd knocked off already in my mind, you know. It was the second one in. I'd had one before, a Wolseley I mean, and I thought, this'll hold me up. You have to be careful with them you see because of the air bubbles.' He paused. She waited, the ink drying on the nib, letting the story unfold gradually in front of her as he wanted it to, sharing its slow progress to a climax she wouldn't even guess at, content to let it come, as she'd said, like unwrapping a present. Nothing she did or said would alter it now, would make it not happen. It existed as surely as if she held it in her hand.

'If it'd been this afternoon I wouldn't even have been there. I'd have been out with the van collecting spares. That's funny isn't it? Coincidence I mean. It never fails to surprise us no matter how often it happens. We ought to be used to it. You know, eight million people in London and you happen to bump into just the one, way outside the laws of averages and statistics. I went over to ask the driver what he wanted. Shouldn't even have been my pitch but I knew Alice was busy in the hut about something. "Yes sir?" I said and he leant out of the window towards me. "Good God!" he said. "Is it you? What the hell?" and then, "Put me in three gallons of the best if that's what you're here for." I felt like a naughty boy who's been smacked. When I'd finished I went back to him and he said, he was laughing now, "Let's see if you can count as well," and he gave me a pound. When I took him the change he said, "Now what's all this bloody nonsense about? I want to talk to you. When are you off? You must have a lunch break or something." I said I'd be free in a few minutes and I'd meet him at the Fox, down the road. I'd have taken him to the café. He wouldn't have minded, wouldn't even have noticed. He's like that. But he's got such an upper class yak on him. He can't help it of course but by the time he's finished the whole world knows the story. I washed my hands and combed my hair, even took my overalls off, not really a concession. I'd have taken them off to go out in the afternoon any- way. I got the list of spares from George, told him I'd go straight off after lunch and then I drove down to the Fox. He was sitting there with a couple of halves in front of him, fidgeting and jerking about like he always does. 'You took a bloody long time,' he said. 'Still I suppose it was worth it. You look a bit more human out of that fancy dress. Never mind about that now. What is all this eh? I thought, when I thought about you at all which wasn't often mind you, I thought you'd have yourself a cushy little number in adult education by now, lecturing to the old ladies in the evenings, and instead I find this.' He's just the same, so exactly the same it almost felt as if there hadn't been any gap and yet it must be seven years since I saw him last. I always said it'd be like that, that we'd pick up just where we left off if we ever met again.'

'Who is it? You haven't told me yet,' she said gently.

'I'm sorry. I forgot. It's Finlay. Alan Finlay.'

'Dr. Alan Finlay, the Etruscan man? The one you worked for in Italy?'

'That's it. Dr. A. Gordimer Finlay as it says in the books. Only I can't think of him other than as old Finlay. He's been back several times of course since I was with him that time and he's starting a new dig in a month from now. Should have gone before but he's been held up over funds. Now he's ready and he wants me to go with him.'

'What did you say?'

'He said, "You're wasting your time. You can do more than this." And I suddenly saw myself as I must look to him. "You know I never fancied sitting in front of a class for the rest of my life," I said. "You don't have to. There are plenty of opportunities, plenty needs doing God knows." So I told him just what opportunities there are for someone like me. He saw it at once as soon as I explained. That's one of the things I've always liked about him. 'You're not rich yourself, you're not married to a wealthy intellectual who'll let you go off and have your own life while he has his, you're not on the old boys' bandwaggon and you won't compromise. I wasn't far out when I said adult education was I? For someone like you society doesn't offer much else. But I was joking of course. I realise it wouldn't really do. I did think when I didn't hear anything of you, you might have changed, might have settled for less. You're mad, you know that don't you? But then so am I. We always got on well together. Some of your ideas are a bit cracked but that doesn't matter. At least you have ideas, in fact I always thought we sparked each other off and that's always a good thing. Why don't you come back with me? It might lead somewhere, who can tell?' "There's just one thing," I said. "I thought there might be," he was laughing again. "It's not just me. How long would it be for?" "Several months," he said, "to do any good. There's work there for years one way and another if you want it. I can even pay you now the trust has come up with something. What can she do?"

'He knew then?'

'Oh yes. He's always known. There couldn't have been any relationship otherwise. You work too close together on site and you have to live with each other for months or even years on and off.'

'What does he think?'

'Finlay finds all manifestations of human behaviour fascinating, and of almost equal value. He's got a wife and two children he keeps in Cambridge. That way he stays a happily married man.

The job's his main interest. I don't know how she feels about it all. She's probably a woman who finds most of what she needs in her home and family, and then they haven't any money worries and there's always something to do in a university town. Anyway I said you worked for the museum and then he asked if you could draw on site. I said I was sure you could but I'd ask and give him a ring tomorrow. It's a bit of a rush but now he's got his grant he'll want to be off as soon as possible. I know him. You can, can't you?'

She nodded. 'Did you tell him what I'd been drawing lately?'

'Yes. He liked that. Thought it was a great joke. Said he wasn't sure if the Etruscans used them but with an expert on tap we'd probably soon find out.'

She looked at him for a moment and then, 'Why?' she said. 'Why suddenly like this?'

'You will come won't you? Tell me you'll come and then I'll try and explain.'

'Of course I'll come.'

'It'll be stinking hot. Perhaps you won't like it.'

She laughed. 'Quite honestly I can't think of anything I'd like better at the moment than to go off to somewhere completely different, where you can be yourself as you should be and yet be doing the sort of job you should. It's what I've wanted, you just don't know how much.'

His face cleared. 'That's alright then. You'll get on with old Finlay in a distant sort of way. He'll probably treat you much the same way as he does his own wife.'

'How does he treat you?'

'Oh he's got some mad idea that he and I are very similar, even look a bit alike he thinks. It's a difficult relationship to define. You'll see. Most people'd say it couldn't exist, that you can't have a relationship without sex coming into it somewhere but I honestly think this one's different. That's partly why I've never been able to settle for anything less because I knew it was possible.'

'Will you tell me now?'

'If I can. I'll try. It isn't just Finlay turning up like this of course. It helps; it solves the immediate economic problem of how and where but I think I was due for a change anyway. It would have come somehow if you know what I mean, because I was ready for it. You know that don't you? What you want to know is why am I ready now, at this particular point in time, when I haven't been before. I've known it was coming, that there was something going on inside that would lead to a change like I said to you the other day. Going away helped the process on a lot, and then one or two things happened today that have happened dozens of times before, a lorry driver wanting me to cook the books with him, something Alice said, the words of a song going through my head, the way the mechanics laughed among themselves when I went into the repair shop; all bits that fitted together. I have to go back a few years to tell you how it all started before you can understand. When I first found out about myself I wasn't shocked or frightened as some people are. Instead I looked around for an idea that would cover the situation, make sense of it. You'd say it was a typical reaction of course, just what you'd expect of me. Anyway I conceived this idea of the rockpool, of the gay world as a universe in little where you could find all the human processes, life and death and love, rich and poor, successful and otherwise, moral and a-moral, just as in a pool on the shore you can find crustaceans and fish, dozens of different forms of plant and animal life in as many colours, a microcosm if you like. And you can sit beside the pool day after day studying them until you become an expert in your own little field. Then I found I wasn't studying them from a distance, from a nice safe seat on the rocks but swimming about down there among them, subject to all the same laws and problems and I accepted this for a long time because at the back of my mind there was another idea too which I can't explain without either being drunk, and then it doesn't matter, I wouldn't care, or sounding so pretentious I couldn't bring it out in cold blood. But it's something to do with involvement and what Steve's father, the vicar, would call suffering. Does any of this make sense to you?'

'Go on.'

'For a time this was right and necessary because I still had enough consciousness of what I was doing for it to be valid but gradually I began to lose that consciousness and become a tiny organism in the life of the rockpool, gasping for an existence like all the rest, adding to the problems instead of helping to solve them and just as frightened of the open sea as everyone else. We're terrified of what's out there, of the competition, of being laughed at, of having to stand up and hold our own and so we make this little world for ourselves where we can be safe and comfort each other with what a dreadful life it is and how handicapped we are until being queer becomes a full-time occupation and there's none left over for anything else. But it's a fallacy. There's no such thing as a microcosm. You're walking along the shore and you come across the rockpool. You think it contains all you want, all varieties of human experience and just as you're becoming thoroughly absorbed in it a great wave washes over it and you realise it's not complete in itself, it's only part of the whole and all the little fishes who've been swimming frantically round and round, and the crabs who've been hiding under the stones half buried in the sand with only a pair of frightened eyes peering out, have to make a run for it out into the open sea because that's the only place they'll ever grow up, and the only ones who are left in the pool are those who're too slow-moving, too firmly attached to their rocks and their way of life to get out. We're part of society, part of the world whether we or society like it or not, and we have to learn to live in the world and the world has to live with us and make use of us, not as scapegoats, part of its collective unconscious it'd rather not come to terms with but as who we are, just as in the long run it'll have to do with all the other bits and pieces of humanity that go to make up the whole human picture. Society isn't a simple organism with one nucleus and a fringe of little feet, it's an infinitely complex living structure and if you try to suppress any part of it by that much, and perhaps more, you diminish, you mutilate the whole.

And there's one more thing, just one more. Not only can you say that the microcosm doesn't exist but it shouldn't exist because it's an idea that springs from the fragmentation of experience and knowledge. We don't learn do we? We develop all our sciences, archeology, cosmology, psychology, we tabulate and classify and cling to our sacred definitions, our divisions, without any attempt to synthesise, without the humility to see that these are only parts of a total knowledge. I suppose it's hard when you can't even begin to touch most fields of human activity today. Coleridge was the last man who was supposed to have read almost every extant book wasn't he and even he wouldn't be able to keep up now. But somehow we ought to be able to keep the idea of the totality of experience and knowledge at the back of our minds even though the front's busy from morning til night with the life cycle of the liver fluke.' He paused for a moment and then went on, 'Some people would say I'm running away, refusing to acknowledge the facts of our life as they are, not taking my share in the common suffering but that's not true. I'm not running. I'm just taking up my whole personality and walking quietly out into the world with it. We'll see what happens.'

'It'll be alright,' she said. 'I know it'll be alright.'

'How do you know?' he said, and then he laughed. 'I'm going to stop asking that question.'

EVENING. The set is in semi-darkness. Spot on centre, Cy lean behind the bar polishing glasses which she holds up to the light from time to time. She is singing quietly to herself. Charlie comes from a door off Right, crosses to the fruit machine and begins to feed in sixpences, pulling the handle mechanically, dispassionately after each one, occasionally collecting from the open mouth below. There is the sound of a car drawing up outside and then the slam of the door. Feet are heard on the wooden stairs Left leading down from the street. A figure, anonymous in pants and jacket enters jauntily. The lights go up a little with a faintly greenish glow. The figure crosses to the bar, feels in a pocket and brings out a coin which it puts down carefully on the counter. Cy looks up from her glass, nods and moves towards it. The evening is beginning.

AFTERWORD

The Microcosm began as all my books do with a hand-sized idea which gradually swelled to fill my whole inner horizon. The difference was that this was an idea for a non-fiction book, a treatment of female homosexuality which would delineate the state of the heart in the early sixties when we were presumably in the middle of a sexual revolution towards a more open society.

To this end I took a tape recorder to a number of women forming a grid of age, class, occupation and geographical spread, typed up the interviews, wrote a synopsis and chapter headings and passed the lot to my agent, Jonathan Clowes, to peddle. When he had collected a series of rejections from the major non-fiction publishing houses, including Hutchinson who had published my first two novels, he passed on an invitation to lunch and discuss the project from Anthony Blond of Blond and Briggs. Money, and lunches, were in short supply so I went along.

Blond's message was quite clear: no reputable house would commission me to write a non-fiction book on such a risky subject because I had no academic qualifications in the sociology or psychology of sex. Why not then write a novel about it? He would pay me £15 a week for as long as the job took, even if it was two years.

Even as he was talking I could see at once how the material might become a novel. £15 was security; not riches but enough to live on. I felt that rush of excitement that comes with a new idea. Scenes and characters began to shape themselves in my head and then I heard what he was saying, for his mind had been working along those lines too and he was suggesting the kind of novel he would like to commission, and what he thought should be in it. Lunch turned into drinks from which I went away with my head buzzing to ring my agent and report. I didn't take the £15 a week, and Hutchinson who had an option on my next novel published *The Microcosm* when it was finished. However I shall always be grateful to Anthony Blond for his initial suggestion because it did more than turn me from a non-fiction to a novel idea. It gave me the opportunity to think more deeply about the nature and structure of novels themselves.

I had more or less given up novel reading at the age of eleven when our girls' school syllabus required us to move on from Sir Walter Scott to Austen and the Brontës, which represented for me a declension from the free imaginative life of the individual to the narrower world of a woman's supposed place in the marriage stakes, though much later I was to come to admire Austen for other things. From eleven until just pre-university when I discovered Woolf and the two Joyces, James and Cary, my passion for literature was largely expressed through plays and poetry. As I've told already in the preface to the Virago Modern Classics edition of *That's How It Was* I was persuaded to begin my first novel virtually against my will. The second had followed almost automatically on commission but I had begun to find linear narrative very limiting.

I resisted the then received doctrine that 'the novel' had been invented at the beginning of the eighteenth century for a new middle-class female reader with time on her hands, and chose rather to emphasize its roots in earlier fictions in myth, saga, romance and fairy tale. I wanted to use a language for fiction that was capable of rising to poetry, and that had all the sinewy vigour and flexibility of the London demotic I had been brought up on. I saw and still see an energized realism as a literary mode in which concrete images function like metaphor in poetry. I wanted a structure in which the parts would take their meaning from being juxtaposed to each other rather than chronologically consequent on each other. I wanted a novel that could put on any dress not just a sober suit; it was possible on stage and I thought it should be possible on the page too. I invented for what I wanted to do the term 'a mosaic style' that would break the tyranny of linear narrative, and that consciously harked back to Joyce.

The Microcosm seemed an ideal place to try this out. I had a subject calculated then to make any publisher nervous: why not fit it with an equivalent style and structure. The result was to be dubbed by one critic 'wilfully experimental'. It gave me however the freedom to be within and without my characters at the same time and to include not only a geographical spread but also historical reconstruction, pastiche, as part of the book's thesis that there's nothing new under the sun.

It was only when the letters began to arrive that I realized that I had tapped into that deep well of loneliness in which thousands of women still felt themselves to be sunk. Some wrote and said I had changed their lives and given them courage to be openly themselves which was a frightening responsibility. Others asked for the names of clubs and organizations which would ease the loneliness. Many were married with children. One in her seventies wrote that although it was no doubt too late for her to find a partner she felt liberated by the mere fact of seeing her sexuality evoked in print.

Since then feminism has moved in and on, and the model for The House Of Shades has closed. Women now see their aspirations mirrored more in the Black struggle for equality than in a politicized psuedo-homosexuality. The closet and the ghetto however haven't been dismantled and for many people the problem of how to be homosexual in a heterosexual society remains almost as acute as ever, in a country where tolerance of eccentricity is used as a justification for conformity, and where young adults of the same sex can still be prosecuted for 'behaviour likely to cause a breach of the peace' by kissing at a bus-stop.

Maureen Duffy, London, 1988

FOR THE BEST IN PAPERBACKS, LOOK FOR THE Ⓟ

FOR THE BEST IN PAPERBACKS, LOOK FOR THE ⓟ

☐ **MILLENIUM HALL**
Sarah Scott

First published in 1762, *Millenium Hall* was one of the first novels to show that marriage need not be the only ambition for a woman. In it, six women come to the mansion and establish a utopian community based on female friendship and support.   *224 pages*   *ISBN: 0-14-016135-X*   **$6.95**

☐ **THE RECTOR AND THE DOCTOR'S FAMILY**
Mrs. Oliphant

These two short novels will delight all who love Austen, Eliot, and Trollope's *Barsetshire Chronicles*. The setting is Carlingford, a small town not far from London in the mid-1800s. The cast ranges from tradesmen to aristocracy to clergy . . .   *212 pages*   *ISBN: 0-14-016151-1*   **$6.95**

☐ **HESTER**
Mrs. Oliphant

Catherine Vernon is seen as a none-too-benevolent despot by her dependent relatives living in the "Vernonry" near her home. Then fourteen-year-old Hester arrives, and as Hester grows up, Catherine finds she has met her match.   *528 pages*   *ISBN: 0-14-016102-3*   **$7.95**

☐ **FAMILY HISTORY**
Vita Sackville-West

Since her husband's death in World War I, Evelyn Jarrold has behaved impeccably. Then she meets Miles Vane-Merrick, a rising Labor politician who is fifteen years her junior, and embarks on a love affair that will change her life forever.   *336 pages*   *ISBN: 0-14-016156-2*   **$6.95**

FOR THE BEST IN PAPERBACKS, LOOK FOR THE 🐧

☐ **A GAME OF HIDE AND SEEK**
Elizabeth Taylor

In her youth, Harriet falls in love with Vesey and his elusive, teasing ways. But when he goes to Oxford, Harriet never hears from him again. She marries the respectable, steady Charles, and is happy for years, until Vesey enters her life again . . .   274 pages   ISBN: 0-14-016137-6   **$6.95**

☐ **TAKING CHANCES**
M.J. Farrell (Molly Keane)

First published in 1929, *Taking Chances* perfectly captures the leisured Anglo-Irish lifestyle of that era, but most of all it explores allegiances and love, as orphaned Roguey, Maeve, and Jer search for love and happiness.
                    288 pages   ISBN: 0-14-016173-2   **$6.95**

☐ **NO SIGNPOSTS IN THE SEA**
Vita Sackville-West

Edmund Carr is an eminent journalist who learns he has only a short time to live. So he leaves his job and buys a ticket for a cruise—for Edmund knows that Laura, a women he secretly admires, will be on board.
                    160 pages   ISBN: 0-14-016107-4   **$6.95**

☐ **MY NEXT BRIDE**
Kay Boyle

Young American Victoria John comes to Paris in 1933. In her Neuilly lodging-house she meets artists and eccentrics, and finds herself drawn into an artistic community with alcoholism and emotional chaos close behind.
                    336 pages   ISBN: 0-14-016147-3   **$6.95**

☐ **A STRICKEN FIELD**
Martha Gellhorn

Mary Douglas, a detached American journalist, arrives in Prague in October 1938 and finds the city transformed by fear. Through her friend Rita, a German refugee, Mary becomes irrevocably involved with the plight of the hunted victims of Nazi rule.   *320 pages*   *ISBN: 0-14-016140-6*   **$6.95**

☐ **THE RISING TIDE**
M.J. Farrell (Molly Keane)

An absorbing tale of three generations of an Irish family in the first decades of the twentieth century, *The Rising Tide* centers around Garonlea, the huge gothic house which holds each family member in its grasp.

336 pages   *ISBN: 0-14-016100-7*   **$7.95**

☐ **DEVOTED LADIES**
M.J. Farrell (Molly Keane)

It is 1933. Jessica and Jane are devoted friends—or are they? Jessica is possessive, has a vicious way with words and a violent nature. Jane is rich and silly and drinks too much. And when Jane goes off to Ireland with George Playfair, the battle begins.   *320 pages*   *ISBN: 0-14-016101-5*   **$6.95**